THE GREAT DISRUPTION

an Earth Rebirth book

Steven K. Smith

THE GREAT DISRUPTION Copyright ©2024 Line By Lion Publications
www.pixelandpen.studio
ISBN 978-1-948807-34-0
Cover Design by Thomas Lamkin Jr. .
Editing by Dani J. Caile

For more information, email www.linebylionpublications.com

LINE BY LION
PUBLICATIONS

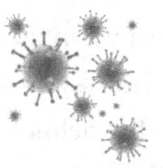

Chapter One

Visitor

"SARA," Jonathan shouted. "We have a visitor." He breathed a quick, silent prayer that this was one of his wife's good days.

Sara responded from the front room of their cabin. "Oh, shit. I'll get the rifles."

The security monitor alert flashed over the novel Jonathan had been reading on his pad's screen, and he hit the "acknowledge" key before it sounded the klaxon. The video showed a ragged-looking figure at the tree line bordering their mountainside farm. Long black hair stuck out in unkempt tufts, but there was no facial hair. "Report," he said to the computer.

"A single intruder just emerged from the white pines at the northeast perimeter. Probably a woman. Possibly a boy. She's limping and may be carrying a rifle."

Jonathan zoomed in on the image as the computer spoke. Even at maximum zoom, he couldn't make out features. Whoever it was carried something that might be a rifle. He ran his fingers through his short-cropped, graying hair, then stood to get his tactical helmet. "Any others nearby?"

"I'd have said if there were. There are none within either visual or infrared range."

Sara met him in the hallway and handed him a 30.06 hunting rifle. She took another one with a telescopic sight and climbed up to the sniper's nest in the attic.

Jonathan set the rifle aside while he strapped on his ballistics vest and put on the helmet. He activated its heads-up display, retrieved the rifle, and stepped outside. "Plan view," he sub-vocalized. The helmet display brought up a stylized map of his mountain hideaway, showing his position with a glowing green icon and the intruder's with a red one.

He'd decided that it probably was a woman. She hadn't moved since the security monitor had detected her. He made his way toward her position, keeping the tool shed between himself and her until he reached it. Then he slid along the side of the shed with his back against it, moving toward the corner. He paused to take a few deep breaths and slow his heart. He worked up some spit and swallowed.

"Video," he commanded the helmet display. It showed the view from the camera mounted on a mast above the cabin. "Zoom in on the person."

She was still approximately where she'd been when the motion detectors first sensed her. She appeared to be surveying his makeshift mountainside farm. Her rifle, if that's what it was, rested with the stock on the ground while she gripped the barrel like a walking stick. It might actually be a walking stick, but he didn't want to assume that. It was too far away to be certain.

He raised the gun to his shoulder and took another deep breath. "Display off," he commanded. He didn't want to be distracted while aiming.

He spun around the corner, the rifle leveled toward her. "Drop your gun," he said, shouting to be heard over the distance, about thirty yards.

She turned to face him and froze.

"Drop it!"

She shook her head. "I don't have a gun."

"Whatever you're holding, drop it."

She let go of the stick, and it fell beside her. She wore a blue and green plaid shirt and tan pants, both of which were stained and torn. A small black belt-pack hung around her waist. "I need food," she said.

"Don't we all. Turn around and walk slowly away, and I'll let you live. If you come back, I'll shoot you. No second warning."

She sank to her knees. "Please! I hurt my ankle. I can't walk without the stick. You're the first person I've seen in more than a month."

Jonathan caught his breath and looked at her above the gun's sights. If she was telling the truth, she was free of the virus. It had an incubation period of less than a week.

Then he shook his head. There was no way to know if she was telling the truth. He looked back through the sights. "Not my problem. On your way."

She struggled back to her feet. After a second she tried taking a step. As soon as she put weight on her right leg she fell, crying out in pain. "Just sh—shoot me," she said through her sobs. "Go ahead. Everyone else is gone." She dropped her face into her hands.

Jonathan set the sights on her forehead, but he had trouble keeping a steady aim. His hands shook, and his heart pounded. This wasn't like the last man he'd killed, more than six months ago. That one had been in the act of raising his rifle, a clear, immediate threat. This would be murder. Assisted suicide at best.

He lowered the rifle. "Wait there, and I'll try to help you. Don't move. I have cameras monitoring you. If you so much as twitch in the wrong direction, I'll kill you."

"I underst—stand."

"Video on," he sub-vocalized to the helmet display. "Monitor the intruder, and sound an alarm if she moves toward the house."

"Program set up."

He backed around the corner of the shed and then jogged back to the cabin, careful to keep the shed between himself and the woman as long as he could.

"Jon, what are you doing?" Sara asked in his earpiece.

"Were you monitoring?"

"Yes, but you're not planning to bring her inside, are you?"

"No. But I can't just kill her in cold blood, and I can't leave her to starve to death either."

He entered the cabin and opened the storage closet. After a brief search he found a tarp and a length of rope. He brought them out to the kitchen and opened the tarp a couple of folds, spreading it out on the floor. From the pantry he took a summer sausage and a bag of dried apple slices and placed them on the tarp. He filled a two-liter bottle with water and added it to the pile. Finally he found an old blanket that was destined to be cut up into rags and added it as well. He rolled it all up in the tarp and tied it together with the rope.

"We need that stuff, don't we?" Sara asked.

He looked up. Sara stood in the doorway to the kitchen, arms folded, her rifle leaning against the doorframe. Her tactical helmet hung from one hand; her wavy gray hair had been disheveled by it.

He checked the video feed in his helmet display. Their visitor hadn't moved. "If she really hasn't seen anyone for a month, then she's virus-free. In a week we'll know. She's not a threat otherwise, with that bad leg."

"You don't know that she isn't faking that injury."

"No I don't. That's why I need you to cover me when I take this to her."

Sara's eyes went wide. "Don't you dare get that close to her! We don't know if she's virus-free or not. She's too far away for me to be sure of a fatal shot from the cabin if she tries something."

"You'll need to come out with me. I'll throw the package to her. I won't get closer than twenty yards or so, and I'll stay upwind."

Sara scowled and tilted her head. "Are you sure this is a good idea?"

"No, but unless we're going to live the rest of our lives here alone, we have to start reaching out at some point. I'm not ready to declare the human race extinct yet."

Sara dropped her gaze to the floor. "Oh, so that's it. She can give you children." A tear trickled down her cheek.

He pulled a knot tight on the package and looked up at her. "Sara, you know good and well that I had a vasectomy. There surely aren't any surgeons left who can reverse the procedure at this point."

Sara shook her head hard, as if trying to dislodge something stuck to it. She took a deep breath. "I'm sorry. Of course I remember. I apologize for the implication." She wiped her eyes with the back of her hand.

"It's okay." He checked the knots on the bundle to give himself something to do. These mental lapses of hers were becoming more and more frequent. "Let's take this out to her, okay?"

Sara put on her helmet and ballistics vest, then picked up her rifle and cradled it like a pro, holding it safely in control, so that she could quickly bring it up to aim. Jonathan slung the bundle over his shoulder and picked up his own rifle. Sara went out first, cutting across the vegetable garden to the tool shed, with Jonathan close behind.

Then, stepping out from behind the shed, Sara leveled her rifle at the intruder's position. "Lift your arms over your head where I can see them and stand up."

The woman lifted her hands in the classic, reach-for-the-sky gesture. "I'm not sure I can stand without using my arms to steady myself."

"You'd best make a good try. Don't give me an excuse to shoot you. It won't take much."

The intruder managed to get on her knees and push herself up with her left leg, gasping and whimpering as she steadied herself with the right leg. She wobbled a bit but made it upright.

Sara cast a glance toward Jonathan and said softly, "My God, Jon, she's just a girl."

Jonathan nodded. He tested the wind direction and set out with the bundle to get upwind of her. The intruder looked at him, then back to Sara, then back again as he walked partway around a circle with her in the center. When he judged that he was directly upwind of her, he approached to where he thought he could throw her the provisions and stopped, twenty or twenty-five yards away.

"Here are a few provisions. It's not much, but it might help. If you're still here and alive in a week, we'll take a look at that leg and see if there's anything we can do."

He swung the package a couple of times and threw it toward her. It landed four or five yards from her position.

"Can I get my stick to go over to it?"

"What do you think," Sara asked, keeping the woman in her sights.

Jonathan unslung his rifle and aimed it at the intruder. "No sudden moves. Slowly pick it up by the barrel end with your right hand, and hold it out where we can both see it."

"I swear, it's just a stick."

Jonathan checked that his rifle's safety was off. "Show us."

She gave a little hop to get closer to where the stick lay, then slowly bent over, balancing on one leg as she grasped it. With the end in her hand, she straightened up and held it out.

Sara had an eight-power scope on her rifle. She spared a glance at Jonathan to be sure he had the intruder covered, then shifted aim to look at the stick.

"It's a stick," Sara said. "Go ahead and use it. But no sudden moves."

"Thank you," she said, and hobbled toward the bundle. "My name's Rita. Rita Ballard."

"If you're still alive in a week, we can do introductions," Jonathan said. "We're going back in now. Don't come any closer to the cabin than you are now. We have a camera monitoring you, and it'll sound an alarm if you try to get to the cabin. It'd be the last mistake you ever make. It works in both visible and infrared, so don't think you can sneak in after dark. We'll have no trouble seeing you, regardless of how dark it is."

"O—okay," Rita said.

"You must have a pack somewhere. Where is it?" Sara asked.

"I lost it when I fell crossing a stream two days ago. That's when I hurt my ankle too."

"Oh. Sorry to hear that. Where are you from?"

"New York. I was on a backpacking trip in the Smokies when the plague hit."

Jonathan returned to Sara's position. Throughout her conversation with Rita, she had kept the gun aimed at her chest.

"Okay, let's get back." He moved behind the shed.

Sara joined him, keeping the rifle aimed at Rita until the last moment, when she ducked behind the shed too.

"Do you think she's telling the truth?" Sara asked as they walked back.

"It doesn't matter at this point, but I have no reason to doubt her. If she's virus-free, then it'll start to matter."

"I guess so."

They re-entered the cabin, and Jonathan opened his laptop to set up the alarm. "I hope she lives," he said. "Especially if she has information about other survivors."

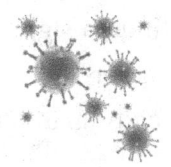

Chapter Two

Quarantine

"SHE'S built a fire," Sara said. She stood by the table, watching the monitor over Jonathan's shoulder as she sipped her morning tea. "Did you give her any matches?"

"No. She must have some kind of fire-starter in that belt-pack of hers. I noticed she'd built the fire not long after you'd gone to sleep."

"We should have made her show us the pack's contents. She might have had a gun in there."

Rita had pitched the tarp into a crude shelter, using some poles she'd collected from the white pines at the field's edge and some smaller sticks to stake down the tarp's edges. A small campfire burned in front of the shelter's opening.

"Too late to worry about that now." He reviewed the video on fast reverse and found the place where she'd made the fire. "Looks like she had a magnesium block and a sparker. That's a common backpacker's gadget."

Sara shrugged. "Well, so far she seems to be doing okay."

Jonathan picked up a bow and a quiver of arrows. "I'm going to see if I can get us something for dinner. Should be back soon. I'll take a walkie-talkie and give you a call on it before I come back in. I'll be out of range pretty soon, though."

"Why don't you just take your cell phone?"

He winced and stifled a sigh. "The cell system stopped working a year ago, remember?"

Sara shook her head again. "Oh, yeah, right. Guess I forgot."

He slipped on a shoulder holster containing a .22 semi-automatic pistol. He checked the clip and chambered a round, then put the pistol back in the holster. "I'll be back soon. Stay inside and keep a gun handy, okay?"

*   *   *

Rita had been camped at the edge of the clearing for five days when the perimeter alarm jolted Jonathan awake. It was after two in the morning, and he'd dozed off while sitting up, supposedly keeping watch while Sara took her turn to sleep.

The monitor showed a bright infrared glow where Rita's campfire burned, but there was another, dimmer figure moving along the tree line in her vicinity. "Infrared signature and image consistent with a black bear," the security program said.

Jonathan rolled his eyes. "Yes, I can see that."

"Just being sure."

The bear approached Rita, wary of the fire. It raised its head, sniffing the air.

Jonathan grabbed his helmet and activated it. He took

his rifle. "Sara! There's a bear after Rita." He stiff-armed the door and checked the safety. "Night vision," he commanded the helmet. He left the cabin at a dead run.

He passed the tool shed and saw the bear standing opposite Rita. She'd crabbed around to keep the little campfire between herself and the bear. It turned toward Jonathan as he came around the shed. He dropped down on a knee, thumbed off the safety, and aimed. His first shot missed, but the gun's report startled the bear, and it ran back toward the trees. He got off another shot and hit it. The bear turned and reared up on its back legs, bellowing its pain and rage, its front legs spread out. Jonathan aimed carefully and fired two rounds in quick succession. The bear fell to the ground.

Rita had been screaming for a while, but he'd been too preoccupied with the bear to notice before. He stood, took his time to aim, and shot another round into the bear's skull, even though it lay still. Then he clicked on the safety, squeezed his eyes shut, and blew out the breath he'd been holding.

He opened his eyes. "It's dead. You're safe."

Rita continued screaming an inarticulate wail. She sat by the fire, her fists up by her face shaking, her eyes wide.

"Jonathan, get away from her!"

He turned. Sara stood some twenty yards away, her own rifle cradled in her arms, her nightgown blowing in the breeze, her face obscured by her helmet. He looked back at Rita. She was less than fifteen feet away. Suddenly feeling shaky, he walked over to join Sara, choosing his steps carefully.

Sara looked him up and down. "Are you okay?"

"Yeah. Stressed, but okay."

Rita continued to scream, though the note became a little less piercing.

"It's okay." Sara shouted to be heard over the distance.

"The bear is dead."

"A bear killed David! Oh God, I couldn't help him. It knocked his head right off. It killed David, and I just ran away. Oh God, I ran away from him, oh God, I'm sorry—"

"David wants you to calm down. You have to keep in control to survive. David wants you to survive."

Rita stopped yelling and stared at Sara. For a moment there was no sound but the chirps of crickets and tree frogs, and the wind rustling in the white pines. She heaved a sigh and said, "Thanks," just loud enough for them to hear. She gave a loud sniffle and wiped her eyes. "David was my fiancé."

Sara nodded. "Our condolences. We're both terribly sorry."

"Thanks."

"How's your leg?"

"A little better. I still have to use the stick to walk."

"If I bring out some tea and leave it over here, can you get it?"

"Y—yes, I think so. Thanks."

"I'm Sara Rillman. My husband's name is Jonathan."

"Thank you for saving my life."

"You're welcome," Sara said. "Two more days of quarantine. If you're still alive then, you can join us in the cabin."

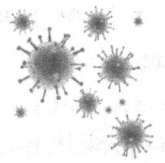

Chapter Three

Then There Were Three

ON the morning of the seventh day, Sara and Jonathan went to Rita's camp together. They stopped by the spot where they'd been leaving her tea and plates of bear meat, and Sara called out to her, shouting over the distance. "Rita, are you awake?"

For an uncomfortable few seconds nothing happened. Sara turned to Jonathan, and he met her gaze, then cast his eyes downward.

Sara was about to try again when the blanket moved as Rita rolled over.

"I'm awake." She pulled back the blanket, wiggled out, and yawned. "I'm still alive."

"Cough hard into a bandana or something, and then show it to us," Sara said.

Jonathan said softly, "Is that necessary? Everything we heard said the incubation period was less than seven days."

"It can't hurt."

Rita searched around and then pulled up a corner of the blanket and gave a couple of good coughs into it. She held up the corner for Sara and Jonathan to see. The pale blue cloth of the blanket was unstained.

Sara nodded. She and Jonathan helped Rita back to their cabin. She was still rail-thin, but generous helpings of bear meat over the previous two days seemed to have improved her health. Her color was better, and her cheeks were less hollow than when she first arrived.

Sara helped Rita wash up and wrapped her ankle, which didn't appear to be broken but was still badly sprained. She found some clothes for her that were only a little too big. The shirt ballooned around her, and the pants had to be cinched at the waist, but they'd work until they could get her own washed and mended.

Jonathan spent most of the day outside, tanning the bearskin and tending the smoldering fire that was smoking strips of bear meat.

Sara gave a final check of the Ace bandage on Rita's ankle and rolled an oversized woolen sock onto her foot. "How'd you find us? We've made an effort to hide this place."

Rita nodded. "You did a pretty good job of that. A few days before I got here, before I sprained my ankle, I climbed an antenna mast to get a look at the country. I noticed the clearing and the smoke from your chimney. The black of your solar panels showed up in the distance. It still took me a long time to find it. Spraining my ankle didn't help, of course." She gave a humorless little laugh. "Or maybe it did."

Sara was washing her hands at the kitchen sink and turned to Rita. "What do you mean?"

"If I'd been able to walk, you'd have just chased me off, right?"

Sara dried her hands, stepped over to the window, and

sighed. "I'm truly sorry about that, but we have good reason to be cautious. We used to have neighbors across the hollow, more than a year ago. Zeke and Linda Anderson and their two little boys, John and Mike." She turned back to face Rita. "They were good folks—kind-hearted, down-to-earth hill people. Some time not long after the plague hit, a couple came up the road, fleeing the city, and stopped at their house, asking for shelter for the night. Zeke and Linda took them in, fed them, and gave them couch space."

Sara ran fingers through her graying hair and looked out the window. Rita could still see her face as a ghostly reflection in the window glass.

"The next morning, Linda found them dead of the plague. Zeke panicked. He called Jon and asked him what to do. I was in the kitchen when he took the call. He said, 'Oh God, Zeke, no.' Then he started crying. We knew by then that there was nothing to do. In about five days the hemorrhaging would begin in their lungs, and they'd drown in their own blood fifteen or twenty minutes later. Zeke was a strong man, both in spirit and body. A lesser man would have just dissolved. He and Linda spent the next five days clearing trees away from their house. Then they let the cows and horse out into the pasture. Linda died first, by a couple of hours, and then the two boys. When Zeke started coughing up blood he called Jonathan to let him know, doused the place with gasoline, and lit it, still inside."

Sara closed her eyes tight, then grimaced and opened them again.

Rita shook her head. "How awful."

Sara nodded. "Yes. All the more so because it's compounded by billions of other awful deaths." She sighed. "We've had a handful of people stop by since then. We've chased them all off, or"—she pursed her lips—"or shot them. Last spring Jon used Zeke's tractor to break up the driveway entrance at the road, and we moved some rhododendron bushes in front of it. That seemed to help. Or maybe everyone else is already dead."

Rita made no comment when Sara finished. Sara just seemed to be glad for someone new to talk to, despite the gloomy subject. Rita looked around the little kitchen and through the short hallway to the main room while listening. The kitchen was comfortably equipped, not modern, but not rustic, either. There was a gas range, but a wooden cutting board lay on top, fitted to completely cover it. The sink was stainless steel, and the water worked in the faucets. They had re-purposed a full-size refrigerator as pantry space. That was where Sara got the Ace bandage she'd used to wrap Rita's ankle. A working dorm-room-sized refrigerator sat on the counter next to it. A microwave oven hung over the range, but it too seemed to be used just for storage.

In the main room, framed by the hallway, a bookcase completely covered the wall, as far as Rita could tell from her seat. It was crammed to overflowing with real paper books. A couple of boxes filled with books sat in front of it as well.

Rita turned to Sara. "If you don't mind me saying, this doesn't look like the sort of place where 'down-to-earth hill folk' would live, with all the antique books, the modern computer equipment, security system, and all. What did you and your husband do before the plague?"

Sara walked back from the window and took a chair at the kitchen table opposite Rita. "This was sort of a summer home. Jonathan taught computer science at the University of North Carolina in Charlotte, and I taught English Literature and Creative Writing there. When they closed the University due to the riots over the infant mortality scandal we came here so I could work on an overview and critique of Margaret Atwood's work and ride out the riots. Then the plague hit and they banned travel. Then the government fell and travel became suicidal, so here we are." She heaved a sigh. "What about you?"

"David and I were students at Cornell University. Sort of like you, when the riots heated up and they closed the University, we decided to hike the Appalachian Trail. Then we heard about the plague and hid in the woods off the trail."

"What'd you do for food?"

"Lived off the land and got thin, mostly. We found some canned food in an abandoned house, once. Got some new clothes there, too. When we stopped getting any access to the internet we waited another month and headed back to civilization. At least, back to where civilization was.

"All the towns we passed were burned out. Cars littered the road with bodies either in them or around them. After a few days of walking along a highway and stepping around corpses, we headed back to the woods. Going was slower, but we just couldn't take it anymore." Rita shrugged. "Not that there was anywhere to go."

"You're lucky you didn't get the plague."

Rita gave a snort and her eyes teared up. "David wasn't lucky. Dead is dead, whether from the plague or a bear."

Sara brought a hand up to her mouth. "Oh, I'm sorry, I've gone and put my foot in it, haven't I?" She got a dish towel from a drawer by the sink and gave it to Rita.

"Thanks."

Rita wiped her eyes and face, looking toward her lap. After an awkward few seconds Sara stood. "I'm going to make some tea. Would you like some?"

Rita nodded and Sara filled a kettle at the faucet. "I'll be right back."

Rita lifted her face toward Sara. "Where are you going?"

"To the fireplace to heat the water." Sara stepped to the hallway.

"Why don't you use your stove?"

Sara turned back toward her. "We haven't had gas for months."

*   *   *

That evening Jonathan cut a thick slice of roasted bear meat and set it on Rita's plate. "So where did you see this other person a month ago?"

Rita gave him a wary look and picked up her fork. "What other person?"

"When you first showed up you said something about having seen someone a month before." He cut a slice for Sara and another for himself.

Rita cut off a chunk of meat and put it in her mouth. She chewed slowly and swallowed. "It was about six or seven weeks ago. East of here, maybe a hundred or a hundred twenty miles. He chased us off too. David tried to argue with him, and he shot at us. We didn't stick around to argue more." She took a bite of her potato and took her time chewing again. "He was old. I mean, older than you. White hair and a long beard."

Jonathan took a drink of water and wiped his mouth. "I guess I can't blame him for being careful with the plague."

"David thought the plague was over."

Lifting her brows, Sara turned toward her. "What? How could he have known that?"

"I don't suppose he really knew for certain. David had been taking pre-med at Cornell. He said that a plague that deadly with a short incubation period would burn itself out after the number of hosts gets small enough."

Sara shook her head. "That sounds like rank speculation."

"He followed the subject on the internet when it started coming up in the news. As long as there was an internet, anyway. The virus was specific to humans for its host. It couldn't survive outside a living body for more than a short time. Minutes or less. And there didn't appear to be any animal vectors. There wasn't enough time to engineer a vaccine and distribute it before most everyone had already died."

Jonathan shrugged. "That chain of logic hangs together, but I don't think I'd bet our lives on it."

"David thought it was a biological weapon that backfired."

"Well, I guess we'll never know." Sara sighed and speared a piece of roasted potato with her fork.

"I don't expect so, no," Jonathan said. "I'm glad you escaped it, at least." He reached over to pat Rita's arm. She jerked away from him and pushed her chair back from the table, shoving the table back a few inches as she did. Some of the water sloshed out of their glasses, leaving puddles on the table around them.

"Ow," Rita cried as she pushed with her bad leg by reflex. Her fork clattered to the floor. She covered her face in her hands.

"What happened?" Jonathan said, turning from Rita to Sara, and then back to Rita.

Sara scowled. "Jon, you can be such an insensitive jerk

sometimes. A week ago we pointed rifles at her and threatened to kill her. That's not something you just forget."

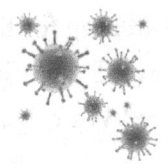

Chapter Four

And a Fourth One Coming

JONATHAN dropped an armload of weeds onto a pile next to the garden plot, and wiped sweat from his forehead with a red and white bandana. "Assuming David was right, that the plague is over, we'll need to start locating other survivors." Rita had finished her quarantine three days earlier and they were taking advantage of good weather to work in the garden plot.

"Well, I don't think it'd be a good idea to go out searching for them," Sara said. "You're likely to get shot before you introduce yourself."

Rita snorted an ironic laugh from where she sat on the ground between rows of vegetables. "Yeah. That matches my experience." She pulled a weed from beside a tomato plant and dropped it onto a pile next to her.

"Don't discard that one," Sara said. "That's lambs quarters. It tastes a lot like spinach if you cook it, and it's high in vitamins."

"Oh." Rita retrieved the plant and set it aside.

Wiping his hands on his trousers, Jonathan re-joined the other two. "If there's any chance to rebuild civilization, we need to find others."

"Yes, but if we're going to find other survivors, we're going to have to get them to come to us," Sara said. "It's not going to work if we go searching for them."

Jonathan wiped sweat from his face again. "How are we going to get them here? We can't exactly put an ad up on Craig's List."

"Signal fires," Rita said.

Sara and Jonathan turned to her.

"Three smoky fires. It's a universal distress signal. If anyone responds, they'll be less likely to be violent."

Jonathan and Sara exchanged a glance, then Jonathan faced Rita again. "Or it'll attract predators who think they'll find an easy victim."

"Then you'll have your surveillance system to detect them."

Sara lifted her eyebrows and shrugged. "It's worth a shot."

"While we still have ammo, at least. But I still want to quarantine visitors for a week."

Sara nodded. "I guess that's safe."

Rita picked up the pile of lambs quarters she'd pulled while they'd talked and grasped her stick to pull herself upright. Sara hopped over a row of peas to help her up.

"Thanks," Rita said as she stood. Then she dropped the greens and staggered. She gasped as Sara braced herself and tightened her grip to steady Rita.

"What's wrong?"

"I just got a little dizzy. It's passed now."

Jonathan came over and picked up the bunch of greens. "You didn't eat much at breakfast. Are you feeling all right?"

"I felt a little queasy this morning, but it's better now."

Sara raised her eyebrows. "How long has it been since you had a period?"

"I have an implant, if you're wondering if I'm pregnant. I've only had intermittent periods over the last year, I guess due to poor nutrition."

"How long ago did you get the implant?"

Rita looked skyward for a second and then her eyes grew wide. "Oh. It's been six years at this point. It's been worn out for a year."

Jonathan sighed. "Well, we can't do an early pregnancy test, so we'll just have to wait to find out for sure."

"Oh God. If I'm pregnant, who's going to deliver the baby?"

"I guess we will," Sara said as they walked back to the cabin.

"You're an English Lit professor, and he's a computer geek." Rita's voice grew shrill. "You don't know how to deliver a baby!"

"Before the internet failed I downloaded all the medical information I could get ahold of," Jonathan said. "I'm sorry, but right now, we're all you've got."

Rita rolled her eyes. "Oh, great. You'll look it up on the internet. Shit! I lost David, and now I'm going to lose his baby." Tears ran down her cheeks.

Sara pulled her up in a hug as they stopped by the door to the cabin. "We've got months yet, even if you are pregnant, and we don't know that for sure. If you are, I promise we'll do all we can to get ready, and to keep you and your baby safe."

Rita sobbed openly now. She said nothing when Sara

embraced her, just buried her face on Sara's shoulder while Sara stroked her back. Jonathan stood beside Sara holding the pile of lambs quarters in one hand, his mouth hanging open.

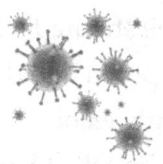

Chapter Five

Reaching Out

JONATHAN threw a double handful of wet leaves onto a fire burning in an old oil drum, then bent down to the wheelbarrow beside him and gathered another batch. Satisfied by the plume of smoke that resulted, he moved the barrow to the next fire, about fifty feet from the first one, and repeated the process.

He'd been doing this every afternoon for a month when it wasn't raining, and still no one had shown up. He stood by the third one for a moment, hands in his pockets, scanning the tree line around the field. Of course, the sensors he'd set would do a better job of detecting visitors, but making his own survey gave him a sense he was doing something.

So far, all they'd detected were some deer, and once, a bear. The mid-June weather was partly cloudy, hot enough to make him sweat freely. He wiped his face on his sleeve and pushed the wheelbarrow back.

About halfway to the cabin his earpiece chimed.

"Accept," he told it.

Sara shouted in his earpiece. "Jon, get back inside. Someone just came into the clearing and he's heading toward you."

Jonathan dropped the wheelbarrow and ran. Faintly from behind him someone shouted, "Hey, wait up."

He made it to the porch and ducked inside. Rita handed him his helmet, and his rifle leaned up against the table.

"Where are you," he asked Sara over the radio.

"In the sniper's nest. He's about half way across the field. He's alone."

"Video on," he commanded the helmet as he strapped on the ballistics vest. An image appeared in the upper left of his field of view, helpfully centered on the figure approaching at a trot. He wore ragged blue jeans but his chest was bare. A scraggly beard covered his face and his long, brown hair hung behind him in a ponytail. He had a rifle. "Are any other intruders present?" Jonathan asked the security monitor program.

"Sara already asked that. It's just him, or I'd have told you by now," it said.

Rita handed him the rifle. He took it and said, "Thanks."

Rita nodded. "Be careful."

"I will. Keep away from the door. Video off."

Jonathan pushed the door open with his foot and stepped out with the gun at his shoulder. The man halted as soon as the door swung open, about thirty yards from the cabin.

"Drop your rifle," Jonathan said, shouting to be heard

over the distance. "Don't come any closer."

The intruder slowly bent at the knees until he could place his rifle on the ground beside him, then straightened up just as slowly with his arms outstretched, his hands empty. "Do you always show visitors this kind of hospitality?"

"Until we know you're virus-free, that's as close as you need to come."

"There's been no sign of the plague around here for almost a year. We stopped quarantining visitors a couple of months ago."

Jonathan took in a sharp breath. "We? We who?"

"About fifty of us have a little village started about thirty miles from here. Northeast off of old highway 215."

"A village?" Jonathan's aim wavered, but he recovered before the stranger could react. "How do I know you're telling the truth?"

The stranger shrugged. "You don't. You set a distress signal. Do you need help or not?"

"We were trying to attract other survivors."

"Looks like you succeeded. My turn to ask, 'We who?'"

"My wife and I live here, and we've taken in another survivor as well."

Sara spoke up in his earpiece. "Don't give out information you don't need to, but don't drive him off, either. If there's a village of survivors, we can't afford to anger them."

The stranger cocked his head to one side while Sara talked to Jonathan over the radio. "Solar cells, body armor, tactical helmet. That's a security monitor system on the mast over your house, right? You're in radio contact with the house too, I'll bet. Doesn't look like you're one of the local folk."

"Never mind about that. What are you doing around here?"

"I'm scouting the area looking for salvage. I saw your

signal a couple of days ago and came looking for you. My camp's a mile or so away, next to a creek." He pointed behind himself with his thumb, but kept his eyes on Jonathan. "We might be able to use someone with technical skills, if you're interested in joining us."

"We'll think about that."

"Good. If you don't need any help and don't want me to approach closer, I guess I'll get on my way. I'm betting you're not the type who would shoot a man in the back. I'm going to slowly turn around and pick my rifle back up. If you want to join us, it's northeast on highway 215, about a mile past I-40. If you get that close, you'll find the village. I won't be back. You'll have to come to us if you want to take this further. I suggest you moderate your attitude, in that case."

He turned slowly in place and squatted back down to get his rifle with his right hand, leaving the other one up in Jonathan's view. He straightened back up with the barrel of the gun clutched in his fist. Taking his time, holding the rifle away from his body as he went, he walked back to the tree line and disappeared into the brush.

Jonathan lowered the rifle, but stood there for a long minute, staring at the spot where their visitor had disappeared.

*   *   *

"I think we should go," Sara said. "We'd be better off as members of a community than we are alone, just from the safety standpoint, if nothing else." They'd gathered around the kitchen table for an impromptu conference after Jonathan came back inside. He'd shed his helmet, but he still wore his ballistics vest. His laptop lay open on the table with the security monitor program showing six video windows that covered the whole perimeter of the clearing.

Jonathan nodded. "I agree, but we might want to wait a while first. I'm a little surprised to hear you say that, though. You've always been so careful about avoiding contact in the past. Thank you," he added as Sara poured tea into his cup.

"You're welcome. Then I was thinking of personal survival. If we have the chance to be a part of a community again, I want to take it."

The thought struck him then that Sara hadn't had one of her lapses of memory for a long time now. The last one he could remember was shortly after Rita had shown up, before she finished the quarantine. She used to have one several times a week at least, and now it had been more than a month.

"Why should we wait?" Rita asked. "I agree with Sara, and the sooner we go the better."

Jonathan turned to Rita, brought back to the subject at hand by her question. "If we just arrive at their gates at this point, we come as beggars. That guy mentioned that they could use someone with technical skills, but I somehow doubt that they'll have much need for an expert in Javascript III programing and network security. They probably don't really need an English Lit professor, or—what was your major, Rita?"

"International Studies."

"Yeah. I'm not even sure there is an 'international' anymore. If we wait until after some of the crops come in, we can bring food with us, at least enough to support ourselves over winter, so we don't become an immediate strain on their resources."

"The tomatoes are already starting to come on," Sara said. "We'll need to start canning them soon."

Rita took a sip from her mug. "How do we bring all that to them? That's a long way to pack that much food. My ankle's a lot better, but I still limp on it a little."

"We can use Zeke's hay wagon and pull it with his tractor," Jonathan said. "I think there's enough gasoline in his tank to get there." He shrugged. "Probably. I bet they'd be glad to have a working tractor as well."

"If that guy's scouting for salvage, might they not be cleaning out Zeke's barn? It's not like we have a legal claim on it, after all. Not that there's a sheriff to enforce a claim anyway."

Jonathan grimaced. "I hadn't thought of that. We might need to bring some of that stuff up to our place."

"What about using your horse," Rita asked. "Wouldn't that work?"

Jonathan tilted his head. "We don't have a horse."

"I've seen one grazing in the field. He used to show up in the mornings while you had me quarantined. It's a bay draft horse of some kind."

"That's Zeke and Linda's horse," Sara said. "I haven't been able to get close to him."

"I used to do some riding in high school. Worked at a stable for a while. Let me try."

Jonathan took a sip of tea. "I suppose that can't hurt."

Sara rubbed her eyes. "That village might prefer to have a horse rather than a tractor. Tractors need gasoline, and have such a slow rate of reproduction."

Jonathan chuckled. "I guess I can't argue with that. Assuming they have a mare."

"It at least makes it a possibility."

"Do you know his name?" Rita asked.

Jonathan nodded. "Johnson."

Rita tilted her head and squinted at him. "Johnson?

That's a strange name for a horse."

"It's a male, and he's big. Zeke didn't have a subtle sense of humor."

"Oh," she said after a second and snorted a little laugh.

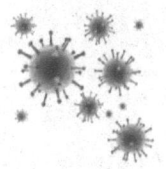

Chapter Six

Too Quiet

ERIK Kinderman had just passed the ruins of Wilmington when he saw a bomb crater beside the road. It spread about fifteen feet across and maybe four feet deep, and it took a bite out of the pavement. He pulled the car to the side of the road, got out, and looked around. Cracked, dried mud coated the bottom of the crater, and there was no sign of vegetation growing in it. There weren't any buildings nearby, nor even any burned out remains of buildings.

It was quiet. He scanned the horizon, turning in place beside the old Ford Focus hybrid he'd managed to get running. The sun shone from a clear sky and it was unseasonably warm for early October near the North Carolina coast. The countryside was flat around here, with farm fields overgrown with weeds. He was used to quiet at this point, but it seemed too quiet, somehow.

He shrugged and brushed hair from his face. A few

volunteer corn plants stood in the field not far from the crater, though they seemed stunted. Some drying ears clung to them, so he pulled a canvas tote bag from the back seat.

As he wandered through the field and collected the corn that remained, he realized why it seemed too quiet. There were no crickets or any other insects chirping or buzzing. Odd, he thought, then shrugged again.

He pulled the car keys from his pocket and rattled them to dispel the unnatural silence as he walked back to the car. The fob of the keychain was a polished brass plate with a name stamped into it: "Tom." He assumed that was the name of the previous owner of the car. Erik had left a house key and a few other keys on the ring, though he had no use for them. It just seemed normal for there to be several keys on a keychain, and he clutched at anything with glimmer of normality.

Whoever he was, Tom had had the courtesy to close the car's door behind him before he died by the side of the road. This kept the weather from destroying the interior, and the only problem had been finding the keys among the bones next to the car, scattered by buzzards and other scavengers.

He put the bag of corn in the car and peered down the road, shading his eyes. It looked as if there might be a gas station up ahead that wasn't burned out. He might be able to pump up some gas. He climbed into the car and drove up to it, maneuvering around debris scattered on the road by the crater.

In the year that Erik had been driving around the Southeast he hadn't seen anything like that crater. Lots of burned out buildings and whole cities that had been reduced to blackened ruins, but nothing that looked like a bomb attack. He shook his head, remembering when he first hiked down from his cabin in the hills of northwest Georgia. He'd run out of basic supplies, but when he reached the town, it was burned rubble, and the country seemed deserted. He'd only seen one other person since then, and he'd shot at Erik when he tried to approach. Since then he'd stayed clear of any contact. He wasn't sure what he was looking for as he drove, he just felt compelled to keep moving. He'd been an engine mechanic in the Navy so he was able to keep the car running, and his survival training kept him fed, if thin.

He parked beside the pumps and pulled his tool kit and a length of hose from the back of the car. It took about an hour to coax off the cap to the underground tank and fill some gas cans with his hand pump. By the time he finished he felt nauseated, but didn't quite have to vomit. Odd. Gas fumes had never done that to him before.

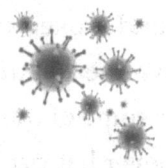

Chapter Seven

Highwaymen

JONATHAN turned toward the cabin when he heard the door open as Sara stepped onto the porch. The sun, bisected by the eastern hills, lit their farm with a ruddy glow. The dew lay heavy on the autumn remains of their garden plot, stripped bare of any remaining vegetables. The maples along the edge of the field showed red and yellow, made all the richer by dawn's light. Leaves swirled in the air when the wind blew. He and Rita were securing a load of provisions on Zeke's hay-wagon and adjusting the harness on the horse.

Hoisting a box of books, Sara made her way through the wet grass to the wagon. She set it on the bed of the wagon, and Jonathan eyed it, a frown forming. "We don't have room for a lot more stuff, and Johnny has to be able to pull it up the hills." "I just can't bear to abandon everything. I don't want Shakespeare and Whitman to go extinct as long as humans remain."

Jonathan pulled a book out of the box and considered it. "Nor Margaret Atwood either, eh?"

"She's an author who's been under-appreciated, but I think future generations will consider her to be one of the great writers of her time."

"I'll defer to your judgment on that." He put the volume back in the box and looked through it a little more. "I agree that we should save these, but we might have to make another trip back here for some of this stuff."

"Jon, that might never happen. I want to be sure to save some of them."

"We'll probably be back for the solar cells and batteries. We can get them then."

"If that happens, that'd be great. But I want to be sure I save some of them first."

He sighed. "Okay, I guess a box of books won't make that much difference in the load."

"I, uh—I have another one to bring out."

He rolled his eyes. "One more?" he asked, lifting his index finger in front of his face.

"Just one more, I promise."

"I guess. Go for it. But you owe Johnny."

"Thanks." She gave him a quick kiss and hurried back to the cabin. He shook his head as he watched her go.

Rita tightened the girth strap on Johnny's harness and turned to Jonathan, brushing a loose strand of hair from her face. "Why don't you just bring them in digital form? That'd weigh almost nothing and take up a lot less room."

"Of course, and we're doing that," he said, gesturing toward the case holding their computer equipment and the portable solar charger. "The thing is, in a few years the electronics will start to fail, and then all those e-book versions will be gone. It's not like we can just hop over to the Computer Market and get replacements, after all. The paper books'll last longer, but even they'll fall apart in fifty years or so. Most of them are on acid pulp paper and weren't intended to be heirlooms."

"Oh." She went back to adjusting the harness on the horse's collar. They never did get used to calling him "Johnson," and had settled on "Johnny" instead. The horse didn't seem to mind. Rita had had little trouble befriending him, with the help of some apples and carrots, and a lot of patience, but he just tolerated Jonathan and Sara.

She stroked the horse's neck. "I think Johnny's all set."

"Good. I think we're about loaded up too, except for Sara's second box of books." He helped Rita onto the wagon. In the last month her pregnancy had become obvious, but hadn't slowed her down much. Her ankle no longer bothered her.

As she settled onto the bench they'd improvised at the front of the wagon to wait, the door to the cabin slammed shut. Sara locked it and then struggled toward the wagon with a box that was easily twice the size of the first one.

Jonathan watched for a couple of seconds, and then shook his head. "'Just one more,' she said." He sighed. "Well, I'd better go give her a hand."

*   *   *

As their shadows began pointing noticeably eastward on the second day of their trip, the I-40 overpass started to creep up in the distance, closer and closer each time they topped a hill as they made their way north. The state road was in good shape, but it had been a stressful journey nonetheless. The ditches, and occasionally the road itself, were littered with wrecked cars with skeletal remains either in them or beside them.

As they passed an old Hyundai Elantra, Rita pointed to it. "The gas cap is open. The last several gas powered cars we've passed were like that. Someone's been here to siphon the gas out of the tank."

"I guess that means we're getting close," Sara said.

Jonathan nodded. "Yeah. That guy we saw last summer said it was only a mile past I-40, and from the looks of things, I-40 is less than a mile away." Jonathan scanned the horizon to the north and pointed. "Is that smoke over there?"

Rita shaded her eyes and looked. A gray smudge hung over the trees to the north. "I think so. I guess we're headed the right way." She pulled on the reins to guide the wagon around a pile of bones on the side of the road and they continued.

*   *   *

As they approached the Interstate underpass two men with rifles appeared from behind the concrete pillars.

"Stop there, and drop your gun," one of them said as the other aimed his rifle at them.

Jonathan laid his rifle on the wagon's bed and Rita pulled the reins to bring the wagon to a halt.

"Hands up where we can see them."

They did as they were ordered.

The other one stood back, covering them with his rifle and the man talking approached the wagon. He was a little shorter than average, with a round face. His jacket was dirty and had a green and black camo pattern. He appeared to be in his thirties. Whoever had trimmed his straight brown hair had been totally innocent of barbering skills.

"Well, look at what we got here. A wagonload of supplies, a geezer, a granny, and a young chick." He looked Rita up and down. "A pregnant one. A little old to be diddling girls that age, ain't you?" He leered at Rita and laughed.

"I'm not the father. We're coming to join the village up ahead."

"Oh, I don't think you'll make it. They're particular about who they allow inside. Wouldn't let George and me stay, for instance."

Sara gave a little gasp. Rita turned back toward them. Jonathan's eyes were wide, but he stared straight at the man, his gaze unwavering.

"How old's the horse?" the man asked, moving in front of it to check its teeth.

Rita gave a kick, catching the reins with her foot, giving Johnny a sharp jerk back. He reared up and knocked the brown-haired man down, striking him in the face with a hoof. Rita went down on the bed of the wagon and George fired a shot. Jonathan pulled Sara down and lay over her, shielding her with his body.

Rita came up with a .22 pistol. She shot George, hitting him in the right shoulder. She tried to fire again, but the ejector had jammed with the spent cartridge still lodged in the chamber.

Before she could clear it there was a rifle crack from above them. George fell back and lay still with a red spot blooming on his chest. Another shot fired from above them and the other man's head exploded.

Sara screamed. Rita spared a quick glance upward and saw a red-haired man with a rifle leaning out through an opening cut in the fence. Then Johnny reared and lurched forward. Rita grabbed for the reins. She gave them a whiplike shake. "Go!"

Johnny pulled the wagon forward and it shuddered violently as the left side wheels crushed the headless body on the road. Rita shouted and shook the reins again and again to urge Johnny up to gallop, but it was too heavy a load for him to continue at that pace for long. Before they'd made a quarter mile he'd slowed down to a trot. When they came around a bend in the road a group of six men and women faced them with rifles leveled. Rita pulled the reins up to stop the wagon. She raised her hands and sobbed. "Oh God, I'm sorry."

From behind her Sara shouted, "My husband's wounded! Please, for the love of God, don't kill us."

Rita spun around toward them, her hands still in the air. Jonathan's right pant leg was soaked with blood.

"We're not going to kill you," one of them said, "but get off the wagon with your hands up."

"He's bleeding massively. I can't let go."

A couple of people approached the wagon from either side with rifles pointed toward them while Rita climbed down, careful to make no threatening moves. They led her a short distance from the wagon and searched her for weapons. Rita submitted without a struggle, but she kept her attention on Jonathan and Sara.

Tears ran down Sara's face. "Please help us. Don't let my husband die."

There was a short silence.

"Jamal's going to climb up there and take a look," a middle aged man said. "No sudden moves or it'll be the last move you make, understand?"

Sara nodded. She tried to wipe tears away against her shoulder while still pressing on Jonathan's wound.

"Jay, check it out."

"Right." A massive dark-skinned man with dreadlocks flowing over his shoulders hopped up on the wagon and evaluated the situation with quick efficiency. "He took a bullet to the thigh. I don't think it broke his leg, but I can't be sure. He's bleeding a lot, but I don't think he's in grave danger just yet." He pulled a knife from a sheath on his belt.

Sara gasped.

"I'm just going to cut away the trouser leg so I can get a better look," Jamal said as he knelt down beside Jonathan, opposite Sara. "Hey guy, you still with us?"

"Yeah," Jonathan said through clenched teeth.

"His name's Jonathan," Sara said.

Jamal nodded, dreadlocks swaying as he cut the cloth away from the wound. "Okay, stay with us, Jonathan. Can I call you Jon?"

"What—whatever. Just don't hurt my wife."

"No one's going to hurt her. My name's Jamal." He turned his neck to face the others around him. "Is the first aid kit on the way?"

"It's coming," someone said.

Jamal turned back to Jonathan. "We're going to take care of you, Jon. It's going to be okay."

"All right."

"Was that your daughter driving the wagon?"

"No. She's—she's a survivor that happened—on our place."

"Oh."

A pickup truck skidded to a halt not far away. Someone jumped out and came up to the wagon with what looked like a fishing tackle box. He set it on the bed of the wagon next to Jamal. As he moved away from the wagon he blocked Rita's view. She shifted a little so she could see them.

The man beside Rita grasped her arm. "Stay put." He

wasn't rough, but Rita didn't test him further. After a few seconds he let go.

*   *   *

Jamal opened the box and pulled on a pair of latex gloves.

"Okay, ma'am, I need you to let go for a second so I can take a better look."

"But he'll start bleeding again."

"It'll be okay for a second."

Sara looked into Jonathan's eyes, her mouth hanging open.

"It's okay, Sara. You've done—what you can." He took a couple breaths. "I love you."

Sara sobbed new tears. "I love you too."

She let go and a woman behind her helped Sara stand, and then helped her climb off the wagon. She led her toward where Rita stood, next to a group that included the leader. Another man climbed up on the wagon to assist Jamal.

Rita took a step toward Sara, but the woman leading Sara held up a hand to stop her, and the man standing beside Rita grasped her arm again.

"I'm terribly sorry, ma'am," the man said, "but we have to search her for weapons first."

Sara's eyes went wide. "Oh."

Rita glanced toward the man, then turned back to Sara. "They took my pistol."

The woman leading Sara said, "Please stand with your arms outstretched and your legs separated."

Sara's eyes flickered over the crowd. More people had gathered since they had first stopped. There were at least a dozen now. They all had either rifles or side arms. After a moment's hesitation, she submitted to the search.

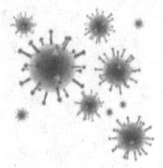

Chapter Eight

Swift Justice

"JAKE was dead when we got to the lookout post on the Interstate," a young man testified. He was maybe twenty-five years old with dark skin, frizzy black hair, and a sparse beard.

"It looked like he'd been shot in the back," another young man added. He also had short hair, but his was red and he was fair-skinned.

They'd gathered in the community center of a gated complex of upscale homes and condominiums where these survivors had set up their village. A laptop computer sat on a table in the middle of the room with an omnidirectional microphone attached. It was early evening, only four hours after Jonathan, Sara, and Rita had arrived.

Sara scanned the room. Twenty-five or thirty people had gathered there, mostly men but eight or nine women as well. After so long alone, with just the three of them, it was almost dizzying to see so many other people together all at once. The one presiding over the meeting was a somewhat-past-middle-aged man with shoulder length graying hair tied in a ponytail. He'd introduced himself as Jim Henderson at the start of the meeting, which he'd called a "Determination of Facts."Jonathan lay on a cot by Sara's side with his head propped up by three pillows, and Rita stood on his other side. Jonathan's injury wasn't as severe as it had first appeared. The bullet had torn a nasty furrow in his right thigh but had missed any major blood vessels or tendons. He'd have an impressive scar.

"So what happened next?" Jim Henderson prompted.

"As I was checking Jake out, we heard voices from underneath the Interstate," the young black man said. "Couldn't understand what they said, just that there were voices. Tyler had his rifle ready and started toward the edge where we'd cut the fence open. Then we heard gunshots."

"There was this wagon there and the older couple was lying on its bed, and this younger girl had a pistol out, when I got there," Tyler continued. "I recognized John and George Gibson. John was on the ground in front of the horse, and George had fallen too. He was trying to bring up his rifle one-handed. I shot George, and then John. The girl grabbed the reins and the horse took off under the Interstate like all the demons of hell were after them."

"Why'd you shoot George and John, and not the ones on the wagon?"

"Huh?" Tyler jerked his head back and his eyes widened. He glanced to the black man, then turned back to Jim. "Well, we'd just run the Gibsons off a couple months ago, didn't we? You said we'd shoot 'em if they came back, so that's what I did. I shot 'em."

"How did you know John and George were the aggressors, and not the others?"

"George fired the first shot," the black man interjected.

"How do you know that? By your testimony you didn't see it happen."

"I heard the rifle crack first, then the pop from the pistol. The girl shot second, for sure no doubt, after George Gibson shot his rifle."

Tyler nodded. "Bill's right. I remember that too, now that he tells it."

"Besides, it just stands to reason," Bill said. "John and George were fucking criminals. We all know that. That's why we ran them out."

Shaking his head, Jim said, "Opinion. Keep to the facts, please. You said both John and George were on the ground, but you only heard one shot from Ms. Ballard's pistol, is that right?"

Tyler scratched his cheek. "Yeah, I guess so."

"How do you think that happened?"

Tyler glanced at Bill again, then turned back to Jim and shrugged. "I have no idea." He looked back to Bill. "Besides, they must have been the ones that killed Jake. The Gibsons must have, that is. He was hit by something high powered, judging by the hole it tore in him. The girl—Ms. Ballard, I mean—just had that little pop gun, and the rifles on the wagon ain't been shot recent."

"How do you know that?"

"Why, I smelled 'em," he said, as if it should have been obvious. "There was no smell of powder on the guns in the wagon."

"You didn't know that at the time you shot the Gibsons, then. You determined that later. Is that correct?"

"Uh—Yes sir, I guess that's right."

"Okay, so you heard voices, then the rifle, then the pistol. You shot George and then John, and the wagon took off.

Then what?"

"Then I shouted to Bill to call an alarm on the radio," Tyler said. "I left Bill on watch and followed after the wagon. By the time I caught up with it, Jamal was doctoring up the man. The two ladies were off the wagon and it was all over. I checked their rifles, like I said, then waited till Jamal was done and led the horse over to the stable."

"Is that everything?"

"Pretty much, I reckon."

"How about you, Bill? Anything to add?"

"No, I guess not. Just that we're all better off without the likes of those two assholes around."

"Keep your opinions out of it. We're after the facts."

"Yessir."

Jim turned to the three newcomers. "Okay, your turn. Who's your spokes-person?"

"I guess I am," Jonathan said, preempting Sara's response.

Sara squeezed Jonathan's hand and gave a small shake of her head. She didn't want to argue with him here, but she worried for him taking this responsibility right now. She pursed her lips. How like a man. Jonathan hadn't had any painkillers when they worked on him, and sewing up his wound had been hard on both of them. That was three hours ago, however, and now he seemed to tolerate the pain okay, as long as he didn't move his leg.

Jim Henderson tilted his head. "Are you sure you're up to telling your side, Mr. Rillman?"

"I'll manage."

"Go ahead then."

"Okay," Jonathan said, "well, we were on our way to your village and these two men stopped us as we were coming up to the Interstate. One of them covered us with the rifle, and the other came over to inspect our wagon. He made some threatening remarks, like he intended to rob us. He asked how old the horse was and tried to check his teeth. Johnny—uh, our horse, that is—reared up and struck the man in the head with a hoof. He went down, and the other guy shot his rifle. He hit me in the leg, and then Rita shot him with that .22 pistol. The next thing we knew someone had shot the two men who stopped us and Rita had Johnny up at a gallop heading away from there. We met your welcoming committee a short time later."

"Why did your horse rear up at that point?"

Jonathan shrugged. "I don't know, but he's particular. He likes Rita, but only tolerates Sara and me, for instance. He might not have liked that guy poking his fingers at his mouth."

"What sort of threatening remarks did he make?"

"He looked Rita up and down like she was a piece of meat for sale. I told him we were coming to your village, and he said, 'Oh, I don't think you'll make it.' I was sure he had rape on his mind."

"Keep to the facts."

Jonathan narrowed his eyes. "It is definitely a fact that I was sure he was considering rape."

Jim raised his brows and after a second he gave a nod. "Noted. How did you find out about our village?"

"We'd set signal fires last summer, and someone came by and told us about it. He said he was scouting the area looking for salvage."

"That was me," a man in the back of the room said. He'd trimmed his beard since his visit to their cabin, but Jonathan recognized him at once when he spoke. "They had a cabin with a high tech security system, solar panels, and tactical gear. It was in my report."

"We recognize Jacob Skinner," Jim said to the recording, then continued, "I remember. You'd mentioned that he didn't seem friendly."

Jonathan's eyebrows shot up. "I was being cautious about the plague. I didn't mean him harm, but I was going to safeguard my wife and Rita."

Jacob shrugged. "That's consistent with what I saw. He wasn't friendly, but he didn't act like an outlaw, either."

"Anything to add to what your husband said, Ms. Rillman?"

"No sir."

"How about you, Ms. Ballard?"

"That man—the brown-haired one—was going to kill us. I'm sure of it, I could see it in his eyes, and from his comment about us not going to make it to the village."

"Opinion. Keep to the facts, please."

Rita shook her head. "No sir. Not opinion. It was a judgment. No disrespect, sir, but I had to make a judgment of him in what was obviously a life-or-death situation, and that's the one I made based on previous—" she pursed her lips while a quiet second passed. "Previous experience." She kept her eyes on Jim's face, but Sara noticed a slight twitch under her left eye.

Jim's eyebrows lifted. "Previous experience?"

"Yes sir. I was—I was raped once before, in my freshman year in college. I recognized the look in his eyes."

Rita wiped a hand over her eyes, but she stood ram-rod straight. Sara reached over Jonathan to Rita and took her hand, squeezing it. Jonathan laid a hand on her forearm.

Jim gave a single nod, his lips pressed in a tight line. "I see. Does anyone else have facts to relate about the homicides of John and George Gibson?"

He waited for several seconds and no one spoke up. He nodded. "Very well. My impression of the facts is that the homicides of John and George Gibson were justified under the circumstances as an act of defense of our community." He spoke formally, with careful diction, facing the microphone on the central table. "It is also my impression that these three people— Jonathan and Sara Rillman, and Rita Ballard—acted in their own self-defense in response to an attempted robbery, and were justified in their judgment that their lives were in danger. I propose that no action be taken against them, nor against Tyler Hopson for the homicides. Does anyone have a dissenting impression of the facts?"

Again he waited a long time and no one spoke up. "We have a quorum of the adult members of our community present," he said. "If there are no dissenting impressions of the facts in the matter of the homicides of John and George Gibson, I move that the impression I have previously stated be accepted as the judgment of this community. Is there a second?"

Multiple people around the room replied, "Second."

"All in favor say, 'Aye.'"

A chorus of "Ayes" arose.

"All opposed say, 'Nay.'"

No one spoke.

"The motion is unanimously carried. Thank you for your service. The matter of the homicides of John and George Gibson is ended."

Sara shook her head, dazed by the realization that what she'd at first assumed was an informal fact-finding meeting was instead something that these people took as very formal, very serious, and very final. The whole process had taken less than a half hour. Apparently they intended justice to be swift.

People got up from their chairs and conversation started up in various corners of the room. Jim stood and raised his voice. "Excuse me, please, everyone. We have another matter to discuss: whether we allow these three people to settle here or not."

Sara turned to Jonathan. His mouth hung open.

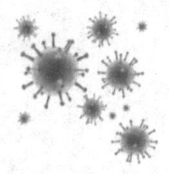

Chapter Nine

A Visitor in Distress

JONATHAN sat at a desk in the back corner of the community center. He peered intently at the screen of his laptop computer, occasionally typing in code for the security program. Though they had spent a few uncomfortable moments at the end of the "Determination of Facts" meeting when they first arrived, it turned out that the question of whether they'd be permitted to settle there was *pro forma*, at least on a probationary basis. Mostly, it was a discussion of what their skills were, to determine their roles in the community workforce.

They'd moved into one of the smaller homes in the complex, a one-story house with a basement. It had a solar power system and a gas furnace. The gas had stopped flowing long ago, so they relied on a wood-burning fireplace for heat. Nights were getting chilly.

A week ago, when Jamal declared that Jonathan's leg

had healed sufficiently, Jonathan led a salvage team back to his cabin. They brought back the security system, the solar panels and household battery, the inverter, and six boxes of books. It had taken three days for five people to disassemble and pack it all, then two days for a four-horse team to pull it all back to the village.

Now Jonathan worked to adapt his security system for the village and Sara was setting up a library for the community. Rita worked in the stable, and they were all expected to help with the community vegetable gardens.

More than half of November had passed. They'd celebrate Thanksgiving in about a week. It was only late afternoon, but the cloud-covered sky was already as dark as dusk. In the main room behind him some of the people moved tables around to put up decorations for the coming feast. He tried to concentrate on modifying the security program he'd had for his cabin in the hills for the village here, but the activity behind his back distracted him. The work progressed slowly in any case. The camera wasn't intended for a site this large, and the range he needed taxed the equipment's capabilities. It was okay for the section facing the front of the community next to the road, but there wasn't enough resolution for the back section. He'd have to add input from other cameras for that, and that was proving to be a challenge. They didn't have another 360-degree surveillance camera system available, so he had to adapt other consumer-grade cameras they had found left in the village for the task. At his cabin, the camera mounted on the mast above his house had had a clear view of the clearing's perimeter. Here, trees and buildings were in the way, so camera placement was critical. Not only that, so far he had units with five different sets of sensor resolutions to integrate into the system.

Before it failed, Jonathan had downloaded a large

section of the internet onto a couple of 16 Petabyte drives. Other projects of his were making a local network with the internet subset available to the residents, and adapting the community's cell repeater for stand-alone use. He hunched his shoulders against the distraction behind him and kept working.

Sara had nearly finished setting up the library. She shuttled back and forth between a stack of boxed books and shelves along the wall across the room, arranging the books. Between the books they'd brought back from the cabin and some others that were in houses here already, a nice little library was taking shape, though it was heavy on literature and pop fiction, and light on technical books.

Most people had had e-books before the plague, however, and there were relatively few on paper. Almost all of the e-books were lost. Even when the devices still worked, they were usually password protected. In a few cases the passwords were easily guessable, or had been written on the back, but by and large, the readers and computers they found needed to be wiped and re-initiated to be of any use.

As Jonathan worked, Jim Henderson came in and took a seat beside him. "How's it coming?"

Jonathan leaned back and rubbed his eyes. "Slowly and with great difficulty. I think I'm getting there, but it's taking a lot of work."

"Well, keep at it. If this works it'll be a real boost to our security."

"I'll get it. It's just going to take some time."

"Okay, good." Jim gestured at Jonathan's laptop. "Are you going to ultimately load the security program onto one of the center's computers?"

"I'll do that for the sake of having a backup copy, but

the program will have to run from my laptop."

Jim raised an eyebrow. "Oh? Why?"

"This computer was one of my research projects before the crash. It has some experimental, enhanced hardware features and dedicated processors that allow the artificial intelligence persona to run effectively. If it'd run at all on one of the other computers is doubtful, and if it did run, it'd be too slow to be worthwhile."

Jim nodded, then shrugged. "Okay, then." He turned on a computer on the desk beside Jonathan.

"I've never been clear about the—I guess you'd call it the political structure of this community," Jonathan said. "How do you choose the mayor, and so forth?"

Jim grimaced. "I'm not sure 'structure' is the right word in that context. We haven't had elections, or anything like that, and I'll deny with my dying breath that I'm the mayor or any other such formal officer."

"You seem to be pretty much in charge, as far as I can see."

Jim rolled his eyes heavenward. "As much as anyone is in charge, I guess so." He swiveled his chair to face Jonathan. "In a group this size, mutual consensus is workable. Has been so far, anyway. I had experience with management and conflict resolution, and I just seemed the best able to moderate meetings. We make decisions together, though."

Jonathan shrugged. "If it works, it works. How many live here altogether?"

"Forty-five adults, thirty-one men, fourteen women, seven of them post-menopausal. Seven children ages two months to fifteen years."

Jonathan arched his brows. "Pretty much on top of the statistics, for someone who's not the leader."

"Old habits die hard. If you'll excuse me, I want to

write up some notes before I go home."

"Of course."

Jim went back to work. Just a few minutes later though, the radio clipped to his belt came to life. He pulled it off and answered.

"This is Tyler," The radio said. "There's a car coming in on the interstate from the east. It's weaving pretty bad."

"A car? Keep close to cover until you know their intentions, but make sure they see someone's there. I'll send some others for backup." He adjusted the radio and said. "This is Jim Henderson. We have a visitor approaching by car on the interstate. Tyler needs backup at the lookout post." He clipped the radio back on his belt and stood. "Gotta go."

Jonathan held up a hand. "Jim, wait a moment. If people get here on foot, it's a good bet that they're virus-free, just from the amount of time it takes for travel. That's no longer a good assumption if they come by car. We should quarantine whoever this is."

Jim nodded. "Of course. That's how we've set up our protocol, though this is the first time we've had a survivor arrive by car."

* * *

When Jim arrived at the Interstate outpost about twenty minutes later, a battered Ford Focus sat some distance away from the checkpoint shack. It had a single occupant—a bald man—who sat with his head back against the back of the driver's seat, panting. A little crowd stood some twenty five yards from the vehicle.

Jim leaned his bicycle against the median divider and approached the crowd. "So what's going on?"

Tyler scratched his head under a watch cap. "Not sure.

He 'pears to be sick, but it don't look like the plague to me. He ain't coughing up blood, anyway."

"He have anything to say?"

"No, not much. Says his name's Erik Kinderman, and he came from Georgia."

"Okay." Jim walked toward the car, but stopped a good distance away. "Erik, can you hear me?"

Erik nodded. "Yeah, I hear you."

"Do you know what you're sick with?"

"I think so, yes."

Jim waited a couple of seconds, but Erik didn't elaborate.

"So what are you sick with?"

"Radiation poisoning."

Jim looked back at the others, eyebrows raised. They took a few steps back. He turned toward Erik again. "Did you say, 'Radiation poisoning?'"

Erik turned more toward Jim and raised his voice. "Yes. Radiation poisoning."

Jim turned to Jamal, who was standing beside Tyler. "What do you think?" Jamal had the best medical credentials in the village, though he wasn't a doctor. He'd been a medic in the army during the Afghan war, twenty years ago.

Jamal shrugged. "About radiation poisoning? I don't know. The plague wouldn't make him sick in that manner, though. Not saying I know he's plague-free, just that what's making him sick now isn't the plague."

Jim shifted his gaze to Tyler. "Hand me the binoculars." Tyler retrieved them from the outpost shack. Jim focused on the man in the car. He was totally bald, including eyebrows. Purple splotches stained the skin over his scalp.

Jim lowered the binoculars and called out to Erik,

"What makes you think that?"

"I used to be in the Navy, on a—a nuclear powered aircraft carrier. The *Clinton*. Worked in the engine room." He panted a few breaths. "We all got training on the effects of rad—radiation exposure. I've got all the symptoms."

"Okay, how were you exposed?"

"Not sure, but—but I stopped by a blast crater near the coast about five or six weeks ago. There were no crickets or flies around it. It was—probably contaminated."

Dan Kiner's eyes grew wide. "We got nuked? Oh Lord."

"It wasn't a nuclear blast. Too small. Was only about fif—fifteen feet across. Must've been a dirty bomb."

"Where was this?" Jim asked.

"East, near the coast. Not—not far from the ruins of—Wilmington, North Carolina."

"At least 250 miles from here," Dan Kiner said.

Jim nodded to acknowledge Dan. "What do you need at this point?"

"A place to rest would be good."

"We'll have to quarantine you for a week to be sure you don't have the plague. There's a house across from our village where you can stay, but don't try to approach anyone. There'll be guards, and they'll have instructions to shoot if you try to get out."

"I don't have the plague, but—but I doubt I'll last the week anyway. I'd—I'd appreciate a comfortable place to die, at least."

Jim glanced at Dan Kiner. Dan dropped his gaze, not meeting Jim's eyes. Jim raised his radio to his face and keyed it. "This is Jim Henderson. We need someone to set up the guest house."

After a second George Hardy, the manager of the

community's vegetable garden plots, responded. "I'll take care of it. Right now?"

"The sooner the better. Our guest is waiting outside the lookout post on the Interstate now."

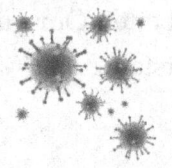

Chapter Ten

Peril in the East

SIX days later Jonathan called up a satellite image on a wide screen monitor mounted to the wall of an office in the community center. "This is the crater that Erik mentioned," he said. Six of them besides himself crowded into the office, selected by he-knew-not-what criteria. Jim Henderson, Jamal Johnson, Janet Haskel, Dan Kiner, and George Hardy were there, but so was Tyler Hopson, the young man who'd shot the Gibson brothers on the day that Sara, Rita, and he had arrived at the village. Jonathan had assumed that Tyler was an uneducated country hick based on his dialect, but now he was less sure.

The screen showed a small, brown, circular feature at the edge of a green field by a road. "The crater is about fifteen feet in diameter," Jonathan said, "and this picture spans about two-thousand feet across the width. It was taken last August." He zoomed the picture out until the crater was just a dot marked by an arrow in the center of the image. "This one spans ten miles. If you look closely, you can see how the vegetation around the crater has a different, more yellow color, compared to that more distant from the crater." He pressed a key on the computer. The screen went to a false-color representation. The corners of the image were a mottled black, gray, and brown, while the area around the crater for a few miles became more garishly splotched by bright colors the closer it was to the crater. The roads were a web of vivid red stripes on the map.

"This highlights the difference. I took the chroma code from some pixels near the corners of the screen, averaged them, and subtracted the result from that of the other pixels. It clearly indicates that there's a difference in the plant health near the crater, as opposed to distant from the crater.

"If, as Erik speculated, this was due to a 'dirty bomb' explosion, that would make sense. To be consistent with the amount of exposure he said he might have gotten there, and his level of illness now, it would have to be a pretty high degree of contamination, though."

He hit another key. "This is a more recent image. It all looks brown in this one due to the season, but here's the difference image." He pressed another key and an image similar to the first one appeared. Though the colored area around the crater wasn't as garish, it was larger, and noticeably tear-drop shaped, with the tail pointing east.

"This shows that whatever is contaminating this area is spreading as the wind and rain scour the site. The prevailing westerly winds have spread the contamination eastward, but the affected area is larger in every other direction as well."

George Hardy raised a hand. "How'd you get these pictures?"

"The weather satellites still work, and some of the newer ones keep an archive of images. I managed to connect with some of them using equipment left by a previous resident who was an amateur radio enthusiast."

Janet Haskell, a Christian minister who also taught

school there, shifted more upright in her chair. "So Erik was just unlucky, and blundered onto this site, then."

Jonathan gave a slow shake of his head. "I'm afraid it's worse than that." He typed a bit on the keyboard and hit the enter key. "This is a time lapse of weather satellite images from February a year ago, before the Internet failed. I put it together from images archived on one of the drives where I'd saved the internet subset." The image showed the east coast of the United States from Washington, DC down to Columbia, South Carolina. Thin clouds flashed across the screen for a moment, then a series of bright pinpricks lit up in a line following the coast. Over a few seconds they faded out.

"One of these exactly correlates with the crater that Erik found. Here's an image of one of the others." He typed a few keys and another still image appeared. This one showed another crater in the middle of a forested area.

He hit another key. "Here's the difference image for this site." It showed the same sort of contamination pattern as the first one. "There are one hundred and seventeen of these sites from Portland, Maine, to Miami, Florida, averaging about fourteen miles between each. Of course, they're not evenly spread, exactly, but there's no more than thirty miles between any two."

He switched to a view of the entire east coast, set in false colors to highlight the contamination. Large parts of a strip along the coast were affected, with only narrow corridors between them. "At the rate the contamination is spreading, in about another year it won't be possible to get to the east coast without exposing yourself to significant radiation poisoning."

George winced. "Who did this?"

"I haven't a clue. It was obviously an attack, but by who, or why, I don't know."

Brows furrowed, Jamal shook his head. "I don't understand what the motive would have been. This would have poisoned the coast for any occupiers as well. It doesn't make sense."

Jonathan nodded. "Then too, the plague was rampant on the coast at that time. Any occupiers who landed on the coast are likely dead at this point. Besides— " he turned back to the keyboard and typed some, brought up a menu and clicked on one of the selections, then typed some more. The image zoomed in to an area around the mouth of Chesapeake Bay. "I think the Navy got them right after they launched the missiles. Look here, carefully," he said, and pointed with the mouse to a spot near the Virginia coast. After a few seconds they saw a dim flare and a puff of smoke, with multiple vapor trails streaking toward the ocean. In the time-lapse sequence they were only visible for a few seconds before the wind dispersed them.

"Now watch." He scrolled the image window over the ocean, and a moment later two bright spots flared for a couple of seconds, then disappeared.

"There were rocket launches like that all up and down the coast. I've found twenty-nine of those little flares in the ocean. In a couple of spots I was able to identify small boats in those locations, but no details that would give a clue about their origin."

He brought the false color image of the east coast back on the screen and leaned against the backrest of his chair. "That's all I got."

"So what do we do about this?" George asked. Sweat had beaded up on top of his bald head despite the cool temperature. It glistened under the lights, a sharp contrast to his brown skin.

Jim had been sitting quietly, intent on Jonathan's presentation and the video images, leaning forward toward the screen with his elbows on the table, his chin cupped in his left hand. Now he leaned back in his chair. "There's nothing for us *to* do," he said. "We're nearly three hundred miles from the coast. At one time that would have been a day trip, but now it's a multi-week expedition. We have no pressing need to go to the coast, and it looks like now we couldn't go there and survive the trip, anyway. This was interesting, Jonathan, and I appreciate the effort you put into this presentation, but as far as what we do going forward, I don't see that it changes much of anything. I guess it's good to know that we can't send an expedition to the coast, but that's about it."

"Salt," Janet said.

They turned toward her. "Excuse me?" Jim asked.

"Eventually we'll run out of salt. I'm not sure how soon, but we'll need a source for food preservation, particularly for meat."

"We got time to figure that out," Tyler Hopson said. "There's lots of salt blocks at the feed store out away from the old town. Bet they got a ton or more of it."

Janet raised an eyebrow. "The feed store?"

"Sure. Livestock needs salt, too."

Janet grimaced and her face flushed.

"There's probably mineral salt deposits other places too," George said. "I'm sure there's information about that stored on one of Jonathan's drives. Or maybe we can get to the Gulf of Mexico."

"Okay, that's a subject we'll have to deal with, but not immediately," Jim said. "Anyone have anything else to add about this?"

George straightened up in his chair. "We've got to dispose of Erik's car somehow. It's probably contaminated. Maybe we could tow it away from town on a long chain, or something. Leave it someplace where rain run-off won't get into the ground water."

"We'll have to seal it in concrete, then," Tyler said. I think there's enough left at the old Home Depot."

Jim nodded. "Anything else?"

Jonathan pushed the keyboard toward the center of the table. "Just an observation: If the whole east coast is contaminated, that means no one from Europe or Africa will be able to reach us, if there are any survivors there. We're isolated."

Shaking his head, Dan Kiner, Jim's *de facto* second-in-command, said, "Not an issue. Definitely not in the near term, anyway. The plague seems to have started in North Africa and spread from there. There was no radio or network response from Europe, Africa, South America, or Asia for some time before the plague finished with North America. If there are any pockets of survivors left there, they'll be too busy surviving to try to cross an ocean to reach us."

Jonathan tilted his head. "I never heard that. Where are you getting that information?"

"Gloria worked in a law office with political connections. It was classified at the time, but I guess that's moot now."

"I guess so," Jim said. "Anything else?"

"How's Erik?" Jonathan asked.

Dan Kiner tilted his face toward the table. "He didn't answer the radio this morning. He wasn't coherent most of the time yesterday, either. It doesn't look good."

Jim ran his fingers through his hair. "How long until the quarantine's over?"

"Tomorrow afternoon."

No one said anything for a while. Jim looked around the table, but no one suggested that someone should go help him, or even that someone should check in on him. Finally Jim heaved a sigh. "Well, I suppose we'll find out tomorrow afternoon, then. I guess that's it, if there's nothing else." He stood, and the others followed his example. "I'll see you tonight at the Thanksgiving dinner."

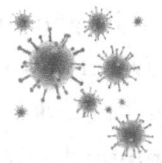

Chapter Eleven

Thanksgiving

"...IN Jesus' name we pray, amen," Janet Haskel raised her face and people began moving up to the buffet line. Sara nodded and murmured "amen," with the others as Janet limped back to join her husband, Bob. Her black hair was streaked with silver and pulled into a ponytail that waved behind her as she went. A soft buzz of conversation started up around the meeting room of the community center and a light rain rattled against the windows.

A couple of roasted wild turkeys rested on platters on the table along with chicken and ham from the farm. Potatoes, squash, and home-canned peas rounded out the meal. A platter of corn bread cut in squares sat on the table next to several loaves of dense, dark brown bread cut into slices. Several bottles of wine and liquor salvaged from before the plague sat on a table nearby.

Jonathan and Sara filled plates and carried them back to the table. Rita joined them, sitting across the table.

A short time later a man of about thirty years old came over, holding a plate stacked high with chicken, vegetables, bread, and potatoes. "Mind if I join you?" he asked.

Sara looked him over. He was of medium height with broad shoulders. His straight black hair was parted on the left, and his beard had been trimmed, but was starting to grow out. He wore a green plaid flannel shirt and blue jeans. His boots were well worn, but sturdy. "No, of course not," Sara said. Jonathan and Rita nodded agreement.

He took the seat next to Rita and offered his hand. "I'm Allen. Allen Jacobs."

Rita took his hand and said, "Glad to meet you, Allen. I'm Rita Ballard." She introduced Jonathan and Sara.

"I don't recall seeing you before," Jonathan said. "We've only been here a little less than two months now."

"I haven't seen you either," Allen replied, "but I heard about the incident with the Gibson brothers when you arrived. I live a little outside the village itself, across the road and out a half mile or so. I manage the livestock. The cattle, sheep, and pigs. Me and three other people, that is. I don't have much to do with the chickens." He spread some butter on a slice of bread. "You have me to thank for the butter, for instance."

"Well, thank you, then." Sara sighed. "As terrible as times have been, it's good to take some time to acknowledge the things we have to be thankful for."

Allen shrugged. "Yeah, I suppose so." He speared a piece of a roasted potato, put it in his mouth, chewed slowly, and swallowed. "I'm not one to turn down a good meal, but I'm not sure our previous traditions have served us well enough to keep carrying them on."

"Giving thanks is always appropriate, regardless," Sara said.

He shrugged again and continued eating.

Sara took a drink of water and set her glass back down. "I'm thankful that we've survived the plague, and for the opportunity to be here with these other survivors, anyway."

Allen raised his eyes back up at her and swallowed. "If we're going to continue to survive, we have some hard lessons to learn, and it doesn't seem to me like, collectively, we're being good students. We almost destroyed the Earth, but she finally had enough and solved the problem in her own way. At this point, the worst thing we could do is to try to re-create the society we had before. If we do that, we're just inviting the Earth to try again, and do a more thorough job of it."

Sara glanced at Jonathan. He gave no sign as he spread butter on a slice of bread. She turned back to Allen and nodded. "God destroyed the world in the Great Flood, and then it was prophesied that the next time the world would be destroyed by fire. So it was. Not in a great, world-wide conflagration, but in millions of little fires filling the air with poisons. Then came the metaphorical fire of the plague, and the literal fires they set in the cities to try to contain it. Is that what you mean?"

"That's one interpretation. Look, I'm sorry I got set off. I guess I'm just bitter."

"We all have something to be bitter about," Sara said, "but bitterness doesn't move us forward."

"I suppose not. I'm just not sure which way forward is, at this point." He turned to Rita. "So, when are you due?" He took a bite from a chicken drumstick.

Rita didn't seem put-off by the personal question as she answered him. Sara took it as Allen's attempt to change the subject, so she let it be. Rita and Allen chatted amiably together, and they all kept to neutral subjects for the remainder of the meal.

*   *   *

That evening Jonathan and Sara lay together in a bed that they'd moved to the family room of their ranch-style home. It wasn't really set up well as a bedroom, but at least it had a fireplace to provide some warmth.

Under a thick quilt Jonathan held Sara close and stroked her back through a flannel nightgown. Like usual she'd given him a kiss as they settled into bed together. She nuzzled her face against his chest and he ran the heel of his hand down her spine from her shoulders to the small of her back, then back up. Usually she sighed with pleasure when he did this, but now she was silent. Not quite stiff, but not responsive, either.

"What's the matter?" Jonathan asked, whispering. Rita's bed was in the den, which shared the fireplace on the other side of a wall lined with stonework, and he didn't want to disturb her sleep. It was something of a damper on their sex life.

"He might be right," Sara whispered.

"Who might be right? You mean Allen Jacobs?"

"Yeah. It's an idea that's been floated for a long time, that the Earth as a whole is a living, conscious being, and the biosphere is a collection of elements of her body. Maybe she got tired of the pollution and did something to eliminate it. Maybe we humans are just a disease on the Earth's skin."

"Even if true, it's a hypothesis that can't be tested. At least, not by us." He held her a little tighter and kissed her forehead. "We have to go on. It's what we humans do. Hopefully we'll do a better job of it in the future."

"Yeah. We can hope." She sniffled, and Jonathan realized that she was crying.

"Sara, it's okay. We still have each other." He gave her a tight hug.

"I'm sorry we never had children." She sniffled again, louder. "I know it seemed like the right thing at the time, but now I'm sorry."

"I know. Me too."

"You are?" She pulled back to look at him. Without her glasses he knew she couldn't have made out much of his face in the dim, flickering light of the fireplace.

"Yeah. But it's too late now, so I try not to think about it."

"Well, we can be surrogate grandparents for the children here, then," she said. She wiped her eyes with her sleeve, then settled back into his arms. He held her tight.

Jonathan reflected that he knew of only one other pregnant woman in the village besides Rita, and another two-month-old infant. "You'll be a great surrogate grandma."

"You will be too. A grandpa, that is."

"Me? I'm a crotchety old curmudgeon. They'll run screaming to get away from me."

"Oh, you are not a curmudgeon."

"Am too. It's a requirement for the computer science doctorate."

Sara laughed, quickly suppressing it to a chuckle to avoid disturbing Rita, then gave him a kiss. "Okay, well, if you're a curmudgeon, you're a lovable one. I love you."

"I love you too."

"We should try to get some sleep."

"Yeah, I suppose so. Good night."

Sara's breathing went soft and regular a short time later, but sleep evaded Jonathan. In his mind he saw the map of the east coast splotched with the indications of contamination while the thought echoed inside: Sixty-two people was an awfully small population to rebuild a civilization. Especially if only seven of the women were able to bear children. He grimaced. Eight, if you counted Dan and Gloria's fifteen-year-old daughter.

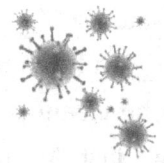

Chapter Twelve

Burial Detail

A week following Thanksgiving Jonathan volunteered to join the crew to remove Erik's body and clean up the guest house. After seven days following Erik's death, cleanup would be a grim job, but any plague virus would be gone by that time. There were four of them, all dressed in plastic coveralls, masks and latex gloves. It was a relatively warm day for early December, above freezing at least, and the sky was clear.

Three of them entered the house and fanned out, looking for the body and opening windows as they went, while the fourth, Bill Stevenson, built a fire in the yard to heat wash water. After less than a minute, while Jonathan was in the bedroom, Dan Kiner shouted. "Found him. He's in the bathroom."

The rest of them crowded into the small room. Erik's remains lay curled up on the floor of the shower, fully clothed, badly decayed. Concentrated in the little bathroom, the stink caused them to gag and their eyes to water.

Jamal brushed a dreadlock from his face as he bent to peer at the body. "Well, dead is dead, I guess, but it doesn't look like he died of the plague. There'd be blood stains around his mouth and nose in that case."

"The hair loss and the nausea he reported are characteristic of radiation poisoning, according to the research I did recently," Jonathan said.

Dan nodded. "I'm glad he came to the bathroom to die, at least. That'll simplify the cleanup. Remember the one who didn't make it a year ago last August? We had to burn the mattress."

Jonathan tasted bile trying to come up in his throat. He swallowed hard. "I'm sorry, but I've got to get some fresh air." He hurried out of the house, then walked across the yard to stand by the fire, where Bill Stevenson stood with a couple of jerry cans of water nearby. Bill poured one into a cauldron hanging from a tripod over the fire as Jonathan walked over to the fire-pit. Some plastic buckets, a pile of rags, a couple of mops, and some scrub-brushes lay on the sidewalk nearby.

"How bad is it?" he asked as Jonathan approached.

"Jamal says he didn't die of the plague. The stink was getting to me, but I guess it's not as bad as it could be. He died in the bathroom, lying in the shower."

Bill nodded. "Nice of him." He poured another jerry can of water into the cauldron.

Jonathan only nodded in response. Just the sight of the corpse had made him squeamish. This rather surprised him. He'd seen many dead bodies before, two of which he'd killed himself. Those were ones who'd been threatening him and Sara, though. At least, he'd had every reason to believe that at the time.

Seeing Erik's body was different. He'd spent time talking to him on the radio, getting what information he could about the dirty bomb attacks so he could research the extent of the contamination. He'd come to like Erik, at least a little, and he felt guilty that he'd made no attempt of help him. He knew that there was nothing he could have done without endangering himself, but that didn't make him feel much better.

Bill put another log on the fire and straightened up, dusting his hands on his coveralls. "What'd you think of Allen?"

Jonathan turned back to Bill. "What? Oh, Allen Jacobs? He seemed okay. Why?"

"Oh, he's a good enough guy. Folks seem to be put off by him, sometimes. Won't join in any of the group functions, unless there's food. Been a great help with his work at the farm, though. Saw you all sitting with him at Thanksgiving, and I wondered."

Jonathan warmed his hands by the fire. "He seems, I don't know, angry, or bitter, or something."

"He's got a right. He killed his wife."

Jonathan's face snapped up towards Bill's. "What? Killed his own wife?"

Bill gave a single, grave nod. "She had sugar bad. When the plague hit they hid out in his hunting shack, but they didn't have enough insulin. She went blind, then her foot started to rot. He tried to cut it off, but it didn't help. Just got infected worse."

"Oh God, what a terrible way to die. That wasn't his fault, though. Sounds like he did his best to save her."

"He shot her."

"Oh."

"Couldn't stand for her to suffer, I reckon. She was twenty-eight."

Jonathan stared down at the fire, and Bill stuck a couple more logs under the pot. After a moment he straightened up and continued. "Jim and Dan saw him digging the grave when they were out hunting, as I heard it. That was before I got here, back a year ago last July. Persuaded him to come back and mind the livestock. He doesn't want to live in the village."

"That's—informative." Jonathan tried and failed to imagine a scenario where he'd commit a mercy killing on Sara and then not turn the gun on himself afterwards.

"Thought you should know," Bill said.

Jonathan nodded. "Well, I guess I'll head back in."

"The fire's set. I'll go on in with y'all."

*   *   *

Bill helped Jamal and Jonathan wrap the body in a heavy plastic sheet for transport to the graveyard. Jamal drove the wagon while the rest of them cleaned up the house, using liberal amounts of bleach and hot water.

The kitchen was almost unused. Most of the food they'd provided before Erik took up residence was still there. Bill shook his head in dismay at the waste as he gathered the unused food for disposal. Couldn't take a chance with it, especially if Erik died from radioactive contaminants.

As he took the sheets and blankets off the bed, Bill noticed a journal on the nightstand and flipped through it. It covered a period from several years before the riots over the male baby deaths up to two days before his own death, though for long periods the entries were infrequent. He brought it outside to the fire heating the cleaning water.

"Look at what I found," he said, holding it up.

Jonathan was standing by the fire taking another fresh air break when Bill came outside. As Bill approached, Jonathan's eyes narrowed. "What is that?"

"Looks like Erik's diary. It covers about six years."

Jonathan's eyes went wide. "Bill, take that away from here and leave it alone!"

"Huh? What for?"

"It's probably contaminated with what killed Erik. Get rid of it!"

Bill started to throw it on the fire, but Jonathan shouted, "No!"

Bill managed to keep his grip on it, and he turned back to Jonathan. "Now what?"

"If you burn it it'll just spread the radionuclides. Fire won't neutralize them." Jonathan looked around the yard, turning in place. "Put it over there," he said, pointing toward the upside-down bowl of an abandoned birdbath on the other side of the yard. "We'll have to bury it with the body."

Bill ran over and dropped the book as if it were hot.

"Take off your gloves and leave them with it," Jonathan said.

Dan came out of the house at that point. "What's going on?"

Jonathan filled him in while Bill returned to the fire. Bill took another pair of gloves from their box of supplies.

"Jon, I don't disagree with you," Dan said, "but there could be important information in that journal. I think we should keep it. It would have been closed up in the car, so its contamination would probably be minimal. He wouldn't have had it out by the crater."

"I don't think that's a good idea. He'd have handled it, and I doubt he washed his hands first," Jonathan said.

"I still think we need to keep it. You didn't touch it with your skin, did you, Bill?"

Bill snorted. "Of course not. I'm not stupid."

"It should be okay, Jon. The gloves would have

protected him from any residual contamination that has been left on it."

Jonathan frowned, then heaved a sigh. "All right. Let me get a phone and take some pictures of the contents."

"I'll do it," Dan said.

"No. You're still young and have a daughter. I'm almost sixty and childless. I'll do it." He headed back to the house. "After we're done here."

*   *   *

Their usual custom was to bury the body just wrapped in a shroud in the graveyard they'd established at the edge of the village. In Erik's case they mixed three yards of concrete and sealed his body inside, along with his clothing and the bed linens he'd used. They added the mop heads, rags, and scrub brushes as well as their protective clothing, the unused food, and the journal to the sarcophagus. They used the wash water to help mix the concrete.

Jonathan stood by the grave with a few others as Janet Haskel read a short service. He bowed his head for Janet's prayer and had a clear view of the semi-liquid concrete mass in the bottom of the grave. Future archeologists should have fun with that.

They shoveled soil over the capsule when Janet finished, making a wide and tall mound over it. The sun had set and stars had started to appear by the time they were done.

As they walked back toward the village, Jim Henderson came up beside Jonathan. "Dan told me about the journal. It was good of you to do that."

Jonathan gave a brief nod as they walked along.

"Thanks. I just hope it was worth the risk." The air had started to cool down as evening came on and his breath billowed in fleeting white clouds. "I'll download the images to the local network when we get back."

"Let's meet at my place tonight and take a look at it before you do that, okay? I want to discuss this with the ones who've seen it so far before we make it public. Say, seven-thirty?"

Jonathan checked his watch. 6:15. He shrugged. "Okay, I guess."

"So did you see anything interesting?"

"Maybe. There are at least two occasions where he'd made an entry about seeing smoke, like from a chimney. One of them he thought looked like several chimneys. I was just skimming it as I photographed the pages. I didn't take the time to read it in detail. I just wanted to get done and get rid of it as soon as possible. By 'interesting' I assume you don't mean detailed accounts of sessions with prostitutes from back before the riots began."

Jim gave a brief snort. "No, that wasn't what I meant."

"Well, there are several of those in it."

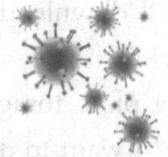

Chapter Thirteen

What the Diary Revealed

JIM lived alone in one of the smaller dwellings in the complex, a two-bedroom condominium. Still, it would have rated as an upscale home before the plague. More so than Jonathan's old place in Charlotte, anyway. The rooms were large and the kitchen was lavishly equipped. Jim's condo was one of the few residences without solar panels. It seemed a shame that none of those kitchen appliances worked.

Jonathan arrived early with his laptop and Jim sat to read through the diary image. He flipped through the pages rapidly, taking only five or six seconds for each one. Jonathan lifted an eyebrow. Either Jim was a speed reader, or he was just giving it a cursory look. Most of the diary entries were brief, with the exception of his reminisces of encounters with prostitutes. Erik had taken some time with those.

While Jim read, Jonathan surveyed the room. It had comfortable furnishings, but nothing fancy. A wallet-sized picture in a home-made wooden frame on the mantle showed a younger version of him with a woman and a boy of perhaps ten. Other than that, no pictures were present.

Jonathan pointed to the picture. "Your wife and son?"

Jim glanced up at Jonathan, then turned his attention back to the screen. "That's past. I'm concerned with the present and the future."

Jonathan lifted an eyebrow, but Jim's expression didn't invite further questions. The next couple of minutes passed in awkward silence.

It seemed incongruous to Jonathan that they were going to gather there around his laptop computer to look at the diary while the room was lit by candles and the flickering glow from the fireplace. Over the next ten minutes after Jonathan got there, the rest of the ones who had been in the clean-up crew arrived. Tyler came in with Bill too, and sat next to him on the couch.

They crowded together to read the screen. The laptop lay on a coffee table in front of the fireplace, and Jonathan scrolled the pages as they read. They skimmed past Erik's sexual exploits and his time alone in the hills and concentrated on the section after the plague, when he was driving around the country.

"Apparently Erik didn't feel the need to seek out other people," Jim said.

Dan smirked. "How do you account for the prostitutes, then?"

"He said he had a 'crisis of conscience'—his words—a month or so before the riots started, and went to his father's cabin in the hills of north Georgia to, 'get his head straight'— his words again." Jim coughed. "Took enough basic provisions for a year, gathered wild edible plants and fruit, and hunted for meat. Didn't take a phone or a computer."

Dan scratched his beard. "Doing the Walden thing, eh?"

Jim nodded. "So it seems. Anyway, he's noted two times where he saw what could have been a settlement of some sort after he finally came down from the hills. One in January of this year not far from Harrisonville Virginia, and the other — " Jim flipped the display forward a dozen pages or so, " — about twenty miles west of Roanoke Virginia in May. He didn't try to contact them either time. To the contrary, he went out of his way to avoid them, once he recognized them as possibly being a settlement."

Jonathan shook his head. "I wonder why he did that?"

"He dropped out." Tyler said.

They turned to him. Jonathan raised his brows. "Dropped out?"

"Yep. Looks clear to me. He'd had enough with other people, so he went out to live alone. He just came back out when he ran out of salt and sugar." Tyler gave a sort of half smile. "Just like me."

Jonathan tilted his head. "Like you?"

"Yep. I dropped outta high school and hid out in the woods when I was seventeen, after my mom and dad got killed in a car wreck." He shrugged. "Mad at the world, I guess. Difference between me and Erik is, when I came out and saw how about everyone else was dead, I joined back up with them as I found. Don't look to me like Erik wanted to, though."

"Then why'd he stop here?" Dan asked.

Jonathan shrugged. "That's obvious, isn't it? He was dying and he knew it. He didn't want to die un-remembered."

Tyler nodded. "Good a guess as anything I could offer."

"That fits with a couple of things he wrote toward the end," Jim said, and then coughed again.

The rest of them turned toward him, and then they all shared a glance among themselves as Jim wiped his mouth with a handkerchief.

"Are you okay, Jim?" Jamal asked.

Jim opened the handkerchief and showed them that there was no blood on it. "I've developed a cough over the last couple of weeks that comes and goes." He stuffed the handkerchief into his back pocket. "It's not the plague, or I'd be dead already. I should see a doctor, I guess. If there were any doctors left to see. It's probably bronchitis, or something."

Jamal grimaced. "Yeah, I guess. Take it easy, okay, Jim?"

"I will."

"Okay, well, what do y'all think we should do about finding these other groups?" Bill asked.

"I'll see if I can find any indication from the weather satellite imagery," Jonathan said, "but this time of year I'll be at the mercy of the clouds. It may take a while to get a good recent image."

"I'm not sure how good an idea it is to send someone off on a trip like that in the first place," Jim said. "It's not like we have a lot of people here with nothing better to do. It looks like the closer of the two sites is more than a week away, if the traveling is good."

Bill shook his head. "We don't know whether they'll appreciate visitors, either. It'd be a dangerous trip for several reasons."

"Winter wouldn't be the best time to go, anyway," Jim said. "How about we see what Jon can come up with from satellite images, and make a decision then?"

"Sounds good," Dan said. The others nodded as well.

Jonathan typed on his laptop and then pulled a thumb drive from the port on the side and held it out toward Jim. "Here's the file with the diary image. Should I post it on the network?"

Jim took the drive from him. "I guess, go ahead."

Dan lifted a hand. "Uh, Jim, could we redact the sections about the prostitutes? I have a teenage daughter. Erik got pretty explicit for some of those."

"Maria's fifteen years old, and I've seen her in the library reading Harlequin romances," Jim said. "I doubt that anything in Erik's diary is going to shock her."

"Still."

Jim turned to Jonathan and after a second Dan faced him too.

"It'd be easy to cut those sections," Jonathan said. "What'd be harder to do is to make a version that the adults can see, but keep the sexy parts away from the kids. I personally don't think it's wise to put only a redacted version of this on the network. That would just arouse suspicion, and I don't think you want to do that."

"When I was a kid we never had much trouble getting past the barriers the adults put up around the X-rated stuff," Tyler said. "It wouldn't surprise me if she's already seen some of that." He smirked a little. "I noticed there's some of that kind of literature on the network already."

Dan turned back to Jonathan with arched eyebrows. "You posted *pornography* on the network?"

"Not on purpose, but I cast a pretty wide net when I copied what I could of the internet. I couldn't review everything, there simply wasn't time."

Tyler shrugged. "There's not much of anything with pictures or movies that I found, but some of the literature is— uh—interesting."

Dan shot Tyler a glare. "You obviously need a heavier workload. You've got too much time on your hands."

Jim sighed. "Jon and Tyler both have a point, Dan. If

you and Gloria still need to have that talk with Maria, it's probably about time."

Dan scowled and a flush came up on his cheeks.

"Should I put an 'Adult Content' warning on it?" Jonathan asked.

Dan's eyebrows shot up. "What, and alert her that it's there?"

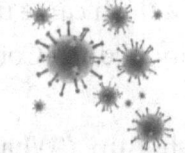

Chapter Fourteen

Allen's Visit

AT about eight-thirty Jonathan trudged up the steps to the house he and Sara and Rita were using—he still didn't think of it as "his" house—and opened the door. Voices drifted from the kitchen as he hung his coat in the hall closet. A deep male voice sounded, laughing, and Jonathan stopped short. He cocked his head to listen for a moment. He couldn't make out the words, but he hadn't expected a man to be there.

"Jon, is that you?" Sara called out.

"Yes, it's me." He continued to the kitchen.

Sara met him as he entered the room and gave him a kiss. He looked past her. Allen Jacobs and Rita sat at the table with mugs of tea in front of them, looking up toward him.

"Hi Allen," Jonathan said. "I hadn't expected to see you tonight."

"Allen brought over a cheese for Rita," Sara said, "and we were just having some tea. Would you like some?"

"Some tea would be great. Thanks."

Allen stood and came over to shake Jonathan's hand. "I just thought that with Rita's—uh—condition, she could use the extra calcium. I hope it came out okay. I haven't been making cheese for long, and I'm not that good at it yet. It probably should age more."

Jonathan nodded and looked Allen up and down. He pursed his lips, remembering Bill's report about Allen and his wife. "That was a thoughtful gesture, Allen. Thank you. I'm sure the cheese is fine."

"Allen's going to have a bonfire at the farm to mark the Solstice," Rita said. "It's going to start at sundown on the 21st."

Jonathan nodded and cocked an eyebrow, but he didn't crack a smile. "New traditions?"

"Actually, that's a pretty old one, but one not widely observed for a long time. At least not in the United States. I think it's an appropriate marker for the beginning of longer days, as the sun comes back to the Earth. It just seems more in tune with the Earth's cycles to me."

Jonathan nodded again and stepped around Allen to sit at the table. Allen took his seat again too. Sara poured a cup of mint tea for Jonathan, and sat beside him.

"Thank you," he said to her. He sipped his tea and shifted in his chair to face Allen, looking into his eyes. "Bill Stevenson told me about your wife earlier today. I want to say how sorry I am."

Rita gave a little gasp and Allen tilted his face down toward the mug of tea resting on the table in front of him. "Thanks," he said quietly. "That's a painful memory. I don't like to talk about it much."

Jonathan kept his gaze fixed on Allen's face. "I'm sure that was hard for you. I can't imagine how she must have suffered. I just wanted to express my condolences."

"Thanks."

Sara shot a glance over to her husband, then turned back to Allen. "Let me offer my condolences as well. I hadn't known."

"Thanks." He picked up his mug and took a big gulp, draining the tea. "Well, I have to get up early to do the milking, and it's starting to get late for me. I better head on back." He stood and Rita levered herself upright as well.

Allen pulled his jacket off the back of the chair and put it on. "Thanks for the tea. I hope you'll all come for the Solstice."

Sara nodded. "Of course."

Rita took his hand. "I'll see you to the door." As she followed Allen out of the room she shot a glare at Jonathan.

Sara turned to Jonathan when Allen and Rita left the kitchen, her brows furrowed. "What was that about?" she whispered.

"There's more to him than he's letting on," he said, just as quietly.

The front door closed and a moment later Rita stomped back to the kitchen and halted at the doorway. "What the *hell* were you trying to do?" Her eyes flashed anger at Jonathan and she'd clenched her fists at her side.

Jonathan said, "Rita, there's something you should know about Allen Jacobs—"

"You mean about how his wife was a diabetic and they ran out of insulin and then she went blind and got gangrene in her foot and he tried to amputate it but it only got worse and he eventually shot her to end her suffering? Yeah. I know all that."

Jonathan's jaw dropped. He glanced at Sara. Her mouth hung open too.

"He's been coming to see me while I've been at work at the stable for the last week, since Thanksgiving," Rita said. "Andrea told me about his wife on Monday, and I confronted him about it when he came over on Tuesday. He told me everything and cried his eyes out the whole time. I don't know that I'd have done anything different in his position, and you have no god*damn* right to judge him either."

She sat down at the table, took a slurp of tea and set the mug back down with a loud thunk. Some of the tea sloshed out. She glared across the table at Jonathan.

"I—I was just trying to protect you."

"Protect me!" She gave her head a quick shake and leaned back in the chair. "Protect me?" She gave a snort. "That's pretty damn funny, coming from the man who pointed a rifle at me and threatened to kill me, the same one that I saved from the Gibson brothers when we got here."

Sara met Rita's stare. "Rita, you can't judge us for that, either. You know good and well why he did that, and didn't he kill the bear that was after you?"

Rita said nothing for a few seconds, sitting there with her teeth clenched and her hand still clutching the mug's handle in her fist. Then she lowered her gaze to the table and licked her lips. "All right. I'll give you that. But let's get something straight." She raised her face and locked eyes with Jonathan. "I don't need to be protected from Allen Jacobs, and I can *damn* well choose who I want to associate with without asking for your approval. Clear?"

"Yes, and I apologize for implying otherwise."

"Okay. Apology accepted. But we understand each other, right?"

"Yes. If I hadn't mentioned it before, thanks for taking care of George Gibson that day, too. I guess I owe a 'thank you' to Johnny as well. If he hadn't happened to rear up and knock down the other guy, George's shot might have been more on target."

Rita gave a little, tight-lipped grimace and turned her face back down toward the table. "I did that too."

"What?" Sara tilted her head. "What do you mean?"

"I guess you weren't paying attention to me at the time. While George had his rifle pointed at you, and the brown-haired one, Jim, or John or whatever his name was, checked Johnny's mouth, I arranged my feet on the reins and kicked out to jerk Johnny's head back." She looked back up at Jonathan. "I knew it'd make him rear up and give me a chance to get the pistol and shoot George while they were distracted. I didn't know Johnny would hit the other one in the head. That was just good luck.

"I'm sorry, but I took a calculated risk that George would be distracted from his aim. I figured at worst only one of us would get killed, instead of all three. There was no doubt in my mind that they intended to kill us."

Jonathan and Sara turned to each other, stunned to silence for the moment, then Jonathan turned back to Rita. "Why didn't you say anything about this before, in that Determination-of-Facts meeting?"

"It didn't seem wise at the time. I wasn't sure how those people were going to react and I didn't want to confuse matters. You were right, in a sense, that Johnny probably didn't like that asshole poking fingers at his mouth, but most likely he'd have just tried to nip at him in response. That wouldn't have had the effect I wanted."

Again they were silent for a moment. Eventually Sara nodded. "You may have been right. At this point, there's nothing to be gained by bringing it up outside the three of us."

"No, probably not." Rita took another sip of her tea and grimaced. "Ugh. It's gone cold." She set it down and pushed it away.

Jonathan sighed. "Well I guess I owe you a bigger debt of gratitude than I knew. Thank you. Sorry for threatening you when you first showed up, but my priority then was to protect Sara and myself from the plague."

Rita grimaced again and gave a brief nod. "Yeah, yeah. I understand that. It's hard to forget looking down a rifle barrel from the wrong direction, though. Thanks for helping me anyway."

Jonathan nodded too. "You're welcome. Look, it's been a long, difficult day for me, and I think I'm going to turn in."

"I'll join you after a little while," Sara said. "I want to read some more before I go to bed."

"Okay, good night." He stood and gave Sara a kiss.

"Good night, Jon," Rita said too, then gave her head a slight tilt. "Look, no hard feelings, okay?"

"No. Thanks for clearing the air."

He walked around the table to head to the family room where they had their bed. After putting on pajamas and fresh socks he turned out the light and climbed into bed. He was asleep before he remembered his head hitting the pillow.

Sometime later Sara opened the door and turned on the light. "Jon, wake up. I think Rita's in labor."

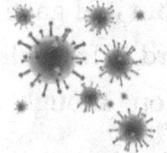

Chapter Fifteen

Allen's Second Visit

JONATHAN knocked on Jamal Johnson's door ten minutes after he woke. A minute or so later Jamal came to the door, wrapped in a bathrobe, holding a candle. As soon as he cracked the door open Jonathan blurted, "Rita's in labor!"

Jamal froze with his mouth open, as if he'd been about to say something, then closed it. "I'll be right there. Go get Gloria Kiner too."

"Huh? What for?"

"Gloria's been through natural childbirth. She was a big help with the Carpenter's baby last September." He closed the door.

Jonathan scanned the surroundings for a second, getting his bearings, then ran off.

* * *

Jamal and Gloria left Jon and Sara's house as the sun rose over the bare branches of the tree tops bordering the complex the next morning. Rita's contractions had stopped around three a.m., and she'd shown no signs of labor starting back up for another three hours. She'd finally fallen asleep. Jamal and Gloria waited another hour to make sure it was safe to leave, and went home to get some sleep too. Jonathan promised to come and get them right away if her labor started again.Jonathan crawled out of bed near mid-day after no more than four hours of sleep. He felt hungover, as though he'd drunk a whole bottle of wine the night before, but he hadn't had a drop. Sara had taken a blanket to Rita's room and spent the morning asleep in a recliner by her bed. Careful to be quiet, he put some more wood on the fire and went to the kitchen. The day had been sunny yesterday, and so far, it was sunny today, so there should be a good charge in the battery. He set a kettle of water on the electric range to heat for tea, wishing for the thousandth time that there was coffee available somewhere.

He'd been up for less than an hour when there was a knock at the door. It was a little past noon. Allen stood on the porch and stared down at his feet when Jonathan opened the door. He stammered, "H—Hello Jonathan. They told me that Rita went into labor last night when I went to see her at the stable just now. How is she?"

Jonathan nodded. "She's fine. The contractions stopped around three in the morning, and she's sleeping right now. I suspect it won't be much longer till the baby's born, though." Jonathan had the image of himself committing a mercy killing on Sara flash into his brain again, then he reflected that if the situation were reversed—if he were the one needing a release from his suffering—he'd want Sara to carry on.

Allen brushed a gloved hand over his chin, wiping condensate off his beard. "Oh. Well, could you—could you tell her I stopped by and asked about her when she wakes up?"

"Of course."

"Okay, well—well, thanks."

Allen turned to leave and Jonathan said, "I'm sorry about last night. I want you to know that I don't blame you about your wife."

Allen turned back to Jonathan for a moment, then tilted his head back down toward the floor. "Thanks. Well, that"—he sniffled—"that makes one of us." A tear rolled off his cheek and splattered onto the porch.

Jonathan didn't know what to say. He just stood there with the door open and Allen standing there wiping his eyes. Allen's breath puffed in little white clouds as he stood by the open door. After a few seconds Jonathan said, "Why don't you come in and warm up a little? I've made some tea, but we'll have to be quiet so we don't wake Rita or Sara."

Allen nodded and wiped at his eyes again with his coat sleeve. "Look, I'm sorry. It's just—hard, remembering."

Jonathan nodded. "I know. You have nothing to apologize for." He stepped aside for Allen to enter.

*   *   *

Allen sipped his tea and chatted with Jonathan at the kitchen table, keeping to safe subjects for their conversation. Allen described the extent of the dairy herd he husbanded, along with the pigs, sheep, and goats, while Jonathan talked about the security program he was setting up for the community.

Allen pointed to Jonathan's laptop, which lay on the table to the side, the screensaver running. "Is that what you're working on now?"

"No, not at the moment. Erik—the guy who had arrived recently by car, that is—had commented in his journal that he'd seen some other settlements on his travels, and I'm trying to tap into the weather satellites to see if I can find them. One in a polar orbit should be passing overhead in a couple of hours."

Allen cracked a bit of a smile. "A settlement in a polar orbit?"

Jonathan laughed and then quickly stifled it to keep from waking the women. "No, the satellite. Guess I should have phrased that more carefully."

Sara stepped into the kitchen wearing the rumpled clothing that she had on last night, rubbing her eyes and yawning. "Good morning, Jon. Hi Allen." She yawned again and looked at the clock. "Good afternoon, I guess." She sat at the table next to Jonathan.

Jonathan kissed her cheek. "Good—uh—afternoon. Sorry if we woke you." He poured a mug of tea for Sara.

"It's okay. I need to be up anyway."

"How's Rita?" Allen asked. "Andrea told me she went into labor last night."

"She's still sleeping as of a couple of minutes ago. She should probably get all the rest she can at this point."

"Yeah, I guess so. It's early for her to be going into labor, isn't it?"

"Possibly a little, but it's hard to know for sure. She told us her periods had been intermittent for a while before she got pregnant, so we don't know for sure when she conceived. Neither Jamal nor Gloria thought the baby felt undersized. Again, it's hard to be sure."

"I sure hope everything goes okay," Allen said. He leaned over in his chair and touched the floor with his right hand, then straightened back up.

Sara's eyebrows furrowed and she looked at the floor by Allen's chair. "Did you drop something?"

"Oh—ah—no. It's just sort of a—well—I'd guess you'd call it a ritual I've become accustomed to." He reddened. "I touch the Earth for—well—good luck, or something. At least I'll touch the floor symbolically if the Earth herself isn't in reach at the moment." He stared down toward his teacup.

Sara nodded. "A connective gesture."

Allen lifted his gaze. "Excuse me?"

"It's like when a Catholic crosses himself, or a Muslim bows toward Mecca. It connects you with your faith."

"It's not part of a religion. It's just something I started doing myself after Brenda—after Brenda died." He took a sip of his tea and set it back down on the table, taking his time, staring down at the cup. He shrugged. "She became part of the Earth."

"Okay, so your faith is personal. That's wonderful. It's a beautiful gesture. I like the symbol, affirming your connection to the Earth."

He nodded, still looking toward his tea. "Thanks."

"Do you want something to eat? We have bread and jam, and we could—"

"Sara!" Rita cried from her bedroom.

The three of them stood as if in one motion and rushed to Rita's room. Sara made it there first, with Allen and Jonathan close behind. Sunlight streaming through the south window gave a bright glow to the room. They found Rita sitting up in the bed.

"I just had another contraction," she exclaimed as they came in.

"I'll get Jamal," Jonathan said and he turned toward the door.

Rita shook her head. "Wait until we time the contractions."

By reflex, Jonathan checked his watch. "Are you sure

we should wait?"

"Give me your watch," Sara said. "I'll time the contractions while you get Jamal and Gloria."

Rita shook her head again, harder. "I don't want to drag them back here if it's another false alarm."

Allen hurried to Rita's side and took her hand. "Darling, let him get them. It's not like they're that far away. I don't think you should take chances."

Jonathan did a double-take toward them. Darling...? He shook his head. "I'm going. I promised to get them if your contractions started again, so that's that." He gave Sara his watch and a quick kiss and left the room.

*   *   *

Jamal and Gloria arrived with Jonathan within a half hour and took up stations in Rita's bedroom. Allen got Jamal to call Jim Henderson on the radio and round up his helpers to take care of the farm chores. The next twenty-eight hours passed in a haze of long periods of boredom punctuated by moments of panic and feverish activity. Gloria and Jamal alternated two-hour shifts of watching Rita overnight while the other napped. Jonathan and Sara tried to help when they could, but otherwise just tried not to get in the way. Allen was a nearly constant presence by Rita's side, holding her hand, wiping her forehead, and doing his best to coach her to breathe properly through her contractions, based on some quick instruction from Gloria. As far as Jonathan could tell, Allen didn't nap for more than ten minutes at a time during the entire period of Rita's labor.

At about four p.m. the following day, Jamal placed a healthy, apparently full-term baby girl on Rita's stomach. He tucked a blanket over them both while they waited for the cord to stop pulsing so they could cut it and deliver the afterbirth. Jonathan and Sara watched from the doorway and gave each other a hug. Sara's grin seemed too wide for her face and her eyes were moist. Allen kissed Rita on the forehead as she gazed into her daughter's face with a mixture of wonder and exhaustion.

"What's her name?" Allen asked.

Rita raised her eyes to him. "Davina. I wanted to name her after her father."

He smiled and stroked Rita's hair. "It's a lovely name."

"Thanks. Davina Stewart Ballard." She brushed a finger over her daughter's forehead.

Allen tilted his head. "Stewart?"

"It was David's last name."

*　　*　　*

By sundown Davina had taken her first feeding and she and Rita had fallen asleep. Davina lay in a cradle next to Rita's bed wrapped in a baby quilt. The rest of them sat in the kitchen with bowls of bean soup that Jonathan had made during Rita's labor. Everyone was exhausted and there were many yawns, but not much speech.

As they ate, Jamal's radio came to life. He pulled it from his belt and keyed it. "This is Jamal."

"Jamal, this is Dan. Is this a bad time?"

"No, it's okay. We're basically done here. Rita had a healthy girl a couple of hours ago, and we were decompressing after she and the baby went to sleep. Thanks for letting me borrow your wife. Gloria was an enormous help."

"Yeah, she's great, isn't she?"

Across the table, Gloria huffed a derisive laugh.

"Flatterer," she said, smiling.

"I'm sorry to bother you," Dan said, "but Anita Carpenter's worried about her baby. Seems he's been spitting up his milk and crying a lot, but he doesn't have a fever."

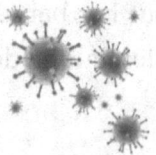

Chapter Sixteen

A Funeral

JANET Haskel presided over Harold Carpenter's funeral in the main meeting room of the community center twelve days later. Jonathan hated funerals, but Sara persuaded him that they needed to attend.

Anita Carpenter sat in the front row next to her husband, Steven, with tears streaming down her cheeks. Janet assured them that their baby's soul rested in Christ's keeping in heaven. Such was the reward of all innocents and of those of good faith who believed in the risen Lord.

Steven sat holding his wife's hand, his face an impassive mask. Every so often he'd give a sniff and wipe at his eyes. His afro-cut hair would give a little shake as he moved his head to look at Anita, or back to Janet. Their surviving son, Jimmy, eleven years old, sat by his father, fidgeting and looking nervously around the room. The whites of his wide, brown eyes contrasted sharply against the dark walnut hue of his skin.

Most of the village attended the service in the community center's meeting room. Jim Henderson sat next to Anita in the front row of seats, and Jamal Johnson sat next to him.

The service was short. Afterward they filed out to walk to the graveyard for the interment ceremony. Low gray clouds augured for snow that afternoon. A light layer of snow from yesterday already covered the lawns, but some of the residents had cleared it from the path to the graveyard earlier that morning. Gloria stayed by Anita's side as Anita's husband and son and four other villagers carried the small bier holding her infant son's shroud-wrapped remains.

Janet said some more words at the graveside, but Jonathan wasn't paying attention to her. He and Sara stood facing the Carpenters across the open grave in the group surrounding it. Steven stood with Anita grasping his hand, a vacant look in his eyes. Every once in a while Anita wiped tears from her cheeks with a white handkerchief. Several times Jonathan saw her clench her teeth and shake her head, the hand clutching her handkerchief balled into a fist. Janet concluded the service and stepped over to give them each an embrace, first Anita, then Steven, and finally Jimmy, though he looked like he'd rather she didn't. When the rest of them turned back to the community center, Tyler, Bill, and Dan shoveled earth back into the grave.

On the way back Sara tapped Jonathan on the arm. "Doesn't look like Rita or Allen have joined us out here for the burial service."

Jonathan looked around, surveying the group. "I think you're right, but that's not surprising. I'm sure she didn't want to take the baby out in the cold."

"That explains Rita, but not Allen."

"Well, he's sweet on her. He probably wanted to be with her."

"Yeah, probably. I hear he generally doesn't participate

in other religious services, so I wondered. He's having that Solstice bonfire next week, and I noticed that Janet has scheduled a competing service at the community center that evening."

Jonathan raised an eyebrow. "Oh? That's interesting."

"I don't think she and Allen get along."

"I haven't particularly noticed, but I haven't really paid attention either. Are you sure you're not reading more into this than is there?"

"I couldn't rule it out, but I don't think I'm completely wrong, either." People were filing into the community center now. Jonathan held the door for Sara and followed her in.

Rita sat in one of the chairs toward the back of the room nursing Davina. Allen sat a discreet distance away with his hands in his lap. Several other women gathered to admire the baby and chat with Rita as the room refilled. Jonathan and Sara joined Rita and Allen, Sara taking seats by them.

Anita sat on the other side of the room with her husband standing beside her, his hand on her shoulder. She'd stopped crying and sat still, nearly oblivious to any of the activity around her.

Janet made her way through the crowd to Anita and laid a hand on her other shoulder. Jonathan watched from across the room as Janet bent down to say something to her. Anita shook her head, her face still bowed toward her lap. Janet patted Anita's arm and straightened up. She shook Steven's hand, then shook Jimmy's hand as well, clapping him on the shoulder. Janet left them to limp toward the front of the room. "We have some soup and bread to share that the Kiners and Jamal were kind enough to provide," she announced. "Please join me in saying grace and we'll start serving."

Most people stood and bowed their heads as Janet said

a brief grace for the food, ending with, "In Jesus' name we pray, amen."

At the prayer's end Allen bent over and touched the floor. Janet did a double-take when he did that and frowned. Jonathan noticed her reaction and glanced to Allen. He faced away from Janet at the moment, looking toward Rita and Davina, and as far as Allen could tell, he didn't notice Janet's reaction.

Allen and Rita sat with Jonathan and Sara as they ate their soup, and Davina slept in a baby carrier on the table next to them. Bill Stevenson came over and tapped Allen on the shoulder.

"Excuse me," he said, "I was wondering if you're still planning to have the bonfire next week on the 21st?"

"Yes, we're going to have it. Hopefully the weather will cooperate, but it'll go on regardless."

"Okay, well, I was just wondering if you rescheduled it 'cause of the service Janet scheduled for that evening too."

Allen's eyebrows went up. They furrowed. "This is the first I've heard of that. What sort of service?"

"I think the title is 'A Christian Welcome to Winter' or something. There's a notice on the bulletin board." He turned and pointed toward the door.

Allen looked toward the door for a second, then faced Bill again. "It's scheduled for the twenty-first too, at sundown?"

Bill nodded. "At five-thirty."

Allen sighed. "The solstice occurs on a fixed date. Sunset is a little before 5:30 that day. We can't reschedule it for the sake of convenience. The bonfire will go on as announced."

"Okay, I was just wondering."

"I hope to see you there."

"I hope to be there too, but we'll see." He shook Allen's hand and went back to the table where he sat with Tyler Hopson and Jane Fulk.

Allen watched him go, then leaned over in his chair and touched the floor.

"That's discouraging—" Jonathan said, but Allen cut him off.

"This isn't about competition. I hope everyone gets whatever meaning that works for them from this transition. It's not like either she or I own the date."

Jonathan gave a slight nod.

An hour later, while Jamal and Gloria packaged the remaining soup and bread for the Carpenters, Janet stood and announced, "Thank you everyone for your attendance and support. It's important to act as a community in times such as these. As we go back to our homes, let us leave with this prayer in mind."

She raised her hands and intoned, "May Christ grant us peace in these times of troubles, and may we all work together to form a loving, cooperative community. We offer Anita, Steven, and James our comfort for their grief, our support for their healing ahead, and our love, just as Christ offers his love, his healing, and his comfort to us all. May we all find hope in the Lord's saving grace and power, and use that hope to rebuild the world with Christ's love as its foundation into a better home for all mankind. In Jesus' name we pray, and let us say, 'amen.'"

Most of the assembly joined her in saying, "amen."

Janet lowered her hands. "Thank you," she said. "On Monday, the twenty-first we'll have a service here at five-thirty p.m. to mark the start of winter. The Christmas Eve service will start at eleven p.m. on the 24th and conclude at midnight. I hope you'll all attend."

Allen sat still for a few seconds, his face blank. Then he stood. "The bonfire at the farm will occur as previously announced at sundown on the solstice. That's at 5:21. Janet's right, it's important that we all work together as a community. There'll be fellowship available at the farm into the evening for those who may wish to attend after Janet's service, and I'm hoping that Janet will provide fellowship as well for those who choose to attend the sunset service at the farm to mark the Solstice there, and then join her later."

Janet leveled her gaze toward Allen, her eyebrows pressed together in anger, as she locked onto his placid expression. But before either Allen or Janet could say anything further, Anita Carpenter stood. "I don't believe this. I just buried my baby and you two are—are arguing about who's going to show up at your parties." Steven put a hand on her shoulder, but she shook it off. Her voice grew shrill. "You talk about community but you don't have a clue about what that means. To hell with you both!"

Rita shifted in her seat as if to stand, but Allen laid a hand on her arm to stop her. He turned to Anita. "You're right, and I apologize."

"To hell with you both!" Anita stormed out the door. Her husband and son followed her out, hurrying to catch up. The door's slam echoed in the sudden silence that filled the room.

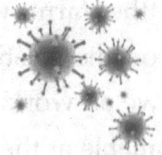

Chapter Seventeen

The Winter's Solstice

ON the evening of the Solstice, as the sun touched the western horizon, Allen put a torch to the base of a pile of wood on the lawn of the farmhouse. It took a few minutes to start burning well, but soon flames caught and climbed throughout the stacked branches. Twenty-five or thirty people gathered in a partial circle around the fire. Jonathan and Sara stood in the crowd a short distance from Allen, holding hands.

The day had been clear, but the temperature had never gone above freezing. With sunset, the air chilled further. A nearly full moon hovered low over the eastern hills. As the fire grew, people on the up-wind side moved a little closer to the warmth. Those downwind shifted away from the smoke. Allen tossed the torch into the bonfire and dusted his gloved hands against his trousers.

"Thank you all for coming," Allen said. "I'm not much of a public speaker, so I hope you'll forgive me if this is brief. We're—uh—at the start of the longest night of the year, which means that now the days will start to lengthen as spring approaches. May the light and warmth of this fire help sustain you and—uh—serve as a reminder of longer days and warmer weather to come." Allen stammered and shuffled his feet as he spoke. The fading light from the evening sky and orange glow of the fire partially camouflaged his reddened cheeks. Still, Jonathan could tell he was blushing more than the chilly air could explain.

"The Earth has helped us survive these terrible times. I want to take this occasion to express my personal thanks for Earth's blessings, and recommit my dedication to helping Her heal so that we all heal as well." He stopped for a second, then continued, almost as an afterthought, "Both personally and as a community."

He glanced at Rita, who stood next to him, then faced the crowd again. He bent over to touch the ground. He stood and Rita knelt down, carefully supporting Davina, whom she'd wrapped in multiple layers of blankets, and touched the ground as well.

People around the circle shared a confused glance with one another. Sara locked eyes with Jonathan for a second, eyebrows raised, then she bent over and touched the Earth. Jonathan helped her back up and then he touched the Earth too. Someone else followed their example, then a few others, then more, until everyone had touched the ground.

Allen nodded. "Thank you. There's heated spiced cider in the kettle by the barn. Please feel feel free to help yourselves." No one moved. Allen shrugged and held out his hands, palms up "That's all I have. I told you it'd be brief."

A couple of people laughed and the crowd headed toward the barn by ones and twos. A few of them clapped Allen on the shoulder or shook his hand as they went.

Sara and Jonathan walked around the fire to join Allen and Rita. As they passed a group heading toward the cider Jonathan overheard someone say, "Well, that was fast."

"Yeah. Better than a long-winded sermon, though," his

companion replied.

Allen and Rita stood together with his arm around Rita's waist. When Jonathan and Sara reached them he shook Allen's hand. "Good job. Short, to the point, and sincere."

Sara nodded. "It was a lovely service."

"Thank you." Allen surveyed the line of people heading toward the kettle of cider hanging over a small fire near the barn door and furrowed his brows. He pointed. "Is that Jimmy Carpenter over there?"

The others turned to check. A five-foot tall figure with dark skin showing above the muffler wrapped around his neck stood by the kettle with a cup of cider.

"I hadn't noticed him earlier, but it must be him," Sara said.

Jonathan scanned the crowd. "I don't see either Steve or Anita around, do you?"

Allen shook his head. "No, neither do I. Excuse me." He set out toward the group surrounding the cider. Rita, Sara, and Jonathan exchanged a glance among themselves, then they followed.

*　　*　　*

Allen ladled out a cup of cider for himself and stepped over by Jimmy. "Thanks for coming. I hadn't noticed you before just a minute ago. Are your parents here?"

"No. I—uh—I came by myself. I got here while you were talking a little bit ago." He stared down at his feet.

"Oh." Allen studied the boy, considering how to handle this when he'd had little experience with children. "How are they?"

"They're okay." Jimmy mumbled his response and

didn't raise his eyes.

Allen glanced up as Sara stepped over beside him, then turned back to Jimmy. "No offense, but that didn't sound convincing. I remember, when my wife died, I cried for months. I still cry for her every once in a while."

Jimmy lifted his face. A tear trembled at the corner of his eye. "Mom either cries or she yells," he said. "Dad just sits at the table or goes off walking. I had to get away for a little while."

"I can understand that," Sara said. "Do your parents know where you went?"

He lowered his gaze again and shook his head. "I didn't tell them I left."

Allen laid a hand on Jimmy's shoulder. "I don't mean to run you off, and I'm glad you came, but you should go back home. Your parents will be worried."

Jimmy broke into outright sobs. "No they won't! They're too busy being sad about little Harry to care about me."

Sara wrapped Jimmy in a hug. "That's not true. They love you, even though they're sad about your brother. It's hard to be yourself when you're grieving, but it'll get better."

"All my friends are dead." Jimmy sobbed and wiped his sleeve across his eyes. He pulled away from Sara's embrace, but didn't leave. "How's it going to get better? There's no one here my age. The closest is Maria Kiner, and she's fifteen. Besides, she's a *girl*."

Jonathan faked a cough in an attempt to stifle a laugh. Sara shot him a glare and turned her eyes back to Jimmy. "We've all lost most of our friends and family. Believe me, I know that's hard. But we're here, and we all survived. We need each other's support to keep on surviving."

Jimmy stood there with tears filling his eyes. After a few seconds he shrugged and lowered his eyes again.

"Have another cup of cider, and Jon and I'll walk you back home, okay?"

He wiped his eyes with his coat sleeve again. "Okay."

Allen took the ladle and handed it to Sara. He gave Jimmy's shoulder a squeeze. Jimmy's eyes were still moist, but he'd stopped crying. "Thanks again for coming. You're welcome any time, but in the future, you should tell your parents before you come."

* * *

As Sara dipped another cup of cider for Jimmy and one for herself, motion at edge of Jonathan's vision drew his attention. Jamal and Jim Henderson stood talking some distance apart from the rest of the crowd. Jamal seemed agitated. Jonathan couldn't hear him, but Jamal used sweeping, emphatic gestures as he spoke.

"Excuse me a moment," he said to Sara. "I'll be right back." He wandered toward Jim and Jamal, approaching them from behind Jim as he and Jamal talked.

When Jonathan drew closer, he overheard Jamal say, "Yeah, just like the other ones." Then Jamal noticed Jonathan and said, "Hi Jon. Beautiful night, if a little cold."

Jim spun around and looked him up and down. "Hi Jon."

"Hi," Jonathan said. "Just like what other ones?"

Jamal stood wide-eyed behind Jim, who was facing Jonathan at this point and didn't see Jamal's expression. Jim stood silent, his brows furrowed as if considering something.

Jonathan raised an eyebrow. "State secrets?"

Jim grimaced, then sighed. "No, but not far off the mark, either. Jamal was just telling me that Harry Carpenter's symptoms were about the same as another infant death we had before you got here. By the reports from before the plague, they were the same as the baby boy deaths from the infant mortality outbreak that sparked the riots."

"I thought those were linked to the insect resistant strain of corn they introduced a few years before."

Jamal nodded. "Yeah, that was the rumor, but no one ever proved it, at least not that I ever heard. We're not using that strain of corn, so I don't know."

Jim coughed a couple of times. "Look, we've only had two infant deaths here since the plague ended. That's not enough to determine anything conclusively. Even if it is due to the same cause as before, maybe it needs some time to work its way out of the environment. In any case, I don't want there to be a panic over this."

"Two out of two boys," Jamal said. He looked past Jonathan. "Sara's coming toward us."

"So anyway, like I was saying, I should head over to Janet's meeting," Jim said as Sara joined them.

Jamal nodded. "I guess I'll go with you."

"We're going to walk Jimmy Carpenter back home," Sara said, "and we should probably do that before his parents get worried."

"Yeah I suppose so," Jonathan said. "Good night, nice talking with you." As he followed Sara back to the cider kettle he twisted around to look toward Jim and Jamal. Jamal met his glance and raised a finger to his lips.

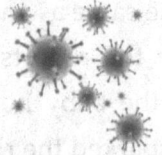

Chapter Eighteen

Personal Revelations

JONATHAN and Sara made it back to their house not long after 7:30 by the light of a nearly full moon. Jonathan built a fire from the coals he had banked in the fireplace earlier, while Sara filled a kettle for tea and set it by the fire. Rita wasn't back yet.

They sat at the table and waited for both the water and the room to heat up. Sara looked Jonathan in the eye. "So what is it that you and Jim and Jamal were really talking about back there at the farm?"

"Huh? What do you mean?" He turned his face toward the table for a moment, then forced himself to lift his gaze back up to her.

"Don't play dumb with me. You don't do it well."

"Uh, well—"

"Out with it, Jon."

He sighed. "Okay. Jamal thinks Harry Carpenter's symptoms were the same as another baby boy's who died before we got here, and that they both seemed like the infant mortality syndrome that sparked the riots before the plague. They're afraid of a panic if the word gets out. They didn't intend to tell me, but I overheard some of their conversation, so they filled me in."

Sara shook her head. "It's better that the word gets out quickly, rather than people think they're hiding something," she said.

"Maybe. If people get the idea that no boys are going to survive—that the human race is doomed anyway—it's hard to guess how they'll react."

"As I recall, not every boy died from that illness," Sara said. "A few of them lived."

"That's not going to be much of a comfort to many people. We just don't know enough yet. There have only been two baby boys born in this community since the plague ended, and both of them died. It's still possible that they died of something else."

"I suppose that's possible, but no one's going to believe that. Not right off the bat, anyway. Not without convincing evidence. You don't, do you?"

He grimaced. "No."

"Well, Jane Fulk is the next one due to give birth in, I think, February or March."

The tea kettle whistled and Jonathan retrieved it from the fireplace. Sara poured some into a white ceramic teapot with some dried mint leaves and set it on the table to steep.

A few minutes later while they sipped their tea, Rita pushed the front door open with the baby carrier. Sara and Jonathan went to greet her as she entered. Sara took Davina and Rita unwrapped her scarf.

Davina slept in her basket. Sara set it on the coffee table in the front room. "She didn't get chilled did she?"

Rita hung her coat in the closet. "She's wrapped in two blankets and Al gave me a hot water bottle to tuck in beside her for the walk back. If anything, I'd be concerned that she's over-heated."

Sara gave a little laugh. "I guess I worry too much. I never had children myself."

"I came from a big family, and I'm the eldest. I learned a lot about babies along the way."

"It shows. You're great with her," Sara said.

Rita took Davina from the carrier and cradled her in her arms, then turned back to Sara. "I thought you were great with Jimmy earlier tonight. If you don't mind my asking, why didn't you ever have children? You seem to like them."

Sara had been smiling at Davina and snapped her gaze back up at Rita's face. Her smile melted. She turned away and brought a hand up to wipe her eyes.

"Sara and I both carry the gene for Tay-Sachs," Jonathan said after a few seconds. "There was a high probability that our children would have died of it. I had a vasectomy not long after we discovered that, back when I was twenty-four."

Rita's eyes went wide. "But couldn't they have edited the gene if the baby was affected?"

"This was in 2004. Before that technology existed."

"Oh." Rita glanced at her daughter, then turned back to Sara. "Oh, I'm so terribly sorry."

Sara nodded, still not facing Rita. "Thank you."

Jonathan stepped up beside Sara and laid a hand on her shoulder. She covered his hand with hers. Forcing a smile, she raised her head to meet Rita's eyes. "Maybe we could be surrogate grandparents for Davina. If that's okay."

Rita smiled back. "Thank you. I'd like that." She gave Sara a one-armed hug.

Davina squalled and Rita checked her diaper. "I think she needs changing." Rita went to her bedroom with the baby.

Jonathan kissed Sara on the cheek. "You okay?"

"Yeah, I'm fine." She wiped her eyes with her sleeve. "Thanks."

He tilted his head. "Thanks for what?"

"For being you." She turned around and gave him a quick peck on the lips.

He smiled. "I'm glad you like that, since I can't be anyone else." He bent to kiss her again, but the perimeter alarm on his laptop blared. He glanced toward the bedroom where it lay on a desk, turned back to Sara and kissed her quickly, then half-ran to the bedroom.

"Report," he ordered the computer.

"Three individuals are approaching the northwest perimeter. At least one has a firearm."

"Not village members?"

"It wouldn't be noteworthy if they were, now, would it?"

Jonathan grimaced. "Notify Jim Henderson."

"Message sent. Awaiting receipt confirmation."

"Notify Dan Kiner."

"Message sent. Awaiting receipt confirmation. Anyone else you want notified?"

"That'll do for now."

Sara came up behind him and laid her hand on his shoulder. He didn't look up.

"Video," he commanded. The video window on the screen expanded to fill the whole display. Three blurry forms in infrared showed, occasionally eclipsed by trees as they headed toward the village.

"Have Jim or Dan responded?"

"No. I'll let you know when they check in," the computer said.

"They're probably still at Janet's meeting," Sara said.

Rita came to the door holding Davina to her breast. "What's going on?"

Sara spared her a glance and turned back to the video feed. "Looks like an attack, or a raid." Jonathan opened the closet and put on his ballistics vest and helmet. Sara squeezed past him and grabbed her own.

"You stay here with Rita," Jonathan said.

"Forget the macho bullshit, Jon. You aren't going out there by yourself."

Jonathan locked eyes with Sara and a second later he sighed. He turned to Rita. "Turn off the lights and stay away from the windows once we leave. Keep your pistol with you and keep trying to reach Jim and Dan. Watch the monitor and keep us informed."

"Right."

Jonathan turned toward his laptop. "Paladin, Rita has access permission."

"I took that as implicit months ago."

Sara raised an eyebrow. "Paladin?"

"I decided the AI needed a name."

Sara rolled her eyes. "Whatever." Jonathan activated his helmet, and a second later Sara did too. The security monitor program acknowledged the connections. Sara handed Jonathan his rifle and took her own. She checked the safety and pocketed some extra cartridges, then followed Jonathan toward the door.

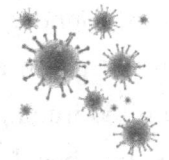

Chapter Nineteen

Intruders in the Night

JONATHAN and Sara made their way toward the intruders through the ghostly green and black night-vision version of the village. Windows were bright, the house frames less so, and the trees were a dim green-on-black outline.

"Plan view, inset," Jonathan commanded his helmet. A stylized map appeared in the upper right of his field of view. The AI had helpfully suppressed icons for other people besides the three who had entered from outside the village. It showed his and Sara's positions as green squares marked J and S, and the three unknowns as numbered red 'x's in the plan view window. Sara had moved ten or fifteen yards to his right as they made their way to the trees bordering the village, close enough together to be available, but far enough apart that anyone seeing him might not see her too.

About the time he first made out the light green speckles of their targets by night vision, Rita called. "Jim Henderson just answered. He's sent Jacob, Tyler, Jamal, and Bill to back you up. He's going back to the community center to warn everyone left there to stay put."

Sara acknowledged the call and then he did too. Some

new red blips appeared on the map from houses in the village and moved toward him and Sara.

"The new targets are friendly," Jonathan sub-vocalized to the program. They turned green and changed into circles. The helmet system had limited intelligence, and there was only one audio channel available besides the short-range inter-helmet channel. He'd chosen to use it to communicate with Rita, rather than directly with the security monitor on his laptop.

He and Sara were 84 yards from the intruders, according to Paladin, and the reinforcements were still 296 yards off for the closest one. In the night vision display, the image of the intruders began to appear as human forms. They picked their way along through the trees, spaced by a few yards between them. Sara and he continued to make their way forward but slowed their pace to allow the others to catch up.

Abruptly the three strangers stopped advancing. One of them pointed toward Jonathan, and another raised a rifle to his shoulder. Just before he fired, Jonathan ducked. Splinters exploded from a tree beside him and clattered against his helmet and vest. Some struck his hand with a sharp sting. Despite himself he jumped and shouted. He landed on his butt in a patch of crusty snow.

To his right three rifle cracks sounded in quick succession. Two of the intruders fell. The third one brought his gun around toward Sara, who fired again. That one fell too.

Jonathan got back to his feet and noted in the plan view that the icons for Bill, Jacob, and Jamal approached at a pace that must have been a dead run.

"Jon, are you okay?"

Jonathan stood and shouldered his rifle. "Yeah. Some

splinters, maybe." He crept to the nearest of the intruders. Even by the grainy night vision image it was clear that he had a neat hole punched in his chest. He kicked the rifle lying beside the body out of reach, and then went to the next one. The top of his head was missing. Jonathan fought the urge to retch and went to the third, where Sara stood with her rifle pointing toward the figure on the ground.

It was a woman and she was alive, clutching at her shoulder as she sat against a tree with her teeth clenched. Blood—black by night vision—coated her side from her shoulder to her waist. He kicked her rifle away just as someone else burst into the clearing. Automatically Jonathan raised his rifle toward him and he halted in his tracks, hands raised.

"Don't shoot! It's me, Bill." His old-fashioned night vision goggles made him look like something out of a cheap science-fiction movie. Jonathan lowered his gun.

"You're sure you're okay, Jon?" Sara asked, keeping her aim on the woman.

"Yeah. He missed. Thanks."

"Check her for other weapons."

Jonathan removed a revolver tucked in the prisoner's belt and a hunting knife from a sheath at her side as Jacob and Jamal appeared. Jacob had night vision goggles too, but Jamal relied on only the light of the moon.

Sara nodded toward Jamal, still keeping the woman covered. "She's alive for the moment."

Jamal glanced toward Sara's helmet, then to her rifle, then to the woman bleeding on the ground. He shrugged off a backpack. "I'll need some light if I'm going to do anything."

"On mark, headlight on," Jonathan commanded his helmet. He looked to be sure the others had turned off night vision. "Mark."

"Where's Tyler?" Bill asked. "Jim said Tyler was gonna

be here too."

"I have no idea," Jamal replied as he pulled supplies out of the backpack and started treating the wound.

*   *   *

Tyler was on his way to the lookout post on the interstate for the overnight shift when his radio squawked.

"Tyler, this is Jim. There are some intruders at the northwest corner of the compound, maybe a couple hundred yards east the road. They're armed. We need you to go back-up George and Bill. Sara and Jonathan are there too."

"I'm almost to the interstate, and that's all the way on the other side of the village. It'll be at least twenty minutes to a half hour before I could get there."

"I know, but you've got one of the few night vision goggles we have, and you're the best shot in the village." He coughed a couple of times, then continued. "Andrea can wait to be relieved at the lookout."

Tyler shook his head and sighed. "As you wish." Tyler turned around, clicked off the radio, and started jogging back toward the location. "It'll probably be all over by the time I get there."

He had the goggles off to conserve batteries as he jogged along the road, relying on moonlight and on his memory of the road. As he passed the main entrance to the village he heard gunshots in the distance. He broke into a run.

He'd just topped a low rise in the road when a rifle blaze appeared ahead of him. A split second later, at the same time he heard the rifle crack, a hot pain seared his left upper arm. He dropped to the road and rolled to the ditch, cursing his stupidity. The radio popped off its belt clip and clattered away across the pavement.

*   *   *

"There's someone else coming up the main road from the south," Rita told Jonathan and Sara.

Jonathan turned plan view back on. A fourth red x had appeared just north of the main entrance. "There's another one coming north up the main road," he told the others. "He's a little past the main entrance."

Jamal turned his head toward Jonathan for a second then looked back to the woman as he continued working on her. "That doesn't make sense. If they're attacking up here they wouldn't have come up the road from the south. You'd have seen them earlier in that case."

"Probably, but we're still checking out the system installation. It isn't fully functional yet. We can't rule it out."

Jamal shook his head, still keeping his focus on the woman's wound as he put on a field dressing and immobilized her shoulder. "Then why would it suddenly start working now for no reason? It doesn't make sense."

A gunshot sounded in the distance, coming from the road. Sara and Jonathan doused the lights and they all dropped to the ground.

"Okay, we've got at least one more visitor," Jacob whispered.

"Over here!" the woman shouted.

The smack of a fist hitting flesh sounded. The woman went silent.

"What was that?" Jonathan asked as he turned on night vision.

Jamal kneeled next to the woman with his fist clenched.

"I shut her up."

Jonathan's helmet radio came on. "Are you all right?" Rita asked.

"We're okay," Jonathan said.

"There was a gunshot from the road about two hundred yards east of your position. Your program thinks it was a high-powered rifle, but can't tell what direction it was aimed. There's no visual at that location. It's going by sound triangulation from the rifle shot."

An icy knot formed in Jonathan's gut. Tyler. Did he shoot someone, or was he shot? He checked plan view. A red question mark appeared on the road where the AI had determined the shot had originated. The fourth red x was stationary by the road. The shooter couldn't be Tyler. He was too far north.

"Video of X4." Jonathan sub-vocalized. The map disappeared, and a shaky, over-magnified IR video replaced it. At first he saw no one, then he noticed a faint glow of body heat from the ditch by the road, almost hidden from the camera's view.

Jonathan didn't want to voice his fears that Tyler had been shot yet, so he whispered only, "Either the one coming up the road got hit, or he's hiding."

Rita spoke in his earpiece. "Jim says he can't raise Tyler on the radio. He got him earlier and told him to join you, but now he's not responding."

Jonathan gulped. He relayed the message to the others.

"It was Tyler," Bill said, his voice rising. "Oh my God, it was Tyler!"

"Keep quiet," Jamal said.

Bill ignored him. "He was on for lookout duty tonight

and Jim must've called him while he was on his way there. Oh, shit. Those motherfuckers shot Tyler!"

Jamal grabbed a giant fistful of the front of Bill's coat and pulled him to his face. "Shut the shit *up!*"

As Jonathan watched the video, the figure in the ditch slowly raised his head and pulled goggles down over his eyes. "He's still alive. He's got night vision and he's taken cover in the ditch. I can't tell if he was hit, but he's not out of it."

Jamal released Bill's shirt, and Bill fell to his knees on the ground. He let out a whoosh of breath. "Oh thank God."

"Another intruder has appeared walking south down the road," Rita reported.

"Plan view." In Jonathan's display a fifth x had appeared just north of the fourth, slowly approaching it.

"Looks like the shooter is approaching Tyler," Jonathan said.

"We've got to go help him," Bill cried.

Jonathan shook his head. "We'd never make it in time."

"Well if I can't save his life then I'll avenge his death!" Bill's voice cracked as he started to stand.

Jamal laid a giant hand on Bill's shoulder and pushed him down. "Or you'll get killed yourself."

"We can't just sit here."

Jamal turned to Jonathan.

"I'll go," Jonathan said. "I have the right equipment, and I'm in contact with the security system. It just makes sense."

"I'll back you up," Sara said.

"No. You stay with the others."

"Jon, stop with the macho bullshit—"

"It's not macho, it's common sense. One of us needs to stay here to relay intelligence from Paladin—the security system, I mean—to the others, and I can make better time than you. That's just a fact. I'm the logical—the only—choice."

He couldn't see it through her helmet, but he knew from long experience that Sara had pursed her lips. She nodded. "Be careful."

* * *

Tyler eased his head up and pulled the goggles over his eyes. A horse and wagon stood ahead of him in the darkness of a stand of fir trees. Just south of it a figure walked toward him holding a rifle with a starlight scope in one hand by his side.

Tyler furrowed his brows. Whoever it was must be crazy or stupid. Anyone with a lick of sense would have the gun shouldered.

The intruder made his way along the cracked pavement toward him. Tyler slowly brought his rifle up to his shoulder, wincing and gritting his teeth as he pulled his left arm up to support it, but careful not to make a sound. His left arm throbbed, and a wet chill from the blood on his arm competed for his attention with pain from the wound. He pushed those sensations away.

At the point where he was sure of his aim Tyler shouted, "Drop your gun and raise your hands."

The figure halted, but he didn't drop the gun.

"Drop it!" Tyler said. "I could shoot y'all through the heart without trying hard, and I wouldn't mind."

For a few seconds the man stood still, then he jerked the gun up to his shoulder.

Too slow. Tyler shot him square in the middle of his chest before his would-be attacker completed the motion. The intruder spun around and flung the rifle aside as he fell. It went off as it hit the pavement. Tyler flinched, but the bullet went harmlessly off into the night. The intruder lay still, face down in the road. Tyler got to his knees and another man came out the woods with a rifle at his shoulder and turned toward him. By adrenaline-fueled reflex Tyler shot this one too.

*   *   *

Jonathan tried to be quiet as he hurried through the trees lining the road. He heard voices up ahead when he got closer, but they were still too far away for him to make out what they said. He spared a glance at the IR display from the nearest camera. A person stood on the road with a rifle at his side. Tyler was still mostly concealed in the ditch from the camera's position. Then the intruder tried to raise his gun. An infrared flare burst from Tyler's position and a split second later the rifle crack sounded. The intruder flung away his rifle as he twisted around, falling face down onto the pavement. His rifle went off as it hit the ground.

Jonathan emerged from the trees lining the road a few seconds later and hopped over the ditch, his rifle shouldered. Tyler turned toward him and fired. The impact on his ballistics vest felt like someone hit him with a baseball bat. It pushed him back a couple of feet and knocked him down on his back. He kept his grip on the rifle until he fell but lost it when his head hit the road. The helmet absorbed most of the blow against the blacktop, but he still saw stars. "Tyler, don't shoot! It's me, Jonathan."

"Jonathan! Are you all right?" Tyler got to his feet and ran toward him. At about the same time Sara echoed Tyler's question in Jonathan's earpiece.

"I think so," he said, answering both of them. He stood

up, groaning. "Thank God for body armor, but I feel like I've been punched in the chest by Muhammad Ali."

Tyler shook his head. "Who?"

"Never mind."

"You're sure you're okay?" Sara asked in his earpiece.

"I'm fine," Jonathan said as he picked up his rifle. "The body armor held. You were watching, right?"

"Yes."

"I'll be in touch." He cut the audio.

They approached the fallen figure and Jonathan felt for a pulse while Tyler stood with the rifle aimed at him. Jonathan let go of the intruder's wrist and sighed. "He's dead." Jonathan turned the body on its back and his jaw dropped. He let out a gasp. Even by night vision it was clear the corpse was a child, thirteen years old at most.

"Oh shit," Tyler said, then he vomited.

Jonathan walked back to Tyler. "You couldn't have known, and it wouldn't have been different if you did."

Tyler retched, bent over, standing on the pavement supporting himself with the rifle, its butt on the ground, clutching the gun by the barrel. "Oh fuck, I killed a boy!"

"He'd have killed you if you hadn't shot him. Look, Tyler, you've got to pull yourself together. We don't know if there're others out there or not." Jonathan laid a hand on Tyler's shoulder and Tyler cried out. Jonathan jerked his hand away. Finally he noticed the blood on Tyler's jacket sleeve. "You're hit!"

Tyler straightened and wiped his mouth against his right shoulder. "He grazed my arm."

Jonathan reopened the audio channel. "Sara, Tyler's wounded in the arm. Doesn't look too bad but I haven't really checked it yet. We'll need Jamal to take a look at it as soon as he's available."

There was an empty second before Sara replied. "Field-dress it the best you can. Bill's on his way to assist." She sighed. "Jamal hit the woman a little too hard when he shut her up. He broke her neck. Right now he's a mess."

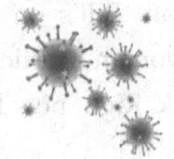

Chapter Twenty

Determination of Culpability

JAMAL sat in the main meeting room of the community center with the majority of the village members gathered around. The others who had defended the community against the raid last night sat nearby. Though afternoon, the day hadn't warmed since dawn. The frigid weather kept the room chilly despite the fire stoked in the massive stone fireplace on the back wall.

The determination-of-facts meeting concerning the attack the previous evening and the homicides that had resulted ground through its course. Jonathan scanned the crowd. Some were grim-faced but many regarded Jamal with obvious sympathy. Festive decorations around the room for the upcoming Christmas celebration were a stark contrast with the somber mood in the room. They'd killed four of the attackers last night. The only ones left were a six-year-old girl and a ten-year-old boy, who they found huddled and shivering in their wagon. The boy wasn't talking much, but the girl told them their names were Amberlynn and Clayton Tolliver.

The community had already judged that Sara and Tyler were justified for the homicides they'd committed based on the video from the security system and Jonathan's and Sara's tactical helmets. For the homicide that Jamal had committed, however, neither Jonathan nor Sara had yet turned on night vision after they'd doused the lights, so the helmet video was useless. The video from the security system was inconclusive due to the distance from the camera and the tree cover.

Jim Henderson faced the laptop's microphone and said, "So, you followed Jacob and joined Sara and Jonathan where they guarded the wounded woman. What happened then?"

Jamal stared at the floor while Jim spoke. He didn't look up as he replied in a monotone. "Sara said the woman was still alive. They turned on some lights and I went to work dressing a bullet wound in her right shoulder. It didn't look life-threatening. Then there was a gunshot from the road and they doused the lights. The woman called out to whoever had fired, and I punched her to try to knock her out and keep her quiet."

"How did you see to hit her if the lights were out?"

"I still had a hand on her from where I was tying the bandage. I estimated the position from that."

"Why didn't you just cover her mouth?"

Jamal sighed. "I guess I panicked. There were already two fatalities, and then someone else was shooting. As far as I knew she was trying to direct their fire. I just wanted to shut her up." He shook his head. "I didn't mean to kill her, I swear it. I over-reacted, I know. I'm sorry." Tears erupted and trickled down his cheeks. "Oh God, I'm so sorry."

Bill spoke up. "Look, it sucks that she died, but they were trying to kill us. They shot at Jonathan, and for all we knew, they were shooting at us, too. It was self-defense, no doubt. We were lucky to have Jonathan's system. Things could've been a lot worse, otherwise."

"It was a reflexive act," Sara said, "straight from the

instinct for self-preservation."

"Opinion," Jim said. "Keep to the facts."

"Jay made a judgment call that our lives were jeopardized by the woman calling to her friends," Jonathan said. "He was the one by her at the time, and he acted in the most direct manner he knew to keep her from calling reinforcements on us. We had no way to know what others might be out there. I don't believe he intended to kill her—" He noticed Jim about to object, and he added quickly, "Okay, it's my opinion—my impression of the facts as we knew them at the time—that he didn't intend to kill her. It was a horrible accident, but it was an accident."

"All right, we're after facts," Sara said. "Here are the facts." She ticked them off on her fingers as she spoke: "One. We were under attack. They'd initiated the use of deadly force. Two. The prisoner called out to her companions, logically putting us all in danger. Three. Jamal was the only one in position to react immediately to the threat she posed. Four. It was an adrenaline charged, life-or-death situation, and the lights were out. He had no time to do anything nuanced, and in the darkness, no real ability to be nuanced anyway."

She ran her fingers through her hair. "Like Bill said, it sucks that she died, but she brought it on herself."

Jonathan took in a sharp breath. Last May he'd been afraid Sara was slipping into dementia. Now she spoke with steel in her voice and crystal clarity in her words.

Jim nodded, then coughed. "Excuse me. Does anyone else have facts to relate about the homicide of the female prisoner by Jamal Johnson?" He waited several seconds and no one spoke. "Very well. Would anyone like to propose an impression of the facts regarding this homicide?"

Andrea stood. "I have an impression."

Jim nodded. "We recognize Andrea Morfield. State your impression."

"My impression of the facts is that the homicide was accidental, that Jamal acted reasonably under the circumstances and should not be held criminally responsible for her death."

"Thank you. Does anyone have a dissenting impression of the facts?"

There was silence for a few seconds, then someone in the back of the room, whose name Jonathan didn't know, said, "What's your impression, Jim?"

"Jamal is my friend. I don't want to state an impression that might be viewed as biased."

A murmur rose in the room. Someone said, "C'mon, we all know each other," but Jonathan didn't see who it was. Jim ignored him. He rapped on the table. "Order, please." He coughed again. "Does anyone have a dissenting impression of the facts?"

Silence filled the room.

Jim scanned the assembled villagers for nearly a quarter of a minute, then said, "We have a quorum of the adult members of our community present. If there are no dissenting impressions of the facts I move—"

Janet Haskel stood. "I have an impression to state." Her husband, Bob, rolled his eyes and stared at the floor.

"We recognize Janet Haskel. State your impression."

"It's clear to me that this whole incident was brought about by some elements of our community who reject the teachings of the Lord, and whose actions threaten to visit God's judgment upon us all."

Rita scowled. "By 'some elements,' you're referring to Allen, right? Say what you mean."

"Order!" Jim said, rapping on the table. "Janet, I don't

see how your impression relates to the issue at hand."

"Well, obviously, the only life is through Christ, so if we as a community reject Him, then death and destruction will surely be the result. It can't be a coincidence that this occurred on the night of Allen Jacobs' Pagan bonfire."

Steven Carpenter glared at her. "So my baby died because we didn't believe strongly enough, is that right?" He'd clenched his teeth and his shaggy afro cut quivered as he locked his eyes on Janet's face.

A buzz of conversation erupted.

"Order!" Jim repeated. He coughed several times as he rapped on the table.

Finally the noise died down. Jim turned toward Janet. "Janet, your impression is not germane to the issue at hand."

"It most certainly is!"

"Janet, sit down," Bob said. "You aren't helping your cause."

She shot him a look that could have withered poison ivy, but she retook her seat.

"Does anyone have an impression of the facts other than the one that Andrea Morfield has stated?" Jim asked, unperturbed.

People turned back toward him, but no one spoke.

"Very well. If there are no dissenting impressions of the facts I move that we accept the impression Andrea Morfield has stated as the judgment of our community. Is there a second?"

"Second," Rita said.

"All in favor, say Aye.'

A chorus of "Ayes" sounded.

"All opposed say Nay."

No one spoke. Jonathan watched Janet, but she sat still

with a scowl on her face without responding to the motion. "The motion is unanimously carried. Thank you for your service." Some of the people got up to leave, but Jim continued. "Before we adjourn I'd like to make a proposal regarding the two children who were orphaned in the attack, Amberlynn and Clayton Tolliver. Gloria and Dan Kiner have agreed to look after them, at least for the time being. I think we should not tell the children who specifically is responsible for the deaths of their relatives."

Most people sat back down, but Andrea remained standing. "With as many who know, that's going to be a hard secret to keep."

"I know, but I think we should try, regardless. We're a small enough group that their knowing could only be disruptive, and it would keep them from integrating into the community."

Andrea frowned. "I don't disagree, but they're surely going to ask. They'll find out eventually, won't they?"

Steven stood. "The Tollivers were responsible for their actions, the same as we are. I agree that it wouldn't be helpful at their ages, which are..."

"Six and ten," Jim said.

"Right. At such a young age it wouldn't be helpful to tell them that their parents and other relatives were responsible for their own fates. My suggestion is to tell them that we as a community bear some responsibility, that we're all sorry that they died, but not be more specific about it than that."

George Hardy spoke from the back of the room. "I'm not sure I have a better suggestion, but I doubt that will satisfy them. Particularly not the boy. I'll bet he's too old to accept that kind of rationalization. I don't think it's a good idea to pretend that their parents weren't outlaws. I think we need to be honest with them about that. I guess I can go along with not being specific about who actually pulled the triggers."

"If the Kiners are going to be caring for them, they'll need to buy into any decision," Steven said. "They're most likely to be the ones who'll have to address the issue."

"Okay," Jim said, "how about if I bring this up to the Kiners and see if they agree. If not, I guess we'll have to have another meeting. Any objections to that plan?"

He surveyed the crowd for at least fifteen seconds, but no one spoke.

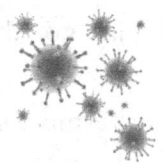

Chapter Twenty-One

Foster Arrangements

GLORIA Kiner put bowls of bean soup in front of Amberlynn and Clayton Tolliver. They were thin and looked younger than the ages they reported. Gloria had managed to get Amber cleaned up well, but Clayton had refused to get undressed for a bath. He had, at least, washed his hands and face. His hair was brown and cut short. Amber had stringy blond hair down to her shoulders, which Gloria had tied in a ponytail. She noted some bruises on Amber's arms and back when she bathed her, but Amber had refused to explain them.

Amber took the spoon after a glance at her brother, then started shoveling in the soup as fast as she could swallow. Clayton eyed Gloria suspiciously, then looked down at the bowl, but didn't touch the spoon. He glowered at Dan, but fear showed in his eyes. Dan watched from the door, leaning against the jamb.

"It's okay," Gloria said. "It's for you. Go ahead."

Clayton shot a glance at her when she spoke, then shifted his eyes back to Dan.

Gloria turned to Dan. "I think we need some more

wood split for tonight. Could you do that please?"

"I just split some this morning."

"I'm sure we need more."

He glanced at Clayton and nodded. "Yeah, I guess we do." He left the kitchen.

Clayton watched him go, then turned back toward Gloria.

"It's real good, Clay," Amber said.

"Mom and Dad are dead! How can you eat?"

Amber took another spoonful with a loud slurp. "They're just asleep. They'll wake up tomorrow."

Gloria froze in place, her mouth hanging open.

"You stupid idiot." Clayton turned his head and spat on the floor. "They're dead. They're not waking up again." A tear ran down his cheek.

"You're lying!" Amber jumped out of her chair, and it fell on its back behind her with a bang. She glared at her brother with a defiant pout on her lips.

Gloria knelt to Amber and wrapped her in a tight embrace. "I'm sorry, honey, but your brother's right. They're not waking up again."

"But the sleeping pills will wear off tomorrow," she wailed. "That's what they said."

"Sleeping pills?"

Clayton snorted. "They told her the guns shot sleeping pills. They said the people they shot were gonna wake up again the next day. She's dumb enough to believe it."

Amber shook her head and tried to squirm away, but Gloria held her tight. "I'm sorry, Amber. I'm so sorry." Tears trickled down her own face now.

"You're lying," she repeated with less conviction.

"I can't tell you how sorry I am, but it's true. I promise

we'll take care of you."

Clayton gave another snort. "Like you took care of Mom and Dad? Like you took care of Trevor and Uncle Quincy?"

Gloria clutched Amber and stared at Clayton with wide eyes, not moving for a moment. Finally she said, "I promise we'll do all we can to keep you safe."

Clayton glanced toward the door, and for a second Gloria feared he'd make a break for freedom. He stayed in place, though and turned back toward them. He kept his eyes fixed on her and his sister. Amber buried her face on Gloria's shoulder and sobbed. Gloria stroked her hair but kept her eyes on Clayton. "I know you have no reason to trust us, but we really mean you no harm."

Clayton glared at her and folded his arms. "So we can go if we want?"

She shook her head. "That wouldn't be a good idea. It's cold out there and food is scarce. We can feed you and give you a warm bed to sleep in. When you're grown up no one will keep you from leaving if you still want to go, but until then you're our responsibility."

He glared at her a moment longer, then shifted his eyes toward his sister, who still sobbed on Gloria's shoulder. His expression softened and he cast his eyes downward.

"I'm sorry I called you a 'stupid idiot,' Amber."

"I want my mommy!"

"I know you do," Gloria said. "I'm sorry."

"I'm still here, Amberlizzy. I won't leave you."

"Why don't you sit back down and finish your soup?" Gloria said. "Your mom would want you to eat, right?" She set the chair upright, and the two children sat.

Clayton still watched Gloria with suspicion in his eyes,

but he took the spoon and swallowed some soup. Amber sat still with her hands in her lap. She still wept, but the tears had slowed.

"Eat, Amberlizzy," Clayton said. "Mom wants you to eat."

She faced him, then Gloria, and finally turned to the soup. Hunger prevailed. She took the spoon again.

"We have more, if you're still hungry when you finish that," Gloria said.

*　　*　　*

Before Amber and Clayton finished their soup Jim Henderson came to the house. Dan let him in, and Jim stopped at the doorway to the kitchen.

"Hi," he said. "It's Amberlynn and Clayton, right?"

Clayton eyed him over a spoonful of soup, a scowl on his face, his eyes narrow slits. Amber spoke up, grave faced. "My name's Amber."

"Okay, Amber it is. I'm Jim." Clayton took another spoonful of soup, but his eyes didn't leave Jim. "I want to say how sorry about your parents, your uncle, and your brother we are. The Kiners will be taking care—"

Clayton made a loud slurp and swallowed. "Go get fucked."

Jim's jaw dropped. He coughed. Gloria shooed him into the dining room, standing in the doorway with her back to the children. "Not a good time for insincere expressions of sympathy," she whispered.

"But it is sincere," he said, whispering himself, then he coughed again. "Excuse me."

Gloria sighed. "Jim, you've got a lot to learn about

kids."

"Maybe so, but I'm going to have to talk to them anyway. Hopefully without swearing at each other. Does he even know what that means?"

"I thought his meaning was clear. What's so all-fired important that you have to talk to them right now?"

Jim coughed. "I need to explain that you'll be taking care of them at least until some other arrangement is made, and I want to (cough) question them about what they've seen on their travels."

"They know the first, and now isn't the time for the second. Leave them be for now."

Jim frowned. "We need to know what they've seen as soon as possible."

"It'll wait, Jim."

"But—"

"It'll wait."

He considered her expression, and after a second he nodded. "Okay. But take note of anything you find out, okay?"

"All right, but I'm not going to interrogate them, understand?"

"Yeah, I understand." He turned away from her and coughed, covering his mouth with his elbow.

Gloria furrowed her brows. "Your cough is getting worse. Have you let Jamal check you out?"

Jim made no indication that he'd heard her. "We exonerated everyone at the meeting just now. Jamal's still pretty broken up"—he turned to cough again—"still pretty broken up about it, though."

"I can imagine, but you didn't answer my question."

Jim leaned to her ear and whispered, "For now, don't tell them specifically who killed their relatives. If they ask, tell them something like, 'they died when we defended ourselves against their attack.' I'll stop by later. Message me when they're asleep and we'll talk some more."

"Okay, but Jim—"

"I'll talk to you later." He left her standing there.

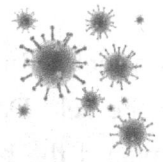

Chapter Twenty-Two

Christmas Eve

DECEMBER 24th dawned cold and clear. Sara had been up since five, and now she stood by the front window watching the sunrise. The yellow band along the horizon lightened minute by minute while she gazed out the window. Maybe the batteries would get a good charge today. Cloudy weather for the previous couple days had left the batteries low.

The morning light reminded her of her father, now dead more than twenty years. Mornings had been his favorite time of day. He'd been a life-long pacifist, a physician who had regularly donated time at the free clinic. What would he think about what his *maideleh* had become?

The baby's squall interrupted her reverie. She walked back to the kitchen.

Rita held the tea kettle under the tap with one hand as she cradled Davina to her breast. She looked up when Sara came in.

Sara joined her by the sink and took the kettle. "Here, let me help you with that." Sara filled the kettle and stepped out to set it by the fireplace to heat. Jonathan barely looked up from his laptop as she placed the kettle.

Rita still stood by the counter when Sara returned. "Is

Jonathan up?"

"He's trying to contact a weather satellite. One's going to pass over soon."

"Oh." She pulled a loaf of bread from the box by the range one-handed while she held Davina, careful to keep the baby at her breast. She placed the bread on a cutting board, then stared at it for a second and laughed. "I guess I'm not going to be successful at cutting bread one-handed while nursing, am I?"

Sara chuckled and pulled a bread knife from the block next to the breadbox. "Still adjusting to motherhood, eh?"

"So it seems." Rita sat at the table and adjusted the blanket wrapping Davina. "I guess I'm preoccupied at the moment anyway."

Sara put a slice of bread spread with raspberry jelly on a plate in front of Rita. "Preoccupied? About something besides nursing your daughter?"

Rita took a bite and swallowed. "I just feel for those kids. Orphaned now, after all they've been through. It's just so cruel. And—" She reddened and turned her face toward the table.

"And that I'm the one who killed their father and uncle, right?"

Rita nodded, tight-lipped, her eyes downcast. "I understand that you had to. I'm just reminded of it every time I see them."

Sara pulled out a chair and sat. She sighed. "You and me both." She spread jelly on a slice of bread for herself. "I'm sorry their family members died. I'm not sorry that I shot them, though. They attacked us, and I reacted to protect Jonathan and myself. I'd do it again." She considered the slice of bread she'd just prepared, then she put it back on the plate before her. "Look, it's no different from when you shot the Gibson brothers. Survival. Him or me and better him than me." She pursed her lips. "It just seems different this time because there are children involved."

Jonathan came in carrying the teakettle. He poured hot water into the teapot and sat beside Sara.

Sara gave him a quick kiss. "Well, did you make contact?"

"Yep. Downloading images as we speak."

Rita adjusted Davina's position. "Anything interesting?"

"Oh, I haven't seen anything yet. I've just initiated the download. I'll have to process the files afterwards to see what's there."

Sara pointed to the plate before her. "Do you want some bread and jelly?"

"Sure. I'll get it." Jonathan pushed the chair back to stand, but Sara slid the plate she'd prepared for herself in front of him.

"I decided I wasn't hungry after all."

"Are you feeling okay? You didn't sleep well last night."

"I'm fine."

"You should eat something. Here, I'll split it with you."

"Not right now. I'll get something later."

"Are you sure you're okay?"

"I'm *fine*, Jonathan." She poured tea for the three of them and took a sip. She set her cup back down on the table with a distinct thud. A few drops sloshed out.

Jonathan locked eyes with her for a second, then he dropped his eyes and picked up the slice of bread. "Okay. Thanks."

Rita's eyebrows lifted, and an awkward few seconds

passed with Sara rotating her cup on the table, staring into it. "Are you going to the Christmas Eve service tonight?" Rita asked.

Jonathan shook his head. "No, I don't think so."

Sara snorted a brief laugh. "I gave up Christmas for Lent."

Rita tilted her head. "Excuse me?"

"We're nominally Jewish, though we haven't been observant for a long time. We never got into celebrating Christmas."

"Well, I guess Allen and I are going."

Jonathan sat up straighter in his chair. "Really? I didn't think Allen got along well with Janet Haskel. How'd you convince him?"

"He's the one who suggested it. He says he doesn't want to be a source of divisiveness."

Sara took another sip of tea. "I hope that works out okay. 'Cause it was my impression that it was Janet who didn't get along with Allen, rather than the other way around."

Rita nodded. "We talked about that some yesterday. I agree with you, but Allen doesn't want his Solstice celebrations and such to become a competing ritual to Christian observation. He keeps saying it's not about competition."

Sara set her tea cup down. "I'll take Allen at his word, but I'm not sure Janet agrees."

"Do you want us to watch Davina for you tonight?" Jonathan asked.

Rita shook her head. "I appreciate the offer, but she's been needing to nurse around that time. I'll take her with me."

*   *   *

Janet Haskel knocked on the Kiners' door at 10:15. Dan answered the door and invited her in. She set a canvas tote bag on the floor by the door and unbuttoned her coat. "Are Amber and Clayton available?"

Gloria came out of the kitchen behind Dan. "They're upstairs at the moment. What's up?"

"I brought them some Christmas gifts."

"Oh." Gloria nodded. "That's nice. I'll get them." Gloria climbed the stairs and Janet turned to examine the Christmas tree in the front room. Most of the decorations were commercial plastic balls with winter scenes and Santas and such. She frowned. There should be more of an emphasis on Christ for the decorations. Gloria returned a couple minutes later followed by the two children.

"Merry Christmas, Amber and Clayton," Janet said.

"Merry Christmas," Amber replied. Clayton stood beside his sister, a frown besmirching his face.

Janet pulled a couple of thin packages out the tote bag. "I know it's a day early, but I brought you some gifts for Christmas." She handed them over. "You can open them now if you like."

Amber ripped her package open, dropping the paper on the floor. Inside was a picture book, The Golden Book of Bible Stories. She regarded it, turning it over, then back. She lifted her face to Janet's. "Thank you."

Gloria said, "We can help you read that if it's too hard for you."

Clayton picked at the string wrapping his package and crumpled the paper as he pulled it off. He stared at the book inside for a moment and then he turned to Janet. "Charlotte's Web?"

Janet said, "It's a classic story about friendship and—"

Clayton rolled his eyes. "I know what it's about. I read this when I was eight."

"Oh." Janet shot a glance toward Gloria, who stood at Clayton's side.

Gloria shrugged. "He's been working his way through Dan's collection of Robert Heinlein. He reads really well."

Janet scowled. Science fiction wasn't the best choice of reading material for a youngster in his state. Should be something more positive.

Clayton flipped through the book and grimaced. "Well, thank you, I guess."

"You're welcome. We might have some other books that are more appropriate in the library at the school."

Clayton lifted his face. "School?"

"We'll start again after the first of the year. There's not too many students, five other children altogether, but there's another boy about your age."

"I've never been to school," Amber said, "'cept pre-school when I was little."

"I saw another school last winter," Clayton said. "Dad and Uncle Quincy shot the teachers who came out when Mom threw a torch through the window. The kids all ran into the woods. We had chicken for dinner that night. I ate till my belly hurt. I had three drumsticks, and we had potatoes too."

Janet's mouth fell open.

After a brief, shocked silence Gloria said, "That's interesting, Clayton. Could you tell us more about that?"

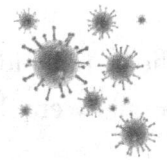

Chapter Twenty-Three

Chicken Dinners

"FROM a tactical standpoint it makes a certain amount of sense," Jamal said. "They ran the children off, which forced the surviving adults to go searching for them. That left the place empty, so the Tolliver gang could raid the community's supplies unhindered."

Janet shook her head. "That's reprehensible. Totally depraved."

Jamal nodded. "I agree. But efficient."

Jim coughed. "Clayton didn't have any useful information about where this was, though?"

"No. It was a year ago, and anyway, his parents didn't tell him anything specific about where they were," Gloria said. "He said there were a lot of pine trees around, but that doesn't narrow it down. It was hilly. That might mean it was west, rather than east. The most noteworthy thing from Clayton's viewpoint was that they got to eat chicken."

Jamal shrugged. "Well, even on foot, during a year they could have covered hundreds of miles. This doesn't help us locate that settlement."

"No," Jim replied, ""ut at least we know that there is another settlement. By the way, I'd prefer that you don't ever refer to them as 'the Tolliver gang' again."

Jamal gave a surprised shake of his head at Jim's tone. "Okay. Why?"

"I don't want those kids identifying themselves as outlaws. Maybe their parents were, but we're going to try to give them a fresh start."

Jamal nodded. "Okay, sure."

Gloria stood and moved closer to the fireplace. She rubbed her hands together and held them toward the fire. "Jonathan was going to try to find some evidence for other settlements from the satellite imagery, wasn't he? Has he found anything yet?"

Jim shook his head. "Not that I've heard. I should've invited him too, I guess." He coughed again, several times, bending forward in his seat, and pulled out a handkerchief to hold over his mouth. "Excuse me."

Jamal squinted at Jim. "Your cough isn't getting better."

"No it's not. I should go get a chest x-ray, and maybe a bronchial endoscopic exam."

Jamal grimaced. "If only."

"Look," Jim said, "this information from Clayton was interesting, but there isn't enough to act on. I'll tell Jonathan what we learned, and in the meantime keep your ears open for any other clues Clayton and Amber might drop."

* * *

Janet and Gloria left shortly afterward, but Jamal stayed behind. He closed the door behind the two women and faced Jim. "Look, you're not dumb, so I'm sure you know why I'm concerned about you."

"Yeah, I know."

Jamal retrieved his coat and pulled a stethoscope from the pocket.

Jim coughed and gave a wry smile. "Don't leave home without it?"

"That's right. Unbutton your shirt." Jamal performed a brief examination and asked a few questions, then pulled the stethoscope from his ears and draped it around his neck. He frowned. "It's impossible to be sure, but your symptoms sure make me suspect lung cancer."

"Yep."

"'Yep?' That's all you have to say? Jim, this is serious."

Jim coughed, covering his mouth in the crook of his arm. "Yes it is, and what do you propose to do about it?" He pulled out a crumpled, wadded-up handkerchief and wiped his mouth.

Jamal opened his mouth, but nothing came out.

Jim nodded as he buttoned his shirt. "Yeah. That was my assessment too." He coughed again, so hard he bent over and clutched at his chest.

Jamal stepped closer in case Jim fell, but Jim waved him off. Jamal's shoulders sagged as his hands dangled at his side. It struck him then that Jim had become visibly more frail than he'd been just a couple of weeks ago. "I can't just do nothing. There's got to be something I can do."

Jim straightened up and wiped his mouth with the handkerchief once he'd caught his breath. Jamal listened for signs of wheezing, but there were none just then.

Stuffing the handkerchief back into his pocket, Jim said, "Fine. Here's what you can do: If it metastasizes into my brain—if I lose who I am—I want you to kill me."

"Jim!"

"You asked."

Sweat beaded up on Jamal's brow. He wiped it off with his sleeve and locked eyes with Jim. "You're serious."

"Yes. I am."

Jamal ran his fingers across his dreadlocks, pushing them away from his face. He shook his head. "I'm not going to promise to do that. Not now. In any case, you'd have to get another witness to that decision before I'd even consider it. At least one other witness." He fell into an armchair by the fireplace.

Jim nodded and sat too. "That's reasonable. I'll ask Dan, and maybe George and Andrea."

Jamal raised his face toward Jim's. "Maybe it's just bronchitis."

Jim nodded again. "I couldn't rule it out. But there's no fever, and the cough's not productive. You don't really think that's what it is, do you?"

Jamal closed his eyes and grimaced. "No."

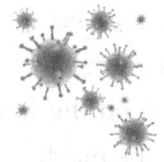

Chapter Twenty-Four

Angels on High

"AND *there were in the same country shepherds abiding in the field, keeping watch over their flock by night.*

"*And, lo, the angel of the Lord came upon them, and the glory of the Lord shone round about them: and they were sore afraid.*"

Janet read the Gospel of Luke from a battered, leather-bound Bible with gilt-edged pages, though she didn't need the text in front of her for this passage. She spoke with expression and emotion as the hour advanced toward midnight.

She finished with, "*Glory to God in the highest, and on earth peace and goodwill towards men.*"

Janet closed her Bible on the lectern. The clock over the door said 11:52. She surveyed the crowd assembled in front of her—about thirty people altogether—seated in the main room of the community center. She noticed Allen Jacobs straighten back up in his chair after touching the floor, and she quickly suppressed a frown. Jim Henderson and Jamal Johnson sat near the back of the rows of chairs. Jim coughed, holding a handkerchief to his mouth to muffle the sound. He had been coughing occasionally through the whole service, sometimes bending down in his seat as he tried to clear his lungs.

Janet turned back to the task at hand. "That's the true meaning of Christmas," she said. "Peace on earth, goodwill toward men. Let us join together in a song of praise for the newborn king, 'Hark! The Herald Angels Sing'." She touched a virtual key on a pad lying on the lectern. The opening chords of the carol swelled from the meeting room's speakers, and the people sang.

When the music started, Davina woke in her carrier and cried. Rita picked her up and rocked her in her arms for a moment. When Davina didn't quiet down, Rita pulled up the front of her shirt and offered her a breast.

Janet did a double-take toward Rita when she began to nurse her baby, and she bobbled the words to the song. She caught up with the rest of the group's singing after a second. Rita and Allen sat near the front, off the center aisle. Janet looked around at the others to gauge whether they were disturbed by Rita's conduct. No one made an outward sign, but she was sure most of the other people could see Rita nursing, and it must be a distraction from the service. If she'd do *that* in public sitting next to a man she's not married to, what else might they be doing behind closed doors? This community really needed some moral guidance.

Rita touched Allen's arm and whispered something to him. He picked up the tote bag at Rita's feet and sorted through it. After a brief search he pulled out a baby blanket and helped Rita cover the baby and herself. Janet averted her eyes while they finished the song. It was now 11:58. She tapped another key on the pad's surface and the text of her concluding remarks appeared.

"Christmas is a time of joy, a time of glad tidings for the coming of the Savior and his message of peace on Earth for all mankind. We all have had much sadness in these terrible times, but let us not forget to be joyful as well. Even though the grief is there, and I wouldn't try to deny that, let the joy of Christ's love fill your hearts until it overflows and spills out into everything you do, and everyone you see. May peace be with you all, may love be the guide to your days, and may joy light your life with Christ's saving grace. May you all have a very merry Christmas.

"Let us end with 'Silent Night' as we pass on to Christmas day." She touched the pad again and the music started. Again the people sang. At the start of the song Allen bent down to touch the floor, and Janet struggled to contain her anger. How *dare* he defile this service with his pagan rites! She had to close her eyes to settle herself and continue with the song.

*　　*　　*

Allen re-packed the tote bag for Rita while Janet wished the attendees a merry Christmas as they filed out following the service. Rita and Allen were the last ones to leave, aside from Janet and her husband, Bob. After Davina finished nursing it took a few minutes to get her settled into her carrier and to get everything packed for the walk back home.

Janet gave Allen a tight-lipped smile when he and Rita came to the door. "Thank you for coming. I'm sorry the service wasn't more to your liking."

Allen tilted his head and furrowed his brows. "Excuse me? I thought it was a lovely service. What made you think I didn't like it?"

"You kept substituting your own rituals for the Christian ones all through it."

Allen pulled his head back a notch. "Are you referring

to when I touch the Earth? I don't mean any disrespect by that. Quite the contrary. It's something I do as a response to a moving emotional experience."

"Well, I don't think it was appropriate for a Christian service. I'd appreciate it if you'd not do that again. I'd also appreciate it if you'd be more discreet about breastfeeding in the future, Rita. I saw that you finally remembered to cover up, but it'd be better if you excused yourself for that."

Rita's eyes narrowed. "I asked Allen to give me the blanket because I felt a draft, not because I felt a need to hide. And I don't need to excuse myself from *anything* because my baby needs to nurse, thank you very much."

Allen shifted the tote bag to his left hand and clasped Rita's hand in his. He noticed that Bob had returned to the meeting room after replacing the lectern in the storage closet down the hall. Bob stood frozen across the room, watching them, his eyes wide. Allen turned back to Janet. "It was a lovely service, Janet. We should be going. I need to milk the cows in the morning whether it's Christmas day or not." He pushed the door open.

Janet sniffed. "Oh, are you two living in sin now?"

Rita and Allen came to a halt, half-way through the door. Rita turned toward Janet and fixed her with a cold stare. "Not that it's any of your business, but no, we're not living together. Yet. If and when we decide to, that won't be none — any — of your business either. The only sin I see here is that of you judging us. Merry Christmas."

The door swung closed behind them. A few steps down the path Allen stopped and bent to touch the ground. Rita handed him the baby carrier once he'd straightened again, and she touched the Earth too. Allen turned toward the community center when he handed the baby carrier back to Rita. Janet frowned at them, framed by the window in the door.

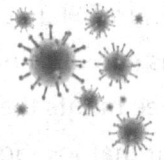

Chapter Twenty-Five

A Distant Settlement

"THE High Resolution Polar Orbit Weather and Reconnaissance Satellite has both infrared and visible cameras. It orbits at a height and inclination that takes it over the whole Earth's surface each day, recording visual images by day and infrared on the night side." Jonathan looked around the table. They all listened intently, and Jim was taking notes. Jonathan smiled. He missed teaching, and these sessions allowed him to recapture the experience.

He clicked the mouse button, and a map of central Virginia appeared, showing the major roads and towns from before the plague. "This shows the area where Erik Kinderman's journal indicated there might be a settlement." He clicked again and an almost featureless black image filled the monitor mounted on the wall. The roads were dimly outlined in dark gray on black, and a couple of lighter patches appeared on the screen as well. "This is the infrared image of that area, from around 10:00 p.m. local time two weeks ago, on December 23rd. The light patches are clouds. When it's clear during the day the Sun heats the pavement, and the roads glow in IR for a while at night." He zoomed in and moved the mouse pointer to a patch of dim light near one of the roads. "This, I think, is another settlement."

"How can you be sure?" Janet asked.

"I didn't say I was sure. I think it is, but only because it glows in IR, it has for three nights that I was able to get images for, and there's a house at that location." Jonathan changed the image to a daytime photo. A large house with a barn and several smaller out-buildings showed from a bird's-eye perspective. "You can see it's a big place from the satellite image and from the size of the shadow, given the time of day, about 10:00 a.m. It turns out, though, we don't have to guess about the size." He clicked the mouse and an advertisement came up for a Bed and Breakfast Inn which also offered tours and demonstrations of a working farm for school groups and such.

"I found this in the internet subset I'd downloaded. This is the house at that location." He pointed to a line in the advertisement. "Fifteen rooms, each with its own working fireplace. Looks like it would be a good place for as many as thirty or forty people."

"How far away is this?" Tyler asked.

"A little more than a hundred and twenty miles."

Tyler looked up and to the right for a moment, "Probably a week each way. Six days, if the weather's good and there are no delays."

Jim pulled a handkerchief away from his face. "Winter's no time for such a trip."

Tyler ran his fingers through his shock of unruly red hair. "Jane's due in February. I don't want to take a chance on being away when she delivers, anyhow. I'd want to either leave right away, or wait till well after the birth."

Janet sniffed. "Don't trust your boyfriend to handle

things while you're away?"

Coming to his feet, Tyler glared at Janet. His face flushed. "Do you have some kind of problem with our arrangement?" He'd clenched his fists at his side.

Jim coughed. "Janet, that was uncalled for. I hope you can be respectful and stay for the rest of the meeting. Tyler, sit down, please."

Jonathan arched his brows, but kept quiet, glancing from Tyler, over to Janet, then to Tyler again. Tyler sat, but the stormy expression didn't leave his face.

"That area is relatively flat," Jamal said, "and there's not much in the way of pine forests right by it. Besides, I didn't see any signs of a burned-out building in the satellite image. This doesn't look like the settlement Clayton described. There must be another one."

George shifted in his seat. "Or maybe if there was, the Tollivers killed them all."

They all stared at George. He'd been quiet during the meeting up to that point.

"Clayton never said they massacred them all," Janet said, "just that they shot the teachers in the school."

George shrugged. "He might not have known. His parents wouldn't have told him, I don't suppose."

Jim turned to Jonathan. "This is the only candidate you've found?"

"So far, yes. I had to do some processing to pull out this one. Because of the size of the building, it has a brighter infrared signature than individual houses would have. Especially if they're well insulated. For example, even knowing where our village is, I had a hard time finding it in the IR image." He typed some and clicked on a couple of drop-down menus. A nearly blank, black and dark gray image filled the screen. "This is our village."

George furrowed his brows. "I don't see anything."

Jonathan moved the mouse pointer over the picture. "Here's one of the houses." A tiny rectangular group of pixels on the screen were dark gray instead of black. "I'd never have found it if I didn't know where to look."

"Could you show us the day-time view of the village?" Tyler asked.

"Of our village? Sure. Hang on a second." He made a couple of clicks and the image came up. "The visible light images have higher resolution than the IR. You can see the houses easily, but there's no way to tell that they're inhabited."

Tyler walked in front of the screen and pointed. "Look over here. This is where we planted corn last year. Now look over here." He moved his hand to one of the other fields. "See how the cornfield has an even, uniform appearance, and this other field we didn"t plant is all mottled? I'll betcha that's an indication the first one was recently worked and planted. That people live nearby."

Jonathan nodded, his lips in a thoughtful pout. "Hmm. You may be right about that." I'll search again on that assumption."

"Okay, good," Jim said. "In the meantime—" A sudden cough came up, then more, and still more. Jim had been coughing off and on during the entire meeting, but not like this. He pushed his chair back and doubled over, hacking and wheezing into a handkerchief. Jamal jumped to his side and thumped his back a couple of times, but it didn't seem to help much. Finally the spasm passed. Jim sat upright in the chair and stuffed his handkerchief back into his pocket. "In the meantime let's wait to see what Jonathan comes up with, rather than send out people to that other site right now."

The rest of them passed a glance around at each other.

After a few seconds Jonathan asked, "Jim, are you all right?"

Jim surveyed the group around the table and sighed. He pulled his chair back up to the table and ran his fingers through his hair. "No. I'm not all right. From what I've read about my symptoms, I probably have lung cancer. Jay agrees."

George gaped at him. "Oh shit, Jim! Are you sure?"

"No, but I can't just pop over to the clinic and get a chest x-ray now, can I?" He coughed a couple more times, but relatively mild ones this time. "Jay thinks that's what it looks like."

They all turned as if connected to the same linkage to stare at Jamal. After a couple of seconds Jamal lowered his head and gave a little nod. "Yeah. That's what I believe it is."

*   *   *

The meeting broke up soon after that. Dan and George stepped up close to Jim to question him further, and Jonathan waited behind them for a moment. Then he noticed Jamal leaving. It didn't appear that Dan and George were going to finish soon, so he left to try talking with Jamal instead. Jonathan ran a few steps to catch up with him. The sun had just set, but the sky was clear and there was still plenty of light. Their breath came out in white clouds in the chilly air. Jonathan tapped Jamal on the shoulder and asked, "Is it as bad as it sounds, with Jim?"

Jamal closed his eyes and grimaced. "Yeah, probably." He opened his eyes as he continued walking. "We don't have the equipment to make a definitive diagnosis, and I don't have the training to do that anyway, but yeah. Probably."

"What are you doing about it?"

Jamal came to an abrupt halt and clenched his fists at his sides. For a moment Jonathan was acutely aware of how big a man Jamal was, half again his weight, a hand-span taller, and no spare fat. His fists were something a heavyweight boxer would envy. Jonathan stopped a step past Jamal and turned to face him. A tear trickled down Jamal's cheek. He wiped his eyes. "Nothing."

"Nothing?"

"What the fuck do you want me to do? Three years ago they'd have inoculated him with tailored viruses to attack the cancer, and he'd be fine in a few months. That technology's gone, and probably gone for good. I can't even cut him open and take out the tumors. I'm not a surgeon." He wiped his eyes again.

"It's all right, Jay."

"God dammit, it's not all right. People look at me like I'm supposed to pull some kind of medical rabbit out of my hat, and I fucking don't have one. I'm just good at putting on Band-Aids."

"You were a medic in the Afghan war, weren't you?"

"During the war I only had to keep soldiers alive until they got to the hospital at Kabul. Then for twenty years I taught Phys. Ed. and coached high school soccer. I'm not a goddamn doctor."

"You did a great job with Rita's delivery. We really appreciate that."

Jamal sniffled and wiped a hand over his eyes. "Thanks, but that was as much Gloria's doing as mine."

Jonathan gave a curt nod. "It was both of you."

"Thanks."

They started walking again, staying silent for a little while, then Jonathan said, "To change the subject, what was going on there between Janet and Tyler?"

Jamal rolled his eyes. "I guess it's not a secret. Tyler's

gay. Bisexual, anyway. He and Bill Stevenson and Jane Fulk are in a three-way relationship. Apparently that's a problem for Janet."

Jonathan tilted his head. "That's the sort of thing I usually say is none of my goddamn business."

"Yeah, that's what I'd say too, but it seems Janet doesn't feel that way."

"So Jane's baby is either Tyler's or Bill's, and they don't know which?"

"From the conversation we had when I examined Jane, Bill and Tyler consider themselves to be equally the baby's father in practice, if not by genetics. Maybe it'd be more accurate to say they'll both equally be the baby's daddy. We'll probably know whose sperm got there first once the baby's born, but frankly, that's not a big issue to me."

"Me neither. Hmm. So that's a problem for Janet."

Jamal grimaced. "So it seems."

Jonathan sighed. "Well, I can't help that."

"It's something of a problem for Bill, too. He was raised Fundamentalist, and deep down, he's conflicted about the relationship."

"Oh? Being gay is a sin? Something like that?"

Jamal rolled his eyes and sighed. "Yeah. Something like that."

Jonathan scratched his beard. "Well, it's obvious from the way he reacted during the Tollivers' attack that Bill feels strongly for Tyler."

Jamal nodded. "That doesn't mean he isn't conflicted."

They reached Jamal's house and stopped on the steps outside the door. Jamal brushed a dreadlock from his face. "Tyler's a smart guy, but sometimes over-confident. I hope he doesn't decide to head out to that settlement on his own. For one thing, his arm hasn't totally healed yet."

"Do you think he might do that?"

"I don't know. I certainly hope—" Jamal stopped and furrowed his brows. He pointed behind Jonathan. "Looks like we'll be able to ask him ourselves in a moment."

Jonathan turned. Tyler ran toward them, less than half a block away. His watch cap was missing and his red hair stuck out in wild tufts. A few seconds later he reached Jamal's front yard and halted, grabbing a lamppost to absorb his momentum. "Jane's bleeding!"

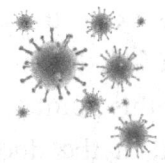

Chapter Twenty-Six

Childcare

ON the afternoon of February 16th Sara stirred a bubbling pot of chicken soup by the fireplace in their room and said, "Jon, could you see if we have any basil or thyme? Something like that?"

Jonathan pulled his gaze from his laptop. "Sure." He hit the "save" key and headed to the kitchen. A minute later he came back with a small jar. "Oregano?"

"That'll work. Thanks." She sprinkled some into the pot and stirred it again.

He took a critical look at the pot. "That's way more than we can eat for dinner. Is that all for us?"

"I'm taking most of it to Jane, Tyler, and Bill."

"Oh. How's Jane doing?"

"She's stir-crazy. Tyler and Bill have been great about doing everything they can so she doesn't have to get out of bed, and she's about ready to kill."

Jonathan snorted a laugh and sat back in front of the computer. "A month of bed rest will do that. She must be close to her due date by now."

"Pretty much there. The dandelion tea seems to be

helping her blood pressure, at least."

"Good. I'm glad that worked."

Sara put the lid back on the pot and wiped her hands on a cotton towel with a faded sunflower print. "Me too. She just wants it to be over at this point."

A knock sounded at the door and Jonathan went to answer it. Clayton Tolliver stood on the porch, his blue plaid coat unbuttoned and red mittened hands at his sides. Jonathan's eyebrows shot up when he saw him, but he recovered quickly. "Hi Clayton, what brings you here?"

"Mrs. Kiner asked if you and Mrs. Rillman could come over for a while. Mr. Johnson wants her to help with Ms. Fulk while she has her baby."

"Oh sh—" He censored himself. " —Oh sure. Let me get Sara." He turned back to the interior. "Sara!"

"What is it?" she shouted from the bedroom.

"Clayton Tolliver is here. Could you join us, please?" Clayton still didn't know that Sara was the one who had killed his father and uncle. Jon and she had talked about this at some length. Sara was torn between feeling compassion for him and Amber, and the desire to keep the secret from them. While she agreed with the practical necessity for the secret, it seemed dishonest to her.

Sara came to the door a moment later. Jonathan thought she controlled herself well when she saw their visitor. "Hi Clayton," she said.

"Jane Fulk's in labor," Jonathan said. "Gloria would like us to look after Clayton and Amber for a while at their house."

Sara stood motionless for a second, her expression frozen. "Sure. Let me get some things together. Come on in, Clayton."

Sara pulled coats out of the closet and handed one to

Jonathan. "Where's Dan?"

"He and Mr. Hardy and Mr. Robertson went to the forest to cut down some trees for firewood."

"I see. Is Maria home?"

"She's watching Amber. Mrs. Kiner made me promise to come straight here and not stop anywhere else."

"Thank you for your diligence," Sara said. "Your careful effort at carrying out Mrs. Kiner's instructions, I mean."

Clayton rolled his eyes. "I know what 'diligence' means."

*   *   *

At 4:24 the next morning Jane Fulk delivered a healthy boy. Tyler hugged Bill and they dampened each other's shirts with happy tears. Tyler let Bill give Jane the first kiss, then he bent to kiss her too. She lay on the bed, exhausted, but gave a hundred-watt smile despite her fatigue as Gloria put the baby into her arms. He calmed down when Jane cuddled him to her, his light brown skin and wavy black hair a sharp contrast to her nearly milk-white skin and red hair.

Tyler thumped Bill on the back and rubbed his kinky black hair. "Congratulations. You're a father."

"We both are. Congratulations to you too."

Tyler shrugged. "You're obviously the father, but we can both be his daddies."

"I can go along with that. That doesn't get you out of changing diapers, though."

Tyler laughed. "I wouldn't want to miss it. It's what daddies do."

Gloria tucked the blanket closer around the infant. "What's his name?"

Jane pulled her gaze away from her baby to look at Gloria. "Grayson. It was my grandfather's name."

"And the last name?"

Jane furrowed her brows. "We haven't discussed that." She glanced toward her two partners. Tyler still had his hand on Bill's shoulder, but they had gone silent, their eyes fixed on her. "I guess traditionally it'd be either Fulk or Stevenson," Jane said. "I'm not sure we need to continue that particular tradition, though."

Tyler lowered his gaze and put his hands into his pockets. "Whatever you all decide is fine with me. I'm happy to be his daddy—" he shot a glance back to Bill, "—his co-daddy—regardless of what his name is."

Jane shook her head. "I'm too tired to think about it right now. Grayson is sufficient for the time being."

Gloria nodded. "Fair enough."

Jamal stepped up and put a thermometer into Jane's mouth, curtailing further conversation for a couple of minutes as he and Gloria gathered their equipment. The thermometer beeped and he pulled it out. "Thirty-six point nine. That's about ninety-eight point four Fahrenheit. Normal, by either scale." He and Gloria helped get Jane cleaned up some more and supported her as she walked to their main bedroom. Bill carried Grayson, looking scared half to death that he was going to do something wrong. Grayson slept peacefully during the short trip.

Bill laid their son in a cradle by the bed and turned to Jane. Tyler had just tucked her in, and she seemed half-asleep already. Tyler gave her a light kiss on the forehead, and Bill leaned down to kiss her, too. Jamal and Gloria went back to the other bedroom, which they'd used as the birthing room, to finish packing. As the bedroom door closed, Bill took Tyler into his arms and kissed him. "I love you."

"I love you, too. Congratulations again."

"You, too."

Tyler gave a bit of a sideways smile. "Jane did all the work. We just stood by and tried not to faint."

Bill shrugged. "Yeah, whatever. Let's go see Jamal and Gloria out. Then I wanna get some sleep myself."

As Tyler followed Bill out he turned back briefly to admire Grayson, lying asleep in his crib. A shiver traversed his body. Oh God, he's so beautiful.

*　　*　　*

Gloria returned to her house a few minutes before seven o'clock. She invited Jamal in for tea and they joined the rest of her family in the kitchen, where they were having breakfast. It was almost time for the children to be off to school.

Dan stood and shook Jamal's hand, then greeted Gloria with a kiss. "So how'd it go?" He poured tea for them.

"She had a boy," Gloria said. "They're both doing fine."

Jamal sipped his tea. "Thanks, Dan." He yawned.

Maria turned to her mom. "What's his name?"

"Grayson. They haven't decided on a last name yet," Gloria said.

Maria furrowed her brows. "Huh?"

Gloria met Maria's gaze. "Don't worry about it right now."

Maria tilted her head but remained silent.

Amber gave Jamal a bright smile. "Good morning, Mr. Johnson. We're going to draw pictures today in school."

Jamal forced himself to face her and smile. "That's real nice. Are you learning to read, too?"

She nodded, yellow pigtails flapping. "I already know

my letters. Mrs. Haskel and Mrs. Kiner are helping me with words. Maria helps too."

He nodded, careful to keep the smile painted on his lips. "That's great." He glanced at Clayton, who had a book— *Citizen of the Galaxy*—propped up behind his plate, reading as he ate a slice of bread with jam.

Gloria tapped Clayton on the shoulder. "Clayton, it would be polite for you to greet our guest too."

He lifted his eyes to look at Jamal. "Good morning, Mr. Johnson. How are you?"

Jamal gulped and refreshed his smile. "I'm fine. Tired, but fine, thank you. How are you?"

"I'm good." He turned back to his book.

"Hurry and finish breakfast," Dan said. "It's almost time for school."

Clayton frowned, but he closed the book and finished the last of his bread in two giant bites. A few minutes later Maria led the other two out the door.

Once the door slammed behind them, Jamal heaved a sigh. "Thank God that's over. So they still don't know, I take it?"

Gloria still sat at the table with a cup in her hand. She lifted an eyebrow. "That you killed their mother?"

Jamal winced, then nodded.

"No. They don't."

"Well—. Their manners have improved."

"Thanks. That was something of a struggle. They've had a hard time of it. Both of them have nightmares."

Jamal winced again. "Me too."

Dan stepped up beside Jamal and patted him on the shoulder. "It'll get—well, not better, but easier to handle, at least."

Gloria sipped her tea. "Let's not dwell on sad things we

can't change, okay? Let's think of happier things. Our population is one greater this morning."

Jamal grimaced. "For the time being, yes."

Gloria set her mug on the table and turned to Jamal. "What's that supposed to mean? You don't really think that syndrome's still active, do you?"

"I don't know. I hate to be negative, but both of the other boys born here died young, and their symptoms sounded like the male infant mortality syndrome that sparked the riots before the plague hit." He scratched the back of his neck. "I just don't want to get my hopes up about—Mason, was it?"

Gloria rolled her eyes. "Grayson."

"Yeah. Grayson. Guess I'm tired. I don't want to get my hopes up about Grayson and then have them dashed down again in a couple of months."

"My sister lost a baby from that." Gloria sighed and turned to stare down into her mug. "Of course, a few months after that they all died from the plague, so it became moot." Dan took her hand and gave it a squeeze. She turned her face up to him and nodded once. "Thanks."

Jamal straightened in his chair and stretched, yawning. "Excuse me." He yawned again and shook his head. "We're not using the strain of corn that was supposed to be responsible, so I don't know."

"I did some research online about that using the law office's search engines after Regina's baby died. There was no solid evidence at the time about that link to the GMO corn. It was all anecdotal. Of course, shortly after that the plague hit, and there was no more research at all."

"Well, we don't know enough yet. I hope my fears are unfounded. In any case, if our little colony is going to survive long term, it needs to grow. We really need to make contact with those other settlements."

Dan tilted his head. "What do you mean?"

"Inbreeding. I don!t know how many individuals are needed for a healthy gene pool, but I bet we!re nowhere near it. And if eighty percent of all boys are going to die, like before the plague, it makes the gene pool that much smaller."

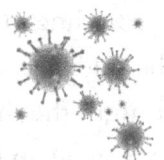

Chapter Twenty-Seven

Baptism Arrangements

JANET parked her golf cart and climbed the steps to Jane, Bill, and Tyler's house after school on the afternoon following Jane's delivery. She took the steps one at a time to favor her bad leg. Standing before the door, she stopped and rubbed her eyes a moment, then gave her temples a quick massage and finger-combed her hair. She'd had a headache off and on for several weeks, and at the moment it throbbed like drumbeats between her ears. She composed herself and knocked on the door.

*   *   *

Bill answered the knock at the door, wiping his hands on a dish towel. "Oh." He frowned. "Good afternoon, Janet. What brings you here?"

"Hi, Bill. This morning at school Maria Kiner told me that Jane had her baby, and I wanted to express my congratulations. May I come in?"

Bill grimaced. "Maybe for just a little bit. Jane's still pretty tired after her labor and feedings and all."

Janet stepped in and slipped out of her jacket, handing it to Bill. His eyes narrowed a little, but he took it. He hung it on a coat tree that was standing by the door, beside Janet. "She's in the bedroom," he said, pointing.

Janet walked through the house ahead of Bill and entered the bedroom. Grayson lay in his crib sleeping, and Jane opened her eyes when Janet came through the door.

"Hi Jane. Congratulations," she said. "How are you feeling?"

"Tired. I was just going to take a nap since Grayson was sleeping."

Janet leaned over the crib. "He's a healthy looking one. He takes after Bill."

"Be careful not to wake him. I just got him to sleep."

Tyler came into the room. He had a dish towel draped over his shoulder. "Oh." He grimaced. "Thought I heard someone come in. Hi Janet."

Janet straightened and turned back toward the others. "Congratulations, Jane and Bill. He's a fine looking baby."

Tyler narrowed his eyes. "Thank you, Janet. Jane really needs to get some rest. Maybe you could stop back sometime in a week or so?"

Bill nodded. "Yes, that would be best. We're all tired right now."

"Well, I also wanted to ask when you want to schedule—Grayson, is it?—Grayson's baptism."

Jane shifted a little more upright in the bed. "Baptism?"

Bill winced. "I—uh—mentioned the possibility to Janet a little more than a month ago."

Jane turned toward him. "Shouldn't we have discussed that among ourselves, first?"

"I'm sorry. I'd just asked her if it's something she does,

and right after that you started bleeding, and things got crazy. I forgot all about it." He stared at his feet. "I'm sorry."

Jane shook her head. "I don't want to think about that right now. Not when we're all tired and frazzled."

Bill patted Jane's shoulder. "Of course. Janet, thanks for the visit but we'll get back to you about the baptism sometime later, okay?"

Janet frowned. "Okay. I guess, I'll see myself out. Good night." She left the room, and a moment later the front door opened and then closed again.

Tyler scowled. "Jerk."

Bill wasn't sure whether Tyler was referring to Janet, or to him.

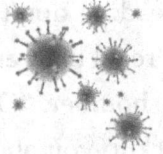

Chapter Twenty-Eight

Medical Issues

BOB Haskel knocked on Jamal's door at about 9:00 a.m. on March 3rd. A minute or so later Jamal answered.

"Hi Bob. Come on in, but give me a few minutes, okay? I've got another visitor just now."

"Sure," Bob said. He took a seat in the front room and Jamal went back toward the bedrooms. Bob surveyed the room, which was originally the parlor. Chairs and a couch lined the walls and some old magazines lay on a coffee table. Bob picked one up and gave a wry smile. A four-year-old copy of Better Homes and Gardens. Just like a waiting room. He laid the magazine back down.

About ten minutes later Jamal came back and invited Bob to one of the bedrooms that he'd set up as a rudimentary examination room. They'd plumbed in a sink, and it had an examination table and some equipment collected from a clinic nearby that had escaped the fires. Jamal washed his hands and turned to Bob. "What seems to be the problem?"

Bob sat on a chair beside the exam table. "Well, it's not about me. It's about Janet. She's been complaining about headaches a lot lately."

Jamal raised an eyebrow. "Oh? Did she ask you to come

and talk to me about this?"

Bob turned away and gazed out the window. "No. She thinks I'm going to inspect the reservoir and the sand filter system." He shrugged. "I really do need to do that, anyway." Bob ran his fingers through his thinning brown hair. This was harder than he expected. He shook his head. Going behind her back like this twisted his stomach in a knot.

Jamal grimaced. "Okay, HIPAA2 is a thing of the past, but obviously you're concerned. I'm not going to tell you anything she's told me before, if I'm not sure she wants me to share it with you, anyway. You also know there's a severe limit on what I can do, right? I'm not really a doctor."

"Yeah, I understand that. It's not like I'm going to sue you for malpractice."

Jamal gave a brief, unamused snort. "No, but I have no desire to be the subject of a determination-of-facts meeting again." He leaned against the sink and folded his arms. "So she's having headaches. Tell me more."

"Just about every day when she comes home from school she has to lie down with a damp cloth over her forehead for an hour or so. She's been irritable, which I guess is understandable if her head hurts."

"Any visual effects? Spots, halos, flashing lights, that sort of thing?"

"Not that she's told me."

Jamal frowned. "It could be any of a number of things, from tension and stress, to migraines, to a brain tumor."

"A brain tumor!?"

"Relax. I'm just saying there's not enough to go on. Especially second hand, like this." He sighed. "For now, unless something more significant happens, there's nothing I can do." He grimaced and closed his eyes. "Not that there's much I can do anyway."

Bob was silent for a few seconds, then he turned his gaze back to the floor. "There is something more."

"Oh? What?"

Bob faced Jamal again. "Her sermons have become simplistic, almost to the point of cliché. She used to write the most beautiful, elegant sermons, with lessons woven in so cleverly that you didn't notice them till they burst on you at the end. But lately they're getting much more ordinary. Boring, even."

"I see. Anything else?"

Bob lowered his gaze again. He grimaced. "Yeah. She's—different—lately."

"How so?"

"Well, she's always been strong in her faith. It's something I've always admired about her, the strength of her convictions. But before—you know, before—she was never—well— intolerant."

"I'm not sure I follow you."

"She comes from an Evangelical tradition, but she'd always said before that other faiths had to be respected as well. She even wrote an article for *Guideposts* to that effect. But—like—after the Christmas Eve service, she ranted until two a.m. about Allen defiling her service with pagan rites."

Jamal furrowed his brows and tilted his head. "I was there until just after midnight, and I didn't notice Allen doing anything unusual."

"It's that touching-the-ground thing he does. She's almost obsessed by it, speculating that Allen's capable of all manner of depravity. And then there was that rant she gave at the meeting when you—well, you know when." He ran his fingers through his remaining hair and grimaced. "She actually swore at me on the way home. She's never done that before."

Jamal sighed. "Well, it's still hard to say what's going on. All that could just be a response to stress. God knows we're all under a lot of stress." He sighed. "Try making her a tea from willow bark. That might help the headaches."

"Willow bark?"

"It contains the active ingredient for aspirin. I'll point out a tree for you, one I've been using."

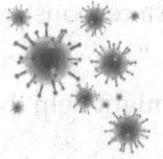

Chapter Twenty-Nine

Male Infant Death Syndrome

A final swing of the hammer secured the manger's loose board. Allen straightened and surveyed the herd, released to graze after the morning milking. He stepped clear as Jack forked hay and drew a few customers. Hints of green in the pasture signaled an early spring. Good thing. Hay supplies ran low. They needed the fresh grass now that calving had begun.

Jack was tall and muscular. At one time he'd played big-ten college football. He could fork in hay twice as fast as Allen could, so he was happy to let him have that task.

Allen's gaze rested on a cow, one with a month-old calf, that hadn't joined the rest. The calf lay on the ground and the cow licked it around the face. The calf raised its head, then laid it back down. Allen slid the hammer into the loop on his jeans and tapped Jack Rockford on the shoulder. "I think we're going to lose another calf."

Jack pitched a final fork-full of hay into the manger and frowned. "Another one? Damn." He leaned the pitchfork against the manger and followed Allen.

Allen patted the cow above the shoulder. "Hey there, girl. Let me take a look."

The calf turned a glassy eye toward him as he checked

it. Its ragged breathing came in weak puffs, and it was underweight for its age. Allen twisted around to Jack. "Yeah. We're losing this one. Another male." He sighed. "I'll get a cart, you lead the mother away."

By the time Allen had brought out the cart and a couple of shovels, Jack had the cow out of sight in the barn. Allen knelt by the calf and touched the ground. "Sorry, boy," he whispered. He pulled the hammer off the loop on his pants and gave the calf a sharp blow on the forehead. It slumped, limp and still.

Jack returned and helped load the body onto the cart. He sighed. "Another one to bury, then."

They both grabbed the cart's T-handle and headed toward the edge of the field. "Don't want to attract coyotes," Allen said.

Jack nodded. "I know. Seems like we're doing a lot of this lately."

"Yeah. At least the piglets and lambs are easier to bury." Allen stopped near the pasture fence. "Good a spot as any." They picked up the shovels and started digging.

"Heck of a way to start spring," Jack said and dumped a shovel-load of dirt onto the growing pile. "This is what, the third calf to die this year so far?"

Allen nodded. "Yeah." He scooped up another shovel-full. He didn't say anything else, but his thoughts were of the two baby boys who had also died as infants in the last year.

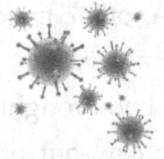

Chapter Thirty

The Vernal Equinox

THE day of the Vernal Equinox dawned cool and damp, but the clouds broke by mid-morning. The afternoon warmed into a pleasant spring day. As the Sun touched the horizon that evening, Allen lit the bonfire and straightened as soon as it was burning well. He turned to face the group of about thirty.

"Thanks for, uh—Thank you for coming. The equinox is here, and now the days will become longer than the nights. Already it's getting warmer, and we're planting the next season's crops. We trust that—that Earth will sustain us, and I want to personally give my thanks to Her for blessing us with an easy winter." He looked at his feet for a moment, then turned quickly back up as he remembered Rita's advice to keep eye contact with the audience.

"We mourn the ones we've lost, and we rejoice in the ones who were born to us. We look forward to the rebirth of the Earth: the flowers and the green of spring, to the growing season, and to the harvest to come. I personally look forward to working together with all of you to build our community together, to sustain each other, and to sustain the mother of us all: Earth." He crouched and touched the ground, and most of the others followed his example.

"Thank you, everyone." He hooked a thumb toward a huge stock-pot sitting on a grate over a small fire near the barn. "Rita and I baked some bread, and we have some lamb stew. I think there's enough for everyone to have a bowl, if you want."

He shrugged. "I'm not much of a public speaker, that's all I've got."

The people applauded. Rita gave him a kiss on the cheek. "Nice job, Honey."

"Thanks."

Jamal came over and shook Allen's hand. "Yeah, good job. Thanks for hosting this."

"You're welcome. How's Jim?"

Jamal's smile melted. "Well, a little better today, actually, but it's still only a matter of time. And probably not that much time. The garlic and turmeric seem to be helping, rather to my surprise."

Sara and Jonathan joined them. "Did I just hear you say Jim's doing better?" Sara asked.

"He's breathing a little easier today, but I don't think he's going into remission. I've been reading up on herbal remedies and trying whatever seems like it's not dangerous." He sighed. "We all need to be prepared to lose him soon."

Allen bent and touched the ground.

Jamal nodded. "Thanks, Allen. I'll take help from whatever source offers it." He bent at the knees and touched the ground too, then straightened back up. "We need to think about succession."

"Jim once told me that he isn't a leader, but just moderates meetings where we reach a group consensus," Jonathan said.

"Yeah, that's what he says, but people rely on him to

resolve conflicts whether they realize it or not."

Sara touched Jonathan's arm. "Speaking of conflicts, something's going on with Tyler, Jane, and Bill." She pointed across the yard where those three stood holding bowls of stew. A baby carrier lay on the ground next to Jane. Bill stood next to Jane, talking to her, and Tyler stood apart from them, looking down into his bowl of stew.

Jonathan turned toward them, then back to Sara. "What do you mean?"

"Tyler doesn't seem to be engaged with Bill or Jane."

"They were over for Grayson's first month checkup a few days ago," Jamal said. "Jane did most of the talking, but Tyler did seem a little—well—out of it at the time." He grimaced. "Uh, that should have been private. Please don't pass that around."

Rita's brows furrowed as she observed Tyler and his partners. "Allen, could you watch Davina for a moment?"

"Of course," he said. "What are—" He stopped speaking. Rita had already left, heading toward Bill, Tyler, and Jane.

*   *   *

"Hi Jane," Rita said as she approached, "May I take a look at Grayson?" Without waiting for Jane to swallow her spoonful of stew and reply, she bent over and peered into the carrier. Grayson lay sleeping, wrapped in a blanket. "He's really growing fast. How much does he weigh now?"

Bill grinned. "Ten pounds, two ounces. Jamal thinks he's doing great, right on schedule."

"He's a beautiful little boy. You must all be overjoyed."

They all smiled and nodded.

"Tyler, if you're finished with your stew, could you give me a hand for a moment? I want to take some of the used bowls and spoons back to the kitchen."

"Sure."

She led Tyler to the table by the stewpot and handed him a tray. She loaded it up with the used bowls people had left there, grabbed a stack herself, and headed to the house with Tyler at her side.

"So how are you adjusting to parenthood?" she asked.

He shrugged, careful to keep the tray level. "Like you say, it's an adjustment. Grayson's a gorgeous little boy, and Bill and Jane are really happy."

"How about you? Are you happy?"

He grimaced. "Sure."

She opened the door and pointed him toward the kitchen. "Let me put the bowls in the sink." He held the tray while Rita unloaded it. "You don't sound particularly happy, if you don't mind my saying so."

He glanced up at her face with quick shake of his head, as if surprised, then he dropped his gaze toward his feet. He sighed. "I feel like a third wheel, lately. Bill and Jane are so happy together, and I—" He shrugged. "I don't seem to fit in anymore."

"Are you able to get any time for intimacy?"

He turned back up, his eyes narrow. "That's a little personal, isn't it?"

She nodded. "Yes, it is. So are you?"

He grimaced again. "Yeah, a little. Jane's tired a lot, and Bill just seems less into it, most of the time." He cracked a bit of a smile. "There have been exceptions."

Rita smiled too. "Well that's good. It's a big change, having a baby. You can't expect things to go back to normal.

They won't. Normal is going to be different now."

He nodded. "Yeah, I guess I know that."

She took his hand and gave it a squeeze. "Let's head on back to the others."

Tyler carried the tray at his side as they went back through the house. As soon as they came out the back door, Tyler stopped in his tracks. Rita almost ran into him. She followed his gaze across the yard, where Bill and Jane stood in an embrace together, kissing. She laid a hand on Tyler's shoulder. "The three of you all kiss each other. It's good that your two lovers love each other, too. It's okay."

Tyler took a deep breath. "Yeah. It's okay."

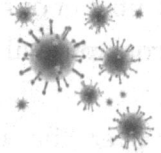

Chapter Thirty-One

The Start of Lent

"...THIS is the time of year we remember Christ's journey in the desert, 40 days of fasting and temptation by Satan." Janet scanned the small crowd of about villagers gathered before her on Sunday morning a week following the Equinox. She was nearing the end of her service. "Like Christ in the desert, we will all be tempted from time to time. It is our challenge to remain strong and resist the temptations of sin, to resist the impulse to stray from the path of righteousness. Let us all remember that the way of God's love is shown by Christ's example on Earth. Though tempted by false idols we must remain resolute in our faith in the risen Lord. The devil's face is comely, but the way of Christ is the way of everlasting life."

She lifted her arm and gave an all-encompassing wave toward the sky. "Accidents of astronomy: solstices and the equinoxes, are mere markers of our planet's journey around the sun, and are of no fundamental importance in God's plan for us. Only Christ has the power to show us the path to salvation. We must all resist the temptation to worship such false idols, just as Christ resisted Satan's temptations in the desert."Those who would tempt us away from the path of

Christ are surely as evil as the devil himself, despite seeming to be kind and helpful. It is our duty as Christians to reject their false promises with every fiber of our being. Despite the devil's comely face, it hides a corrupt, evil soul. The devil must be stopped."

She looked out over the crowd, and noted with satisfaction the widened eyes and gaping mouths of many of them. Good. She was getting through.

"Let us end with a hymn of praise," she said. "'A Mighty Fortress is Our God,' and may Christ's love ever guide you on your way." She pressed a virtual button on her pad and music swelled from the speakers. The gathered faithful sang.

As she joined in the song, she heard the words, "Allen must be stopped," from her left side, as if whispered in her ear. She turned quickly, but no one stood beside her. Some of the congregation faltered in their singing, seeing that she'd stopped. She gave her head a brief shake and got back into the song. The others continued as well.

She'd heard it distinctly, a low pitched male voice that reminded her of her father, who had died of the plague. She shook her head again, a quick, small jerk that she hoped was inconspicuous. Her headache had suddenly become worse. The song came to an end.

Janet raised her hands. "May the peace that comes from Christ's love be with you all, and let us say, 'Amen,'" she said.

As fast as her bad leg would permit she limped out of the meeting room. The back hallway was not lit, and she didn't turn on the light. She retreated to one of the offices instead of taking station by the door to shake the congregants' hands on their way out, the way she usually did. She closed the door and sat in the first chair she encountered. In the semi-darkness she buried her face in her hands.

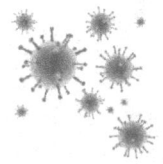

Chapter Thirty-Two

A Voyage of Discovery

April 18, 5:00 a.m.

TYLER guided his horse along the road by the light of a nearly full moon. Jacob rode by his side.

"So, you doing okay?" Jacob asked, breaking a prolonged silence since they'd left.

"Yeah. I'm fine."

"No, you aren't. You've been silent as stone since we left. And you left notes all over the place. I think you regret leaving."

Tyler frowned, but the pre-dawn darkness concealed his expression. "We have an important mission for our community. That's enough, right?"

"One that two-thirds of the village didn't agree to."

"You and I both think it's necessary. Otherwise you wouldn't be here."

"Yeah, I'm here," Jacob said. "But you're sorry about leaving your lovers."

"None of your business."

"It is if it means you're not committed. Are we doing this or not?"

The image of Jane and Bill kissing at the Equinox

bonfire without him participating flashed into Tyler's brain, and he winced. "Yeah. We're doing this."

"Okay then."

*   *   *

5:40 a.m.

Jane opened her eyes. The soft cry of her baby, a slight dampness on her breast, the dim light in the predawn skies, sunrise might be yet an hour away, but the day begins now. She slipped on a dressing gown and padded bleary-eyed and yawning across the hall and into the nursery. Grayson needed a change. Once done, she swaddled him with his arms free, and offered him a breast. He suckled as she stroked his cheek with her thumb. Her eyes fell closed for a moment, and she allowed herself a few moments alone with him before rising to her feet.

She walked into the kitchen and furrowed her brows. No sign of Tyler. He often awoke before either her or Bill, but usually she found him in the kitchen with a mug of tea, reading.

She turned on a light and poured water into a kettle. The sun had been bright all day yesterday, so the house's batteries should have a good charge. She put the kettle on an electric hot plate and pressed the start button. Stretching while holding Grayson to her breast, she pulled three mugs from the cupboard, and then she noticed a sheet of paper lying on the counter. She read the first line on it and shouted, "Bill! Get over here."

Grayson released her nipple and bawled.

Bill stumbled into the kitchen, ricocheting off the doorway, still nude. "What's wrong? Are you okay? Is

Grayson—"

"Tyler's gone!" She held the paper out to him.

"Huh?" He took the sheet and scanned it. "Oh, shit."

*   *   *

7:10 a.m.

Dan Kiner laid the letter down on his dining room table and raised his eyes to Jane and Bill. He sighed. "I'm sorry, but no, we can't send anyone after them." Gloria picked up the letter and read it again.

Jane's eyes, already red from crying, threatened to spill over again. "Why not? You said just last week it wasn't time to go. We all agreed on it."

Gloria laid down the letter. "As I recall, Tyler voted against that. So did about a third of the community."

"But don't we all have to abide by the decision of the majority?"

Gloria pushed the letter across the table to Jane. "Tyler has the freedom to act on his own without our support if he chooses. I don't think it was wise of him to do so, not to mention being irresponsible, inconsiderate, and selfish. But for the same reasons we decided not to send a search party to that settlement during the planting season, we can't send a party after Jacob and Tyler. Especially not now, since we're down two workers with them gone."

Bill glared at Gloria. "I'll go myself, then."

Gloria nodded. "You could choose to do that, but do you really want to leave Jane alone with a new baby right now? And make us three workers short, instead of two?"

Bill glanced at Jane, then he cast his eyes downward. He sighed. "No. I guess not."

"Look," Dan said, "Tyler knows how to take care of himself, and so does Jacob. You have every right to be upset that Tyler took off this way without discussing it. I'm upset too. But the greatest likelihood is that they'll be back safe and sound in two or three weeks with some valuable information." He scowled. "I'm still going to propose they get extra work details for a long time when they return, though."

New tears ran down Jane's cheeks. She wiped her eyes with a blue bandana. "*If* they return."

Bill clasped her hand. "Tyler lived off the land for almost two years with no help before he joined us. He'll be okay."

Andrea burst into the dining room. "Tyler and Jacob took their horses and left last night." She slapped a sheet of paper on the table next to Jane and Bill's letter. "They left a note."

The four of them just stared at her for a moment. Andrea shifted her gaze to Jane and Bill. Jane wiped her eyes again. Andrea flushed and her eyes widened. "Oh."

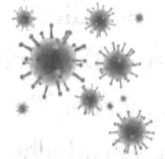

Chapter Thirty-Three

Practical Lessons

April 22, 6:30 a.m.

A knock sounded at the door and Gloria answered it. Bob Haskel stood there, back-lit by the morning sun over his shoulder, his face lined with worry. "Bob, what's the matter?"

"Janet isn't feeling well, and she's not going to make it to teach school today. She was hoping you could cover for her."

Gloria pursed her lips. "I guess so. I really need to help with the planting today, though. We're short-handed. Is her headache worse?"

"Yeah." He sighed. "She's really not up to it today. She could hardly get out of bed. I'm sorry to ask, but I don't know what to do. The willow bark tea isn't helping."

"Well, I was scheduled to help with planting the vegetable gardens today, but I guess I can work out something. I'll go over with the kids in a bit."

"Okay, thanks. We really appreciate it. I better get back home."

*   *   *

Bob's concern weighed on Gloria as she returned to the kitchen. Dan met her gaze and matched her frown. "Who was that, Honey? Is something wrong?"

"It was Bob. Janet's headache is worse. He asked me to sit in for her with the kids."

Dan shook his head. "Bad timing. We all need to be in the fields while this weather holds."

Gloria sighed. "Yeah, I know. Down three people if Janet can't work."

"This is going to put us in a real bind. There's got to be another option."

Gloria sat and took a sip of rosehip tea, just a hint of honey. On the wall in front of her hung the calendar Maria had made as an art project last December. Today was marked as a minor holiday, the block shaded green. Hmm. "How about this: Today is Earth Day. After I look over homework papers and such, I'll do a short module on that, and then we'll do a field trip to the garden plots for some practical demonstrations. A community service project. I can get some planting done, and the kids can help."

Dan shrugged as he sliced bread. "Sounds like a reasonable compromise."

"Oh, hell," Maria muttered.

Gloria locked eyes with her. "What was that, young lady?"

"I said, 'That's swell.'"

"It better not have been what it sounded like at first, 'cause we don't tolerate that kind of disrespect here."

"Yes, Mom."

Clayton snickered.

Gloria turned to him. "Is something funny, Clayton?"

His smirk vanished. "No ma'am." He went back to his book.

Dan put a plate of sliced bread and a jar of raspberry jam on the table. "Go easy on the jam. We're running low."

"Hurry and eat, everyone. I want to get over there early to get some materials together."

*   *   *

Through a background of pain throbbing between her temples Janet conducted the Good Friday service on the evening of April 23rd. A double dose of the willow-bark tea kept the pain muted, but hadn't banished it.

As she scanned the crowd seated before her, it seemed small. Gloria sat next to Dan in the front row, with Amber, Maria, and Clayton beside them. Jim and Jamal sat in the front too, on the other side of the main aisle. Neither Bill nor Jane were present. Bill, at least, had been a reliable attendee in the past. She hoped she wasn't losing the opportunity to get him to see the light.

Janet kept the service shorter than usual. She read a passage from her Bible, gave a brief sermon, and concluded with an invitation for them all to join her for a sunrise service on Easter Sunday.

On their way out, Janet shook Gloria's hand and said, "Thank you for covering for me the last couple of days at the school."

"You're welcome, indeed. I hope you're feeling better. I sort of improvised a field trip for the kids."

"With as few students as we have, I usually improvise myself."

"Thursday was Earth Day, so I did a short session on

that. Then we went to the garden plots and they all helped with planting. Hands-on reinforcement is always good."

Janet scowled. "I'd prefer in the future that you not indoctrinate them with pagan activities."

Gloria lifted her brows and tilted her head. "I discussed nothing pagan. I just talked about working to protect the Earth. Conservation and the web of life, that sort of thing."

"That's what I mean. I don't think we should be emphasizing the Earth, and not Christ, as the source of life."

"I don't think what I did was inconsistent with that."

Again the voice of her father sounded in Janet's left ear: "You must stop Allen." She shook her head and looked to her left. No one there.

Gloria furrowed her brows. "Are you all right?"

"I'm fine. We'll go over this more, later."

Gloria gave a slow nod. "Sure. Later." She hurried out, pulling Dan and the children with her.

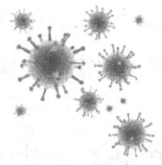

Chapter Thirty-Four

Just Another Day Dawning in Hell

April 24, 6:00 a.m.

BRENDA Jameson woke with a start when Herman Myers groped between her legs. By reflex she tried to sit up, but her wrists were still tied to the bedposts. A strand of straight brown hair landed across her face, and she shook her head to move it out of her eyes. The fire in the bedroom's fireplace had gone to embers. Goose flesh covered her arms and belly. Early morning light—before sunrise—showed through the cracked window pane.

Herman's calluses were rough and his nails untrimmed. "You like that, don't you, sweetheart?" he asked.

Brenda gritted her teeth, but she forced a smile. "That feels good." Best to keep him in a good mood to avoid bruises, or worse.

Herman shifted position to bring his crotch up to her face, straddling her arm. "Suck my cock."

She tried to accommodate his rhythm, but with her hands bound it was difficult to manage. He needed a bath, and he still tasted of last night's sex. Isolate your thoughts. Be mentally elsewhere. Flowering peach trees. Fluffy clouds in a blue summer sky. Apple turnovers.

He made a particularly deep thrust and held it there, deep in her throat. She gagged and pulled her head back to get him out.

His slap caught her on the cheek. She tasted blood. "I'll tell you when you can take it out, bitch."

She forced up tears, and they ran down to the pillow. She'd learned that if he didn't see tears he'd keep trying. "I'm sorry. I'll do better."

He grinned upon seeing her tears. "Damn straight you'll do better, bitch. You want us to throw you off the farm, out where you'll get the plague? You should thank us for keeping you safe."

She wondered if the plague might not be better. "Yes, thank you, Herman. Let me suck your cock some more." Got to get this over with. She fantasized about what she'd do if she could get her hands on a knife.

Eyes shut tight, she concentrated on controlling her gag reflex. Finally he pulled out and ejaculated onto her face. He grunted. The semen landed on her forehead and trailed across the bridge of her nose to her cheek in a warm, sticky line. Some of it threatened to run into her eye, but she was unable to wipe it away. At least she didn't have to swallow. He squeezed out the last drops and slapped his penis against her cheek a couple of times. It stung where he'd hit her.

"That's better, sweetheart." He slid off the bed, pulled on a pair of pants, and grabbed a shirt from a pile on the floor. "You keep performing, you get to stay." He sat on the edge of the bed and tied his shoes. "You want to stay, don't you, sweetheart?"

His use of the endearment made her grit her teeth, but

Brenda nodded. "Yes. Of course." She wasn't lying. She had to help support the others.

"Yeah, fuck yeah, you do. That means you work hard and you play nice. Got it?" He strapped on a holster with a revolver, like a cowboy in a Wild West video. She'd thought about trying to steal it once, but the gun was coded to his fingerprints. It wouldn't fire for her. Might make a good club, though.

Brenda nodded. "I'll work hard."

He walked back to the bed and stroked her breast. "You're good, sweetheart. Nice and tight. I might try you again this evening."

It was a struggle to keep disgust from showing on her face.

"I think I'll go for one of the other girls, though. Maybe Chrissy or Becky."

Brenda's eyebrows rose. Christine was her best friend, and Rebecca was only fifteen.

He laughed. "Don't worry, sweetheart. I'll have you again soon." He untied the scarf binding her right wrist. "Get something to eat but don't take long about it. You need to help with the planting today." He left the room, leaving the door standing open to the hallway as he went.

Brenda untied her other arm and her ankles and picked up a towel from the floor by the bathroom to wipe the semen from her face. She wrapped the sheet around herself and went to close the door.

The room had originally been one of the best in a bed-and-breakfast inn before the plague. Now it was a cluttered mess of soiled clothing in fetid piles and dirty plates and silverware. The fireplace needed to be shoveled out, and one of the windows had a crack covered with duct tape.

Her pants and shirt lay on the floor on opposite sides of

the room where Herman had tossed them when he'd stripped her last night. She put them on and straightened the bed. The toilets no longer worked, so she left to use the outhouse they'd built behind the inn, then headed to the room that she shared with three other girls.

She still thought of them as girls, though the youngest of the four was eighteen now and had already borne a baby. He'd died though, only a month old. Brenda thanked God once again that she'd gotten a contraceptive implant before the plague. She pushed the memory of her boyfriend away. He was surely dead. More than two years ago she'd given him her last kiss the night before she left with her Girl Scout troop for a late fall wilderness campout.

Then the plague hit.

*   *   *

Mark sat by the door to the hallway to the woman's quarters, guarding the exit. He gave Brenda only a perfunctory slap on the butt as he let her pass. Christine looked up from tying her boots when Brenda opened the door to their room. Her blond hair was loose, though usually she tied it in a ponytail, the way most of them wore their hair. The men didn't let them have scissors. It hung down over her shoulder concealing her face as she bent to tie the knots.

Christine turned toward her, and her eyes narrowed. She met Brenda and took her chin, turning Brenda's head to the side to inspect the rising bruise on her cheek.

Brenda pushed her hand away.

As she picked up a tie and pulled her hair into a ponytail Christine asked, "Well, who was it?"

"Herman. How about you?"

"Earl." Christine sighed. "Are you okay?"

Brenda scowled. "Are any of us?" She decided not to tell her about Herman's plans for the coming evening. Why spoil her whole day? Christine had been a teammate on the high school baseball squad as well as a sister scout. They were as close as real sisters.

Christine grimaced. "I'm sorry."

"Yeah, thanks. I'm sorry for you, too." She pulled off her shirt and pants and took fresh clothes from a dresser by the bunk beds she shared with Christine. She had the top bunk this month. At least she did when she wasn't being raped. "We need to get down to the dining room before all the food's gone."

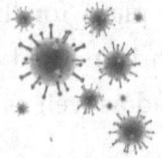

Chapter Thirty-Five

Discovery of Another Settlement

"THAT'S got to be the place," Tyler said. He lay on the ground beside Jacob under the cover of some low pine boughs on a hill above an inn, only fifty yards away. Smoke drifted out of the chimneys. The building was made to look like a rustic farm house, just bigger. Solar panels covering the south facing roof seemed out of place. It stood surrounded by meadows and a tilled field. The yellow glow above the trees to the east showed where the sun was about to rise.

Jacob pointed. "The fields to the east have been worked."

"Yeah. Looks like a good sized group lives here, judging by the size of the tilled fields."

The door opened and some people filed out—five women followed by a man. The man had a sidearm. "Okay, something's happening now," Tyler said. The man opened a tool shed and the women pulled out some tools—rakes and hoes Tyler thought—though it was hard to be certain due to the distance. They headed to the field. The man cuffed one of the women who lagged behind a couple of steps. She fell forward on her hands and knees, then scrambled up and ran to catch up with the others. The man went to stand by a nearby tree. The women dispersed into the field to work.

Jacob tapped Tyler on the arm. "The door's opening again."

Another line of people left the building. Again, it was a group of several women followed by a man with a sidearm. He shouted at them to hurry up.

Tyler furrowed his brows. "Does something look odd to you?"

"You mean that the men are treating the women as if they're prisoners in forced labor?"

"Yeah, that."

"Yeah. That seems odd." A third group emerged, four women followed by a man with a sidearm, like the other two groups. "This isn't coincidence," Jacob said.

"No. It's not."

A fourth group came out less than a minute after the third. Tyler counted them. "Eighteen women, four men."

Jacob shook his head. "No. Eighteen slaves, four masters."

Tyler grimaced and nodded. "Yeah."

"Well, this changes our plans," Jacob said. "It doesn't seem like a good idea to just march down there and offer them an alliance with our village now, does it?"

"No, not at all."

"I guess it'd make sense for us to go back and report our findings."

"I suppose. Should we try to free—" Tyler stopped when the hoe handle one of the women was using broke in two. The man guarding her group strode to her and began to beat her with what looked like a riding crop. She fell to her knees and covered her face. A red blotch appeared on her back.

Tyler froze, his mouth hanging open. "What the hell—"

Before Tyler recovered, Jacob stood and raised his rifle. He fired and the man beating the woman fell to the ground. Jacob shifted his aim and fired again. Another of the slave masters fell. A hail of gun shots from the other two slavers targeted Jacob. One of them got lucky and hit him in the right side of his chest. A spray of blood erupted from his back as the bullet exited. Jacob staggered and grunted, then recovered his stance and squeezed off another round toward the one who'd shot him. That one fell too.

Still lying prone, Tyler aimed toward the last of the four slave masters, but before he could fire, one of the women buried the blade of her hoe in his skull. Two others ran up and beat his corpse with their rakes as he lay across a furrow they'd just planted.

Jacob let the butt of his rifle fall onto the ground, then dropped it as if being careful not to damage his gun. He stood a moment longer, then sank to his knees and fell forward. Tyler crawled to him on hands and knees and turned him over. Jacob gazed wide-eyed into Tyler's face. He coughed and blood sprayed out.

"You got him," Tyler said through tears. He gave his face a quick wipe on his sleeve. "You got the bastard."

Jacob smiled and let out his last breath. His eyes clouded over.

Tyler lifted his gaze. The women ran up the hill toward him, many of them carrying their tools. "Watch out. There's two more men in the house," one of them shouted as she drew closer, then she veered away and ran into the forest.

They all appeared young, no more than nineteen or twenty. Some of them were girls, sixteen years old at most. They scattered into the stand of trees on the hilltop, none of them approaching him. Tyler took another look at Jacob and wiped his eyes. Why the hell did he have to stand up? Searching quickly, he dug a box of cartridges from Jacob's pocket and grabbed his rifle. He crawled back to cover with both rifles.

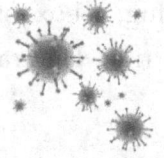

Chapter Thirty-Six

Rescue?

BRENDA and Christine had lined up with two other young women to head out for the work detail when they heard the gunshots. Earl froze in the act of loading his gun and turned toward the door. Brenda took Christine's hand on one side and Tiffany's on the other and pulled them closer. She scanned the room for potential places to take cover.

"What the fuck is that?" Herman shouted from the dining room. He stomped into the rec-room where the rest of them had assembled, a napkin still tucked under his chin.

"I don't know. Gunshots," Earl said.

Herman pulled off the napkin and threw it onto a table. "I can tell they're gunshots, dumbshit. Who's shooting?"

The gunfire ceased. Earl moved to a window and peered out. "Can't see anyone shooting now. Jesus Christ! All four of the others are down, and the girls are running away."

"Fuck! Go upstairs and bring the other girls down here." "The babies too?"

"Yes, dammit, the babies too."

Earl started off.

"Earl!" Herman said.

Earl stopped and turned back, eyes wide.

"Lock the fucking gun safe."

*   *   *

A few minutes later Earl herded two young women into the rec-room, each carrying a bawling infant. One of the women had a bag of diapers hanging from her arm. Herman directed them all to a corner of the room between a pool table and some book shelves lining the corner. The women tried to comfort the babies as they huddled together on the floor.

"Take a look outside and see how many there are," Herman ordered.

"Are you fucking crazy? There's someone out there with a gun. I'm staying in here."

With a motion polished smooth by long practice Herman drew his pistol and pointed it at Earl before he had even tried to react. "There's someone with a gun in here, too. Get the fuck out there and see what's going on."

They stood staring at each other for a moment, then Earl blinked. He spat on the floor. "You motherfucker. You're sending me out to die."

"Try not to get shot."

Earl glared, but he stomped to the door and nudged it open. He stepped to the doorway and then spun around toward Herman, drawing his gun.

Herman shot him before he'd made it halfway around. The women screamed. Earl's gun flew in a high arc and went off when it hit the floor. A window shattered. Earl fell halfway out the door. His body twitched once, then lay still.

The babies cried, and their mothers tried to shush them. Herman picked up Earl's gun and stuck it in his belt. He glared at the women. "Shut the fuck up." He pointed to Christine and then Mary. "You and you. Pull him back inside."

Christine helped Mary up. Careful not to make any sudden moves, they grabbed Earl's body by the ankles and dragged it inside.

"Close the door," Herman said.

Christine stepped over the body and gingerly reached for the doorknob, exposing herself to the outside as little as possible. She grasped it and jerked the door shut, pressing herself to the wall next to the door.

"Back over with the others."

Christine and Mary joined the other four women and the two babies. Herman scowled toward the huddled group. "I guess we wait for them to make the next move."

*   *   *

Tyler crawled out behind the pine tree and crouched in the cover of a maple's trunk as women ran up the hill. "I'll try to help you," he shouted as one of the last ones passed. "Tell me what's going on."

She stopped a moment and stared at him wide-eyed. "I don't want to get the plague," she cried, then ran past.

"The plague is over! Talk to me!"

She stopped again and turned back to him. She was a year or two younger than he, nineteen, possibly twenty. Her red hair swung behind her in a ponytail. Her face was pretty, but her eyes were hard. "The plague's over?"

Tyler stood, keeping the maple between himself and the house. "Yes. We haven't seen anyone with the plague for more than a year."

"You're sure?"

"I'm sure I don't have it."

She hesitated. "How do I know I can trust you?"

Tyler shifted position so they could see each other better in slow, careful steps, trying not to spook her. "You don't know, but you can. My friend—" He wiped his eyes. "—My friend, Jacob killed three of those men out there. He—he died doing it. I want his death to mean something."

A gunshot sounded and Tyler and the woman both dropped to the ground. Another shot followed. They crawled back under the tree so they could see the house, but the woman still stayed a safe distance from Tyler. A brown-haired man lay in the doorway, face up.

"That was Earl," she said. "Herman's the only one left."

After a couple of minutes Earl slid back into the building. An arm grabbed the doorknob and pulled it closed.

"So what's going on here?" He shook his head. "Sorry. I'm Tyler Hopson, by the way."

"Cynthia Jones. They imprisoned us and force us to work for them and—and they rape us. Someone every night." She turned her head and spat. "They said we should thank them for keeping us safe, and threatened to kick us out where the plague would get us if we didn't do what they said."

"All of you are women, and your captors are all men?"

"We're all members of a Girl Scout troop. We were on a wilderness campout when the plague hit. These six men were at this inn when we hiked out the next spring. They killed our scoutmaster and took us all prisoner."

"How many other girls are left inside?"

She shot him a glare. "Women. There are six more women and two babies."

Tyler raised his brows. "Babies?"

"That's what happens when people have sex. Or didn't

they teach that where you went to school?"

Heat rose to Tyler's cheeks. "Yeah, yeah. That just complicates things." He picked up Jacob's rifle. "You know how to shoot one of these?"

Her eyes widened. "I've done some target shooting, but not for a while. Used to be okay at it."

He handed the rifle to her. "Treat it with respect. My friend used it to kill three of your captors."

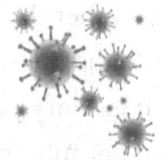

Chapter Thirty-Seven

Negotiations

THE hours dragged on and Herman became more foul tempered as each minute passed. The women stayed quiet, huddled together in the far corner. Brenda kept a close watch on him from the edge of the group, but no opportunity for them to escape presented itself.

She considered the group: Anna and Crystal only thinking about protecting their daughters, Tiffany scowling, ready to fight without thinking and do them all more harm than good. Mary's tall for her age, but physically weak and under-confident. In a crisis she'd just dissolve. Christine's reliable, but it was basically just her and Christine. They had no weapons, and Herman was a dead shot.

Around 12:30 he started pacing the room, talking to himself in tones too soft for Brenda to understand. At 1:17 by the clock on the microwave, he stopped pacing and turned a slow circle. His eyes met Brenda's for a second, then moved on in obvious dismissal. He spat on the floor once again. "Fuck this." He turned toward the huddled group and pointed to Mary. "You. Come here."

Mary's eyes went wide, but she rose to her feet and

approached him. "I'll do anyth—thing you want," she said. She wiped tears from her eyes. "Just p—please don't hurt me."

Herman grabbed her by the upper arm. "Shut up, bitch." He pushed her to the door. "Open it."

Her hand shaking, Mary pushed the door open.

Herman shoved her into the doorway and stood behind her, crouching a little to put his head behind Mary's. He pulled his gun and held it to her temple. "You out there. I've got eight hostages here. They're going to start dying one at a time if you don't bring the truck to the door and give me safe passage out."

"No!" Mary cried, and her knees buckled. He jerked her back up, and she howled in pain.

"I'm not very patient. I won't wait long for an answer."

* * *

Tyler and Cynthia took turns watching the house from the cover of the pine tree. While they waited, Cynthia filled him in about the layout of the building. There was no cover in the meadow in front of the door. He'd be easily visible if he tried to approach. The other doors were all locked, and an attempt to break one down would be easily heard throughout the building. The path to the outhouse was fenced in and covered over, and Tyler had no way to cut it open that wouldn't alert Herman.

She told Tyler the story of their escaping the plague, camped in the wilderness over winter. How one of the other adult leaders had died in her sleep in January. Of her four attempts to make a bow and arrow before she got one that would kill a rabbit. Of their half-starved hike back out the next spring, and then their capture and enslavement. Tyler shook his head in equal parts horror and amazement over what they'd survived.

The door opened while Tyler took his turn to watch. A girl—young woman—appeared in the doorway in front of a man with black hair and a beard. He crouched behind the woman to shield himself and held a handgun to the woman's head. He shouted his demand for a truck and safe passage.

Tyler turned to Cynthia. "What truck? I don't have a truck."

"There1s a truck in the barn over there." She pointed.

"Why doesn't he just get it himself?"

"He probably thinks we're guarding it, and for him to get over there he'd be exposed when he crosses the yard. He doesn't know there's only you."

"Yeah, let's keep it that way." He got to his feet.

"What are you doing?"

"I'm going to talk with him. I don't want him to shoot that woman."

Tyler circled around behind the trees and came out into the pasture away from their hiding place so as not to give away Cynthia's position. He stopped where Herman could see him. He shouted to be heard over the distance. "So you want the truck. We can do that. Just let the hostages go and I'll bring it over. Where are the keys?"

"You think I'm stupid, don't you? Bad assumption, asshole. I'm taking one of them with me as insurance. You try anything, and she's a corpse."

"We don't want anyone else hurt. How do we know you'll let your hostage go after you get away?"

Herman laughed. "You'll just have to trust me. The truck is a PIN number start. 158917."

Tyler went over the number in his head a few times to

memorize it. "Trust is something that's earned. How are you going to earn our trust?"

A second passed before Herman answered. "I'll show you the consequences if you don't trust me." He pulled the trigger.

The spray of blood splattered the door frame a split second before the gun's report reached Tyler. "Shit!" he said and brought up his rifle, but Herman was already back away from the opening. The woman's body lay crumpled across the threshold.

*   *   *

The women screamed and the babies cried. Brenda tried to calm them, but with tears streaming down her own face, it was hard to be effective. Herman glared toward them. "Shut up, dammit." He pointed to Christine, then to Anna. "You and you. Dump her outside and close the door." He pointed to Brenda. "Don't try to get away, or she gets shot."

Anna handed her baby to Tiffany, then she and Christine picked their way to the door, keeping as far from Herman as they could. Anna bent to grasp Mary's legs, then clutched her stomach and vomited.

Herman spat. "God dammit, bitch. You're gonna clean that up."

Christine grabbed the body by the shoulders and dragged it outside. Anna helped, but kept her head turned. They re-entered, and Herman threw a tablecloth at Anna.

"Clean it up, bitch." He pointed to Christine. "Back with the others."

Brenda hugged Christine as Anna cleaned the floor.

Christine's cheeks were wet from tears, but she'd clenched her teeth and glared toward Herman with fire in her eyes. She pulled away from Brenda's embrace and wiped blood from her hands onto her pants. When Anna rejoined the others Christine gave her a hug and tried to comfort her, but Anna couldn't stop crying. Several of the others were crying too. Brenda knelt to hug Anna. She sat with her arms wrapped around her knees, clutching them to her chest as she sobbed.

*   *   *

In his haste to get away Tyler nearly knocked Cynthia over as he ran back to cover. She pivoted out of his way and watched him pass. He bent over and vomited and wiped his mouth on his sleeve. "Oh fuck, oh fuck, oh *fuck!*"

Cynthia stepped toward him and stopped ten feet away. She wiped her eyes and glared. "Nice job negotiating, asshole."

Tyler retched again, but nothing much came out. Tears streamed down his face. "Oh, fuck it all to God damn hell!"

Cynthia heaved a sigh. "Shows you what kind of monster you're up against, anyway."

He wet his lips. "Okay. You—you know him. What do you think we should do?"

Cynthia considered his expression. He really was asking for her opinion. Not a hint of macho condescension. She stared toward the house, but it was almost totally concealed by the pine's branches. She sighed again. "To be honest, I don't know that I'd have been able to do any better. He probably thought he had to show you he was serious about his threat. Mary was probably doomed, regardless. I—I'm sorry I called you an asshole."

He sniffled. "Mary was her name?"

She nodded.

Tyler bent and touched the ground. "Mary, I'm sorry I failed you."

Cynthia raised an eyebrow.

Tears still dampened his face when he straightened up and faced her. Wiping his eyes, he asked, "So what do you think we should do?"

She took a deep breath. "I think our best bet is to go along with his demands, and try to take him out when he gets into the truck. Worst case, we—" she gulped. "—Worst case we save some of them, anyway." She turned to peer through the pine boughs at the inn. How many more of her friends were going to die?

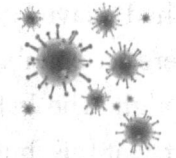

Chapter Thirty-Eight

Killing

HERMAN looked the women over, then pointed to Christine. "You. Come here."

Brenda gasped. Christine turned and stared wide-eyed at the others. They returned her gaze with eyes just as wide.

When Christine hesitated, Herman pointed to Brenda. "Get over here, bitch, or I shoot her." Brenda met his gaze, unflinching. If this was it, she wouldn't give him the satisfaction of seeing her cringe.

Christine trembled as she got to her feet and approached Herman. Like before with Mary, he clutched her upper arm and pushed her to the door, using her as a shield with the gun to her head.

"All right, asshole," Herman shouted. "You want another try at it?"

The women huddled in the back of the room. Brenda strained to hear, but she couldn't make out the voice from outside. She got to her feet, careful not to attract attention, and leaned against the pool table, trying to listen. *He'll do it. He'll kill them all. And then the babies...* She shuddered.

"Damn right, you'll bring the truck. Bring some rope

too. I'm taking three of the cunts for insurance."

A few pool balls lay strewn across the table, left over from a game the men had played the night before. Brenda grasped one and considered a possibility. A little smaller than a baseball, but near enough. The ball had a solid, satisfying heft. She'd only get one try at this, but he was close, and she'd earned trophies for her pitching. She picked up a second one in her left hand too. Their only chance.

"No tricks or you'll have another dead bitch on your conscience," Herman shouted out the door.

Aim for his head, or for his gun hand? The head was a safer shot, especially since it had been a couple of years since she'd thrown a baseball. Then too, a pool ball has a much different texture than cowhide with stitches. But if she hit him in the head, might he not pull the trigger by reflex and kill Christine anyway?

On the other hand, if she aimed at his gun hand and missed, she and Christine both were dead, and likely the other girls too. The head shot was safer. She hoped Christine's soul would forgive her.

Visualizing the pitch the way her coach had taught her, Brenda cocked her arm and fired her best fastball at Herman's head. The ball hit in a glancing blow, above his ugly, hairy ear, ricocheting off into the door jamb. Herman staggered and his gun arm jerked upward. He fired. Thunder echoed through the room.

Christine brought her head back sharply, hitting Herman in the face. She stomped on his instep.

Brenda gasped. Herman's shot had missed. Christine was okay.

So far.

Herman dropped the gun and Christine twisted away

from his grip. She kicked the gun out the door and scrambled outside. Blood poured from Herman's nose.

He groped for Earl's gun, which was still tucked in his belt. Dazed, though, he didn't find it at once. Brenda threw the second ball, but in her adrenaline-charged haste she missed. Herman flinched from the throw, giving them another couple of seconds with Herman unarmed. Anna threw a ball too, hitting him in the stomach, but her throw lacked power. He grunted and glared at them.

As Herman grasped the gun at his waist, Brenda threw the last ball on the table. It caught him in the center of the chest, right below the collar. There was a thud followed by a whoosh of breath escaping. He fell back and moaned, rolling over. His arms and legs flailed as if he were swimming as he tried to get to his hands and knees.

From behind Brenda, Tiffany shouted something incoherent and ran toward Herman, grabbing a chair on the way. She swung it down on his back between his shoulders. Herman fell flat, and the chair splintered. She wrenched a front leg off the broken chair and struck Herman on the back of his skull, swinging her improvised club down with both arms. It made a dent. A spasm shook Herman's body. She struck again.

Tiffany's eyes had gone wide and wild. "Does that feel good, sweetheart?" She struck again. The end of the club buried itself deep in Herman's skull. Blood splattered. She pulled it out, twisting the chair leg to dislodge its square end from the bones. Globs of brain tissue, like fat drops of gray jelly, flew off the end of the club as she struck another blow at the side of his face. Then another.

"Tiffany!" Brenda said.

Tiffany struck again.

Brenda came up behind her and grabbed Tiffany's arm

as she raised the club. "Tiffany! He's dead. You can stop."

Tiffany struggled with Brenda for a second. She turned to her, eyes wide with rage. Then she squeezed them shut tight and blew out a deep breath. She lowered her club and ran her fingers over her forehead, panting. Brenda skirted the body and slipped outside to find Christine.

*   *   *

It was hard, but Tyler did his best to be polite and accommodating as he and Herman shouted their negotiations. Then, without warning, something caused Herman to stagger. The gun went off, but somehow it missed the woman. She jerked her head back and stamped on his foot. Herman dropped the gun, and she kicked it out the door. She twisted away from him and ran off to the side with her hands up.

Tyler raised his rifle, but Herman had moved back from the doorway. After a few seconds the soles of Herman's shoes appeared over the threshold. They jerked as if he were convulsing.

"Something happened. I don't know what," Tyler said.

Cynthia joined him. "That's Christine. She looks okay, far as I can tell."

Tyler nodded. "She's got some pretty good moves, too."

Another woman came out and called for Christine. She wrapped her in a hug when Christine joined her. "That's Brenda," Cynthia said.

Brenda turned toward them. "Herman's dead," she shouted. "The rest of us are okay."

"Oh thank God," Cynthia said. She started toward the house.

Tyler grabbed her arm. "No so fast." He turned back to

the building and shouted, "Pull him out where we can see him."

Brenda turned back to the doorway, and she and Christine pulled Herman out the door by the ankles. His head was a bloody, unrecognizable mess.

Tyler heaved a sigh. He turned toward Cynthia. "That's all of them?"

Cynthia nodded. "That's everyone. We're free." Tears erupted. "We're finally free."

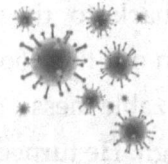

Chapter Thirty-Nine

Emancipation

TYLER followed Cynthia back to the inn. She hugged Brenda and then Christine, tears streaming down their faces. Cynthia introduced Tyler to the others.

"Thanks for helping free us," Brenda said. "There's no way—I mean, I don't know—I mean—just, thank you."

Tyler stared at her face for a second. Her left cheek had a fresh bruise. He pulled his gaze from her bruise and met her eyes as he clasped her hand.

"I'm Brenda, and this is Christine." He shook Christine's hand too.

"Thank you," Christine said.

"You're welcome," Tyler said, "but Jacob's the one who killed those men. Not me. I didn't really do anything, and what I did do, didn't—" He sniffled and took in a breath. "—What I did do didn't help." He released Christine's hand and dropped his gaze. He wiped his eyes.

"Jacob?" Christine asked.

"Tyler's friend," Cynthia explained. "Mark shot him."

"We're sorry for your loss," Brenda said, "but Mary

was done for from the moment Herman pulled her to the door." She wiped her eyes. "He had to—he had to prove to you what a badass he was."

Christine nodded. "Nothing you could have said would have stopped that monster from shooting her."

Some other women came to the door and Brenda introduced them. One of them, a brown haired young woman of seventeen or eighteen years with a jagged red scar on her left cheek, held a chair leg like a club. The end was bloody. She took his hand but there was suspicion in her eyes. "I'm Tiffany. Don't think that 'cause you helped get rid of those assholes you have a right to try anything."

Tyler's mouth fell open. "No. I would never—"

"Tiffany, that was uncalled for," Brenda said. "He proved his intentions are good when he gave Cynthia that rifle."

Tiffany glanced at Brenda when she spoke, then turned back to Tyler. She gave a curt nod. "Okay. Still, don't try anything. Not with me."

"Of course not."

Christine sighed. "We need to take care of Mary and your friend—"

"Jacob," Tyler said. "His name was—was Jacob Skinner."

Christine patted him on the shoulder. "Yeah. We all appreciate his sacrifice. And Mary's. Mary Vickers. We need to take care of Mary and Jacob. The buzzards can have the rest of them for all I care."

"We can get them covered and maybe bring them inside," Tyler said, wiping his eyes with the back of his hand, "but I think our top priority should be to get the other women back here under shelter."

Anna's eyes went wide. "What if they get the plague out there? For that matter, how do we know *you* don't have the plague?"

"The plague's over," Tyler said. "There haven't been any new cases around here for months. More than a year."

"How do we know we can trust you?"

Tyler's eyes narrowed. He shrugged. "I guess you don't know. But my friend Jacob died killing three of your captors. I risked my life to stand out there and try to negotiate with that asshole. I gave Cynthia a loaded rifle. If that doesn't show you can trust me, I don't know what else I can do."

Brenda gave Anna a warning glare and turned to Tyler. "I trust you." She shook her head. "We need to stop wasting time. If he has the plague, we're all exposed now, anyway. I think he's right, we've got to get the others back. It still gets cold overnight."

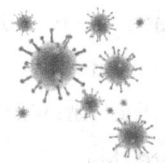

Chapter Forty

Recovery

THEY spent the rest of the afternoon and into the evening coaxing the other women back to the inn. Tyler helped them line up the bodies of their former captors on the lawn by the field and set bonfires on either side of them to show it was safe to return. Christine disconnected the PA system from the stage in the rec-room and they managed to hook it up to the truck through an inverter. Several of them took turns broadcasting a message that it was safe to return.

In the afternoon Tyler hiked back to his and Jacob's camp and brought back their equipment and the horses. Christine met him as he rode back into the yard and helped him settle the horses in stalls.

"More than half of the others have returned," Christine said as they filled buckets of water for the horses.

"That's good. Apparently none of them found our camp. Nothing was disturbed." They each took one of the saddle bags and made their way to the door.

"They wouldn't have gone near your camp even if they had seen it. They're afraid of the plague."

Upon exiting the barn, a woman in torn, muddy

clothing, using a rake as a walking stick, faced them, about twenty yards away. She halted when she saw them, then turned and ran back toward the woods.

"Leila," Christine shouted. "Come back, it's safe."

Leila stopped by the forest edge and turned around. "You said all the men were dead."

"All our captors are dead. Their bodies are over there, by the fires. This is Tyler. He helped us."

"He's still a man."

Heat rose to Tyler's cheeks. He turned to Christine. "I'll just go to the house now. I'm not helping things here. Give me the saddle bag."

*   *   *

Tyler assisted Brenda, Christine, Cynthia, and a couple of others digging graves for Mary and Jacob in the early evening. All the ones who had returned, except for a couple who searched the woods nearby for the stragglers, gathered around as they laid Jacob and Mary to rest by the last rays of the sunset.

Someone said a few words of eulogy, but Tyler didn't recall any of them later. He cried unashamed tears as he helped shovel the earth over the bodies. They placed markers in the form of crosses improvised from picket fence slats on the graves.

In the fading twilight once they finished, Tyler stood a moment before the graves. He bent and rested his hand on the freshly turned soil over Jacob's burial plot. Then he repeated the gesture on Mary's. Brenda stepped beside him and laid a hand on his shoulder. "Thanks for helping."

Tyler wiped his eyes. "Of course. Jacob was my friend,

and I feel responsible for Mary getting shot."

"You're not responsible for Herman murdering Mary. But I meant thanks for everything else you did, too."

He nodded. "I guess. You're welcome." The image of Mary falling in a crumpled pile in the doorway filled the space behind his eyes.

Wiping dirt from her hands, Cynthia joined them. "I do appreciate what you did. And what you tried to do, too."

"Thanks." He sniffled. "Look, there's still a couple not back yet, right? Can I help look for them?"

Brenda grimaced. "I don't think that'd be a good idea."

"Huh? Why not?"

"No offense, but I doubt that they'll show themselves to a man."

*   *   *

At a little after ten o'clock that evening the door to the inn's rec-room swung open and two of the searchers entered supporting the last of the stragglers between them. It was the one whose beating had prompted Jacob's attack on the womens' captors. The back of her shirt was in tatters, and the seat of her pants were soaked with blood. She left a bloody trail across the floor as they helped her in. She could hardly stand on her own, and her pale skin beneath the dirt reminded Tyler of a ghost.

Christine sprang to help them, and Tiffany followed. They led the staggering woman to the closest of the bedrooms to dress her wounds. When they turned toward the hallway, the wounded woman's eyes went wide as she saw Tyler standing near the kitchen door. She and Tyler locked eyes for a second. She struggled with the two supporting her, pointing toward him as they guided her toward the door.

Tyler's face bloomed in a hot flush. He entered the kitchen and ran his fingers through his hair. It wasn't personal. They'd been through more than he could imagine.

He ladled some leftover soup into a bowl. At the door to the rec-room he surveyed the group and stepped up to Brenda carrying a tray with the soup and a glass of water. "Excuse me, but—uh—I figured that woman they just brought in might need something to eat. I probably shouldn't be the one to take it to her, though."

Brenda nodded and put down a book. She took the tray from him. "Thanks. That was thoughtful." Halfway to the door Brenda stopped and turned back to Tyler. "Her name's Alissa."

When they moved the men's bodies together Tyler had seen the wand the man had used to beat her. It was a piece of electrical cable that had been wrapped with barbed wire.

*   *   *

As the hour neared midnight Tyler tried to read a book he'd found on the shelves by the pool table. He found himself reading the same page over and over, not absorbing any of the book, but sleep wasn't a possibility yet. The door leading to the sleeping rooms opened and drew his attention. One of the women he hadn't been introduced to came in with a brown leather briefcase and a cloth bag, probably a pillowcase. She held them up. "Look what I found in Herman's room."

She set the briefcase on the table and laid the bag on a chair beside it. It rattled. Tyler closed the book and stepped up closer, but he stayed at the back of the crowd of women that gathered around. With a flourish she flipped open the latches and raised the lid of the briefcase. Inside were stacks of hundred dollar bills wrapped in neat bundles of a hundred bills each, according to the mark on the wrapper.

"I haven't counted it, but there's probably a million dollars or more," she said.

A gasp arose, then one of the women laughed. Soon they were all laughing. Tiffany pulled a bill from one of the stacks and crumpled it. "Might work as fire starter. A little too stiff to be good for wiping your ass."

"What's in the bag?" one of them asked.

"That's more useful." She emptied its contents onto the table beside the briefcase. A pile of pocket knives and a couple sheath knives spread across the surface.

"Hey!" Christine said. "That one's mine." She reached through the crowd and took one of them, a Swiss Army knife with a red case, chipped on one end.

They sorted through the knives and handed them out. Then one of the knives turned over to reveal the name "Carla" engraved on it. The women all went silent.

Tyler scanned their faces around the crowd. "What is it? What's wrong?"

Some of them glanced at him, but no one said anything for a few seconds. Then Brenda pointed to the knife. "Early on, just after they imprisoned us, Carla tried to resist being raped. She kneed Mark in the groin and tried to run for it. They caught her, tied her to a table, and forced us all to watch while they took turns raping her. Then Mark shot her in the privates and they left her to bleed to death."

Tyler gasped. "Oh my God."

"It seemed like it took her forever to die, but it was probably only ten or fifteen minutes. They made us watch for the whole time."

Tyler's knees went weak. He knelt, half by intent and

half because his knees buckled, and touched the floor. His ears roared and the room spun around him. They had to help him back to his feet.

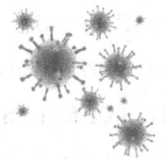

Chapter Forty-One

Group Meeting

THE next day, just before noon, Tyler addressed the whole group. Brenda and Cynthia stood beside him in the rec-room as he faced the other twenty-one young women ranging in age from fifteen to twenty, and two babies. One of the babies was a toddler of just over a year old, and one was an infant of four months. Both were girls.

He described his village and some of its more prominent members. He went over the organization of their government to the extent that they had one, and their system for cooperating to support each other.

"I would never suggest that all y'all 'must' come join us, or anything like that," he said, making air quotes, "and I agree that it'd be a long trip to get there. It's at least a week to hike there on foot. It'd be a hard trip for anyone, and especially those with the babies. I can assure you, though, that all y'all'd be welcome there. There are houses available where you could live, although you'd have to share, and they'll need some clean-up. I can also assure you that all y'all'd be treated with respect if you choose to come live with us.

"I can't really imagine everything you all have been

through," he said in conclusion, "even after you've told me your stories. Jacob and I came here expecting that we'd offer an alliance to another cooperative community. I guess we were naive to believe everyone who survived the plague would be good people, willing and eager to work together. We should've known better, 'specially since we have seen other bad people before." He shook his head. "I wouldn't presume to tell all y'all what you should do. I offer you the choice, for those who want to make the journey."

"Do you know anything about engines?" Christine asked.

Tyler tilted his head. "Some. I took auto shop in high school and I've worked to help maintain the vehicles we have."

She hooked a thumb over her shoulder. "Well, there's an old bus in the garage over there. If we can get it working we wouldn't have to walk and it'd be a day trip to get to your village."

Tyler's eyebrows lifted. "A bus? That'd be perfect."

"There's even a double horse trailer in the barn, and the truck has a hitch for it."

"Is there gas?"

"Plenty in the tank by the garage," Christine said.

"Well. Let's get started."

A buzz of conversation arose. Heads nodded and smiles appeared as the mood in the room became thick with excitement.

Kayla, a dark-skinned young lady with kinky hair newly trimmed close around her scalp stood. "I think we should offer thanks for our deliverance. Especially given that today is Easter Sunday, and it's during Passover."

Tyler jerked his head back in surprise. He'd lost track of

the date. They all bowed their heads.

"We give thanks for our safe deliverance," Kayla began. The prayer wasn't long, but it listed those who had died before from their group, including Jacob and Mary yesterday. She ended with, "In the name of Christ, and in the name of the God of Abraham, Isaac, and Jacob, in the name of all that is sacred and holy, we give thanks. Amen."

"Amen," they all replied.

Tyler bent and touched the floor. Straightening, he said, "Look, I don't mean to disrespect the holiday, but I think we need to post some lookouts. Those bonfires we set yesterday might have attracted some unwelcome attention."

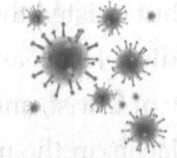

Chapter Forty-Two

Easter Celebration

AS sunrise approached on Easter morning about 30 villagers gathered outside the community center. Janet assembled them facing east by the little formal garden blooming with daffodils and tulips just in front of the main entrance. The morning was pleasantly cool, and the sky was clear, promising to be a beautiful spring day. This year Easter came on the latest date possible, April 25th.

Janet looked over the crowd. Jim Henderson attended, seated in a wheelchair with Jamal at his side. The Kiners with the Tolliver children were there, as were Bill Stevenson, and Jane Fulk, who cradled her infant.

The edge of the sun appeared over the low eastern hills and Janet lifted her arms. "We give thanks for the reshur—resurrection of Christ the Lord this day. As it says in the Bible, there is no salvation except through Christ." She lowered her arms and rubbed her temples.

The voice at her side again said, "Allen must be stopped." She opened her Bible. "I'll read from First Corinthians, chapter 15, verse 12.

"Now if Christ be preached that he rose from the dead, how

say some among you that there is no resurrection of the dead?

But if there be no resurrection of the dead, then is Christ not risen:

And if Christ be not risen, then is our preaching vain, and your faith is also vain..."

The passage took her only a few minutes to read. She took it slowly, reading with expression and passion. She ended with:

"...For he must reign, till he hath put all enemies under his feet.

The last enemy that shall be destroyed is death."

Janet closed her Bible. "Thus Allen must—" She gave her head a quick shake. "Thus all men and women are saved for eternal life in heaven if they accept Christ and believe in the risen Lord."

She took a breath. "Let us praise our Savior with a hymn. *Christ the Lord is Risen Today.*"

She started the song, and most of the others joined in. At the conclusion she spread her arms wide, as if inviting everyone to an embrace. "There is much work left to be done to rebuild our world. With faith in Christ, we will surely succeed. Without Christ, failure is inevitable. Allen Jacobs has been helpful in managing the farm, that cannot be denied. But his paganist beliefs cannot be tolerated either, if we are to survive and prosper."

A murmur rose from the crowd. She noted Bills eyes had grown wide, and a couple others nodded with their eyes narrowed. She gave a slight smile. Lifting her arms to the heavens she intoned, "May the rising of Christ fill us all with hope for the future, to rebuild our world with Christ's love as its foundation and guiding light. Peace and joy be with you all, and let us say, 'Amen.'"

"Amen," the crowd echoed.

"There's bread and jam inside and George Hardy will be scrambling eggs on the grill outside on the patio for those who want some," Janet said. "I want to express my appreciation to him for being here before the crack of dawn to get the fire started and burned down to coals so he could do that for us." She clapped and the rest joined in. Off to the side, by the grill, George raised a spatula in salute. Janet faced the crowd again. "Have a very happy Easter. Thank you for coming."

Bob stepped up beside her and took the Bible. She reached up with both hands and stroked her temples as he put an arm around her waist to guide her back inside.

*   *   *

Jamal observed Janet as Bob settled her at one of the tables and went to get some food for her and himself. He gave his head a slight shake, not sure what to make of Janet's tirade about Allen. She'd practically called for his head. That seemed out of character for her, based on his memory when he'd first met her. That was nearly two years ago now, when he found this community while hiking in the national forest, away from society after the plague hit. He recalled Bob's comment from a few weeks ago about Janet having become, "different."

Even more disturbing, it seemed as if at least a few of the others might agree with Janet about Allen. The last thing he wanted to see among this small group was that kind of division, let alone any threat of violence. Were Janet's constant headaches twisting her thoughts?

At the buffet table Bob cut slices of bread and put

scoops of scrambled eggs on a couple of plates. As he stretched to reach for a glass of jelly across the table, Jamal took it first and handed it to him.

"Let me give you a hand. My arms are longer."

Bob hesitated for a second, then took the glass from Jamal. "Thanks."

"You're welcome. How's Janet?"

He shot a glance to his wife. She sat with her head in her hands, massaging her temples. "No better. I'm really worried about her. The headaches are awful, and the willow bark tea isn't helping."

Jamal closed his eyes and grimaced. "Unfortunately, there's not much more I can do."

Bob pulled out a handkerchief and wiped at his eyes. "I know. I appreciate all you've tried to do, but I guess it's in God's hands now."

Jamal nodded and clapped Bob on the shoulder. Bob took the plates to Janet.

Jamal surveyed the group, and his eyes rested on Ron Culbertson. Ron sat by himself with a vacant grin on his face, which was his typical expression. He worked the farm fields mostly, but George had told Jamal once that Ron wasn't the most productive member of the crew. Jamal meandered through the room to approach him. "Hi Ron," he said as he walked past.

Ron turned his face up and smiled. "Hi Jay."

As he worked his way back to where he'd parked Jim's wheelchair, Jamal nodded. As he suspected, Ron's eyes were bloodshot.

*   *   *

Ron Culbertson shared one of the smaller houses in the village with two other men. The back yard bordered the stream that flowed from the community's water reservoir. A chain-link fence circled the yard, but the gate stood open. A rusting lawn mower sat in the front yard by the corner of the porch, though the grass hadn't been cut for more than a year. No sense to waste gas for something like that.

On Sunday afternoon Jamal knocked on Ron's door. After a few seconds a muffled voice shouted, "Just a minute." Not long afterwards Ron opened the door. He smiled at Jamal. "Hi Jay, what brings you out here?"

"I just wanted to have a chat. May I come in?"

"Sure." Ron stepped aside and Jamal entered. Old concert posters hung on the walls in a seemingly random arrangement, and a couple of shelves stood filled with little ceramic figurines. Incense burned on a holder resting on the coffee table and the curtains were drawn shut. Some daylight leaked past the curtains, but the only other light in the room came from a small LED reading light attached to a real paper book on coffee table. An empty wine bottle stood on the table next to a glass with a dried red stain in the bottom.

"Are your house-mates home?"

"Not right now. Eddie's out back, fishing, and Bryan's visiting some friends. What'd you want to chat about?"

"At breakfast following the Easter service this morning I noticed that your eyes appeared irritated. Are you feeling okay?"

Ron's smile slipped a little and he tilted his head. "Yeah, I'm fine. Why?"

"I just wondered. If this isn't a good time, I could come back a little later. Say, at 4:20."

Ron's smile disappeared. "I don't know what you're

talking about."

"Ron, are you using marijuana?"

"Maybe you should leave now."

Jamal made no indication that he'd heard Ron. "'Cause if you are, I don't care, as long as you keep pulling your weight and don't pass it out to the children. This isn't a drug bust. But there are a couple of people here who are sick in a bad way, and some pot might ease their suffering."

Ron stood silent for a long time. A clock somewhere in the room ticked. He glanced toward the kitchen, then lowered his eyes. "My supply's getting low, and it'll be a while before the plants are big enough to harvest."

Jamal nodded. "What plants? Where?"

"I've got a plot in a clearing outside the village on the other side of the forest, to the east. I just planted this year's crop last week."

"Okay, can you let me have some for a couple of our patients?"

Ron furrowed his brows. "You obviously mean Jim Henderson for one. Who's the other one?"

"I can't tell you that. That's private."

Ron cracked a sideways grin. "Trying to score some for yourself, eh?"

Jamal frowned. "No, I'm not, and you're not going to trick me into revealing who it is." His fists clenched at his side by reflex, then he relaxed them.

Ron glanced at Jamal's hands. "All right Jay. I understand. I can spare a couple ounces, if that'll help."

"That might be enough to see if it works, but if it does I'll need more. How much have you got?"

Ron grimaced. "What I've got is left over from last fall and the potency is down. Not very skunky. I've got less than two pounds to last me till mid summer when the new plants start producing."

Jamal's eyebrows shot up. "Two pounds! Almost a kilo? How much do you smoke?"

Ron shrugged and gave a wry smile. "Like I said. Not very skunky."

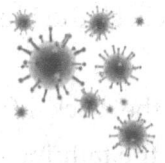

Chapter Forty-Three

The Refugees Arrive

Friday April 30, 2:30 p.m.

TYLER tightened the last of the spark plugs in the bus and re-attached the wire. He connected jumper cables to the battery terminals and wiped his hands on a rag. It didn't help. Black oil covered his arms up past the elbows.

"That it?" Leila asked. She was about as grease covered as he.

"We can hope. Turn on the truck and let's try it."

Leila stepped over the jumper cables that snaked between the two vehicles and climbed into the truck. She punched in the pin number. When the "ready" light turned green she hit the start button. The engine roared to life.

Tyler turned the key in the bus. It groaned a couple of times, then the engine turned over and caught. A plume of acrid black smoke poured out the back. He pumped his fist. "Yes!"

He climbed out of the bus and high-fived Leila as she met him in front of the truck. "We'll let it run for a little bit to get the battery charged up, then see if it starts on its own."

Leila disconnected the jumper cables and coiled them. "So we can leave tomorrow?"

"We still need to check the brakes and the transmission, but probably soon."

Leila pointed to the back of the bus. "There's not as much smoke coming out the tailpipe now."

"We probably got some oil in the cylinders when we cleaned the valves. It's burned off now, mostly." He put the jumper cables into the tool compartment in the bus. The bus had a stated capacity of twenty. The B&B had used it to shuttle tours to various parts of the farm. The logo for "Shady Acres Farmhouse Inn" had faded, but still showed on the side.

Tyler made another attempt to wipe oil from his hands, then tossed the rag onto a workbench. "Let's see if anything useful happens when we put it in gear."

He took the driver's seat, and Leila sat in the front passenger seat behind him. Pulling the shift lever to reverse he eased his foot off the brake. The bus lurched and crept backward a few feet.

"So far, so good." He stopped it and put it in drive. The bus moved forward. He stepped on the brake and stopped it at nearly its original position in the garage. He put it in park and set the brake. "Looks good. We might be able to do this after all. We'll give it a more thorough test when the battery's charged."

Leila wiped her hands on her pants. "Thanks for all your work on this. We owe you big time."

"I didn't do it alone. You deserve credit for this too. I'm glad your dad did such a good job teaching you auto maintenance. How long should we let it charge?"

Leila shrugged. "I'd give it an hour, anyway."

*   *   *

Sunday May 2, 3:15 p.m.

As Bill stood watch at the Interstate lookout post, a flash of light on the highway to the east caught his eye. He squinted at the spot and saw it again, a brief flash at the peak of the hill to the east. He grabbed the binoculars and scanned the road, looking where the interstate crested the hill, nearly five miles away.

Three vehicles approached. No. Two vehicles, one pulling a trailer. The first one looked like a bus. He pulled the radio off his belt and keyed it. A second later Dan answered. "A truck and a bus are approaching on the interstate from the east," Bill said. "They just crested the far hill, about five miles away."

Dan's response took long enough that Bill worried that the radio wasn't working. Then it came back to life. "Did you say, 'a bus?'"

"That's right."

"I'll be there with reinforcements as soon as possible. Stay behind cover."

"Right." Bill put the radio back on his belt and moved behind a concrete barricade. He clicked off the rifle's safety.

Seven minutes later a bus stopped at the lookout post, and a black pickup truck pulling a horse trailer stopped behind it. Bill's heart thudded bass drumbeats in his chest as he crouched behind the barricade. "They're here," he said into the radio. "They've stopped outside the post."

"Still a couple of minutes away. Hold on."

The streaked and dusty glass of the side windows kept Bill from getting a clear view of the faces behind them. The bus appeared to be full, though. The people inside stayed seated as the driver turned off the engine. In the silence following, Bill could hear voices from the bus, but couldn't make out words.

The door of the bus opened, and a man stepped out with his hands up. Bill shook his head in disbelief when his face became visible. Tyler exited the bus. "Tyler! Are you okay? Oh my God, Tyler, we were so worried about you."

"Bill? God, it's good to see y'all again."

They met and embraced. Bill kissed him and tears ran down his face. "Thank God you're okay," Bill hugged Tyler again and then pulled back and slapped him. "Don't you ever do anything that stupid again, you understand?"

Tyler's eyes went wide with shock, then he cast his gaze downward and nodded. "I'm sorry. I just—well—I felt neglected."

"We didn't mean to neglect you. I'm sorry if we did, but you should have talked to us about it. I'm sure Jane feels the same way." He shook his head and gave him another hug. "We'll talk more later, the three of us. I'm just glad you're back safe."

"I'm glad to be back safe too, believe me. How are Jane and Grayson?"

"They're fine. Jane was really upset when you left. Expect to be hugged, kissed, and slapped from her, too. Maybe not in that order."

The pickup truck sped up the ramp toward them. Bill and Tyler waved at it as it ground to a halt in front of the bus. Dan climbed out and approached Bill and Tyler with George and Jamal following.

"Well. Glad to see you back," Dan said. He looked into the bus. "How many did—"

"Get your butts behind cover!" Andrea shouted.

They turned to her. She had taken cover behind the

open door of the truck and had her rifle aimed toward the bus.

Dan lifted his eyebrows. "It's just Tyler and Jacob, back with some more survivors."

"Uh—" Tyler began, but Andrea cut him off.

"We don't know they don't have a gun to Jacob's head and that they're not waiting to attack when our guard's down."

Dan and George shifted their grips on their rifles, but didn't aim them. They just got ready to do so if necessary. Jamal's eyes were wide as he stood behind Andrea holding the first aid kit.

Tyler lifted his hands in a placating gesture. "Calm down, Andrea. I swear, it's okay. I'll ask them to come out of the bus slowly, all right?" He stepped back to the door of the bus and said a few words. Bill couldn't make them out, but he recognized Tyler's tone of voice. He was trying to calm things, be the diplomat.

After a moment they filed out and stood beside the bus. Two of them carried babies and several had side arms. One had a rifle. All of them were women.

"Everything's fine," Tyler said. "They want to join us."

"That's right," one of them said, a tall woman of about Tyler's age with short-cut brown hair. She scowled. "That is, if we're welcome here."

Dan nodded. "You're welcome to stay if you want to join and cooperate with our community. We all need to be confident about the safety of our groups, though. And yes, I know that works both ways." He turned back to Andrea. "I think you can lower your gun."

Andrea nodded and stepped out from behind cover.

"So how many are you?" Dan asked.

"There's twenty-three women and two babies," Tyler

said.

Dan furrowed his brows. "All women and children? No men?"

"That's right."

Dan gave a quizzical tilt to his head and peered toward the truck, squinting against the sun's reflection in the windshield. "Where's Jacob?"

Tyler's face fell. "Jacob didn't make it."

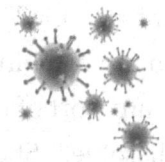

Chapter Forty-Four

Educational Opportunities

May 28, 3:30 p.m.

GLORIA knocked on Sara and Jonathan's door after school let out. No one answered at once, and Gloria considered just leaving. She shook her head. No. Got to do it. She was just about to knock again when Sara answered the door.

"Hi Gloria. Come on in." Sara took Gloria's tote bag of books and set it by the closet. "What brings you here?"

"I was hoping to chat a bit. Jonathan here?"

"He went out with Jack and George on a salvage trip yesterday. I don't expect him back for a couple of days. He got a satellite image of a cluster of intact houses at a cross-road nearby. About twenty miles. They went to check it out. Good possibility for firearms and fuel, and such. Jon's hoping to find technical books, and toner and paper for the printer, too." She led Gloria to the kitchen and pulled out a chair for her. "So what did you want to chat about?"

Gloria settled into a chair. "I guess you know I've been teaching the school lately, while Janet's been ill with her headaches, right?"

"Yeah, that's what I heard. How's that working out

with the new arrivals from the Girl Scout troop?"

"Frankly, not great."

Sara raised an eyebrow. "Oh?"

"Only five of them are showing up with any regularity at all, and they don't take any sort of criticism well. They either get belligerent, or they dissolve." She shrugged. "They're old enough that they don't have to attend if they don't want, but I guess Brenda has been encouraging some of the younger ones to go. It's becoming a problem with keeping order with the other students, though."

Sara nodded. "Yeah, I can see that being a problem. I don't envy you for it."

Gloria nodded too. "Yeah, a problem. Maria was overjoyed at first that there were other girls her age, but she just can't relate to them. Their experiences are too different."

"Yeah, I suppose so."

"For which I'm glad, after a fashion. That Maria didn't have to experience what they went through, I mean. But they're not socializing with the rest of us to any degree that I can tell."

Sara shrugged. "Maybe they should be in a separate group from the others at school."

Gloria smiled. "Exactly what I was thinking. Would you be willing to take on a group of them?"

Sara's eyebrows shot up. She lifted her hands, palms front, as in a warding-off gesture. "Whoa. I don't have any experience with the young ones. All my experience has been with college-level literature and creative writing for the last twenty-some years. I taught high school English for a couple of years before I went back to get my doctorate, but that's about it."

"I don't mean for you to take on the general schooling

for the young ones. I'm suggesting you teach a creative writing seminar. They need to work through their experience, and they can't do that with the others that haven't been through anything similar. Maybe an approach through theatre, or poetry, or something like that would work. You'd be perfect for that."

Sara grimaced. "I don't think I could provide the Christian-centered focus that Janet seems to insist upon."

Gloria returned Sara's grimace. "That no longer seems to be a problem."

"Oh? Why is that?"

"Janet's headaches have pretty much crippled her." Gloria sighed. "I've been the teacher for the last few weeks. She's only barely able to manage the Sunday services too. She's even stopped railing at me about 'pagan indoctrination,' or whatever."

Sara furrowed her brows. "Pagan indoctrination?"

"Apparently anything that doesn't fit with her definition of Christian, is Pagan, if not Satanic." Gloria scratched her ear. "She wasn't that closed-minded, back when she first got here. I mean, she was always a Fundamentalist Christian, but she used to be more willing to get along with others."

Sara pursed her lips. "If I'm going to do this, I'm not going to tolerate interference or censorship of my methods. I've taught Literature and Creative Writing for nearly thirty years, and I know what I'm doing in that field."

Gloria shook her head. "I don't think she's going to be interfering at this point. Jamal's found a source of an analgesic, but it's got her sort of blissed out." She held her thumb and forefinger up to her puckered lips as if holding a joint, and sucked in a breath.

Sara furrowed her brows, then understanding it a

second later. "Ah. Somebody's growing pot. Figures that someone's doing that. Wouldn't surprise me if someone's got a still cooking moonshine, too. I'm glad it's helped her pain level, anyway."

"She seems more comfortable, yes."

"If I do such a class," Sara said, "I don't think it'd be wise to limit it to just the women from the Girl Scout troop. I'd want to open it up to everyone. Maybe everyone over the age of, say fifteen, so all of the Girl Scouts would be included."

"So Maria would be eligible too, then."

"Would that be a problem?"

Gloria tilted her head, considering, and after a second she shrugged. "I guess not. She's starting to rebel about going to school anyway. She might find creative writing to be interesting. I'd like her to continue with other subjects too, but it's hard to argue she needs to stay in school long term, now."

Sara sighed. "I know what you mean. I don't want this to be the start of the dark ages, though. Jonathan's been printing a lot of technical information on farming, engineering, and on medicine and herbal remedies and such. Some on basic math and physics, too. When we can get printer paper and toner, anyway."

Gloria nodded. "That'll help."

"Most of the other books we have are on acid-pulp paper, though. In a hundred years or less they'll be unreadable."

Gloria pressed her lips together in a tight line. "It won't matter, if no one knows how to read, will it?"

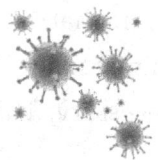

Chaper Forty-Five

Paternal Support

JANET swallowed the final sip of cannabis tea from a white porcelain cup set it on an end-table. She settled back on the couch to wait for it to take effect. Initially she'd resisted using the marijuana when Jamal suggested it, but the headaches had become intolerable and Bob had encouraged her.

Now she looked forward to the doses. Not only did they provide some relief from the pain, but she could see her father visit when she was on it, rather than just hear his voice whisper in her ear. He was a source of comfort to her, even though she knew, in some resting corner of her mind, that he wasn't real.

He put his arm around her shoulders and gave her a gentle embrace. "You're doing a lot of good in the community here, Janet. I'm proud of you. This is the work that God meant for you when He saved you from the plague." He wore the gray cardigan her mother had knitted. The soft, slightly scratchy feel of its loosely knitted sleeve on her shoulders felt like a trip back home.

"I'm having trouble keeping up, between the headaches and the medicine," she said.

"Even so, you stand as an example for others. But it still remains that Allen must be stopped from spreading his pagan message. You still have to do that."

"How can I stop him, though?"

"By any means necessary. This is what God wants you to do."

Bob entered the living room. "Hi Honey. Are you feeling better?"

Janet turned toward him. He seemed smaller than normal somehow, like a child. For a second he appeared beardless. Then his close-cropped, graying beard reappeared and he regained his normal stature. "Yes, I'm feeling better now." She looked to her side. Her father was gone.

Bob sat next to her in the spot where her father had just been and took her hand. "George and Alice have invited us over for dinner tonight. They're cooking a chicken. Isn't that nice of them?"

"Yes, that's very nice. They're good people. Not like Allen."

Bob grimaced. "Yes, they're good people."

"Like I told Wilma Canfield, after services, I don't trust Allen a bit. Wouldn't doubt he's working up to some kind of pagan, human sacrifice at those solstice gatherings. You mark my word. He's evil."

Bob's eyes went wide. "Well—uh—yes, Alice and George are great folks." He stuffed his hands into his trouser pockets and twisted his head to look at the wall clock. "It'll be an hour or so before we need to go over to the Hardys' house. Do you want to take a short nap?"

"I think I'd like to read some. Could you bring me my Bible?"

"Sure." He went to her study to find it. Janet watched

him go, then turned back to her father, who sat beside her again. He gave her an approving nod.

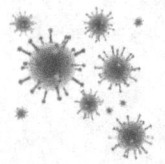

Chapter Forty-Six

Writing Assignment

June 14, 2:15 p.m.

SARA collected the papers from yesterday's assignment that they'd passed forward and set them on the corner of the table in the front of the room. She turned to face the class. Twelve young women and two men sat before her in a meeting room of the community center. Their expressions ranged from interested and attentive to suspicious and guarded. "I want you to think of a piece of clothing," she said. "It can be anything, outerwear or underwear, even just a sock or a scarf. Write a short piece—say, up to a couple of hand-written pages—that concerns that article of clothing in some manner. The piece of clothing doesn't need to be the central focus, but it has to somehow relate to the subject."

She looked at her watch. "In twenty minutes I'll see if anyone has a piece they'd like to share."

Kayla raised her hand. "Should this be poetry or prose?" "Whatever moves you. Either or both. No rules, other than it's concerning a piece of clothing in some manner."

They leaned toward their notebooks, some writing

industriously, some staring at the paper with furrowed brows, tapping their pencils on the table, or chewing on the end, lost in concentration. Sara looked around the room. Gloria and Dan's daughter Maria was one of the ones writing rapidly, as were Anna and Leila, two of the former Girl Scouts. Toward the back of the room Tiffany sat staring down at her notebook with her pencil lying on the table beside it. The scar on her cheek made her expression hard to read. It forced one side of her mouth to curve up, even if she was trying to frown.

Sara furrowed her brows. The first few days of the class Tiffany had written practically non-stop. Her inactivity now seemed odd. Sara stepped toward the back row and looked toward Tiffany's paper from a couple seats away. There were three lines written on it, but she couldn't read them without invading her space. Tiffany didn't look up. She sat as if turned to stone.

Sara moved closer and Tiffany came to life. She glanced up and turned her notebook over, hiding the words from view. Without stopping, Sara continued past her and made her way around the room, then back to the front.

After twenty minutes of writing she asked for volunteers to read their efforts. One of them read a piece that was almost a eulogy for her boots. Another one wrote about a sweater her grandmother had knitted for her when she was in the third grade. Sara glanced at Tiffany, but Tiffany made no indication that she wanted to read her piece.

A couple of others read. When no one else volunteered, Sara said, "We heard some good first drafts. Writing quickly like this is a good exercise to let out words you may not have known yourself that you had inside you. For tomorrow I'd like you continue working on this piece if you didn't come to an end point, or revise and polish it if you did. Keep in mind that, especially for a short piece like this, every word counts. If a word or phrase doesn't advance the story or the point you're trying to make, cut it out. Be brutal. We'll pass them around tomorrow for a workshop session. Any questions?"

She waited for a few seconds, and when no one spoke up she said, "Thanks for coming, and I'll see you tomorrow."

Tiffany grabbed her notebook and bolted for the door.

As the rest of them gathered their books and left, Sara stepped to Brenda. "Could I have a word with you for a moment?"

Brenda lifted her gaze from her book-bag to Sara. She made a gesture as if to brush hair away from her eyes, but her short-cropped brown hair hadn't moved. "Sure, I guess so. What is it?"

Sara waited a moment, considering how to approach this, while the last of the others left the room. "Is Tiffany all right? She only seemed half present. There was something with only three lines on her paper, but she didn't want me to see it. She covered it when I walked by."

Brenda frowned. "I don't know that she isn't okay, but she's been sort of closed mouthed lately, particularly in the last few days." She furrowed her brows. "She's always been proud of her writing. She won a poetry contest in high school when she was just a freshman."

"I thought she'd changed during the last week, too. Did something happen?"

Brenda snorted an ironic laugh and gave an eye-roll. "Yeah. A lot has happened. Most of it you know about, at least in outline."

"You know what I mean, I think. You seem to be the leader of your group of women. They look up to you, anyway. You said you've noticed a change too. I just wonder if there's something I can do to help."

"Tiffany's under a lot of stress," Brenda said. "You knew she was the one who actually killed the leader of the gang that had enslaved us, right?"

"I thought you and she both did."

"I knocked him down, but Tiffany..." She looked out the window and shuddered. "She still has the chair leg she used to beat him to death."

Sara winced.

Brenda turned back to Sara. "Herman—the leader of the gang, that is—is also the one who gave her that scar on her cheek. Jessica stitched it up afterwards. It took three of us to hold Tiffany down. The cut was all the way through to the inside of her mouth. Jessica did an okay job, considering we didn't have anything to deaden the pain."

Sara winced again. "I know you have all been through a horrible experience, one I can't even imagine. I just want to offer what help I can."

"No matter how richly he deserved it, killing a man isn't something you just forget." Brenda shrugged. "I helped her, and I have nightmares, too." She turned her head to gaze out the window again. "I don't think anyone can really appreciate that unless they've experienced it."

Sara nodded. "You're right. And I do understand."

Brenda snapped her head back toward Sara's. She lifted an eyebrow. "You've killed someone?" She gave her head a quick shake. "I'm sorry. I don't mean to pry."

"It's all right. I've killed two men. They shot at my husband."

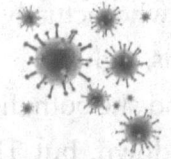

Chapter Forty-Seven

Mental Health Clinic

June 14, 4:15 p.m.

SARA returned home to the sound of sizzling from the kitchen and the aroma of cooking meat and rosemary. Her mouth watered. She found Jonathan standing in front of the range tending something in a skillet before him. She set her bag of books on the table and pressed herself to him, kissing the back of his neck.

"Hi Lover," he said. "How'd it go today?"

"Okay. Is that chicken?"

"Rabbit. We're splitting one with Andrea. Ed Fischer brought it over."

"It smells great. The rosemary was a good idea." She pulled back from him and sat at the kitchen table. "Well, mostly the class went fine. I'm worried about Tiffany, though."

"Tiffany? The one with the scar on her face?"

"I'd prefer you not identify her by that mark, but yes." She shook her head. "Poor girl. As if it weren't bad enough, going through what they did, having to bear that scar, too. Aside from that, though, something's off with her, but she's not talking about it. I asked Brenda, and she didn't know either."Jonathan turned the heat down under the skillet and put on a lid. "Tiffany has an attitude, which isn"t surprising, I suppose. I'm glad she's showing up for your class, but I wouldn't press her. Hopefully, she'll talk when she's ready."

"Yeah, that's pretty much what I decided. I mentioned it to Brenda. Maybe she can get something more out of her."

"I guess we'll see," Jonathan said. "Brenda seems really sharp, and tough as nails. Especially since she's only, what? Twenty?"

Sara winced. "Ugh. Cliché, Jon. Yes, they all had to do a lot of maturing in a short time."

Jonathan laughed as he took a couple of plates from the cupboard. "It's been a long time since you called me out on a cliché. Your writer-reflexes are kicking back in, now that you've started teaching that class."

Sara snorted a brief laugh. "Yeah, guess so." She shook her head again. "I worry about my students too much. But here we've got no support services except ourselves. No counselors, no student mental health center, and I can't call her parents."

"You told Brenda. Next best thing."

"But like you said, Brenda's only twenty."

"Brenda and Kayla, and probably Christine and Cynthia too, kept that group together both physically and mentally through a situation more horrific than I can imagine. Tiffany's got a good support system over there." He bent down to Sara and gave her a kiss. "You wouldn't be you if you didn't care for your students, but let it go for now, okay?"

Sara nodded. "Okay."

"Could you see if there are any greens for a salad?"

"Sure, but it's probably going to be dandelions. The lettuce is about gone till the next crop comes in. I'm sure we have some lambs quarters, too."

Jonathan grimaced. "We should have planted more lettuce. Well, whatever. Maybe cooked greens, then."

*   *   *

Brenda made her way home from the class, cutting through the playground behind the community center. She paused a moment to consider the swings. Not long before they went on that campout, nearly three years ago now, some of her sister scouts might have been playing on a swing set like this one.

She shook her head and continued through Jack Rockford's back yard toward the cul-de-sac where the Girl Scouts had settled in. The light green of her house came into view behind the other white ones as she approached. The glittering black of the solar roofing shingles looked like a piece of the night sky intruding on the bright sunlit day.

The familiar path left Brenda free to consider what, if anything, to do about Tiffany as she walked home. Clearly, stress and previous trauma were boiling up inside Tiffany. She had to defuse it before Tiffany exploded.

The clock in the entry hall showed 4:15 when Brenda entered the house. Too early for Christine and Jessica to be back from their jobs at community farm fields, but Alissa should be home. Brenda set her books on a chair in the front room and went to the kitchen. Alissa stood with her back to the doorway, just starting to cut up a skinned and dressed rabbit on the counter. Brenda's mouth watered in anticipation. It had been three days since they had meat. "Hi Alissa," she said as she entered.

Alissa jumped and yelped. She spun around, clutching the knife in front of her like a weapon, eyes wide.

Brenda took a step back. "Take it easy. It's just me."

Alissa closed her eyes and blew out a breath. She lowered the knife. "Don't sneak up on me like that."

"Sorry. I thought you'd hear me come into the house."

"Sorry I jumped at you too." She turned back to the counter. Her lightweight, white cotton top did little to conceal the red welting scars covering her back. The knife clacked against the cutting board as she forced it through the rabbit's carcass.

Brenda poured herself a glass of water and pointed at the rabbit. "Who do we have to thank for dinner?"

"Tyler brought it over. Hunting was good today. He had one for all the houses in our cul-de-sac." She put the cut-up pieces into a bowl and slid it into the refrigerator. "I'll wait for Christine and Jessica to get back before I cook it. I got some potatoes for helping Bryan fix the roof on his shed, too."

Brenda tilted her head. "Bryan?"

"Bryan Pierce. He lives on the next cul-de-sac to the north."

"A few potatoes in exchange for roofing work doesn't sound like a fair trade."

"He didn't need a lot of help. Mostly, I passed tools up to him and steadied the ladder. It was a small shed. He probably gave me about five pounds of spuds."

"That was nice of him, I guess. Be careful, though."

"Of course. Don't worry. He was a perfect gentleman."

"Okay, just be careful."

Alissa rolled her eyes. "Yes, Mother."

Brenda rolled her eyes too. "Okay, okay, enough on that subject. I'm going next door to visit Tiffany for a little while. I'll be back soon."

Brenda put the glass in the sink and picked up her notebook on her way out. As she walked across the street to

Tiffany's house she was still unsure how she'd handle this. Anna answered her knock, her daughter, Bree, cradled in one arm.

"Hi Anna. Is Tiffany back?"

Anna grimaced. "Yeah, she's here, but good luck in trying to see her. She practically sprinted home from the writing class, and she's been in her bedroom since then."

"I want to try anyway."

Anna stepped aside. "Knock yourself out. Her bedroom's up the stairs, first door on the right."

Brenda patted Bree on the head as she entered and headed up the stairs. Tiffany's door was latched shut. She rapped on it.

"Who is it?" Tiffany asked through the door.

"It's me, Brenda. Can I come in?"

"What do you want?"

"I wondered if you'd look at my writing assignment and give me your feedback."

A moment later Tiffany opened the door, but she stood barring the way in. Brenda was used to reading her expressions and knew that the up-turned corner of her mouth on the left side had nothing to do with a smile.

"It's, 'May I come in,'" Tiffany said.

"What?"

"Whether you're capable of coming in is not the question. What you meant to ask was whether or not you're permitted to enter. If you're going to be a writer, you need to get the usage right."

Brenda nodded, pleased that Tiffany had called her on her error, rather than just ordering her away, but she kept her expression neutral. "Okay. *May* I come in?"

"Yeah, I guess so." Tiffany stepped aside.

The room was small and spare. A twin bed and a desk filled the space between the window and the closet door. Some wall-mounted shelves over the desk held a few books. The sheet and bedspread had been pulled up to the headboard, but that was the only concession she'd made to "making the bed." Lacy pink curtains, ones left behind from a previous resident, covered the window. Didn't seem as though Tiffany would have chosen that style. Brenda tried to ignore the broken chair leg lying on the top shelf, but it kept drawing her eye.

She handed her notebook to Tiffany. "I started writing something personifying a glove, it lamenting its inability to keep fingers warm in the winter." She shrugged. "I'm not sure how to end it."

Tiffany read the piece and furrowed her brows. "I'm not sure where this is going, beyond the exercise for the class, but as I see it, you have a couple of options. You could have an ironic end, with the fingers freezing, and the glove dying in despair with the hand it was supposed to warm, or you could have the glove valiantly fluff its fibers for that last, heroic effort to insulate the fingers from the cold, holding them under your armpits for warmth until the sun's return in spring, or some such." She shook her head. "I gotta be frank. This is something of a stretch."

"In general, I'd prefer the happy ending."

Tiffany gave a brief nod. "Yeah, that's what Hollywood scriptwriters would do."

"Well, thanks for looking it over." Brenda pointed to Tiffany's notebook, which lay on the desk. "Can—er—may I take a look at yours?"

Tiffany froze. For a few seconds Brenda was afraid she'd order her out, but eventually Tiffany cast her eyes to the floor and nodded. "Okay. Sure." She opened the notebook and gave it to Brenda. Just three lines showed on the page:

> *Knitted booties for*
> *the baby growing inside.*
> *Oh, how I hate him!*

Brenda remained silent for a long time as she read and re-read the poem. She re-read it again. She lifted her face to Tiffany's and nodded. "A perfect haiku in form. Five, seven, and five syllables. Nicely formatted with the surprise ending." Tiffany took the notebook when Brenda held it out for her. "Did you ever have Mr. Abbott for composition in high school?"

"No. I heard stories, but I never had him."

"I only had him a couple of months for Senior Comp before—well—before. People tended to either love him or hate him. He was hard, and not exactly warm and fuzzy, but there's one quote of his I remember that seems appropriate right now."

"What was that?"

"He said, 'Never let the facts interfere with telling the truth.'"

Tiffany's eyes widened.

"Do you think you're pregnant, or are you just writing in the voice of one who does?"

Tiffany turned away. A second later she heaved a sob and wiped her cheeks. "I haven't had a period since before we got here, and now my breasts are tender."

Brenda gathered her up in a hug. "It'll be okay."

Tiffany laid her head on Brenda's shoulder. "I don't want a rapist's baby!"

"It's a baby. *Your* baby. It's not at fault."

"That's easy for you to say." Tiffany wiped her eyes with her sleeve.

Brenda nodded. "Yes it is, and no, I don't really understand. But you should have Jamal examine you anyway."

Tiffany pulled away from Brenda's embrace and shook her head. "I'm not about to let some guy poke his fingers in my twat."

"Closest thing we have to a doctor. He's the one who'll deliver your baby."

Tiffany gave her head another, more emphatic shake. She folded her arms. "Not interested. Unless he can abort it."

Brenda sighed. "In either case you'll need to see him."

*　　*　　*

June 14, 4:55 p.m.
Brenda at her side holding her hand, Tiffany sat on the edge of the examination table, fully clothed. She eyed Jamal with a blatant distrust that he found unsettling. He'd looked her in the eyes in the textbook-recommended, "engage-the-patient," manner when she sat, but he quickly had to drop his gaze in response to her glare. Brenda had to coax her to relay her history.

Once she finished, Jamal sighed. "From what you told me, yes, it's likely that you're pregnant. Probably about two months along. There's no need for me to do a pelvic exam at this point. It wouldn't tell us anything more."

Tiffany glanced at Brenda, then turned back to Jamal. "Can you get rid of it?"

He shook his head. "No. I have neither the equipment, nor the knowledge to do that sort of procedure." He sighed again. "I think I can dimly appreciate your feelings, and I'm truly sorry, but no. That's not something I can do." He forced himself to meet her eyes. "Any of the herbal methods you might try are mortally dangerous this far along. Don't do it. I'm sure we can find someone to adopt your baby. Any attempt you might make to abort it yourself is likely to kill you."

Tears came up in Tiffany's eyes. "Maybe that wouldn't be so bad. What, oil of pennyroyal? Do we have any of that?"

Brenda wheeled around in front of Tiffany and grasped her by the shoulders. She shook her, hard. "Don't even go there. You'd be letting Herman win. Is that what you want?" She let go of her shoulders, took Tiffany's chin, and lifted her face to meet her eyes. "You freed us from Herman's control. Are you going to give in to it now after all this?" She shook her head. "Not on my watch. Your baby will be born free and healthy and without any rapist's stain. I'll raise her myself, if necessary. Or him. Whichever. But regardless, your baby— *your* baby—will grow up in a loving family."

Tiffany heaved a ragged sob. "But I'll have to carry that rapist's spawn for nine months, and then see him every day in the village." She ran her fingers through her hair. They rested for the briefest moment on her scar. "It'll be a constant reminder of all the times I was raped. Besides, I'm—I'm probably the one who killed his father." Tiffany wiped her eyes. "Herman was the only one who raped me at about the time it must have happened. The others were put off by my scar, but Herman was fucking proud of it." She turned her head as if to spit, but then restrained herself. She grimaced.

Brenda hugged her. "I'm responsible for killing him too. It wasn't just you."

"Bullshit. I'm the one who broke his skull open, not you."

Jamal lifted his hand to pat Tiffany's shoulder, then

thought better of it. He dropped it back to his side and sighed. "Try to eat plenty of vegetables and fruit. I'll have Allen bring you some extra milk. See me again in about a month, okay?"

Tiffany made no sign that she'd heard him.

Brenda retook Tiffany's hand. "Let's go back and get some dinner, okay?"

It took a few seconds, but finally Tiffany turned to Brenda. After a moment she shrugged and wiped her eyes again. "Okay."

On their way out the door Tiffany stopped and turned back to Jamal. "Uh—well—thanks, I guess. Listen, I don't want this to get out, all right?"

Jamal nodded. "If that's what you want, I'll respect that. I generally try to keep patient confidentiality anyway."

Brenda turned to Tiffany, raising an eyebrow. "Eventually it'll become obvious."

"I'll deal with that when I have to."

Brenda shrugged. "Your choice. You'll need to rewrite your assignment, then."

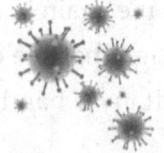

Chapter Forty-Eight

Security Issues

June 16, 4:00 p.m.

"I asked for this meeting to go over some modifications I'm proposing for the security monitor program," Jonathan said. The people gathered in the Kiners' dining room raised their faces to him as they settled into seats. Gloria set a glass of water in front of Jim and pushed his wheelchair a little closer to the table. She took a seat beside Dan.

"The basic problem," Jonathan said, "is that it's a balance between reporting useful information, and over-intrusive monitoring and false alerts. Before, it was set to sound an alarm if someone entered the area from the outside, and also to raise the alert level if they were armed. But I didn't want it crying wolf if someone left the village to go hunting, so I set it to ignore people leaving."

Gloria frowned. "What about when the hunter returns?" "It remembers who left, and tries to recognize them on their return. It can do that by noting their height and build, presence or absence of facial hair, clothing color if it's during the day, their characteristic gait, and so forth. Facial recognition if possible, but they have to be close to a camera for that to work."

Jim furrowed his brows. In a dry whisper he said, "Still a little—" He coughed a few times and wiped his mouth with a handkerchief. He picked up a pen and wrote on a pad, "Still a little Big-Brother-ish, no?" Jamal read Jim's comment aloud for the benefit of the others seated opposite.

"Potentially. I have it set to erase those records after 24 hours unless it's told not to."

"We were glad to have it for the Tollivers' attack," Dan said, "but I don't think we need to know who's sneaking where for a moonlight tryst, for example."

"Not unless someone gets assaulted, no."

Dan grimaced. "Yeah, maybe."

"What'd you change?" Jim wrote.

"I set it to give an alarm if someone takes a horse from the stable after hours. I figured that'd be something we'd want to know. I also set it to note if somebody carries something out of the area but doesn't bring it back."

Gloria tilted her head. "What's the reason for that?"

"I thought it might tell us if someone is taking communal equipment or supplies for private use." He shrugged. "To catch thieves."

"I'm not aware that's been an issue so far," Dan said. "Do we need a solution for a problem we don't have?"

Jim took his pad and wrote, "I don't want to create a police state."

Gloria shook her head. "You're going to catch a lot of people who took a picnic lunch to the woods and had the bag they carried it in folded up in their pocket on their return. I see this as causing more distrust and suspicion than it's worth for any theoretical benefit."

Jim wrote rapidly on his pad, pausing to cough every

once in a while. He crossed out a word and kept going a few times, his head bent down over the paper. Finally he leaned back up and pushed the pad to Jamal. He took a deep breath, wheezing.

Jamal read: "We've built this community on mutual trust and cooperation. We try hard to give everyone of age a say in decisions that affect us. Everyone is invested in the success of our community. If we have a police force that monitors and controls us, we lose that. At some point I hope we'll get big enough that we'll need police of some sort, but I don't want to do anything that will hasten that day's coming till it's necessary."

Jonathan nodded. "I can see that. It's easy to remove that module." He ran his fingers through his graying hair. "My experience is in network security. I guess I have a basic assumption operating in the background that there are bad guys out there who want to attack us and steal our possessions." He shrugged. "For people coming in from outside, I think that assumption has been shown to be valid."

"What about when you and Sara and Rita arrived last fall?" Jamal asked.

"You were correct to assume that about us as well, until you knew otherwise. That doesn't mean that you kill all outsiders, it means you treat them with caution. As I recall, that is how you treated us."

Jamal gave a brief nod.

"How about the change in monitoring the stable?" Jonathan asked.

Dan shrugged. "I don't have a strong feeling about that. It would have alerted us to Tyler and Jacob leaving last April, I suppose."

Jim grabbed his pad and began writing. The others

waited for him. After a minute he passed the pad to Jamal, who read: "Tyler and Jacob were unwise in leaving the way they did, but can't argue rescuing those women wasn't worthwhile. That's why I argued Tyler's penance work be light."

Dan arched his brows. "So the end justifies the means?"

Jim shrugged and nodded. He coughed. "Mitigates, at least," he wrote on his pad.

Gloria leaned back in her chair, a grimace on her face. "The horses are important to our ability to work the fields. We can't rely on having diesel for tractors much longer. I think we're justified in some increased security for the stables."

"I agree," Jamal said, his dreadlocks swaying as he nodded. "I'm just not sure a high tech surveillance system is the best way to do that, if we don't want to create a police state mentality. I think it'd be better to have a person posted there in that case." He frowned. "We should have invited Andrea to this meeting."

"If one person takes one horse, that might not be a big deal," Dan said. "Assuming it's their own horse. Can your security system make that distinction?"

Jonathan frowned. Paladin's facial recognition algorithm would need serious work to recognize horses too. "Not currently. I might be able to make it do that, but it'd take some doing. I mean, of course he—it—can easily see that someone's taking more than one horse, but it'll be much harder to identify that a specific individual is taking their own horse, and not someone else's."

"That's why we'd need someone on site," Jamal said.

"We don't have a lot of people sitting around with nothing to do," Dan said. "Who's going to man the stable all those hours?"

"We just got more than twenty new members of the

community," Jamal said. "With them available, there should be enough to cover that task."

Gloria frowned. "Some of them are only fifteen years old. Do we really want them doing guard duty at night?"

"It wouldn't have to be one of them, necessarily," Jamal said. "But with them available, maybe they could take over some of the other tasks that one of the older, more experienced members are doing. Besides, some of them are almost twenty-one. Not much younger than Tyler. *Older* than Tyler was when he started doing guard duty at the Interstate lookout. I see this as mostly an administrative thing. People signing out their horse, and such. They'd have a radio to call for help, and I think several of them have proven they can handle themselves in an emergency.

"Anyway, George tells me now that the new garden plots are tilled and planted for them, the extra workers are tripping over each other, at least until the harvest. It'd also be a perfect job for the one who's pregnant. Until she delivers."

Gloria's eyebrows shot up. "One of them is pregnant?"

"Oh, shit. That was private. Forget I said that."

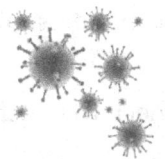

Chapter Forty-Nine

Milk Run

June 17, 8:30 a.m.

ALLEN reined his horse to a stop in front of Anna's house and hopped to the ground. He pulled out a bandana and wiped his forehead. Still early and already getting hot. He pulled out three bottles of milk from the cooler in the back of the wagon, carefully tucking one under his arm, and stepped toward the door. Then he came to a halt. No, not three. Jamal had told him the other day they get four bottles now. Grinning, he went back and got another bottle, putting them into a bag instead of carrying them loose.

He rang the bell, and after a moment Anna opened the door, her baby on her hip. "Milk delivery," he announced, smiling.

Anna glanced at the bottles in the bag. "I thought we only get three."

"Jamal told me you're supposed to get four now." He smiled a little wider.

Anna furrowed her brows. "Why is that?"

Allen blinked. "Well, he didn't say but, but I assumed

that—"

Tiffany came to the door beside Anna. "I'll take those." She grabbed the bag by its handles, pivoted, and stomped back inside.

Anna turned her neck to watch her go, then faced Allen again. "Uh—well—thanks."

"You're welcome. Don"t forget about the bonfire—"

"Don't just stand there with the fucking door open," Tiffany shouted from inside. "You'll let in flies."

Anna winced, then she smiled at him. "Yeah, the bonfire on the 21st. Thanks." She shut the door.

Allen stood there a couple of seconds more before he walked back to the wagon, brows furrowed. He climbed back on the wagon's seat, but didn't take the reins. Then he rolled his eyes. Stupid idiot. They'd only been here six weeks. Hardly enough time to meet someone, get knocked up, and know about it. If one of them had gotten pregnant it was by a rapist during their previous enslavement. Jamal hadn't told him, so obviously he wasn't supposed to know. Didn't look like even Anna knew. Tiffany wasn't surprised by the extra bottle of milk, though.

He climbed off the wagon, knelt and touched the ground, his hand flat on the grass feeling the Earth's peace as the hum of katydids and birdsong filled the air.

*   *   *

9:35

Allen's final stop was at the Canfields' house. They had a six-year-old daughter, Julie, who would be at school at that hour. He knocked on the door.

"Milk delivery," he announced when Wilma Canfield

answered.

She took the bottles. "Thanks." She turned to go back inside.

"Don't forget about the Solstice bonfire next Monday."

Wilma stopped in mid-turn. She twisted her neck to look at him and scowled. "We're a Christian household, and we don't participate in such godless ceremonies."

"But it's not against Christianity—"

"And I don't want you talking to Julie. Is that clear?" She elbowed the door shut with a slam.

After a couple of seconds Allen nodded at the door. "Crystal clear."

Before he climbed back onto the wagon, he knelt once more and touched the Earth.

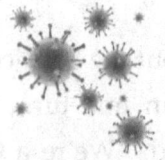

Chapter Fifty

Transitions and Announcements

June 21, 8:49 p.m.

AS the sun neared the horizon, Jonathan surveyed the crowd gathered around the bonfire built to commemorate the Summer Solstice. The number there had nearly doubled over that of the Vernal Equinox, since most of the recent arrivals had joined them. They stood clustered together, a little apart from the rest of them.

He'd hoped this opportunity would aid the survivor's integration to the community, but let things stand for now, as Allen's all too familiar speech threatened to put some to sleep. At last Allen concluded with a welcome to the new members of their enclave.

Everyone expected it this time, and more or less together they bent or knelt to touch the ground when Allen finished. Even the former Girl Scouts joined in after a slight hesitation. Allen straightened up and said, "Thank you, everyone. We've got some yogurt and some wild raspberries that Rita and I picked. There's also some bread and cheese. Feel free to help yourselves, but keep in mind we have a lot of guests to share it with."

Kayla stepped forward from the group of women and faced Allen. "May I offer a blessing for the meal?"

Allen raised an eyebrow and nodded. "Of course."

Kayla bowed her head. "We give thanks for the food we are about to enjoy, for Earth's gifts that we share together. We give thanks for the opportunity to gather as a community to mark this special day in pleasant fellowship. We give thanks for all these blessings, and more not named, but still appreciated. In the name of all that is sacred and holy, we offer our gratitude. Amen."

"Amen," echoed most of the crowd. Allen, Rita, and several others bent to touch the ground again. Kayla joined them in the gesture, and the Girl Scouts joined her after a second.

People headed to the tables with the food, but Jonathan hung back, watching. He surveyed the young women, wondering which of them was pregnant.

Sara bumped his elbow with hers. "If I were the jealous type, I'd be worried about you staring so intently at young women. But I'm not, so I'll just assume you have a good reason to do that. You're going to make them nervous, though."

Jonathan grimaced and scanned the immediate surroundings. Rita and Allen stood nearby chatting with Jamal, Dan, and Gloria. Jim sat in his wheelchair beside them. Steve and Anita Carpenter stood in front of Sara and himself. They watched while their son Jimmy and Clayton Tolliver played a game that seemed to involve trying to not let the other one tag them, while not getting too far away from each other at the same time.

"Let's take a walk." He took her hand and they strolled around the barn toward the fence bordering the cattle pasture.

A couple of wide, black and white splotched faces turned toward them for a moment, then bent back down to graze.

Jonathan checked to be sure they were out of sight of the others and leaned against a fence post, facing Sara. "The other day, at the meeting on the security system, Jamal let it slip that one of those women is pregnant. She doesn't want that to be generally known yet, though. Jamal wouldn't tell Gloria who it was, and he generally clammed up about it afterwards. He asked us to forget he said that."

Sara nodded. "Tiffany."

The startled shake of his head Jonathan made threatened to dislodge his glasses. He pushed them back up on the bridge of his nose. "You knew?"

"Not until just now, no. Remember last week I mentioned that something seemed off with Tiffany? That, plus filling in between the lines on some of her writing, and the fact that she's had to excuse herself to run to the restroom a couple of times and then denied that there was anything wrong." She shrugged. "I guess I don't really know I'm right, but I'd bet you money that I am. If we had any use for money, that is."

Jonathan shook his head again, slow and thoughtful this time. "She's obviously unhappy about this, and I couldn't blame her. Do you think she'll try to abort it?"

"I hope not. I mean, they've been here for what, seven weeks now? Best case she's about eight weeks pregnant at this point. Probably more. Any of the ways that she might try to abort her pregnancy are pretty risky without high-tech medical intervention, this far along."

Jonathan nodded. "Well, in any case, we shouldn't let on that we know—suspect, I guess—that she's pregnant until she's ready to let it be known."

"That's a 'duh' sort of thing," Sara said. "I just hope she

treats the baby okay until it's born. I assume we're going to need an adoptive parent for it."

Jonathan rolled his eyes. "Duh."

*   *   *

After Sara and Jonathan turned the corner by the barn on the way back to the bonfire, Tiffany left the group of newcomers to approach Rita, carrying a cloth bag. Rita looked into the bag and she jerked her head back as if surprised. She turned toward Allen and said something to him.

Jonathan furrowed his brows. "Tiffany isn't the sort to do the 'snake-in-the-bag' prank, is she?"

Sara snorted. "Hardly."

A few seconds later they were close enough to hear Rita and Tiffany.

"I decided I need to get rid of this thing," Tiffany said. "I thought maybe doing it this way would help me—" She turned to look over her shoulder toward Brenda and Christine, who had come up behind her, then turned back to Rita. "— Well, just that it'd help me."

Brenda laid a hand on Tiffany's shoulder, and Tiffany clasped it, still focused on Rita.

Allen took Rita's hand. "What do you think?"

Rita's eyes had gone wide. She looked back to Tiffany, then glanced over to Gloria and then to Jamal. They stood nearby, watching, silent. She bit her lip and took a deep breath. "This fire symbolizes transitions. I think if by doing that it'd symbolize a transition toward healing for you, then it'd be entirely appropriate. Don't you agree, Allen?"

"Absolutely."

Tiffany nodded. She took a deep breath, sniffling.

"Thanks." She pulled a broken chair leg from the bag. She closed her eyes and her lips moved for a few seconds, but no sound came out that Jonathan could hear. Sara took in a sharp breath and clutched Jonathan's hand.

Almost gently, Tiffany tossed her club onto the pile of burning branches. Brenda hugged her, then Christine embraced her as well.

Allen bent to touch the Earth. Like a ripple spreading across the surface of a pond, people around them also bent to touch the ground. Tiffany turned in place watching as they did. Tears overflowed her eyes and trickled down her cheeks. She knelt on the lawn and laid both hands flat on the grass in front of her. Brenda and Christine helped her back up after a moment.

Wiping her eyes with the back of her hand, Tiffany said, "Thanks, everyone."

Rita stepped to her and gave Tiffany a one-armed hug while holding Davina in the other arm.

"Thanks," Tiffany repeated. She dug out a handkerchief and wiped her eyes again. "There's something else I want to say." She looked around and took a deep breath. "I'm—I'm pregnant."

Christine gasped. She turned to Brenda, and Brenda nodded.

"But I—I don't think I'm ready to be a mother," Tiffany continued. "Not for this child. I'd appreciate it if—you know, if someone could—could—"

Gloria stepped up to Tiffany and wrapped her arms around her. "It'll be okay. We'll find someone to adopt your baby. We all understand." Tiffany stiffened, standing there in Gloria's embrace, and Gloria added, "All right, I guess we don't *really* understand, but we can appreciate why you feel that way. We all want to help you."

Sara nudged Jonathan in the ribs. "Told you." She grimaced. "Now we just need to find someone to adopt the baby."

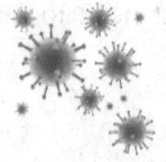

Chapter Fifty-One

Against the Pagans

June 21, 9:05 p.m.

THE sun sank below the horizon and took the heat of the day with it. A cool evening breeze arose, floating strands of Janet Haskel's hair over her face. As she brushed them aside Bob set a glass of iced mint tea on the table next to her lawn chair under the maple tree in their back yard. No hint of the morning rain or the heat of the day remained as Janet reclined in her yellow sundress and sipped her tea.

Bob remained standing by her chair after bringing the tea. "Can I get you anything else?"

"No thank you." He tried so hard to be nice that she found it annoying. Insufficient to provoke a comment, but enough to disrupt her peaceful moment.

Bob took a seat on the other side of the table.

Janet turned toward the opposite side where her father sat in a bentwood rocker, sipping a glass of ginger ale. "You still have to stop Allen," he said. "Even now he's performing his pagan rites. Look toward the farm and you'll see."

The chair creaked as she turned toward Bob. "Which

way is the farm from here?"

Bob stopped with his glass halfway to his lips. He lowered it. "I'm not sure. Why do you ask?"

"This is the day that Allen is having his bonfire, isn't it?"

Bob winced. "Don't worry about that, okay Honey? It's not really important."

Janet set her glass down. "How can you say that? There are dozens of souls at stake. We can't let Allen's paganism lead people away from Christ." She pulled herself out of the chair and swayed a little as a new pulse of pain shot through her skull. Closing her eyes, she massaged her temples and let out a soft moan.

"Take it easy, Honey. It's okay. Just relax, and I'll get you a damp cloth for your head." He set his glass on the table and jogged into the house.

Janet's father leaned forward in the rocker. It creaked. "You have to stop Allen. It's imperative."

She scanned the horizon. In the northwest a plume of smoke rose. As if pulled by a magnet, she limped toward it. When she reached the Hardys' garden she pulled up a branch they'd set as a tomato stake and continued walking, using the stick to support herself as she went. The throbbing in her head pounded with each heartbeat, but she gritted her teeth and continued.

"That's the way," her father said. "God wants you to stop Allen. It's your mission." He walked beside her, keeping pace, but not touching.

"Janet, where are you?" Bob called. Her steps faltered.

"You must stop Allen."

"Janet! What are you doing? Come back."

She turned toward Bob's voice for a split second, then

winced as another throb of pain went through her skull. "You must stop Allen," her father repeated.

She turned back toward the smoke and continued walking.

Bob caught up with her and grasped her arm. "Janet, come back home."

She shook off his grip and swung the branch at him. He dodged away from it and caught her wrist. She dropped the stick. "Let me go! I have to stop Allen!" She struggled for a moment and looked toward her father. "Help me!"

Her father stood unmoving, just a few feet away. "You must stop Allen."

Bob held her wrists as Janet tried to twist away from him. "Who are you talking to? I can't let you hurt anyone. The way of the Lord is love. Isn't that what you always say?"

Janet stopped struggling and stared into his face. She blinked a couple of times. The way of the Lord is love. She'd used that phrase in sermons more times than she could count.

"Honey, come back home with me."

She turned back to her father, but he'd left her again. Her knees buckled. Bob tried to catch her, but her weight carried him to the ground with her. Weeping now, Janet leaned on Bob's shoulder.

He stroked her hair and kissed the top of her head. "It's okay. It'll be fine. I love you."

* * *

Sept 21, 9:10 p.m.

As the bonfire burned down Jonathan chatted with Jamal and Allen. Jim was having a good day, breathing easier, and he joined in the conversation too, albeit in a hoarse whisper. In mid-sentence Jonathan's earpiece chirped. He held up a finger to Jamal. "Excuse me for a second. Yes, Paladin, what is it?"

His computer's synthesized voice answered. "Security monitor alert: Two individuals are fighting near 146 Evergreen Lane. One appears to have a weapon of some sort, a staff or a club."

Jonathan furrowed his brows. The Hardys lived at 146 Evergreen, and they were present at the bonfire. His hand went to his pocket. Empty. Damn, didn't bring the phone. "I have no ability for visual," Jonathan said. "Who are they? Describe the incident."

Sara looked over to Jonathan, "What—" she said, but stopped when Jonathan held up a hand.

"They're too far from a camera for facial recognition. The one with the weapon appears to be female. She's wearing a dress. She limps in a pattern consistent with Janet Haskel's. She swung the weapon like a club at the other one, who has facial hair. He evaded the attack and she dropped the weapon. They're struggling, with the man grasping the woman's wrists."

Jonathan muted the microphone. "Who has a smart phone with them?" he shouted.

Heads turned toward him. Gloria pulled one out of her pocket and held it toward him. "I was going to take some pictures."

He grabbed it. "Send the visual to Gloria Kiner." A second later Gloria's phone rang. The video showed two figures locked together, one grasping the other by the wrists. Then they fell to the ground, sitting upright together.

"The combatants have fallen to a seated position, still grasping each other," the computer said in Jonathan's earpiece.

"Dammit," Jonathan muttered. "Verbal description

off."

"Just following your instructions. No need to swear."

A crowd had gathered around Jonathan, trying to get a look at the small screen. Jamal had an advantage due to his height and the fact that he had been standing nearby when Gloria gave Jonathan the phone. "That looks like Janet and Bob," Jamal said.

Jonathan gave a quick shake of his head. "Janet and Bob are fighting? She swung a club at him? That doesn't sound right."

Jamal's eyebrows lifted. "Swung a club? That's certainly out of character for her."

"They're not fighting now," Sara said. "To the contrary, he's stroking her hair."

Janet's head rested on Bob's shoulder. As they watched in the video, Bob kissed her hair. After a moment he helped Janet to her feet and they made their way toward their house, Janet leaning on Bob's arm as she limped along.

Dan shook his head. "I don't understand that at all."

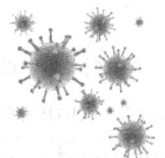

Chapter Fifty-Two

Emergency Conference

June 21, 9:28 p.m.

JAMAL'S dreadlocks swung around him as he shook his head. "It's none of our business. You should erase the video, and we should pretend we didn't see it." Jonathan scanned the faces of the others gathered in the farmhouse to review the video of the incident concerning Janet and Bob Haskel. A couple of them nodded, but most of them frowned in doubt.

Over the last several months Jonathan had come to generally respect Jamal's opinion, but this time he disagreed. Before he made a comment, though, Sara spoke up. "I'm not sure it's any of our business either, but I don't think it was just a marital spat. There was too short a time between Janet swinging a club at him, then crying in his arms. Something else is going on."

Rita put a glass of water in front of Jim Henderson. He took a drink. "I agree that something looks odd," Jim said in a raspy whisper, "but I don't see that we have an interest in terms of community safety to pursue this."

Jonathan shook his head. "I disagree. If someone's

attacking another person with a weapon, it's not a marital spat. It's assault. Attempted assault, anyway. I don't see how we can ignore it."

"So what do you suggest we do?" Jim asked.

"I don't know. Maybe someone should check on them."

"Right." Jim pantomimed knocking on a door. "Knock, knock. Oh, hi Bob. We'd just noticed with our all-seeing surveillance system that Janet attacked you earlier, and we wondered if anyone needed medical attention, or if Janet needs to be locked up for assault." He coughed and pulled out a handkerchief to wipe his mouth. By the end of his speech his voice had faded to a bare whisper. He sipped some more water.

"I'm sure we could be more diplomatic than that," Jonathan said.

Jim coughed and wiped his mouth. "This is what I meant about creating the impression of a police state."

"Unless Bob makes a complaint, I don't think we have a right to intervene," Jamal said, shaking his head.

Jonathan sipped some water. "It doesn't have to be an intervention. We all know that Janet hasn't felt well for a while. Maybe you could stop by to follow-up on how she's doing. A wellness check, or something."

Jamal sat silent a few seconds. His jaw worked as if he were trying to say something but couldn't get it out. Then he tilted his head down and brought a hand up to cover his eyes. "I can't do anything for her." He dropped his hand to get a handkerchief from his hip pocket and revealed tears on his cheeks. He wiped his eyes and face. "She's in near constant pain, and I can't help her. Heaven knows I've tried, but there's nothing more I can do."

Jim reached up and clasped Jamal's hand. "We forgive

you for not being God."

Jamal stared wide-eyed at Jim for a moment, then he dropped his gaze and nodded. He licked his lips. "Thanks." His whisper seemed too soft and meek for someone of his size. He wiped his eyes again and stuffed the handkerchief back in his pocket. He sighed. "Well, I guess it wouldn't hurt for me to follow up on how Janet's doing."

George patted Jamal's shoulder.

"Do you want someone to go with you?" Alice asked.

Jamal shook his head. "That wouldn't look right. Couldn't keep confidentiality if there was someone tagging along."

The image of Janet swinging the branch at her husband still hung in Jonathan's mind. "You'll let someone know if you think she's a danger, though, right? To herself or others?"

"Of course."

"To change the subject," Andrea said, "should you try to get Tiffany to see you for a prenatal exam?"

Jamal grimaced, then shrugged. "I guess, since she's announced it, it's okay. I've already seen her, but she swore me to secrecy at the time. Brenda brought her over last week. As far as an exam's concerned, it's too early for me to examine anything. I told her to eat lots of fruit and vegetables, and drink more milk."

Rita nodded. "That explains the extra milk Allen's been taking there. I asked him about it, but he wouldn't say why. So Allen knew?"

"Suspected, I'm sure, but I didn't tell him, either."

"I guess I can understand why she doesn't want to keep the baby, but I hope she follows your advice."

"So far it seems she's doing that. Far as I can tell anyway." Jamal wiped his forehead. "I don't mean to sound creepy, but those women showing up was the best thing that could have happened for the health of our gene pool."

Sara rolled her eyes and snorted. "You can't be serious."

"I'm sorry if that seemed insensitive, but if we're going to survive long term, that's something we need to think about."

Sara nodded. "You're right, that was insensitive. But that's not what I mean. Those women were brutally and repeatedly raped for two years. They aren't going to want to 'contribute' to our gene pool." She made air quotes. "I'm surprised they interact with men at all."

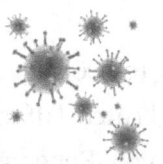

Chapter Fifty-Three

Remedies

June 28, 4:15 p.m.

JAMAL knocked on the door of Tiffany's house not long after the writing class ended. He wiped sweat from his forehead and dried his hand on his trousers. Getting too hot to wear long pants, but he didn't feel fully dressed in shorts.

After a moment Rebecca opened the door. She was a short young lady with close-cropped kinky hair who'd just had her sixteenth birthday earlier that week. The Girl Scouts had held a celebration for her and had invited everyone. She smiled at him, though he thought the smile looked guarded. "Hi Jamal. Can I help you?"

"Hi Rebecca. I was hoping to see Tiffany."

"Becky."

Jamal gave his head a tilt. "Excuse me?"

"Everyone calls me Becky. Unless they're mad at me."

He smiled. "Well I'm not mad at you, Becky. Most people call me 'Jay.'"

"Okay. Anyway, Tiffany isn't back yet. She and Anna should be back any minute, though."

Too early. Should have waited a little longer. "All right. Is okay if I wait for her?"

The guarded expression reappeared, deeper. "Well, I—"

"Actually, I need to see Brenda too. I'll just head over there for the moment and catch Tiffany a little later."

Relief washed over Rebecca's face. "Sure—uh—Jay. She'll be back soon."

Jamal headed across the street toward Brenda's house, though he really didn't need to see her. Anyway, she was in the writing class too and probably wasn't home yet either. Clearly, though, Rebecca—Becky—wasn't comfortable with letting him in. He took a brief walk around the cul-de-sac where the Girl Scouts lived. The grass in the yards was tall and unkempt—like it was in about all the other yards—though in one case a large section of the front yard had been dug up and a "three sisters" garden was in progress. Corn, bean, and squash plants had started to fill the plot. He smiled. A much better use of the space than the grass, but what would the home owner's association say?

He snorted a laugh. Yeah, right. Home owner's association.

Motion in the distance to his left caught his attention. Several women were approaching the cul-de-sac, and a couple of them went into Tiffany's house. He headed back.

Anna opened the door to his knock this time and called for Tiffany. She arrived a few seconds later and looked him over with the sort of half-frown her scarred face was capable of. "Doing house calls? Where's your little black bag?"

"I'm not here to see you as a patient. I have a proposition—ah—proposal you may find interesting, though."

She tilted her head back a little and squinted at him.

"What kind of proposition—ah—proposal?"

He lifted his eyebrows at her mocking his correction of his word choice. She didn't miss much. "Could we sit somewhere and talk for a bit?"

Tiffany gave a brief eye roll. "I suppose we *could*. Is that what you'd like to do?"

He gave an eye roll of his own. "Yes, please."

*   *   *

Tiffany led him around the house where there was a deck shaded by a canvas awning. She took a seat at a folding chair by a glass-topped table and waited for him to sit as well. "So what's your proposal?"

"I've got a couple of questions first, if you don't mind."

She gave a brief nod.

"A couple of weeks ago, when I saw you at the clinic, you mentioned pennyroyal."

Tiffany furrowed her brows. "So?"

"I was sort of vaguely aware of it as an herb that had been used in medieval times to cause an abortion, but that's all I knew at the time. Brenda's response preempted anything else I would have said. I looked it up later. Yes, it can induce a miscarriage, but it's quite toxic. It's also called tick weed 'cause it was used to repel insects, including fleas and ticks. Because it's poisonous. Easy to get a fatal overdose. Especially of the oil, like you mentioned." He pushed a dreadlock from in front of his face. "So I'm curious. How did you know about it?"

Tiffany grimaced. "I found a book on herb lore on the shelves at the B&B. I smuggled it back to my room and was trying to come up with a poison."

Jamal's eyebrows lifted. "A poison?"

"I couldn't very well do any kind of direct attack on all six of those men, could I? Especially not after what they did to Carla." She shuddered.

"Carla? Who's—"

"I don't want to go there."

He nodded. "Okay. Well, did you get anywhere with it?"

She shook her head. "Identified some prospects, pennyroyal for one. Jimson weed. A couple of types of mushrooms. But I couldn't get away to find and collect the herbs. They kept us locked up too tight."

She shrugged. "Mostly I was dreaming. I spent a lot of the little spare time I had reading through it. Helped keep me sane, I guess." The right side of her mouth lifted. "Assuming that I *am* sane."

Jamal returned her smile, happy to see hers. He couldn't recall any other time he'd seen a smile on her face. "That's not something I'm worried about for you."

"Anyway, it did give me some helpful advice for easing menstrual cramps. So it was useful from that standpoint, at least."

Jamal's eyebrows lifted. "Oh? What kind of advice?"

Tiffany tilted her head and narrowed her eyes. "I used fennel and chamomile teas. That seemed to help most of them to some degree. Basil is supposed to work too, but we didn't have any of that in the herb plot at the B&B."

"I've been recommending willow bark tea for the discomfort."

"Not the best choice." She shook her head. "At best a relief of symptoms only, and at worst, it can lead to stomach upset and increase the bleeding."

Jamal gave a slow nod and a smile spread across his

face. "Thanks. Some women here are going to be glad we had this conversation."

Tiffany smiled a little wider.

"So. My proposal: I'm looking for an assistant. You're knowledgeable about herbs, and Brenda said you're good at first aid. I need someone willing to learn with me, and eventually take over from me. Someone not afraid to see blood once in a while, with a good head on their shoulders and who won't fall apart in a crisis. Is that person you?"

Her smile turned into an outright grin.

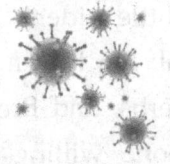

Chapter Fifty-Four

Another Prospect

Aug. 29, 10:30 a.m.

JONATHAN reviewed the satellite imagery from the latest pass of the HIREPOWR satellite and compared it to the last image he had, only a week previous. He'd already verified that the radioactive contamination on the east coast had not spread westward by any significant amount since last fall, but his search routine had flagged him about a different anomaly. A plot of about three acres, only forty miles away, had definitely changed over the last week. He knew of no natural phenomenon that could have changed that field in a neat, rectangular pattern in that period. People had worked the field, almost without question.

He rubbed his eyes and looked again. The image hadn't changed. He saved it to his local disk and uploaded it to the server.

Sara had gone to help pick apples, and he should be out there too. He'd begged off, promising to be there as soon as the image from the satellite downloaded, but then he had to take a look, and when it seemed odd he did some further processing of the image.

Now an hour had passed since he said he'd be there. He shut down the computer and jogged to the orchard.

Sara peered down at him from her perch on a ladder once he arrived and a frown formed. "Nice of you to help out. I thought you were coming right after me."

"Sorry. I found evidence of another settlement, about forty miles away."

"Really? That's great." Her frown deepened to a grimace. "Now take those baskets we've filled to the wagon and start picking the next tree."

* * *

Aug. 30 8:10 p.m.
Jonathan pointed to a small rectangular patch shown on the big conference monitor in the main meeting room in the village's community center. "This is the image on August 29th." He brought up the next picture, split-screen with the first. "Here's the one from August 24th. You can see that this plot looks different over this time frame, and only within the confines of this specific plot." He surveyed the crowd gathered in the main meeting room: more than two-thirds, possibly three-quarters of the population. Few of the beige folding chairs in the room stood empty.

"I think that's a clear indication that someone has worked this plot," Jonathan continued. "I'm guessing that they harvested some wheat, or cut hay, but almost without doubt some people live in this area."

"You found a field that'd been worked," Dan said. "People live around there. That's great, but did you find their settlement? Where they actually live?"

Jonathan shook his head. "No. That area is forested for

the most part. There's a lot of little patches of cleared ground in the area, mostly along the road where there are burned-out houses. The few houses I could find that seemed intact didn't show signs of habitation. This time of year it's hard to get conclusive data on that from the satellite imagery, though." Jonathan caught some people frowning, shaking their heads. He pressed on. "They don't have to heat the houses, so they don't glow in IR. And some could be under tree cover and hard to see. But I think it's safe to assume they'd have to be near that field."

"Three acres is a tiny hayfield," Allen said. "There couldn't be a big settlement there."

"Probably not. But it's only forty miles away. We could get there in the truck in an hour or so, easy."

"You're assuming the roads are clear. There's likely to be a few places where trees have blown over. And we don't have a lot of gas to use for wild goose hunts," Jack Rockford said. "There and back would take at least four gallons. Can we spare that?"

Jamal spoke up before Jonathan responded. "If there's another settlement, I'm not sure we can afford not to check it out. In the greater scheme of things, I'm not sure four gallons of gas would make that much of a difference. We're going to have to go to horse power to work the fields before much longer, anyway."

Jonathan nodded. Exactly his thoughts. There was only one two-hundred gallon tank of gas and another of diesel, neither one anywhere near full. They wouldn't even make it through the next season on gas power.

"We could just send a couple of people out there on horseback to check it out, and then send the bus if necessary," Andrea said.

Dan shook his head. "The harvest is underway. We

need workers to bring in the crops and preserve them for the winter."

Jamal nodded. "All the more reason to contact them soon, both for the sake of the workforce, and the health of our gene pool."

Jonathan took in a sharp breath and glanced at Tiffany. This could get tense. She sat with most of the other survivors of the bed and breakfast inn on the left side of the room. Over the summer, Tiffany's pregnancy had become noticeable. Her face clouded, but she looked almost disappointed, rather than angry.

Brenda stood, red-faced. "We are *not* just breeding stock, dammit. We appreciate the help we've received since we arrived last spring, but we won't condone that attitude." She took a deep breath and scowled. "If that's how you think, maybe we should go join that other group instead."

Some of the women sitting near her nodded, and a murmur rose among them.

Jim Henderson typed on a laptop sitting on a tray attached to the arms of his wheelchair. Synthesized words spoke from the computer's speakers, spaced as he typed and then hit return to speak his words. "Please accept our apologies—for the clumsy way Jamal—made his statement.— I'm sure Jamal didn't mean that the way it came out,—right, Jay?"

Jamal's eyes had widened and he had blushed. He stammered as he spoke. "That's right. That wasn't my intent. I'm sorry for the implication. Please accept my personal apology too."

Jim had continued typing while Jamal spoke, and he hit "return" when Jamal finished speaking. "None of us condones the idea of any kind of coercive relationship. I think Jamal's basic point is that the long-term survival of our community depends on having a healthy and diverse population, and that the bigger it is, the better, from that standpoint. In that sense, all of us are part of the community's gene pool. All of us still capable and willing, at least."

Brenda gave a curt nod. "We'll talk about this more, later." Jonathan heaved a silent sigh as she took her seat. No disasters too big to handle this time.

"As long as we have a regular and friendly relationship with this community, it may not matter all that much if they come here or not, from the standpoint of our gene pool," Dan said, "if we have some kind of regular commerce and exchange of members with them."

Bryan Pierce smirked. "Friendly, or *very* friendly relationships?"

The hall broke out in giggles and a few outright guffaws. Jim rapped on the table and called for order, turning up the volume on the computer. People settled back down. Jonathan didn't know if it had been intentional on Bryan's part, but he was glad the room's mood had been lightened.

Dan's cheeks had reddened. "Well, before we make any rash decisions, we'd need to know more about them. We don't want anyone leaving here to go into a dangerous situation."

Sara raised an eyebrow. "So you agree that it'd be a good idea to send some people out there to take a look?"

"I agree that it would be a good idea, but this isn't the best time for it."

"There's never gonna be a good time," Tyler said. "There's either the harvest, or the planting. Hunting and smoking the meat, weeding crops, repairing equipment, or winter storms making it unsafe. Something's always gonna need to be done. If we wait for the perfect time to go, we'll never go."

"Are you volunteering?" the synthesized voice from Jim's computer asked.

Tyler turned to Bill and Jane, who sat beside him. They met his eyes in turn, motionless except for Bill gently rocking Grayson in his arms. After a couple of seconds Tyler grimaced and dropped his gaze toward the floor. "No. I guess not."

"I'll go."

Jonathan turned to see Andrea Morfield standing in the back of the room.

Jim nodded. "We need another volunteer."

Jack Rockford stood. "I'll go."

Cynthia Jones stood as well, at almost the same time as Jack. "I'll go too."

Andrea locked eyes with her. "This isn't going to be a Girl Scout hike. There won't be much in the way of comforts."

Jonathan raised an eyebrow and turned toward the women. Dammit Andrea, not you too.

Several of the former Girl Scouts gave loud, disgusted snorts. Cynthia pressed her brows together and glared at Andrea, but her voice was even. "We lived off the land over winter in the hills before we hiked out the next spring. I know how to set snares, and I learned how to hunt with a home-made bow and arrow. Then we spent two years as slaves. Believe me, that wasn't comfortable. I think I can handle it."

"I've been working with her on target practice with the rifle." Tyler said. "She's pretty good."

"All right. Sorry." Andrea retook her seat.

Dan Kiner stood, frowning. "I still don't think this is a good time to do this."

Jim typed a bit, and his computer said, "Tyler has a point. There'll never be a perfect time."

Andrea said, "There and back to take a look should

only take about a week. Then, if necessary, we can go back with the bus."

Tyler turned in his seat to face Cynthia. "You can use my horse, and my saddle and saddle bags. I have a tent you can borrow too."

"Thank you."

"Wait a minute," Dan said. "We haven't voted on this yet, and you're acting like it's decided. Shouldn't we take a vote?"

Jim's keyboard clicked as he typed. "We have a quorum present.—Do you have a proposal to present?"

Dan pursed his lips. "I propose that we send a search party to this location after the harvest is in. Say, mid-October."

Andrea said, "I counter-propose that we send a party immediately, as soon as we can make preparations."

"We need seconds for these motions," Jim said through the computer. A confused period followed while people proposed seconds for the two issues. Finally the seconds were recorded and accepted. Jonathan tilted his face down to hide a smile. Not exactly according to *Robert's Rules of Order*, but it seemed to work.

Jim nodded. "All in favor of Dan's proposal, raise their hand."

Hands went up and George counted them. "Twenty-four."

"All in favor of Andrea's proposal raise their hand."

"Thirty-eight."

"Andrea's proposal passes.—Andrea, Jack, and Brenda, get together and plan—your expedition immediately.—To be consistent with your proposal—you should leave within the week,—but take due diligence to plan your trip."

Cynthia furrowed her brows and glanced at Brenda.

She met her gaze with furrowed brows as well.

"Brenda didn't volunteer to go, I did," Cynthia said.

Jim's keyboard clicked. "Sorry, I mis-spoke. Mis-typed. — Andrea, Jack, and Cynthia, I meant."

Andrea nodded and turned to Jack then to Cynthia. They both nodded to Andrea.

Jonathan tilted his head as he regarded Jim. That kind of error was out of character for him. He glanced toward Jamal. Jamal squinted at Jim, a frown on his lips.

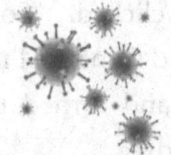

Chapter Fifty-Five

Setting Off

Sept. 4, 6:50 a.m.

A few days after the meeting, Bill stood next to Tyler, holding his hand by the stable just before sunrise. Andrea, Jack, and Cynthia made final adjustments on their saddle bags by the pre-dawn light as Tyler kept up a conversation with them. He worried about Tyler. He seemed far more concerned about the travelers than was reasonable. It had been nearly midnight when he and Jane managed to convince him to turn in, much later than was usual for him. Tyler had tossed and turned most of the night afterwards though, finally settling down some only when Jane threatened to banish him to the couch.

"Don't show yourselves until you're sure the situation is safe," Tyler said. "Then keep two of you out of sight, but watching, while one makes contact."

Andrea adjusted the position of the saddle bags on her horse, standing on a low stool so she could reach. "Thanks for your advice, but I'm sure we'll have to improvise when we get there anyway." She stepped down and moved the stool out of the way.

Jack tightened the main cinch strap on his saddle. "I

know why you're concerned, but no risk, no gain. We'll be careful."

"Tyler's right to be concerned," Cynthia said. "No offense, but you don't have the experience he and I had. We need to assume they're killers until we know otherwise."

"They'll be assuming the same thing about us, won't they?" Andrea asked.

Tyler nodded. "Exactly. Just like we treat visitors, till we know different."

Andrea lifted an eyebrow and gave a replying nod, then turned toward the glow over the eastern hills. "The sun'll be up any moment." Slipping a foot into the stirrup, she hopped onto her saddle with a fluid motion. "We ready?"

Jack checked the cinch strap again and mounted, and then Cynthia mounted as well.

"Let's do it," Cynthia said.

"Be careful," Brenda shouted as they spurred the horses toward the road. Dan and several of the others gathered to see them off echoed Brenda, waving.

"We will," Cynthia shouted back over her shoulder as she waved back. They urged the horses up to a trot, and in less than a minute they were around the bend in the road and out of sight.

Tyler stood watching the place where they'd disappeared for a few seconds, then he bent and touched the ground. Bill touched the Earth too. So did several others.

Standing up again, Bill put an arm around Tyler's shoulders. "Let's go back home. Jane's up by now and probably wants breakfast. I'll make us omelets."

Tyler turned to Bill and gave a nod. "Thanks." He looked back down the road.

"Ty, they'll be fine. You did good, helping Cynthia

improve her marksmanship. That'll help 'em a lot."

A tear trickled down Tyler's cheek. "I keep remembering when Jacob died. I heard his last breath come out and saw his eyes cloud over. And also when Herman shot Mary."

Bill knew that Tyler blamed himself for Mary's death, though he disagreed with him about that. This didn't seem the right time to argue that point, though. He gathered Tyler in his arms. Tyler laid his head on Bill's shoulder and silent tears dampened Bill's shirt. "They'll be fine," Bill said. He patted Tyler's back. "They had the best preparation possible, and you done great to help 'em get ready. Let it go for now."

Tyler nodded, his head still against Bill's shoulder. Working an arm loose, Tyler wiped his eyes with the back of his hand. Bill kissed his neck.

"You okay?" Bill asked.

Tyler lifted his head and gave a single brief nod. "Yeah."

They took hands and walked home.

* * *

Sept 5, 3:20 p.m.

Andrea shaded her eyes from the afternoon sun and peered down the road. She still found it odd that they could ride down the highway with no concern for automobile traffic. The sun came from the left as they went along a two lane highway to the north. Only occasional birdsongs broke the silence, aside from the clop of the horse's hooves on the pavement.

Cynthia dug out a bandana and wiped sweat from her face. "I thought it was supposed to be getting cooler, now that it's September."

Jack scratched his beard. "Make up your mind. Last

night you thought it was too cold."

"Whatever." Cynthia replaced her hat and stuffed the bandana back in her hip pocket. She guided her horse to the west side of the path to take advantage of the occasional shade from trees lining the road. The others followed her.

Andrea cocked an eyebrow. "Not comfortable?"

"I'm fine. I was just trying to make conversation."

Andrea shook her head. Cynthia was trying to get along after the rocky start they'd had in the meeting last week. Bad idea to sabotage that just for the brief pleasure of a snarky remark.

Andrea removed her hat and ran a bandana over her face and behind her neck, pulling her ponytail back into place afterward, replacing the hat. "It is pretty warm for September. Good idea, keeping to the shadier side of the road." She pulled out the map. "As far as I can tell, we've got about another five miles. The field Jonathan noticed is about six miles past Canfield Road. We passed that about ten minutes ago."

"We should get off the road soon, then, shouldn't we?" Jack asked.

"I think we've got a little while before we have to do that." She stuffed the map into her hip pocket and turned in her saddle to face Jack, who was just behind her. "In about another half hour we'll stop and draw lots to see who stays on the road, like we planned. That should put us a couple of miles before the settlement."

Jack shrugged. "A reasonable guess, but it's a guess. I think we should be more cautious. We don't really know where they are."

"Oh shit," Cynthia said. She reined her horse to a stop.

The other two turned to her and stopped too. Andrea looked forward and froze.

"We know where they are now," Cynthia said. She

nodded up the road as she raised her hands. A figure stood there with a rifle pointed toward them. A second one with a rifle or shotgun emerged from the brush by the road and stood near the first.

Jack and Andrea raised their hands too.

"What do we do now?" Cynthia asked.

Andrea cast a quick glance her way, then turned back to the ones ahead with guns pointed at them. Another one came up to the road and pointed a gun their way. "We improvise."

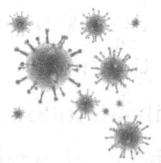

Chapter Fifty-Six

Captured

THEIR captors' youth shocked Andrea. The eldest couldn't have been more than seventeen. The one in charge had black hair and just a hint of darkening peach fuzz on his cheeks. His eyes, pinched into narrow slits, held a palpable intensity as he covered Andrea's group. The other two, a redheaded boy and a blond young woman, disarmed them and tied their hands behind their backs. The blond-haired woman also had an intense demeanor, though the redhead, who appeared a little younger than the other two, seemed nervous. His wide eyes darted this way and that, seemingly at random. Their clothing was salvaged from before the plague. They wore blue jeans that seemed more patch than original material. The redhead wore a cotton button-down shirt that at one time might have been worn by a banker or an accountant. Now stains mottled it between the patches, and mismatched buttons held it closed. Several sizes too big, it bloomed around him.

Andrea would have shaken her head, but she didn't want them to misinterpret the gesture. *They're still just children. Surely they could be reasoned with.* "Listen to me. We're—""Shut up," the black-haired one said. He waved his rifle toward her.

The red-haired boy picked up a game bag with at least one small kill in it, and the six of them continued along the road. The blond guided the horses and the black-haired boy led the way while the redhead followed behind. No one spoke.

After nearly an hour of walking they turned off the main road and followed a gravel driveway overgrown with weeds through a wooded lot. A sprawling brick ranch house stood at the end of the drive, concealed from the road by the trees and the curve of the driveway. Trees near the house had grown to shade the solar cells on the roof. A couple of barefoot children, maybe seven or eight years old, stared at them as they entered the yard, but they didn't approach.

The girl went to hitch the horses to a wooden rail fence and the two boys prodded the three of them into the garage, which stood open. The red-haired boy opened a door in the back to reveal stairs that ran down to darkness.

"Inside," the black-haired guy said.

Andrea took a deep breath. This looked bad. She had to do something to make these folks think of them as people, not just captives. She faced him. "I need to go to the bathroom."

"We'll get you a bucket." He waved his rifle toward the door. "Downstairs."

"How am I going to manage that with my hands tied behind my back?"

The boy grimaced and glanced at the red-haired one.

"Be reasonable," Andrea said. "You haven't given us a chance to explain ourselves. We mean you no harm."

Cynthia nodded. "You're not bad people. We understand you wanting to be cautious, but give us a chance."

The red-haired boy cleared his throat. "We could let 'em use the outhouse, couldn't we, Nate?"

A scowl covered Nate's face as he shot a glance at the other boy. After a second he said, "I guess. Okay. Cover 'em." He pointed to Andrea. "Come over here."

"I have to go too," Cynthia said.

"One at a time. The rest of you, downstairs."

Nate had just gotten Andrea untied when the blond-haired young woman entered the garage. As she came in she said, "I got the horses hitched—." Her eyes went wide when she saw Andrea untied and Nate standing behind her. "What the hell're you doing?" She shifted her grip on the rifle, not raising it, but getting ready to do so.

"I ain't doing nothing. She has to use the outhouse."

The young woman frowned. "I'll take her. Where are the others?"

Jerking a thumb at the door he said, "Downstairs. The other girl needs to go, too."

"Just wait here. Clara's on her way."

Nate's eyes went wide. "Oh, shit."

Andrea furrowed her brows. Who's Clara that Nate's so afraid of her?

The girl rolled her eyes. "Don't give me that, 'oh, shit' crap. You knew she'd be coming." She turned to Andrea and gestured with her rifle. "Let's get going, if you really need to take a piss, or whatever."

*　　*　　*

A women in her seventies stood in the garage questioning Nate when the blond-haired young woman led Cynthia back from the outhouse, having already taken Andrea. Cynthia regarded her with care, memorizing details, as they reentered the garage. She was a gnarled, white haired woman who leaned heavily on a walking stick made from a twisted branch. Her hair, set in a single braid, reached the middle of her back.

She looked Cynthia up and down as they approached. "She doesn't seem dangerous. What's your name? That's not necessary, Ellie," she said as the blond young woman began to retie Cynthia's hands. She turned back to Cynthia. "So what's your name? I'm Clara."

"Cynthia Jones, ma'am." She rubbed her wrists, first the left, then the right.

Clara glanced at the red marks circling Cynthia's wrists and scowled at Nate and Ellie. She turned back to Cynthia and nodded. "Manners. Good. Are the other two your mom and dad?"

Shaking her head, Cynthia said, "No ma'am. My mom and dad died in the plague. We're members of another village, come to make contact with you." She rubbed her wrists again. That had seemed to get a helpful reaction from Clara before. "We don't mean you any harm."

Clara's eyes narrowed. "Of course you don't." She turned to Ellie. "What'd you find in their bags?"

"Mostly camping stuff. A couple of tents, blankets and sleeping bags, some cooking pots, and so forth. Extra clothes. They all had rifles, and the other woman had a pistol. There was a box of about fifty cartridges in one of the saddle bags. There was also this." She pulled a folded sheet of paper from her back pocket and handed it to Clara.

Clara examined it and her eyebrows rose. She lifted her gaze back to Cynthia and turned the paper to her. "How'd you get this?"

"One of our village members can contact weather satellites. That's a picture he got a couple of weeks ago."

"It's got a map overlaid on the image, and our hay

field's marked on it. It was laser-printed. You have a working computer, then?"

"Yes ma'am. Quite a few, actually."

"How many are at this village?"

Cynthia raised an eyebrow of her own. "Members, ma'am?"

"Yes, members."

"I'm not sure. Around a hundred."

Clara tilted her head, regarding her through narrowed eyes. She was definitely the one in charge here. Cynthia held so still it hurt. Best not to act the least bit threatening.

After a moment Clara turned to Nate. "Bring the other two up. Put them all in separate rooms with guards outside. Don't let them talk to each other. And untie them, for God's sake."

"Yes ma'am."

"And you don't need to be so rough with visitors in the future, if they're not aggressive."

"Yes ma'am."

*   *   *

Ellie took Cynthia to a room with a twin bed, a desk, and a chair, and locked the door behind her. Cynthia scanned the room. The bed had been made up and covered with a red plaid blanket, but no bedspread.

At one time the room had been carpeted, but the carpet was gone, showing bare wafer-board flooring where it wasn't covered by oval throw rugs. A candle holder, empty save for some wax drippings on the pan, sat on the desk. She checked the desk drawers. Empty. The shelves mounted on the wall above the desk were also empty.

No curtains hung over the window. An iron grate,

mounted to the outside of the house covered the window and discouraged any thoughts of escape that way. She peered outside. The ground sloped down a hill behind the house, showing a fire ring surrounded by benches in the field below. The view extended clear to the western horizon.

Over the next couple of hours Clara questioned Cynthia several times for periods of a couple of minutes to nearly a quarter-hour per session. Then she would leave for long periods. Ellie stayed at the door outside nearly the whole time with her rifle at her side, except when Clara questioned Cynthia. Then she stood inside by the door with the rifle cradled in her arms. Ellie didn't respond to Cynthia's attempts at conversation through the door between Clara's visits other than to say, "shut up."

After a couple of hours a boy about eleven years old brought in a bowl of chicken and vegetable soup and a piece of corn bread. Ellie eyed the tray with a hungry expression as the boy set it on the desk. Cynthia met Ellie's eyes for a second. Ellie frowned and hurried the boy out of the room, closing the door behind herself with more of a slam than was necessary. Cynthia looked from the door down to the tray, and then back to the door. After a moment she decided she needed to be undistracted by hunger, so she sat to eat. Not chicken. Rabbit.

As she ate, voices from the other side of the door caught her ear. Someone had come to relieve Ellie. Good. Ellie had shown her at least a tiny bit of consideration in taking her and Andrea to the outhouse herself, instead of letting one of the males do it.

*　　*　　*

Orange-red sunbeams painted an image of the grate-covered

window on the wall opposite when Clara entered the room again, sometime well after dinner. She eased into the desk chair, supporting herself with the walking stick as she sat. She locked eyes with Cynthia. "Tell me about Herman."

A fever-hot flush rose to Cynthia's face. The image of him killing Mary flashed behind her eyes. She clenched her teeth and fists and sucked in a breath. "Herman Myers was a murderer and a rapist. He was the cruelest motherfucker I've ever known. I'll thank my friends Tiffany and Brenda with my dying breath for killing that monster."

Clara nodded. "That's enough. I can see you're telling the truth. Ellie, you can leave."

Doubt clouded Ellie's face and she raised her eyebrows, but after a brief hesitation, she left the room. The door remained open.

Clara turned back to Cynthia. "Okay, I believe you. Welcome to New Hope. I'm sorry we treated you this way, but we've learned to be cautious about visitors, since the raid we survived a couple of years ago."

Cynthia put her hands on her hips, her fists balled. "What was that question about Herman for?"

"Andrea told me about your experience. I wanted to be sure she wasn't just trying to get me sympathetic, or something." She shrugged. "Maybe I'm being too self-confident in my ability to judge character, but I don't think you could have faked that flush to your face if that was just a cover story designed to gain my confidence."

"Well, all right." Cynthia grimaced. She ran a hand over her brow. "After my experience, I can understand your wanting to be cautious. Our village suffered a raid too, last December, I guess. That was before I got there."

"Yes, Jack and Andrea told me about that. A minor

experience compared to what we had, with a much better outcome." Clara's eyes narrowed and the intensity of her gaze sent a shiver down Cynthia's spine. "We don't intend to get caught like that again."

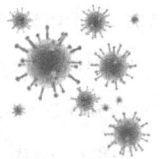

Chapter Fifty-Seven

Invitations

STARS appeared overhead through the gathering dusk, and light from a quarter moon filtered through the trees. Andrea, Jack, and Cynthia joined the community around a fire pit behind the house. A few other members walked up toward the fire pit from some small cabins under the trees downhill from the house as Andrea and her companions arrived. Clara waited until the stragglers made their way up the paths foot-worn through the tall grass on the slope.

Andrea surveyed the crowd and counted fourteen people in the group, some of them pre-adolescent. That included a few latecomers who ambled their way to the gathering. With the exception of Clara, none of them appeared to be more than twenty years old. The young children she'd seen when they first arrived weren't present.

As she scanned the people gathering, she caught one of them, a young lady of eighteen or so watching her intently. Her loose blond hair fell around her shoulders. As Andrea locked eyes with her, the young lady smiled. A tingle went down her spine and settled within her pelvis. Andrea found herself smiling. Couldn't help herself. She was cute. Maybe a little young, but cute. She tore her eyes away. Can't risk an entanglement here. Could torpedo the whole mission.

"The whole group is here, right?" Andrea asked as Clara led her, Jack, and Cynthia to seats by the fire.

"There are a couple of young kids already put to bed, and someone watching them, but otherwise, yes. Oh, and Nate's on watch in front of the house."

Andrea nodded. They're not much of a threat to the village, especially with Jonathan's security system in place.

Clara introduced the three of them to the village members and asked them to speak. Then she hobbled toward one of the nearby benches and eased herself onto it.

Andrea stood with her back to the fire, facing the group and launched into the speech she'd prepared. "We want to extend greetings to you from our village. We hope to have a productive relationship with you. I still don't know the extent or character of your settlement, so I apologize in advance if anything I say seems not relevant to your situation.

"I know how difficult it is to scrape out a living all alone. I applaud you for the job you've done with such a small group. It's a little easier for us, since we have about eighty people in our village. They range in age from babies a few months old to those of over sixty years. We have an established dairy and poultry farm, as well as vegetable plots and grain fields. A water reservoir on the hill above the village supplies running water for the village.

"It's about forty miles from here, and the roads are mostly good between us. Some trees down in a couple of places, but it shouldn't be too hard to clear a path through. We have a bus big enough to take you all and a truck that can carry belongings and supplies.

"But we don't intend to dictate what you do. That's up

to you to decide. In any case, we'd like to establish a cooperative relationship with your community, even if you prefer to remain separate. We feel that both of our communities will be stronger cooperating, whether we join together as a single community, or as cooperating separate communities."

The three of them answered questions about their village and the people there for nearly a half hour. Then one of them, a young man of at least eighteen years, asked, "How do you decide on work assignments for your members?"

Andrea nodded. "Good question. We try to place people in jobs that match any particular skills or interests they have as much as possible. Of course, we all pitch in with the farm work, especially for the planting and the harvest. For the younger kids, they help with farm chores some too, but we also have a school set up where—"

"No! I don't wanna go to school!" A youngster of about eleven had jumped to his feet, fists balled at his side. A young woman beside him, who wasn't old enough to be his mother, stood as well and shushed him.

Andrea chuckled. "School's not so bad. There's a couple of other boys there about your age."

"I didn't like school much at your age either," Jack said, smiling.

"No! I won't go. You can't make me!" He buried his face in the woman's chest and held her tight around the waist.

Andrea furrowed her brows. That was a pretty extreme reaction.

"Enough on that subject," Clara said.

"Okay, but we think education remains—"

"Enough."

The young woman led the boy toward the cabins. The

rest of them seemed subdued now. Andrea scanned the group seated in front of the fire. No smiles, no frowns, just blank masks. What the hell just happened? She'd hit some kind of nerve. "Well—uh—are there any other questions?"

Only crickets and an owl answered. Just a minute ago the questions had been coming fast and free. At length Clara stood and approached them, taking careful steps in the darkness, leaning on her walking stick as she came. "Thank you for sharing this information with us, and for extending your invitation. We'll discuss this among ourselves later. You're welcome to sleep in the house tonight or to set up camp in the yard."

Andrea glanced at Jack, then at Cynthia. "If it's okay with the others, I suggest we accept your offer of hospitality." Excruciating formality seemed safe for the moment.

Clara nodded, then turned toward the crowd of young people gathered. "This meeting is finished." She raised her arms, stretching them wide above her, still holding the walking stick. "Good night everyone. Be well, and be blessed."

"Be well, and be blessed," the group repeated in chorus. Andrea joined in too, tripping over the first couple of words. The young lady Andrea had noticed earlier turned to her and locked eyes for a second. She gave a tentative smile, then turned back and followed the others as they went to the cabins. Clara lowered her arms. Andrea bent and touched the ground, and Jack and Cynthia followed her example a second later.

Clara tilted her head, watching them, but made no comment on the gesture. "I'll show you where the candles are. We can offer you bread and fruit for breakfast in the morning."

They followed Clara as she made her way to the back door of the house. Upon opening the door she shouted, "Nate, it's Clara. I'm coming in the back." She motioned with her free arm toward the other three. "Come on inside."

As Clara led them into the house, Nate appeared from inside with a candle in a brass holder. He carried a rifle in his other hand.

The room had been the kitchen, but Andrea didn't think it had been used that way for a long time. The space for a range stood empty with the gas supply hose lying on the floor. Clara opened a cupboard above the counter and gave each of them a candle. They lit them from the one Nate carried.

"Nate will be on guard duty until midnight," Clara said. "Ellie will relieve him at that point."

Cynthia scowled. "He's going to be here while we're asleep? Pardon my unease, but this is the guy who was going to have Andrea piss in a bucket with her hands tied behind her back."

Andrea lifted an eyebrow. The girl had spunk.

Clara glowered at Nate.

"I wasn't thinking at the time, 'cept about security," Nate said. "I agreed to untie 'em so they could use the outhouse when they objected."

"I'm still sort of uncomfortable about this," Cynthia said. "When do we get our guns back?"

Clara faced Nate and nodded toward the door to the garage. "Get them."

Nate pursed his lips. "Yes ma'am." He went out the door.

"I have a question," Jack said. "Why is there such a gap in ages here? Aside from you, the oldest one here seems to be twenty or less."

"Nineteen." Clara shook her head. "I don't want to get into that now. I'll explain in the morning."

The door to the garage swung open and Nate re-entered carrying a black canvas duffle bag. He eased it onto the table and zipped it open. Their rifles lay inside, along with their box of cartridges, Andrea's pistol, and their pocket knives. Andrea took her rifle and inspected it. The safety was on, and it was still loaded. She handed the other two rifles to Cynthia and Jack, and then pulled her pistol from the bag.

"Thanks," Jack said. "If you don't mind, I have a suggestion. Let us take shifts keeping watch along with Nate and Ellie tonight."

Nate's eyebrows lifted. "Don't trust me?"

Jack returned his knife to his pocket. "You earn trust, and apparently you don't trust us."

Nate glared at him.

"Nate, this is the reason you need to be more courteous with visitors," Clara said. "I appreciate that you wanted to keep us all safe, but there was no reason to tie them up if they were cooperating and you had their weapons. And suggesting they had to use a toilet bucket with their hands tied was just offensive." She turned to Jack. "Thank you for your offer. We'll take you up on that."

Nate's eyes went wide. "Ma'am!"

Clara faced Nate again, her eyebrows pressed together. She shot him a glacial stare. "What?"

It was as if Clara's glare had punctured Nate and deflated him. His shoulders slumped. "Nothing, ma'am."

There it was again. Nate was totally cowed.

"I'll take the first shift with Nate," Jack said.

"I'll take the next," Cynthia said.

Clara nodded. "There are privacy locks on the bedroom doors, but of course, it wouldn't take much of a kick to break them open if necessary. Hope you sleep well. Good night."

Andrea lifted her brows. There's a thought that'll

assure a good night's rest. Clara left by the back door.

Jack checked his rifle. He closed the chamber and nodded. "Well Nate, why don't you show me around the checkpoints?"

the next morning Clara ran to the back door. Jack did not hesitate. He fired the charges, and said he'd "Well, anyway, don't you see, no one attend the operator."

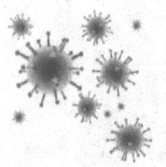

Chapter Fifty-Eight

Explanations

Sept 6, 8:00 a.m.

THE next morning Andrea opened the door to the house at Clara's knock while the sun hovered low and red in the east. She and a brown-haired boy of twelve or thirteen entered, him carrying a basket of apples and pears, and a loaf of bread wrapped in a towel under his arm. He lacked shoes, but his face and hands were freshly scrubbed. At Clara's word he set the basket and the bread on the table in the dining room. Andrea had been up with Arthur, the third shift sentry, since 4:00 a.m. Jack already stood in the door to his room, rubbing his eyes, when Andrea knocked on Cynthia's door to wake her.

Clara settled into a chair at the dining room table while they waited for Cynthia. "Sorry. We don't have any coffee."

"We're out too," Jack said. "I used to love my espresso, but that's a thing of the past."

"It was cappuccino for me," Andrea said as she took an apple. She sighed. "With cinnamon. And a bagel with cream cheese, sitting in the kitchen with Cassie, golden sunlight pouring through the patio doors."

She shook her head to banish the memory and bit into her apple. "Cinnamon trees don't live around here, but we still have a small supply of ground cinnamon back home." She snorted a quick laugh. "'Back home.' That might be the first time I've used that expression to mean our village, rather than my house in Charlotte." She took another bite.

"I had a grandson who lived in Charlotte," Clara said. She gave her head a rueful shake. "I guess he's dead now."

Andrea swallowed. "Charlotte's all burned down, from what I've heard."

Clara cocked an eyebrow. "Heard from whom?"

"Last fall a guy stopped by who'd been driving around the country for a while after the plague ended. There was an entry in his journal about seeing the ruins of Charlotte."

"In his journal?"

"He didn't survive his quarantine period," Jack said, "but he didn't die of the plague. He died of radiation poisoning." He gave her a brief overview of what they'd learned about the dirty bomb attack on the east coast.

Cynthia stumbled in, yawning, as he finished. "Sorry to be a slug-a-bed. I had trouble getting back to sleep after my shift on guard duty." She took a pear and bit into it. "These are really good. Thanks."

The boy brought a knife from the kitchen and Clara cut the bread. The dense, brown loaf still held some of the oven's warmth.

Andrea gave a nod. Someone had to be up at oh-dark-thirty to bake bread. They had a strong sense of commitment to group cooperation here. She glanced up at the overhead light fixture attached to an old ceiling fan. No bulbs. They didn't have electricity, so there must be wood-fired ovens somewhere, and they baked by candlelight.

They didn't speak as they ate breakfast.

Finally Clara wiped her hands on her pants. "Well, I promised some explanations, so let's do it." She pulled herself out of her seat. "You can leave, Bobby. Go see if your sister needs help."

Bobby nodded and left by the back door. The screen door slammed on its spring behind him.

*　　*　　*

Clara led them down a gravel path away from the house through a wooded area leading away from the small cabins where the others lived. Dew still covered the grass, and gravel crunched beneath their boots.

Andrea stepped up beside Clara. "So what's the reason for the gap in ages here?"

Clara shook her head. "Wait."

Andrea furrowed her brows. Why the suspense?

Coming around a stand of white pines, they faced a burned out building. Clara didn't approach it, but leaned on her walking stick, gripping it with both hands near the top. "We used to use this building as a meeting room and as the school. Not quite two years ago someone set fire to it while the kids were inside for lessons. As the kids and the teachers fled the building, raiders shot the adults."

Andrea shared a glance with Jack, eyebrows raised. The Tollivers. Should she mention it to Clara? How would she react? Happy that they're dead, upset that they saved the two children? Better to keep quiet about it for now.

"One of the older kids, too," Clara continued, "who was tall for his age. Others heard the shots and saw the smoke and came running to help. They got shot, too." Clara pointed to some boulders on a rise overlooking the building's remains. "The raiders took cover in those rocks up there." She sighed. "At least they spared the children. All for ten or twelve chickens they stole from the henhouse, some potatoes, carrots, and some bags of beans and dried fruit." She shook her head. "I'd broken my leg a week before and was bedridden in my cabin at the time. I waited there for more than a day before one of the kids found me. All the other adults were dead."

Jack bent and touched the ground, followed closely by Andrea and Cynthia. Clara watched them and her eyes narrowed. "I'm not sure what you mean by doing that, but I'll assume it's a respectful gesture."

"Yes ma'am," Andrea said. "It's an acknowledgment of our connection to the Earth. I do it as a reaction to a moving experience, either happy or sad."

Clara nodded. "Fair enough." She pointed with her walking stick. "This way."

They skirted the clearing around the burned out building and soon came upon an area surrounded by a wattle fence. Clara pulled an aster flower head off its stem as she approached the fence. She didn't go inside, but stuck the stem of the flower cluster between a couple of the branches that comprised the structure. She pointed toward the interior.

"This is where we—that is, where the children—buried their parents. I wasn't able to help. The oldest of them was only seventeen." She gazed inside, then lowered her eyes. "My son and my daughter-in-law are buried here." She turned back to them. "Gary—the boy who protested about going to school last night—Gary's mom was the main teacher at the school. He saw her gunned down right in front of him. He was only nine then. He insisted he wanted to dig his parents' graves, but he was too little to do it. Arthur did most of the digging for him, after he'd buried his own parents and grandfather."

The three of them touched the Earth again.

"Thank you." Clara pointed with her stick again. "This way."

She led them to a clearing nearby with several benches set within it. The grass had been cut and the last drying stalks of some black-eyed susans stood bordering the clearing between the benches and along the path to it. Clara took a seat on one of the benches that faced another one nearby. Andrea sat beside her, and Jack and Cynthia took the other bench.

Clara made an all-encompassing sweep of her arm. "Some of the kids set up this little park the spring following the raid. It's near the burial plot but not actually in sight of it. I've found it to be a quiet place to meditate." She chuckled. "At first they tried to keep it a secret from me, like they thought I'd be angry, I don't know, for taking time from chores to work on it, I guess. I was still limping pretty bad at that point. Nate was quite surprised when I approved." She turned her face toward the ground and sighed, then looked back up. "Well, I'm sure you have questions."

Andrea opened her mouth to speak, but Cynthia beat her to it. "How'd you escape the plague?"

"We were trying to be Back-to-Nature activists." She shrugged. "Hobbyists I guess I'd say, now that I've seen what that really means. A group of us went together to buy a few hundred acres in the hills and we were trying to homestead there, trying to be totally self-sufficient." She snorted a humorless laugh. "Except that we continually had to consult the internet for advice on building shelter, growing food, hunting game, and purifying water. Then the plague hit and we hunkered down to keep out of view of any of the people fleeing the cities."

"How'd you know the plague was over?" Andrea asked. "When we met your welcoming party yesterday, they weren't worried about the plague at all."

Clara grimaced. "One of our members was a retired research virologist. He told us, after the government fell and there was no more need for secrecy, that his real job had been working for an Army lab developing biological weapons and defenses for them. The plague had all the characteristics of a project at his lab, the reason he took an early retirement, as a matter of fact. Couldn't face the implications of his work anymore. He said it had to keep spreading or it would die out as soon as there were too few hosts. Just before the raid, a year ago last January, he said there was no real chance that any plague virus was left."

"This place doesn't look like a homestead in the hills," Jack said.

"We left the settlement the following spring, once the internet and the cell system failed, and resettled here. Subsistence crops didn't grow well in the rocky soil in the hills. We buried the two bodies we found in the house in what became our cemetery back there."

"You said you were going to discuss your response to our proposals with the others later on," Andrea said. "When is that going to happen?"

"We'll meet after lunch."

"Do you want us there?"

Clara shook her head. "I specifically don't want you there, at least not at the start. We'll send someone for you if we want you to attend later. You can wait in the house or in the front yard. Just be close, and be sure we can find you."

"I guess we should have asked this sooner, but I assume someone's taking care of our horses, right?" Cynthia asked.

Andrea rolled her eyes. Right. She couldn't believe she hadn't thought of that before.

Clara nodded, and pointed northward with her stick. "There's a barn where we've set up some stables up the road that way. Randy's good with horses, and he should be there now. You're free to go up there and check if you like."

Cynthia nodded.

After a few seconds with no further questions, Clara said, "If you have no other questions, I'll leave you for now. You're welcome to look around, but be sure to make yourselves available around noon. There'll be bread and vegetable stew for lunch. You're welcome to join us for that by the house. Don't stick around by the fire pit after lunch, though, unless we call for you. You'll know when it's time for lunch, 'cause we'll ring a bell to gather people."

"Will we need an escort to look around?" Jack asked. "I don't want to surprise anyone who's over-concerned about security while we're wandering around your settlement."

"You got introduced to everyone at the meeting last night except for Julia. She was watching the youngsters. Julia's been informed you're okay. Still, I wouldn't sneak up on anyone."

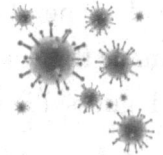

Chapter Fifty-Nine

Downhill

Sept. 6, 6:30 a.m.

JAMAL knocked on Jim's bedroom door and brought in a tray of breakfast without waiting for a reply. Jim sat in the wheelchair by the bed with a book open in his lap. The sun had not yet risen, but blue sky showed through the window.

"Good morning, Jim. Got to the chair yourself, I see. Good." Jamal latched the tray onto the brackets molded into the chair's arms. Jim's breath came in labored wheezes, but he waved an acknowledgement of Jamal's greeting as he set the book on the bed. Jamal picked up his own mug of tea from the tray, and sat in the desk chair.

"How are you feeling today?"

Jim shrugged and held up his right hand in an "Okay" gesture. He stared at the tray and grimaced. Jamal followed his gaze. The scrambled eggs glowed yellow from all the turmeric Jamal had added, and the odor of garlic filled the air. Jim shrugged again and took a bite, lifting the fork to his mouth with a shaky hand.

Jamal sipped some mint tea. "I'm going to check on

Janet Haskel later this morning. Do you want me to get someone to stay with you while I go over?"

Jim shook his head as he chewed an apple slice. He pointed to his chest and made the "okay" sign again.

"All right, well, I guess I'll clean up after breakfast, then."

Jim held up a hand and pantomimed writing. Jamal took a pad of paper and a pencil from the top of the dresser and handed them to him. Jamal had gotten used to reading Jim's shaky scrawl. Jim wrote, "Are Andrea, Jack, and Brenda back yet?"

"No. There hasn't been enough time. And it was Cynthia who went, not Brenda."

Jim furrowed his brows. "What's today?" he wrote.

"September 6th."

Jim's eyebrows lifted, "Thought it was later."

"You mean that you thought the date was later in September than the 6th?" Jamal asked.

Jim nodded.

"They've only been gone two days. Just starting the third day." Jamal furrowed his brows. Jim didn't usually lose track of time. Never that he could recall, in fact.

Jim shrugged, then nodded.

"You must be thinking back from when we had the meeting, or something."

Jim shrugged again and ate another forkful of eggs.

*   *   *

Before going to Janet's house Jamal stopped at the Kiners'. He could have just called Dan on the radio, but he wanted to do this face to face. Gloria and the children had already left for school, but Dan knelt in the vegetable patch, weeding. Jamal noticed him there as he came up the street and cut through the side yard to meet him. Dan stood and shook the dirt off the roots of a plant he'd just pulled and threw it onto a pile of weeds by the edge of the garden. He wiped his hands on his trousers as Jamal approached.

Before Dan spoke a greeting, Jamal asked, "Do you remember last winter when Jim told us his wishes if the cancer spreads to his brain?"

Dan's expression froze, then he blinked. "Yes?" He drew out the word, locking eyes with Jamal.

Jamal grimaced. "Jim's not that bad yet, and I hope I'm imagining things, but he's confused about the date and about who went on the search expedition recently."

"So what do you want to do?"

"Nothing, yet. Just keep an eye on things. I thought you should be aware, though. So you can watch for signs, too."

Dan sighed. "Okay. Thanks, I guess."

"Sorry to ruin your morning."

Dan shook his head and gave a dismissive wave. "I needed to know. You were right to tell me. You going to tell Allen and George, too?"

"Yeah, I will. I have to see Janet right now, though. I'll head out to the farm later."

"You want me to do it? I can get away long enough to take care of that."

Jamal shook his head. "I think I should talk to them myself." His head bowed for a moment, as if contemplating Dan's garden plot, then he lifted his gaze back toward Dan and grimaced. "We need to think about succession. I mean, seriously do something about succession. You've done a good job of filling in, but people still expect Jim to decide things, even if he makes them think they came up with the decision themselves."

Dan returned Jamal's grimace. "I've never liked being a manager. I can do it, but I hate it, listening to complaints, telling people what should have been obvious, that sort of thing."

"Somebody has to. What about Gloria or Allen? Or Andrea?"

"Janet would never accept Allen, and a lot of people respect her opinion. Gloria, maybe, but I don't think she wants that job either. Andrea's an interesting possibility. Have to think about that."

"She's done a great job managing the stables, and everyone likes her. She seems to have good judgment in general. I think Andrea could be good in that role."

Dan nodded. "Yeah. Could be. Should we have an election?"

Jamal's eyebrows shot up. "And split the community in half?" He shook his head. "Only as a last resort."

"Yeah, I see that. Maybe we could get a meeting together with some of the main prospects after the equinox and go over the possibilities. Sort of an executive session."

Jamal nodded. "Sounds like a plan."

"Okay, well, keep me informed."

"Of course." Jamal turned to go, then stopped and pivoted around to Dan. "Uh, we should probably keep the situation with Jim confidential for now, okay? I mean, it's privileged medical information, after all."

"Is that really important anymore?" Dan asked. "We're so tight-knit now, it's all common knowledge anyway."

Jamal squeezed his eyes shut tight for a second, then

opened them and locked his gaze on Dan. "We're not lawless, uncivilized barbarians. The rule of law and respect for privacy still mean something, and I'm not going to let that small bit of civilization lapse."

Dan raised his brows and nodded. "Okay. Point taken."

*   *   *

Ten minutes later Jamal reached Janet Haskel's house, and Bob answered his knock.

Jamal stepped in and shook Bob's hand. "How's Janet doing?"

Bob lowered his gaze. "I'll let you assess that. You're the expert."

Laying a giant hand on Bob's shoulder with a feather touch, Jamal said, "Bob, you know my limitations. I depend on your observations as much—no—*more* than my own. I only want to help her."

Bob met Jamal's gaze for a moment, then dropped his eyes toward the floor again. "I guess we have that goal in common, then." He heaved a sigh and his eyes met Jamal's. "She's no better. In pain all the time, irritable and moody, and I'm not sure the cannabis is helping any more. She seems obsessed more and more with Allen. She's even speculated that he's planning human sacrifices. I know she's said that to some others, too, not just me. She was never like that before."

Jamal lifted his eyebrows, but he didn't interrupt Bob.

"A couple of times I've caught her talking to herself, but she said she was just thinking out loud. She never does it when she knows I'm watching her." He scratched his beard. "I'm really getting frightened for her. Right now she's in the study."

Jamal nodded. He knew the way.

The door stood cracked open already. Janet looked up from a pair of trousers with a half sewn-on patch on the knee when Jamal knocked on the door frame. She set them aside on the back corner of the desk and laid a pair of scissors by the front. A teacup half-full with a milky, pale green liquid sat on the desk beside the computer keyboard.

"Good morning, Janet. Don't get up," Jamal said as she started to rise from the desk chair. "How are you feeling today?"

Janet glanced at an empty chair beside her desk for a second. "About the same." She sipped from the teacup.

"Is the cannabis helping?"

"A little. It still hurts, but the pain's more bearable with the marijuana." She gave her head a single, quick shake. "Makes it hard to concentrate, though."

Jamal nodded. "I know. May I do a quick examination?"

Janet stole a glance at the empty chair for a split second, then faced him again. "Okay. Bob, would you excuse us, please?"

"Um—okay, sure. I'll wait in the living room." He closed the door behind himself.

Jamal did a basic neurological and physical exam and noted that her pulse was a little rapid, but there were no other obvious signs. Her eyes were red, but he expected that.

"I'm sorry, Janet, but I still can't identify why you're having these headaches. Any other symptoms? Visual effects, like flashing lights, halos, or spots?"

"No."

"How about hallucinations?"

Janet's eyes flickered to the empty chair, then she met Jamal's gaze again. "No."

An obvious falsehood, but why? Jamal furrowed his

brows. What was she hiding? Who or what did she see in the chair? "Okay. Anything else you think I should know about?"

She shook her head. "I guess I'll just have to deal with the pain. I appreciate what you've done. Don't beat yourself up about it."

Jamal sighed. He couldn't force her to confide her condition if she didn't want to. "Well, okay. I need to go see Allen, so I guess I'll get on my way."

Janet's eyes went wide. She looked toward the chair and said, "What?" Then a second later she nodded.

As Jamal turned to leave he caught her movement from the corner of his eye—the shears from the desk in her hand, raising them like a knife. Old army combat training kicked in and his arm went up to block hers before he knew what he was doing. "What the hell—"

Janet spun around in the desk chair, then stood and pivoted toward him, still holding the scissors.

He grabbed her wrists. "Janet, put that down! What are you doing?"

The door to the study flew open and Bob barged in. "What's happening?"

"I've got to stop Allen!" Janet said through tears streaming down her face. "Jamal's in league with Allen. With the devil!"

Jamal squeezed the wrist holding the scissors. Janet cried out and dropped the shears, and he kicked them out of reach.

Janet's knees buckled and she fell, kneeling to the floor, with Jamal holding her up, arms over her head. Bob knelt to her and Jamal released her wrists. Janet collapsed in a pile.

"I was just about to leave and all of the sudden she attacked," Jamal said.

Bob wrapped his arms around Janet, oblivious to Jamal.

"It's okay, Honey. Everything's going to be okay." He pressed his face to her hair. Janet sobbed unresponsive on the carpet.

Jamal staggered to the doorway and leaned against the jamb. His heart thundered in his chest. He wiped sweat from his face with a trembling hand. Being cautious, he leaned toward Janet and laid a hand on her shoulder. "Janet—"

She didn't respond.

He gave her shoulder a gentle shake. "Janet, look at me."

No response. Janet was obviously sicker than he'd realized. A brain tumor? Deepening stress-induced psychosis? It didn't really matter. He couldn't treat either one.

Jamal straightened and tapped Bob on the shoulder. "Bob, we've got to deal with this. She's either going to hurt someone, or else herself. This is serious." He pulled out his radio and pinged Dan's channel.

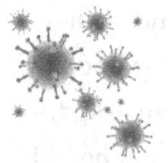

Chapter Sixty

Ambassadors

Sept 6, 1:30 p.m.

JACK, Cynthia, and Andrea sat in the shade of a maple tree on benches that Nate and Arthur had pulled in front of the brick ranch. The meeting for the New Hope residents had started a half-hour earlier, and the three of them had remained quiet as they waited. Birdsong and leaves rustling above them filled the air otherwise.

Andrea's thoughts wove though dozens of scenarios, from ones reasonable to those wildly unlikely. Would the New Hope members go or stay? Would they try anything violent? Andrea shook her head. Clara was without question an authoritarian, but she didn't seem like an outlaw. The grip she had on this group probably was rooted in her being the only adult left after the kids seeing their parents' violent murders shocked them, leaving them unprepared, and perhaps unwilling, to continue. She wanted to protect them, that was clear, but the level of her grip on them still seemed strange. Nate's fear of her didn't seem to fit. Was that due to Clara's

340 | The Great Disruption

actions, or to Nate's psychological trauma? Some of both?

Sitting beside her, Cynthia seemed lost in thought. She was staring at the ground at her feet, idly pushing a pebble around with the toe of her boot. "Cynthia, what do you think about this group?" Andrea asked.

Cynthia looked up at her. "Huh? What do you mean?"

"These people have been through a severe mental shock and are trying to live through it, similar to what you and your friends did. What's your impression?"

"We've all been through a severe mental shock," Jack said. "They have no exclusive on that."

Andrea nodded. "True. But these people and the Girl Scouts both are able to put faces on the perpetrators. That makes them different from you and me."

"It's still different," Cynthia said. "We had people who abused us physically and mentally every day. These folks had a sudden shock, and then the 'perpetrators' were gone." She made air-quotes.

"Still, I'd like to hear your impression."

Cynthia remained silent for a few seconds, then she shook her head. "I still don't think our experiences are comparable. One thing that seems odd to me, though, is the amount of control Clara has over these people."

Andrea nodded. Bingo.

"What do you mean?" Jack asked.

"You were in the basement at the time," Cynthia said, "but when Ellie brought me back from the outhouse when we first got here, Nate acted—well—he acted scared of her."

Andrea nodded. "Yeah, I noticed Nate's reaction too. When Ellie told Nate that Clara was coming, his comment was, 'Oh shit.'"

"That does seem like more than just respect for her

age," Jack said.

"I'm not sure how much we can make of that," Andrea said. "She was the only adult authority figure left after the Tollivers' attack, after all."

Cynthia gave a quick shake of her head. "Still, it seems strange. Look, I'm about the same age as the oldest of these people, and folks my age rebelling against authority is so typical it's a cliché."

"When you were camping over the winter, before you went to the B&B, how did you treat the adult leaders who were with you?" Andrea asked.

"Well, we all had to work together to survive. Mrs. Cohen was knowledgeable and experienced about wilderness survival and hunting, so of course we respected her."

"I suspect the situation's similar for this group," Andrea said. "Clara probably has a lot of knowledge of farming and such, and as the sole authority figure, they defer to her."

Cynthia nodded. "Maybe."

The screen door slammed on the house, catching their attention. Ellie approached them, frowning. "Clara wants you to join us now."

* * *

The rest of the New Hope members watched in silence as the three of them approached. Clara directed them to a bench across the fire ring from the rest of the group. Andrea sat in the middle, flanked by Cynthia and Jack. The intensity of the glares the New Hope residents fixed upon them set Andrea's teeth on edge. They were upset about something.

"We've decided that Arthur will go back with you and

look over your village," Clara said.

Arthur, a tall, broad-shouldered young man with a sparse beard gave a single nod, solemn-faced.

"He'll come back and tell us what he's seen in a week or so, and then we'll make a final decision about joining with you," Clara continued.

"That's fine," Andrea said.

Clara held up a hand. "But we have a condition."

Jack's eyebrows lifted. "Oh? What condition?"

"We want one of you to remain here during that time."

Andrea and Jack locked eyes, then they glanced at Cynthia. Her eyes had gone wide.

Andrea tilted her head toward Clara, eyes narrowed. "A hostage?"

"Not at all. Think of it as an exchange of ambassadors."

Andrea frowned. "Which one of us do you want to remain behind?"

"You can make that decision yourselves. Keep in mind that we'll expect whoever stays to participate fully with us. We don't have the resources to entertain guests long term. The one who stays will need to work with the rest of us to put up the harvest and help with other chores."

Andrea squinted past the fire across the circle to Arthur. He met her gaze, then the young woman sitting beside him took his hand and said something to him. He replied and kissed her forehead. She wiped her eyes.

Andrea focused more closely on her. She was pregnant. Maybe. Yes. A rounded belly contrasted with an otherwise slender frame. Maybe four or five months along.

Andrea turned back toward Clara. "What if we don't agree?"

"Then we'll send you on your way." Her eyes

narrowed and a new shiver rattled Andrea. "We really hope you'll decide to go along, though."

"I think we need to talk this—"

"I'll stay behind," Cynthia blurted.

Andrea eased a smile and turned to her. "That's fine, Cynthia, but we should take a few minutes and talk this through. I'm sure we can come to an agreement. Clara, would you give us some time?"

Clara nodded. "Of course. Is an hour enough?"

Andrea nodded.

"We'll meet back here in an hour. You'll hear the bell." Clara lifted her arms. "The meeting is over for now." The people got up and drifted away. Arthur's girlfriend/partner/wife shot them a glare before she headed off, Arthur at her side holding her hand.

*　　*　　*

Cynthia sat on a bench by the fire pit facing her two companions, her hands folded in her lap. Her gaze shifted between Andrea and Jack, and back again. She scowled. They were going to try to protect her and end up putting the village at risk instead. "There's nothing to discuss. I'm just a garden grubber. I'm the most expendable. It's gotta be me, or we make too big an impact on our village. Or we lose the opportunity."

Jack scowled. "People aren't expendable."

Cynthia grimaced and heaved a sigh. "Andrea, you manage the stables, and Jack is Allen's right-hand man at the farm. They had to get two people to cover for him when we left. I'm the logical one to stay behind, and that's that."

Jack shook his head. "No offense, and I appreciate your experience, but I'm just physically stronger than either you or

Andrea. I'd be safer here."

Cynthia rolled her eyes. "Oh, please. Spare me the macho chest-puffing. There's enough of them to easily overpower you if they want to."

"I'm less likely to get raped."

The memory of Herman tying her to the bed flashed into her brain. She clenched her teeth, and heat rose to her face. She thrust the image away and glared at Jack. "That's a damn cheap shot."

"Sorry."

"If they had rape on their minds, they've had plenty of opportunities since they captured us," Cynthia said. "Clara's a controlling bitch, but I don't see her tolerating rape. Quite the contrary."

Andrea looked over to Jack and frowned. "I hate to admit it, but from a logical viewpoint, she's right. Not that I particularly like it either."

Cynthia shook her head. "Don't you go all mother-hen on me. I can take care of myself." She hoped.

"I don't like the whole idea that they're forcing one of us to stay behind in the first place," Jack turned his head and spat on the ground. "'Ambassador,' hell. It's a hostage."

"I agree," Cynthia said, "but I can also understand them being over-careful, given their history."

"Well, I guess we'd have a hostage ourselves," Andrea said, "one they probably have a strong incentive to get back."

"What makes you say that?" Jack asked.

"You didn't notice that the young lady who was seated by him is pregnant? Or the glare she gave us as she and Arthur left? She, at least, isn't happy with him going, and I assume she wants him back safe and sound, and as quickly as possible."

"Since we're on this topic now, I assume that means I'm

staying, right?" Cynthia asked.

Jack frowned, but before he got a word out, Andrea said, "That makes the most sense, yes." She sighed. "I don't like it, though."

"I still think I'd be the better one to stay," Jack said.

"Cynthia's right. Did you see the look on Allen's face when you volunteered? Even with two people to replace you, he's got to train them before they're useful."

"I don't understand why Arthur's going in the first place, if his wife's pregnant," Jack said. "I'd think he'd want to stay with her."

Andrea shrugged. "I couldn't say, but I don't think he's happy about going either. I'm not sure that he volunteered, so much as he 'was volunteered.'" She made air quotes.

Jack tilted his head. "Huh?"

"He appears to the oldest and physically strongest of the young people here. They probably thought he'd be the safest in this mission. My guess is, Clara decided that he was the one who should go."

Jack rubbed his chin. "It occurs to me that not only do they have an incentive to want him back, but that he himself will have a strong incentive to return too, if his wife's pregnant."

Andrea nodded.

"What about Tyler's horse?" Cynthia asked.

They turned to her. Andrea cocked an eyebrow. "What?"

Cynthia waved. "Hey, I'm still here. We're discussing the fact that I'm staying here as the hostage, remember? So does Arthur take Tyler's horse back, or does he use his own horse?"

Jack frowned. "I didn't think we'd decided that you're

staying."

Cynthia huffed out a sigh. "Oh, for God's sake."

Andrea sat up straight and ran her fingers through her hair. "Jack, she's right, and no, I don't like it either."

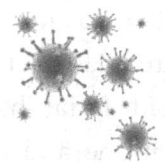

Chapter Sixty-One

Homecoming

Sept. 10, 1:45 p.m.

JONATHAN flipped slices of apples with a spatula on trays laid out in the sun before him, then re-covered them with a piece of cheesecloth as he finished each tray. The trays rested in rows on a line of tables in the clearing by the orchard as he and Ron Culbertson tended them. While Jonathan pulled the cheesecloth from the next tray, his earpiece chimed.

"Yes, Paladin, what is it?"

"Security monitor alert: Three individuals are approaching from the north on horseback. At least two of them have firearms in saddle holsters."

Jonathan gasped, then he remembered that the search party was due back by this point. "Good. Andrea's expedition has returned, then."

"I'm afraid not. Two of the intruders are male, and one of the horses is a dappled gray. That doesn't match the profile of Andrea's group."

A chill shot down Jonathan's spine. "Notify Dan Kiner and George Hardy. Tell them in the first sentence that it's not

Andrea's group." He pulled out his smartphone.

"Messages sent. Awaiting acknowledgement."

"Stream the video to my phone." A hazy, heat shimmered image appeared. He couldn't make out details, but two of them clearly had facial hair, and the gray horse contrasted beside a black one and a chestnut one. Andrea's group had two black horses.

"Important call?" Ron asked.

Jonathan flicked his eyes at him. Ron's smile wavered. Jonathan returned his gaze to the phone. "Yes."

His earpiece chimed again. "Dan Kiner acknowledged the call," his computer said. "He's on the way in the truck with Tyler Hopson."

Ron came up behind Jonathan. "That looks like Andrea," he said, pointing to the screen.

Jonathan spared him a glance, then fixed his attention back at the screen. "How can you tell that?"

"Can't be sure, but she's short like Andrea, has the right hair color, and has a ponytail like Andrea's. And her horse is the right color. The one on the other side could be Jack. He's big enough, anyway. Don't know about the one in the middle."

Jonathan's earpiece chimed once more. "George Hardy acknowledged the call. He's notified Christine Sanders at the stable by radio. He's on his way to intercept the intruders, but he's on foot. Dan and Tyler will reach them first."

Jonathan nodded. Should have thought about the stable. It's nearer to the location of the intruders than to the rest of the village, and the worker there would need to be warned. He'd have to write a subroutine to check for that sort of thing in the future. As he watched on the screen with Ron looking over his shoulder, the three intruders turned off the road onto a path into the woods to the east.

"Visual contact with the intruders lost."

Jonathan furrowed his eyebrows. "I wonder why they left the road?"

"I haven't a clue," Paladin replied.

"They're taking the shortcut to the stable," Ron said.

Jonathan lifted his gaze to Ron's face and squinted. Ron's eyes were clear.

"I know what you're thinking," Ron said, shaking his head. "I ain't smoked since yesterday. They're heading to the stable down the shortcut from the back."

Jonathan nodded. He touched his earpiece. "Paladin, notify Dan, George, and Christine that the intruders are approaching the stable from the back through the woods."

"Messages sent. Awaiting acknowledgement."

"Change the video to the camera viewing the stable." A view of the front of the stable appeared.

"Dan Kiner acknowledges the message," the computer said. A couple of seconds passed. "George Hardy and Christine Sanders acknowledge the message."

"It almost has to be Andrea," Ron said. "Strangers wouldn't have known about the shortcut."

*   *   *

Sept 10, 1:46 p.m.

Dan released his grip on the posthole digger and answered his radio when it squawked. Tyler pulled up another scoop with his own posthole digger, then his brows furrowed as he caught the word "intruders" in the scratchy audio from the radio. Dan's expression went grim.

"Acknowledged," Dan said. "Tyler and I will head up there in the truck right away." He clicked the radio off and he headed to the truck, leaving his digger in the half-dug hole.

'C'mon," he said, pulling off his gloves. "We have some intruders approaching from the north. Three people on horseback."

Tyler's eyebrows lifted. "Not the search party returning?"

Dan shook his head. "Two men and a woman, and different horses."

"Oh, shit." He glanced toward the shotgun in the rack in the pickup. He preferred a rifle, but the shotgun would have to do.

Dan slid in behind the wheel and Tyler climbed in the other side. He lifted the shotgun off the rack and held it so the barrel pointed toward the window. Fence posts lying in the back of the truck thudded against the tailgate as they left.

* * *

"Locate Sara Rillman," Jonathan said to Paladin.

"Sara Rillman is in the community center."

Teaching the writing class. "Ron, do you have a phone?"

"Sorry, no."

The truck appeared on Jonathan's screen, pulling to a jerky stop in front of the stable. Tyler jumped out holding a shotgun, and Dan climbed out the driver's side. He had a pistol of some kind. They headed around the stable from opposite sides.

With a scowl, Jonathan touched the earpiece to alert his computer. "Paladin, send a message to Sara. Tell her of the intruders and warn her to stay in the building with the students."

"Message sent. Awaiting acknowledgement."

*   *   *

The truck skidded to a halt in front of the stable, and Dan winced. They didn't need any extra noise to alert the intruders. Tyler handed him the 9 mm pistol from the glove compartment, then hopped out the passenger door with the shotgun. He headed around the right side of the stable, while Dan went to the left. He took shelter behind a juniper bush where he could see where the back trail opened to the clearing by the stable. Sparing only a glance at it, he pulled out his radio and changed the channel to the stable's. "Christine, this is Dan. Tyler and I are here. Where are you?"

After a pause long enough to worry him, the radio came on and she whispered, "In the loft."

"Stay put." He turned off his radio.

After a couple of minutes he heard leaves rustling from the trail and then saw a chestnut horse approach, half hidden by the sparse underbrush beneath the trees. His pulse pounding bass drumbeats in his ears, he clicked off the safety.

Before Dan could see the first rider Tyler shouted, "Don't shoot, Dan! It's Andrea."

Startled by the shout, Dan almost fired anyway. Andrea reined her horse to a halt and the other two stopped behind her.

"It's me, don't shoot," she said, hands in the air as Dan popped up from behind the bush and Tyler came around the corner of the stable.

"You gave us a hell of a scare," Dan said. He clicked on the safety. Heaving a sigh, Andrea swung herself off her saddle and hopped to the ground.

Jack and a young man Dan didn't know followed

Andrea into the clearing. Dan squinted at the stranger. "Who's this, and where's Cynthia?"

"This is Arthur. He's a representative from the other settlement—New Hope—here to look us over. Cynthia stayed behind until Arthur returns."

Arthur dismounted and held a hand out to Dan. "Hello, sir. Arthur Whetstone."

Dan transferred the pistol to his left hand and met Arthur's clasp. "Dan Kiner. This is Tyler Hopson." As Tyler shook hands with Arthur, Dan shifted his gaze to Andrea, who stood a few feet behind Arthur. "Was Cynthia okay with staying behind?"

Andrea grimaced. "Yeah, pretty much." Jack, standing beside Andrea, rolled his eyes.

Dan glanced at Jack and his eyes narrowed. He turned to Arthur again. "Well, I guess we're going to have to have a meeting to get you introduced."

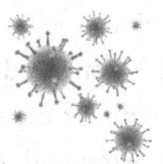

Chapter Sixty-Two

Devotions

Sept. 12, 9:00 a.m.

KAYLA looked over the crowd gathering in the community center the Sunday morning following the search party's return, a sour knot growing in her stomach. Jim Henderson himself had stopped by last Thursday afternoon and asked her to lead the Sunday service. Jamal Johnson had pushed Jim's wheelchair to her house, and he added his encouragement. When she asked why, Jim said nothing to confirm or deny the rumors flying around about Janet. He said only that Janet Haskel was incapacitated, and wouldn't be able to lead the services for the time being. He spoke through the laptop on the wheelchair's tray. Its synthesized voice gave away no clue for hidden meanings.

Now her palms sweated and her mouth felt as if filled with cotton. She laid her notes on the lectern—version 14 of the sermon she'd written and version 9 of her opening prayer. For the last couple of days she'd practically lived in front of one of the computers in the community center, writing. Whatever had possessed her to agree to this? As the chaplain of their Girl

Scout troop she'd led formal prayer services during campouts before, as well as over the winter they'd spent hiding from the plague in the hills. While imprisoned at the B&B she hadn't been allowed to assemble the girls—women—for formal services, but Brenda had encouraged her to do what she could to help keep morale up without attracting attention to herself. Those sessions, however, were with others her own age. Some of those seated before her were old enough to be her grandparents. Her nana Rachel came to mind. She'd always encouraged Kayla to do her best, and to always support the ones less able to support themselves.

She worked up some spit and swallowed. Nana Rachel had believed in her. Kayla set her mouth. "I can do this," she whispered.

People settled into their seats and Gloria Kiner nodded to her, smiling, from one of the front row seats. Brenda sat next to Gloria, and Arthur from New Hope sat beside Dan. Most of her sister scouts attended too. Becky gave her a thumbs-up, grinning.

Kayla glanced up at the clock above the main entry door. Time to start. She looked down at her notes, then back up at the crowd in front of her, took a deep breath, smiled, and began.

After the welcoming prayer and the opening hymn she worked her sermon around the parable of the Good Samaritan. The reading from the Gospel of Luke took only a few minutes, then she expanded on the reading with her thoughts about the meaning of the requirement to love one's neighbor in times when personal safety dictated caution. The hymn she chose to end with was "Lord Make Me an Instrument of Peace." She asked people to stand and join hands as they sang together, following the words displayed on the meeting room's monitor behind her.

At the end she spread her arms to the crowd and said, "May you all find peace and love in the days that follow. In Christ's name; in the name of the God of Abraham, Isaac, and Jacob; in the name of all that is sacred and holy, let us say, 'Amen.'"

The crowd replied, "Amen," on cue, then Kayla bent and touched the floor. A muffled gasp sounded briefly, and the room went quiet. Eyebrows lifted throughout the room, and people glanced from one to another.

Brenda bent and touched the floor, followed closely by Gloria, and then Dan. Then a few more followed their example. Jim Henderson struggled to reach the floor from his seat in his wheelchair, and Jamal helped him, then he touched the floor himself. Soon everyone had touched the floor, though a few of them grimaced as they did.

"Thank you," Kayla said. "Allen and Rita will be hosting a bonfire at the farm to mark the equinox. That'll be a week from next Wednesday, at sunset, but you should plan to be there a little early, of course.

"I also want to welcome Arthur Whetstone today. Most of you have met him already, and you all probably know that he's here from a group of survivors about forty miles away to the north-east, from a village they call, 'New Hope.' I encourage you all to make him feel welcome as well. He'll be heading back soon, and then Cynthia will return. We're looking forward to cooperating with his group whether they choose to continue to live at their site, or they join us here.

"Thank you all for coming. Please pray Janet makes a rapid recovery."

Kayla stepped toward the door to shake hands as people left. She concentrated on keeping her steps even and on controlling the tremors that threatened to wrack her as she went, but she felt triumph, too. Yeesss! Survived the experience.

She nodded at the members as she made her way down the center aisle. Most of them smiled at her, though she caught a few of them shaking their heads.

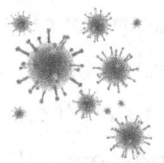

Chapter Sixty-Three

Hunting, Feasting, and Hunting

Sept 15, 8:35 a.m.

NATE held his breath as the deer approached, but he didn't have a clear shot from his stand. Branches in the way. He lifted his eyes over the rifle's sights and slowly turned his head toward Cynthia. Her stand was on the other side of the trail and down a ways. Her eyes flickered up at his after a moment and he gave a slight nod. She had a clearer shot. Cynthia nodded back and dropped her gaze to her gun's sights. After a second her rifle's crack shattered the morning's peace. The deer took a leap and then collapsed. It kicked once and then went still.

"Good shot!" Nate said. They climbed down from their stands and approached the deer, being cautious to determine it was really dead before they got close.

"A four-point buck," Nate said as he looked it over. "Probably a hundred and thirty pounds total, and at least forty pounds of meat. We'll eat well tonight. Good job. Clara will be pleased."Cynthia nodded, her mouth set in a tight line. She patted the deer's shoulder, then bent to touch the ground.

"Thanks," she said.

Nate tilted his head. He wasn't sure whether she was thanking him for his compliment on her marksmanship, or was thanking the deer, but he said, "You're welcome," anyway. "I'll cut a pole and we'll carry it back. I'd guess it'll be around a hundred pounds once it's field dressed. Can you manage that much weight, or should we go back for help?"

Cynthia shot him a glare. "I can manage."

"Okay, I was just asking." Damn. He couldn't even get near first base with her. He shouldn't have treated them so rough when they arrived. He leaned his rifle against a tree. "I'll be back soon."

*   *   *

The trip back to New Hope took much longer than the trip out. The pole holding the deer dug into Cynthia's shoulder no matter how she adjusted its position. She sweated till her shirt clung to her back like wet plaster, even though it was not yet noon and the day was cool. She forced herself to keep up with Nate, even asking if he needed to rest once, when he stumbled on a tree root. Finally they reached the clearing around the brick ranch house and stopped short upon seeing three horses hobbled in the yard, grazing on the tall grass in the unkempt lawn.

Nate wiped his brow with the back of his hand and twisted around to her. He took a couple of breaths. "Looks like Art and—and your friends have returned."

Cynthia nodded but didn't waste any breath to comment. They took the deer to an out-building near the edge of the clearing, and Nate prepared to dress and butcher it. A couple of the others saw them coming and came to help as well.

"Go ahead and see your friends," Nate said as he fastened a strap connected to a block and tackle around the deer's neck. "We'll take care of this."

Cynthia rubbed her shoulder where the pole had rested. "Thanks. I appreciate it."

She stopped at the washstand by the little stream running along the edge of the yard and dipped out a bucket of water to clean up, then headed to the house. When she stepped into the front room, Clara, Arthur, Andrea, and Brenda turned their heads to her.

Clara's eyebrows arched. "Well, there she is now."

Brenda came over and gave Cynthia a hug. "We got here a few minutes ago, and I'd just asked where you were. Clara said you'd gone hunting with Nate."

"That's right," Cynthia said. "We got a deer. Nate and a few of the others are butchering it now."

Andrea glanced at Clara, then faced Cynthia again. "Everything go okay while you were here?"

"Yeah. I'll be glad to go back home, though." She met eyes with Arthur. "So what did you think of our village?"

Before he answered the back door slammed and a second later Arthur's wife appeared in the doorway to the kitchen. She ran to him and locked him in a tight embrace. "Oh Art, thank God you're back safe!" She planted a kiss on his lips.

Arthur held her tight while they kissed, then a couple seconds later he said, "I missed you so much, Jan."

Clara tapped Arthur on the shoulder. "I'm sorry to interrupt, but I want to speak with you privately before we have our meeting tonight. Jan, please excuse us."

Arthur's face fell. "Right now? I just got here."

"I want to do that now while it's fresh in your memory and get it out of the way," Clara said.

Arthur nodded and took his wife's hand, giving it a squeeze as they separated from their embrace.

Jan pursed her lips but kept her peace.

"Jan, why don't you, Cynthia, and Andrea, show Brenda around," Clara said. "Come back here in a half hour or so. Since we got a deer, I guess we'll have a feast tonight, but that'll be late before the meat's butchered and cooked. There'll be plenty of time for you to catch up with Arthur." She pointed with her walking stick toward one of the side rooms. "Come on, Arthur, I'm eager to hear about what you saw on your trip." He followed her in and Clara closed the door.

Jan gazed at the door for a second after the latch clicked, then dropped her eyes. She brushed a strand of brown hair that had escaped her ponytail away from her face as she turned back to the rest of them. She frowned. "Well, let me give you the tour."

*   *   *

Andrea sat with some of the New Hope residents as evening came on. Brenda and Cynthia chatted together on a bench by another table across the central fire, catching up on the developments back at their adopted home. The aroma of roasting venison filled the meeting circle. Several people tended steaks and pots of venison stew around the main fire ring and in portable barbecue units brought into service for the occasion. Nearby a rack holding strips of meat hung over a low, smoldering fire.

Arthur related his impressions of Andrea's village—

which for the sake of conversation Andrea had decided on the spot to call "Hendersonville"—to the rest of the group. She knew that had been the name of another city not far from there before the plague, but what the heck.

Arthur was upbeat about the prospect of moving and had been impressed with the houses that were available for them to use. He also liked that they had rudimentary medical services.

Andrea answered questions from time to time, but mostly the members of New Hope listened to Arthur's account of his trip. They discussed whether to leave, or to stay at their village and set up some kind of regular commerce with Hendersonville. Some of the New Hope villagers wanted to go, but a sizable faction resisted the idea of abandoning the place where their parents were buried.

A nearly full moon rose a couple of hours after sundown. It cast a dim light over the meeting grounds where the firelight didn't reach. People sat in scattered groups discussing the possibility of moving while they feasted on the day's kill. No consensus had emerged as the hour grew late.

Clara had declined to give an opinion, and people grew sleepy between the late hour and the big feast. Some of them headed to the cabins, others stayed up talking and eating. Andrea tried to moderate her feasting, though she didn't abstain from it either. The bowl of stew a young lady had offered her was excellent.

When the moon was high above the eastern horizon the discussion still hadn't ended. Andrea thought about half of them were still up at that point. She sat by herself on one of the back benches enjoying the cool evening by the fire. It felt good to offer help to these people, like she was doing something important and worthwhile. Every cricket's chirp around her was beautiful music, and even in the darkness, every shape stood out in sharp relief.

A young lady holding a white ceramic bowl stepped to her. "Would you like more stew? You seemed to enjoy your first bowl, and there's plenty."

Andrea glanced up at her, then at the bowl of stew. It smelled ambrosial. She'd accepted a bowl of stew from this person earlier in the evening. Against her better judgment she took the bowl. The young woman smiled. "I hope you like this. I added some special herbs."

Andrea took a bite. It was delicious. Even better than the first bowl. Hot peppers, potatoes, greens, onions, basil and other herbs flavored it. Something else she couldn't identify, too. "It's great," she said. "Thanks."

The young woman smiled. She took a seat next to Andrea on the bench, close enough that their thighs touched. Andrea gave her a brief glance but didn't pull away. She was at least fifteen years younger than Andrea. No. Clara had said the oldest of them was only nineteen. That made her more like twenty years younger. Blond hair hung behind her in a ponytail which reached below her shoulders. Her slightly built frame stood a little taller than Andrea's, but that wasn't unusual. Most people were taller than her.

Andrea shook her head. She felt strange. Not bad, quite the contrary. She felt happier and more at peace than she'd felt since the plague hit. She turned back to the young woman, who she guessed was eighteen or nineteen years old. Then recognition hit. This was the one who had smiled at her during her visit the previous week. Her hair had been loose then. Andrea smiled herself. "What's your name again?"

"Bethanna. Everyone calls me Bethy."

Andrea smiled back at her. She took another bite of

stew, then shook her head again. "Beth," she said. "Bethy's a child's name, and you're no longer a child."

Bethanna laughed. "Yeah, I'm old enough to vote now, if that ever happens again. I'll answer to whatever you want to call me. Have another bite of stew."

Andrea furrowed her brows. Some part of her couldn't believe she was talking to this young lady this way. It seemed as if her sensible half were standing beside her, frowning. She's just a girl. Keep some distance here. Remember the mission.

Andrea took another spoonful. "This is great," she said. "What's the spice? There's something I don't recognize in it."

"Just some herbs we grow here. Basil, oregano, fennel, and a few others." She smiled broader and stroked Andrea's thigh up to her hip. "I'm glad you like it."

A shiver tingled Andrea's spine. She hadn't had a romantic relationship since her wife, Cassie, had died in the plague. She felt aroused and guilty at the same time. Andrea shook her head. Cassie was dead, and she'd want her to be happy. She ate another spoonful.

"Do you want more stew?" Bethanna asked.

Andrea glanced at Bethanna, then dropped her gaze to the empty bowl in her lap. Yes, she did want more, but her stomach bulged. She shook her head. "I shouldn't. Thanks, though. It's really good."

Bethanna nodded, smiling. She twisted in her seat and pointed to a cabin down the hill, barely visible by moonlight. "I think I'm going to turn in. I sleep in that cabin over there. It's one of the smaller ones, and I have it to myself." She stood and leaned over to stroke Andrea's cheek with a couple fingers. "It has a double bed." She headed down the hill.

Andrea watched her go and squirmed in her seat. Heat rose to her face and traveled down to her groin. The warm tingle felt nice, and almost unfamiliar after all this time. She looked around to find where to take the empty bowl and noticed a table holding a battered plastic tub filled with dishes on the other side of the fire.

She walked to it, staggering a little in the dark. The tub was stacked so full she couldn't see how to put her bowl in so it wouldn't send the whole pile crashing to the ground. She set the bowl on the table by the tub next to some other dishes there.

Someone tapped her on the shoulder. Andrea turned to find Brenda standing behind her. She grinned. "Hi Brenda."

"Hi. I'm not sure they're going to make a decision one way or the other any time soon. How long do you think we can wait while they make up their minds?"

"Uh—I don't know. A couple of days?" She closed her eyes and shook her head as if to clear out cobwebs.

"Are you okay? Your voice is slurred."

"I'm just tired. I'm going to go to bed."

Brenda tilted her head and furrowed her brows. "Okay. I'll see you in the morning."

Cynthia waved from the other side of the fire pit. "Brenda!"

"Let me see what Cynthia wants," Brenda said. "Good night." She headed around the fire to join Cynthia.

Andrea pivoted on her heel back toward the cabins and almost lost her footing. She recovered and surveyed the cabins down the hill. After a few seconds she identified Beth's. She glanced to Brenda and Cynthia. They talked to each other, making emphatic gestures. Arthur and Jan stood nearby. Andrea peered through the darkness toward the moon-lit cabin and started downhill.

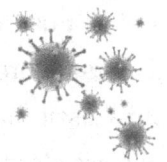

Chapter Sixty-Four

The Morning After

Sept 16, 7:45 a.m.

ANDREA awoke disoriented by the surroundings. She sat up in the bed and surveyed the room. A sliver of sunlight angled through the south window, providing the only source of light. Piles of laundry and stacks of books on the floor cluttered the room, and some potted plants sat on the windowsill. The bed had needed fresh sheets days ago.

She shrugged. At least the bed *had* sheets. She rubbed her eyes and winced as she remembered what happened last night. Then she smiled.

No sign of Beth, and no sounds of anyone moving around in the main room of the cabin came through the bedroom door. Andrea climbed out of bed and found her clothes.

As a lover, Beth had been eager and enthusiastic, but had a lot to learn. Andrea grimaced, but couldn't help smiling. Understandable for her age. Andrea had had to keep asking her to slow down when Beth got excited. A fun romp, but Andrea didn't see her as a prospect for a long term relationship.

Andrea shook her head, not sure why she'd slept with Beth in the first place. She didn't usually jump into bed the first time she met someone. Always before, she'd taken it slow with new relationships. She and Cassie had dated for more than a month before she accepted Cassie's invitation for sex.

Andrea found her last shoe underneath a corner of the blanket that had strayed onto the floor. She tied it, opened the bedroom door, and froze. Clara sat at the table, facing the door, reading a book. A slice of bread on a plate and a jar of honey sat on the table at the place setting beside Clara's seat. Sunlight streamed through the window behind her. Beth wasn't present.

Clara put down the book. "Good morning. Sleep well?" She wasn't frowning, exactly, and her expression didn't appear angry, though no hint of a smile showed either. Backlit by the morning sunlight, Clara's expression was hard to read.

"Uh, yeah. I guess so. Where's Beth?"

"Mucking out the stable." Clara glanced around the cluttered room. "Maybe that'll inspire her to do something about this cabin, too." She gestured toward the chair beside her. "Have a seat."

Andrea joined her at the table. "She hadn't told me last night that she needed to do that in the morning."

"Usually she doesn't work in the stable. I thought that would be a good job for her today." Clara pointed at the bread. "Have some breakfast, if you're not still too full from last night's feast. I've already eaten."

Andrea spooned a little honey onto the bread. "Look, about last night with Beth—"

Clara gave a dismissive wave. "I'm not upset about

that. I saw you and Bethy together last night, and then saw you head off to her cabin. Bethy—Beth—is of age, and it's not like you're going to get her pregnant. No, I'm upset with her, not with you."

Andrea stopped with the slice of bread halfway to her mouth. She lowered it. "Beg pardon?"

"This morning when Brenda asked about you, I told her you'd spent the night with one of the others. Didn't name names. Brenda said that wasn't like you and appeared concerned. She mentioned you acted odd last night, and you slurred your words. That's when I put it together."

Andrea laid the bread back on the plate. She locked eyes with Clara. "Put what together?"

"Beth drugged you. Marijuana in your bowls of stew. It lowers the inhibitions. She admitted it when I confronted her this morning."

Andrea's face flashed hot. All through college she'd abstained from pot, despite the peer-pressure. She rarely even drank alcohol. Then to have some barely legal girl dose her unawares, and then share a *bed* with her.... She gritted her teeth. "That little asshole!"

"Indeed. It wouldn't hurt for you to give her a piece of your mind too. Just consider that the pot doesn't create an attraction that didn't exist before. It just lowers the barriers. I've already had a talk with Beth about honesty in relationships. I thought mucking out the stable for a week or two might give her some time to reflect upon our conversation."

*   *   *

Sept. 18, 8:30 a.m.

Two days later, on Saturday morning, Andrea, Cynthia, and Brenda packed up their horses after breakfast to head back to Hendersonville. The members of New Hope had still not made a firm decision to stay put or leave, though Andrea's impression was that the ones wanting to join them in Hendersonville held a slim majority. Clara hadn't expressed an opinion of her own. She said she wanted the group to come to a firm consensus themselves.

As Andrea checked her horse's tack, Bethanna approached with a rolled up canvas bundle. She gave Andrea a tentative, rueful smile. "This is a sample of some dried herbs we grow, and some extracts we make from them, things we might be able to use as trade goods. I wrote out some notes on their use and packed them with the samples." She held the bundle out to Andrea.

Andrea glanced at it, then looked Bethanna in the eye.

After a second Bethanna dropped her gaze.

"We already have a source of marijuana," Andrea said.

"I didn't include any pot." She met Andrea's gaze again. "There's both medicinal and culinary herbs. My parents were expert herbalists. I learned a lot from them, and I have their reference books, including the one they wrote. Native Medicinal Herbs of North America and Their Use. Rodale Press, 2033. In hardcopy."

Andrea's eyebrows rose. "On actual paper? Wow." She gave her head a quick shake and frowned again. "That's quite impressive. For them."

Beth cast her eyes to the ground. "Thanks." She sighed. "Look, I want to apologize again for giving you pot without telling you. I hope you'll forgive me."

Andrea scowled, but she took the bundle. Stepping up on a bench by her horse, she fastened it to her saddle bags, taking care that the straps were tight. She checked it again. She adjusted its position. Finally, she hopped down and faced Bethanna. She put her hands on her hips. "I accept your apology. I'll work at forgiveness, but I'm not there yet."

Bethanna nodded, still facing the ground. "I understand. Thanks for accepting my apology, anyway." She lifted her face and sighed. "Be well, and be blessed." She walked back toward the house.

Andrea watched her go, then cast her eyes downward and sighed. Under other circumstances... She lifted her eyes and met Brenda and Cynthia's gaze. They stood frozen by their horses, staring at her. Andrea frowned. "What are you looking at? Let's get going."

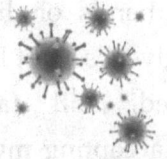

Chapter Sixty-Five

Theft

THEY'D been on their way back less than a half hour when the bushes rustled beside the road ahead of them. Arthur's dappled grey emerged with both Arthur and Jan astride it. Andrea reined her horse to a halt, and the others stopped beside her.

"We want to go with you," Arthur shouted.

"You're welcome to go on your own," Andrea replied. "It's an open road."

"We're asking for your support and help on the trip to Hendersonville. We don't have much in the way of supplies or shelter, but I can hunt, and Jan knows a lot about wild edible plants, and trapping, and she's good with children. We can be productive members of your village."

Andrea glanced at the gun Arthur had in an improvised saddle scabbard. A .22 rifle. Might be okay for rabbits. "You may travel with us, and we'll share our shelter with you. Why are you sneaking off like this?"

"We want Jamal's help with the childbirth, and we're afraid the group will decide to stay separate and we'll have to stay behind too."

Andrea turned to look at Cynthia and Brenda. "Did you

know anything about this?"

"They brought up the possibility to Cynthia and me a couple days ago," Brenda said, "but asked us to keep quiet about it. They weren't committed to going then. Wanted to see what the group would decide."

"Couldn't you have mentioned that to me?"

"We tried. This was the night of the feast. While you were busy. We couldn't find you at the time. Then Jan wanted to keep it down low, and was afraid you'd tell Clara. They never mentioned it again, and we assumed they'd decided to stay."

"We can talk about this later," Arthur said. "Can we please just get going now?"

Andrea scowled. Secrecy, and they were afraid. They weren't telling them everything, but he was right: they can talk about it later if it was that important to get away. She spurred her horse forward. "Okay. Let's get going, then."

*   *   *

Arthur kept his horse moving at a trot much of the time. He kept glancing over his shoulder as they went. Andrea worried he was going to wear it out with the doubled load and kept calling on him to slow down. He'd comply, but soon he'd have it trotting again. Then Andrea would have to catch up with him and chide him to slow down once more.

Andrea shook her head. Jan was a small woman, and while Arthur was tall and broad-shouldered, he was slim in the waist. Even so, she estimated the horse was carrying more than three hundred pounds between them. It was a good-size horse, but still, it would be suffering by the day's end at this rate.

Andrea made two suggestions for places to camp

overnight as evening came on, but Arthur encouraged them to continue until it was too dark to see well. When Andrea finally gave a flat order that they stop, Arthur insisted they camp out of view of the road.

As he pushed past the tall grass and the brambles bordering the forest beside the road looking for a place to camp, Andrea called him back. She glared. "What exactly are you afraid of?" She stood beside her horse, and Cynthia and Brenda stood next to theirs as well.

He hopped over the ditch at the side of the road and moved up near Andrea, so he could see her in the gathering dusk. "I just don't want to take any chances."

"You weren't this worried about security on the way out last week. Why now?"

Arthur glanced over to Jan, who stood beside their horse holding the reins. "Well—uh—Jan's with us now. I want to keep her safe."

"How very macho." Andrea gritted her teeth, but kept her voice even. "Your horse has got to be exhausted by this point. You badgered us to keep going until dark. Now you want us to stumble around blind under the trees to make a camp, and we'll probably end up sleeping in a patch of poison ivy. If you're so goddamn worried about highwaymen, we'll take shifts keeping watch. I'm sure you'll be glad to take the first shift, but we're not going—"

"He's afraid they're coming after us from New Hope," Jan said.

They all turned to her. Arthur stepped toward his partner. "Jan—"

"We should have told them from the beginning." Jan met Andrea's gaze. "As far as Clara's concerned, we're runaways, and we stole a horse, a saddle, and a rifle."

Andrea pulled her head back and furrowed her brows. "You said those belonged to you, didn't you? You kept referring to them as 'my' horse, and saddle, and so forth, last week."

"Art's the one who has use of them," Jan said, "but we don't have private ownership in New Hope. Especially not for things like that. They belong to the community as a whole."

"In Clara's mind, we even stole our own selves from the community," Arthur said.

Andrea frowned. "In *my* mind you're of age to make your own decisions about your life. The horse and the other stuff, maybe that's more of a question. If you both want to continue with us, okay. But I need to know if this is going to become a battle. Do you really think they're coming after you, and do you really think they'll use force to get you back?"

Arthur nodded. "I can't rule it out."

After a second Andrea gave a curt nod. She glanced toward Brenda and Cynthia. Their eyes were wide, but they nodded to her.

She turned back to Arthur and Jan. "I'll help get you to Hendersonville, but if it comes down to a choice, I'm not going to risk anyone's life to do so. Is that clear?"

Arthur's eyes went wide, and he turned his head toward Jan.

She gulped. "Yes. Understood."

They found a place to shelter behind the burned-out shell of a house at the end of a long driveway. They lit no fire that night. Jerky and dried apples sufficed for dinner.

Despite Andrea's threat to make Arthur take the first watch, she took it herself. No way she could sleep yet, under the circumstances.

She looked toward Arthur and Jan lying asleep in each

other's arms, dimly illuminated by the waning gibbous moon, blurred by mosquito netting. She shook her head. So sweet and peaceful. No one would guess they were criminal fugitives.

And she was helping them.

On purpose.

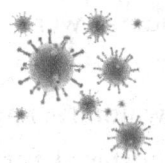

Chapter Sixty-Six

It Becomes a Battle

SUNDAY morning Jonathan sat at home having breakfast with Sara when the perimeter alarm chimed on his laptop. He put down his slice of bread and tomato and hurried to the bedroom and the computer.

"Report."

"Five people are approaching from the North on four horses. At least three of them have rifles in saddle holsters. The profile does not match the group expected to return from that direction."

"Video on main screen." It showed a fuzzy, heat shimmered image of four horses with riders, one with two riders, but no details. Sara came up beside him. "I don't see rifles," she said.

The program highlighted the position of the rifles in red.

Sara nodded. "Thank you."

"My pleasure," Paladin replied.

"Notify Dan Kiner and George Hardy."

"Messages sent. Awaiting acknowledgement. Dan Kiner and George Hardy auto-respond that they're at the Sunday service at the Community Center."

"Shit." Jonathan shook his head. Damn security hole. The computer couldn't do everything. "Notify the worker at the stable." The intruders were approaching from that direction.

"Message sent. Awaiting acknowledgment."

Jonathan stood and faced Sara. "I'm going to get Dan and George." He put on his ballistics vest and grabbed his helmet, but didn't put it on. He pulled his phone from the charger on his desk. "Sync with my phone, but keep the main screen active," he told the computer.

"No need," Sara said as she took her own vest. "I'm coming with you."

Jonathan locked eyes with her, then swallowed an objection. "Okay. Let's do it then." They left together, grabbing their rifles as they went out the door.

*   *   *

Jonathan opened the door to the community center's meeting room, and Kayla stopped her sermon in mid-sentence. The gathered members turned in their seats to face him.

"Five armed people on horseback are approaching from the north," Jonathan blurted. "We need to mount a response."

Dan stood. "Are they acting aggressive?"

"Not yet, but they probably don't know we've detected them. So far they're just coming down the main road."

Dan headed to the door and after a quick word to Maria, Gloria stood and followed him. George Hardy joined them too.

Dan's house was near the center. They stopped there and got some firearms, then they all squeezed into the pickup truck and headed out. After they'd gone only a few seconds, however, Jonathan's earpiece chimed.

"Security monitor alert: The intruders have stopped moving and are near camera N-1b. I recognize Andrea, Brenda, and Cynthia in the group." Camera N-1b. The northernmost camera near the stable. Jonathan pulled out his phone. Andrea, Cynthia, Brenda, and Arthur stood beneath the camera next to the horses. There was also another woman he didn't know. Andrea's pistol was in her holster, and Brenda and Cynthia stood within reach of their rifles.

Jonathan heaved a relieved sigh. "It looks okay. It's Andrea and her group, and she's got Arthur and another woman with her." He showed the image to the others in the back seat, then passed the phone to the front.

Sparing a quick glance at the phone, Dan nodded. "Looks good, but we're still going to be careful." A couple of minutes later he parked by the stable.

*   *   *

Andrea made a point of approaching slowly from the main road, bypassing the shortcut to the stable. Don't want to excite anyone, especially with an unexpected group size. She stopped the group below one of the cameras monitoring the road at the northern border and made sure the camera had a clear, close view of everyone. After a ten minute rest in front of the camera they proceeded to the stable via the main road, even though that required some backtracking.

Dan met them with his rifle leveled as they cleared the line of arbor vitae bordering the road by the entrance to the stable. Andrea led the group, and she reined her horse to a stop when she saw him. "It's okay, it's just us," she shouted, hands in the air.

"What are the other two doing with you?"

"They want to join us."

"Dismount and come forward, hands empty."

Gloria stood beside Dan. She had a rifle too, but held it at her side. "Is that necessary?"

"I hope not." Dan shifted his aim to Arthur as they approached. "I didn't expect to see you back here. At least, not without the rest of your group. What's going on?"

"We want to join you here in Hendersonville," Arthur said. "We weren't sure they were going to decide to come here, back in New Hope, and we didn't want to be stuck there when Jan delivers this winter."

Dan furrowed his brows. "Hendersonville?"

"I—uh—made that up 'cause it was getting too awkward to keep using 'our village' and 'your village' and such," Andrea said. "About time it had a real name, anyway."

"Okay, I guess. Can't imagine Jim'll approve, though." Dan lowered his rifle and turned to Jan. "You're okay with this, right? You're coming of your own free will?"

Jan took Arthur's hand and raised it to her lips to kiss his fingers. "Yes."

"Okay then. We'll set you up with a place to stay once we get something ready. In the meantime we'll find a temporary spot—" he stopped when Jonathan raised a hand.

"Got another alert," Jonathan said. "Two more visitors coming down the road and they have rifles out and ready."

Arthur pointed to the stable. "Get under cover, Jan."

Dan lifted his rifle and locked eyes with Arthur. "What the hell is this?"

Arthur's jaw dropped. "Uh—"

"They're probably people from New Hope coming after Jan and Art," Brenda interjected. "They snuck off without getting approval."

Andrea moved behind Jonathan to see the video and

pointed at the screen. "That looks like it might be Nate."

Brenda nodded. "Let's disperse the ones with rifles under cover around the parking lot and wait for them. I'll meet them as they come in." She pulled her rifle from the saddle holster and got Arthur's too. He handed the .22 to Art and rejoined Jan in the center of the parking lot, holding her rifle at her side.

"I should meet them," Dan protested.

Brenda shook her head. "They know me and are less likely to come out shooting if they see me first. I'm the one least skilled with a rifle here, but I know how to talk. I'll introduce you once they're here and the situation is calm."

Andrea cocked an eyebrow. She had a point. Besides, she'd seen Brenda shoot before, and she was right about that, too. Andrea crouched behind a juniper bush.

"But—" Dan said.

Gloria put a hand on his arm. "She's right. Let's get under cover."

Jan hadn't moved. "Get into the stable," Arthur repeated.

"It'll help Brenda if they see I'm okay, and not a prisoner," Jan said. "I'll stay by her."

"Jan, think of the baby." His eyes had gone wide and sweat beaded his forehead.

"I'm not going to live in fear, dammit, and neither is our baby."

Jonathan had locked his gaze on the phone's video. "They're almost here. Maybe another minute. Probably less." He crouched behind a bush and put on his helmet. Sara already wore hers.

Jan moved up beside Brenda. "Get behind shelter, Art."

"But Jan—"

Cynthia grabbed Arthur by the collar and pulled him behind a tool shed with her.

*　　*　　*

A few seconds later Randy and Nate rode into the parking lot. They reined their horses to a stop side by side a moment after coming into view, just past the bushy trees by the entrance.

"Welcome to Hendersonville," Brenda shouted. "There's no need for guns."

"We're here to take Jan and Art back," Nate shouted.

"Shut up," Randy said. He turned to Jan. "Jan, we need you and Art back at New Hope. There ain't enough workers to bring in the harvest with you two gone."

Jan crossed her arms above the slight bulge of her belly. "And if we choose not to return?"

"Jan, we need you back. Think of the others."

"The others would be better off if they came here."

Brenda licked her lips. She had to de-escalate the tension. "Our offer to transport you in our bus still stands. You'd all be welcome. We can use the truck to bring back as many supplies as you want, within space restraints. It's only about an hour's travel by bus."

"We still ain't agreed on that," Randy said, "'least, not when we left."

"What does Clara think?" Jan asked.

"She told us to come get you," Nate said.

Randy shot a poisonous glare toward his companion. "Nate, shut the fuck up." He looked back to Jan. "Clara sent us to try to persuade you to return. She ain't spoke her mind 'bout leaving or no. She wants everyone's agreement on the decision."

Brenda shook her head. "It's more like coercion than

persuasion, when you have rifles out."

Randy glanced at the rifle he clutched in his left hand and grimaced. He faced Brenda again. "We saw smoke and figured people were nearby. We wanted to be ready if there was a problem."

Brenda shook her head again. "There's no problem. Put your rifles away. Here, I'll put mine down too." She crouched and laid the rifle on the cracked pavement beside her.

Randy scowled, but he clicked on the safety and slid his rifle into the leather scabbard attached to the saddle. They turned to Nate. He still clutched his rifle with a white-knuckle grip. His wide eyes flickered between Brenda and Jan, then to the truck and back. "Clara told us to bring 'em back," he said.

Randy snorted and rolled his eyes. "Don't be an idiot. What are you gonna do, shoot 'em?"

Sweat beaded on Nate's forehead. "If it comes to that—"

Brenda took a deep breath. "There are eight people hidden around the parking lot with guns aimed at you, Nate. That includes Arthur, who's already agitated, and some who've already had to shoot people to defend the village. It'd be a real good idea if you'd put your gun away."

"You're bluffing," Nate said. His voice cracked.

Brenda shook her head as she locked eyes with him. "Not even a little bit."

"Do what she says, Nate," Randy said.

"But Clara said—"

"I'm sure Clara didn't mean for us to drag 'em back against their wills, or to go shooting anyone to do it." Randy sucked in a breath. "Put the gun away."

"You'd be shot at least three times before you could get that rifle to your shoulder," Brenda said. "You won't get them to go back by using the gun. You'd just get yourself killed."

"Put the gun down, Nate," Jan said. "It won't do you any good."

"But Clara—"

"Clara don't want you to get killed," Randy said. "You can't help bring in the harvest for Clara if you're dead."

Nate's gaze shifted between Randy, Brenda, and Jan. He licked his lips. He blinked, still wide-eyed.

Ron Culbertson stepped into the clearing behind Brenda and Jan, stumbling a little. "Hi everyone," he shouted, waving a hand.

Brenda gasped and spun around toward Ron when he announced his greeting, then turned back to Nate and Randy. Nate made a sudden motion with the arm holding the rifle. Was he going to fire? He might have just been startled.

Randy leaned over and shoved Nate's shoulder, ducking his head. Two shots fired. One hit Nate, grazing the top of his shoulder.

The horses reared, dumping both Randy and Nate off. Randy grunted a gasp of pain as he landed. Nate landed across a curb edge and rolled over on his back, moaning. Blood stained his shirt.

When Nate's rifle hit the ground it discharged and spooked the horses further. Randy's, Andrea's, and Arthur's horses took off, panicked.

Jan grabbed the reins of Nate's and calmed it while Brenda knelt by Nate. The others ran up from their hiding places converging on Brenda and Nate. Brenda noted Cynthia checking Randy. He seemed unharmed and she helped him up.

Brenda whipped out a bandana from her back pocket

and pressed it against the wound on Nate's shoulder, which had now soaked the top of his shirt with blood. He cried out as something in his shoulder moved in a way it shouldn't have when she applied pressure. Dan tried to raise Jamal on the radio.

"Should we just take him straight to the community center?" Jonathan asked. He still had his helmet on and looked like a cartoon spaceman. Nate recoiled when Jonathan came up to him, but Brenda, Cynthia, and Randy kept him from moving too much.

"Depends on how long Jamal's going to be," Brenda said. "Something's broken in his shoulder and I'd rather not move him if we don't have to."

"I was just coming to see if you needed any help," Ron said. He stood nearby, his face ashen, his eyes wide and bloodshot.

Dan shot him a glare. He clenched the fist of the hand not holding the radio. "Get the hell away from here. I don't want to see you again until—. Just get away from here."

"I could go get the horses, or something," Ron stammered.

Dan stomped to him and clutched a fistful of Ron's shirt, pulling him up to his face. "Get the fuck away." Dan didn't shout, but he was all the more menacing for that. He pushed Ron back, who fell to the ground, landing on his butt, scraping his palms as he tried to catch himself. He crabbed backwards a couple of steps and then rolled over and scrambled to his feet. He left the parking lot running.

Dan's radio was squawking. He keyed it as he walked to Nate. "This is Dan."

"Finally! This is Jamal. What's going on?"

"Gunshot victim at the stable. One of the intruders.

Shoulder wound. Bleeding and something broken inside."

"I'll be right there. Do you need more backup?"

Brenda listened in to the radio conversation while applying pressure to Nate's wound. "Jonathan, anyone else coming?"

"No sign of others."

Dan nodded and keyed the radio. "Couldn't hurt, but I think it's under control."

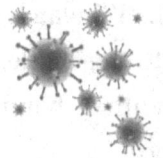

Chapter Sixty-Seven

EMS Run

JAMAL clicked off his radio and stuffed it back into his belt holster. Intruders? He glanced at Jim, who lay curled up on the bed, sleeping. Jim spent more and more time sleeping, and was often confused when awake, sometimes agitated, or even abusive. His periods of lucidity were still more frequent than those of confusion, but the trend worried him. Jim was declining fast, distinctly worse in just the last week, and he dared not leave him alone for any length.

Jamal grabbed his first aid kit and opened the door. The street was empty. Many people were still at the Sunday service. He ran to the Canfields' house beside his and pounded on the front door. "Anyone home?" He pounded again. Nothing. The next one he tried was the Edmunds' across the street. No answer there, either.

While Jamal was halfway to the next house up the road, Anita Carpenter came out her front door, the one next to Jamal's on the other side from his initial path, and shouted, "Jamal! What's the matter?"

"I need someone to watch Jim. There's trouble at the stable."

Steven appeared beside Anita. "What kind of trouble?"

"Intruders, and one of them's wounded. Dan says it's under control but he'd like more backup."

Anita stepped out. "I'll watch Jim."

"I'll go with you to the stable," Steven said. He ducked inside and reappeared with a handgun, a revolver of some kind. "You want a gun too?"

Jamal shuddered. "No."

Steven turned back to the interior. "Jimmy, go to Bill and Tyler and Jane's place and tell them there's trouble at the stable and they need backup. Then you stay put there with Ms. Fulk. You understand? No dawdling, no fooling. I need you to be a man about this."

Jamal didn't hear his reply, but Jimmy burst out the front door a few seconds later still pulling on a jacket and ran south, opposite the direction of the stable.

Steven joined Jamal. "Let's go."

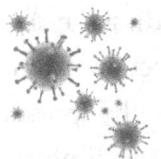

Chapter Sixty-Eight

Preparations

ON the morning of the Solstice, Wednesday, September 22nd, Allen made his way to the front of the barn, Jack's report of last Sunday morning's events filling his head. The drama around Randy and Nate's arrival had dominated the conversation around Hendersonville, as more and more residents were calling their village despite Jim's objections, but the details had just reached Allen. Monday morning Jack and Bryan had only known there had been an incident of some kind with armed intruders from New Hope, and one of them had gotten hurt. Yesterday's news hadn't been much better, but now the story had taken on a consistent, believable character.

Word was, judging from the size of Nate's wound, that the shot that hit him was from Arthur's .22, not Dan's 30.06. The bullet wasn't a hollow point round, so it did less damage than it might have. Jamal also said the bullet hadn't broken his collar bone. The break wasn't in the right place for the bullet to have done that. Most likely the bone broke when Nate fell off his horse and landed across a concrete curb in the parking lot.

The day had dawned cloudy and windy with thunderstorms threatening. Allen surveyed the sky as he stacked firewood by the barn, and shook his head. He stood just in front of the open barn door, which faced east, and watched the clouds scudding the sky. The roof's overhang here would give some protection from any rain, and the barn shielded the area from the prevailing winds. The bonfire would be much smaller this time, but he planned to have one anyway, even if it rained. The previous ceremonies had been at a spot where they could see the setting sun. With the clouds, that wouldn't be an option today.

The wind fought him, but Allen managed to cover a pile of firewood just inside the barn with a tarp. That done, he set a table up inside to hold the snacks he and Rita were going to offer to the participants. Coming out the door, he staggered against a sudden gust. Limbs on the giant maple in the front yard waved in the wind. He decided to get some fire buckets up there too.

There were still chores to do, and he'd promised Rita that he'd help her peel and cook some apples to have after the ceremony. Dusting his hands off against his pants, he went back inside to clean out the milking stalls. Jack should be finished with the milking by now and would appreciate the help.

*   *   *

Sept 21, 9:20 a.m.

Bob Haskel worked alone, cleaning up after breakfast. Janet had sequestered herself in her office, and Ed Fischer sat in the living room reading a book. He'd offered to help, but Bob had declined, saying he'd rather be by himself and wanted to be busy.

He dried the paring knife he'd used to cut apple slices

for breakfast and laid it on the counter. He hung the dish towel and stepped to the door to the living room. "I'm done with the dishes."

"Okay." Ed stood and pulled a key ring from his pocket. He unlocked the knife drawer and put away the paring knife, re-locking the drawer afterwards. He dropped the keys back into his pocket.

Bob frowned. He hated this, but the alternative Dan and Jamal had given them had been to put Janet in detention. He wasn't sure what that'd mean, but surely it was the worse choice. He understood why they didn't trust him with the only keys they had to the drawer lock and the garage lock, but he still resented the denial of control over their house.

The door to Janet's study drew his eye. More and more he found himself staring at that barrier. Janet blamed him for going along with the "protective restrictions," and for not helping her to stop Allen. She hardly spoke to him anymore. He'd been sleeping in the guest room rather than suffer her rejection of his caresses in bed.

Janet spent most of her time either in her office or in the bedroom these days, only coming out to the dining room for meals. Bob wasn't the only one she shunned. She hardly spoke at all, beyond the bare minimum required. Bob found more and more excuses to inspect the water reservoir on the hill and the main water line leading to the village. Anything to be out of the house.

Today, however, he really did need to go check on the reservoir. On his last visit he'd noticed some water leaking around the sluice gate on the dam. If it was getting weak, and with the storm threatening, he didn't want the level to get too high. Ed looked up as Bob came through the living room and took a raincoat from the hall closet.

Ed lifted his brows. "Not raining yet."

"It will be soon. I'm going to check on the reservoir. I'd rather not be caught on the hill without a coat if it starts." Bob slipped on the coat and opened the door. "I'll try to be back before lunch, but if not, don't wait for me."

* * *

Sept 21, 10:00 a.m.

Brenda had her notebook out on the desk in the stable's office working on a writing assignment. She'd already mucked out the three stalls she was responsible for, carried up water for the horses, and put hay in their mangers that morning. Christine hadn't yet finished her stalls. The scrape of the fork as she worked penetrated the wall between the office and the stalls with a rhythmic, gravely rasp.

The wind had picked up as the hour approached noon, when the shift changed. She hoped the rain would hold off until later. She'd brought a poncho but still, it was a more pleasant walk home if it wasn't raining. It'd also put a kink in the plans for the bonfire that evening.

The scraping sound ceased, followed a few seconds later by a thud as Christine hung the fork on its nail and it banged against the wall. A second after that she stopped outside the office to shed the battered rubber over-boots they all shared for that job.

"Whatcha writing?" Christine asked, twisting her neck to peer at Brenda's notebook.

"It's a class assignment. A pantoum."

Christine furrowed her brows.

Brenda put down her pencil and rubbed her eyes. "It's a specific type of poem."

"Oh. Well anyway, are we still planning to go to the

bonfire tonight? Looks like rain."

"I'm sure Allen is going to have one in any case. You know Allen. He'd do it even if no one showed up."

"So we're all going together, like for the last one?"

"I'm not gonna to force anyone to go, but I'll encourage everyone to attend. I think it's good to support Allen in these, especially since Kayla's adopted some of his gestures for the Sunday services, and a lot of people are accepting that. I want to keep up the momentum. Builds community spirit."

Christine raised an eyebrow. "All for one, and one for all?"

"Dr. Rillman would call that a cliché, but yes."

*   *   *

Sept 21, 10:20 a.m.

Jonathan clicked the start button on the screen to initiate the download from the geostationary weather satellite. He confirmed that the progress bar was advancing and swiveled the chair around. "Would you like some tea?"

Sara looked up from the bed where she reclined, marking papers from the writing class. "Sure. Thank you."

Jonathan headed toward the kitchen, but before he made it to the door, the computer chimed an alarm. "Satellite signal lost."

Jonathan turned back toward the computer. "Huh?"

"I said, the satellite signal is lost. Should I boost speaker volume?"

Jonathan shook his head and raised his eyes heavenward. "No." Should have been more careful in selecting dialog examples when training the AI. Anyway, he hoped the satellite hadn't failed.

A quick check behind the receiver confirmed that the

cable connection was good. He stepped to the window and pulled the curtain aside. At the far edge of the back yard, a tree leaned against the dish antenna, knocking it out of alignment. As he watched, the tree fell to the ground, cracking the dish in pieces and flattening the turnstile antenna, which stood next to the dish.

"Oh shit."

Sara looked up from her papers. "What's wrong?"

"A tree has blown over on the dish and turnstile antennas," the computer said. "Video from camera M-2a on screen." The display changed to a shaky view of their back yard from about 100 yards away.

"I've already seen that," Jonathan said.

"Well how would I know where you're looking? You don't have any cameras up in the bedroom."

Sara gave an emphatic nod. "Damn straight."

"I don't know what you think I'd be interested in. It's not like I—"

"Paladin, cancel that subject."

"Sorry."

Sara slid out of bed and joined Jonathan by the window. She laid a hand on his shoulder. "Can you fix it?"

"I hope so," Jonathan said, but he was shaking his head.

Sara shrugged. "Well, firewood, I guess. Can't do anything about it in this wind."

*　　　*　　　*

Sept 21, 10:30 a.m.

Bob Haskel reached the hill just below the reservoir about a half hour after he'd left his house and stopped just below the sluice gate. The water level stood just below the top of the gate and leaked around it in a stream that looked troublesome. He shook his head. If it broke through, the repair would be more difficult, but it wasn't a danger to the community. At most, some basements might flood. It wasn't a large reservoir.

He climbed up to the top of the gate and gripped the turn wheel on the sluice gate. It turned a quarter of a rotation—enough to take up the slack in the mechanism—and stopped. He leaned into it. It creaked open a little and stuck again. A thin slot—less than an inch wide—had opened and a smooth sheet of water streamed from it. Not enough.

Bob released the wheel and stood back, frowning, hands on his hips. He scanned the area for something useful. There. A dead tree down the slope with several stout branches within reach caught his eye.

He tugged on one about as thick as his wrist. The branch broke off with a loud crack on his third try. Wedging it in a fork of the tree, he broke off a section about five feet long and carried his improvised lever back to the sluice gate's wheel. It took some work, but he got it stuck through the spokes of the wheel in such a way he could use it to increase his leverage.

He took a breath and pulled on the branch. The gate groaned a metallic protest, but it crept open. He shifted his position and pulled again. It opened further. Almost done now, just a little more. He adjusted his position again, gripped the branch closer to its end, and pulled, leaning back as he braced his feet on rocks half buried in the bank.

The branch snapped with a report like a pistol shot. The piece in his hands flew away as he fell down the bank. He had a glimpse of the other piece pinwheeling against the thunderheads before he hit his head on a rock.

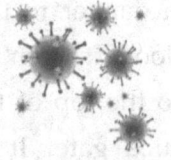

Chapter Sixty-Nine

Confession and Penance

Sept 21, 12:18 a.m.

JAMAL applied a poultice of calendula flowers and plantain leaves to Ron Culbertson's left palm and secured a dressing over it, tying the bandage with a strip of cloth around his hand and wrist.

"Okay, that's done." He gave Ron a jar containing some of the dried herbs. "Change the dressing twice a day." Turning to a file box on the counter behind him, he pulled out a couple of sheets and handed them to Ron. "Here are instructions for making the poultice and for making bandages. Just please bring the sheets back once you're comfortable with the process. Jonathan says we're getting low on paper."

Ron nodded. "Okay."

Jamal stepped up and examined Ron's eyes, pulling down the lower lid, first the left, then the right. "Your eyes are clear. When's the last time you smoked?"

Ron lowered his gaze to the floor. "Not since the—the accident."

Jamal nodded. "Three days, then. How's it going?"

Ron shrugged, still facing the floor. "Okay, I guess. I still catch myself wanting it, but I haven't used since Sunday morning."

"Well, that sounds normal. What have you done with your stash?"

"I asked Bryan to hide it." Ron lifted his shoulders once more and grimaced. "Not that it'd be hard to get more from my plot."

"Hang in there. Keep busy as much as possible. Bryan and Ed aren't using in front of you, are they?"

"No, they've been good about that." Ron sniffled and wiped his eyes. "They were never heavy users anyway. Not like me."

"Okay, good. Well, that's it. If your palm's not better in a week come see me again."

Ron stood and reached for his raincoat. He stopped with one arm in its sleeve. "Look, Jay, I'm real sorry about that guy. The one who got shot. How's he doing?"

"Nate will be all right in a couple of months. Can't say more."

"I hope he heals okay. I never should have interfered. 'Specially not while stoned." Ron wiped his eyes again. "If you like, I can bring you some apples, and maybe some fish." He finished pulling on the coat. "Do you like fish?"

Jamal gave him a tight-lipped smile. "Sure Ron. Whatever you've got will be fine."

Ron slid his other arm into the sleeve and zipped the coat. "You can have as much of my stash as you need for the others, too. Just ask Bryan."

*   *   *

Jamal pulled the sheet off the exam table and dropped it into the laundry hamper once Ron left. Flinching from the hot water, he washed his hands and dropped the hand towel on top of the sheet.

A few steps down the hall and a left turn, and he entered the kitchen. Tiffany was tying up bundles of mint plants to dry and looked up when he came in. "How are we fixed for plantain leaves?" he asked. "I just gave a jar to a patient."

"I think we're okay for now. Eight or nine more jars in the storeroom aside from what's in the pantry. At this point we won't get much more until next spring, will we?"

"Should still be able to find some. Have to take a look after the storm passes."

"Okay."

"Why don't you knock off once you finish that? You'll probably want to go to the bonfire, right?"

"I was planning on it, yes."

"Go ahead. I appreciate your help. I'm going to check on Jim."

*　　　*　　　*

The door to Jim's room already stood open a crack. Jamal pushed it open a little more without knocking to peer inside.

Jim lay on the bed, but he opened his eyes when the door creaked, and he struggled up on an elbow. Jamal opened the door the rest of the way.

"Don't get up. I'm sorry if I woke you."

Jim shook his head, then coughed a few times: hard, wet, hacking spasms that shook his body.

Jamal stepped in and held a spit basin up to Jim's face.

After a moment the coughing subsided, and Jamal gave him a tissue. He examined the contents of the kidney-shaped bowl. Bloody. Jamal set it on the dresser.

Jim took the tablet from the night stand. "When are we leaving for the bonfire?" he wrote.

Jamal shook his head. "The weather's bad. Thunderstorms threatening. I don't think we should go."

Jim gave his head a weak shake. "Want to go."

"Jim, you'll get soaked and chilled. It's a real bad idea."

"Won't hurt me now. I want to go!" He underlined "go" three times.

Jamal shifted his focus from the tablet to Jim's face, and they met each other's gaze for a second, then Jim had to cough again. When finished, he took the tablet and wrote, "Want to go. Use raincoat and woolens."

Jamal sighed. "Okay. Sunset's at 7:28 and we'd have to leave about an hour before that to be sure to make it, considering the weather."

Jim nodded, then he pointed to a makeshift wooden frame that sat on the dresser. Jamal looked where he pointed. "You want the picture?"

Jim nodded again.

Jamal handed it over, a small glossy print the size one would have put in a wallet. It showed Jim standing behind a woman with long brown hair and a boy about ten years old. A rude wooden frame encased it, one that, as far as Jamal knew, Jim had made himself. The joints didn't quite meet square, and the finish was rough.

Jim traced the faces of the figures in the image and tears came to his eyes. Jamal watched for a few seconds and said, "Your wife and son, yes?"

Jim had never talked to Jamal about them before,

always deflecting his questions. Jamal had almost stopped asking. This time, however, Jim nodded. Spurning the tablet, he croaked in a hoarse whisper, "Carol was a lot younger than me. Fifteen years. She was mad I went on the hunting trip, with the infant mortality riots. Been planned more than a year, though, so I went. Me and two other guys. Then the plague hit. Ben was fourteen then." Jim wiped his hand over his eyes and took a few deep breaths, wheezing, then continued. "We'd been about to head home when Carol skyped me. Ben had started to cough blood. Then she started to cough blood too. Watched Ben—Ben die in her arms. Then Carol died too."

"Oh God, Jim. I'm so sorry."

"Couldn't do anything for them. Do what I can for ones who survived."

Jamal nodded. "You've done well by us—"

Jim gave his head a weak, dismissive shake, waving his hand, then coughed. He wiped his mouth. He picked up the tablet again and wrote, "Do what I can. Least anyone can do."

Jamal gave another nod. Checking his watch, he said, "Well, it's about five hours till we'd have to leave. Get some rest before we go, okay? I'll get us something to eat before then."

Jim nodded again and lay back down. Jamal left the door ajar when he left.

* * *

Sept 21, 1:45 p.m.
Ron Culbertson knocked on the Haskels' door, and Bill Stevenson opened it.

"Hi Ron, can I help you?"

Ron blinked surprise at seeing him there. "Uh, hi Bill. I

was hoping to see Janet."

"She hasn't been feeling well. Could I give her a message?" Bill stood in the doorway and made no move to step aside.

"No, I really wanted to talk with her. Uh, privately."

"I don't think that's a good—" Bill said, but Janet walked into the front room and came up behind Bill, prompting him to turn toward her.

She rubbed her temples. "What's going on?"

"Hi Reverend Haskel," Ron said, standing on tip-toes to see over Bill's shoulder. "I was hoping to talk with you some."

"Sure. Come on in."

Bill frowned, but he stood aside for Ron to enter.

"What did you want to talk about?"

Ron glanced at Bill, then back to Janet. "Well, it's sort of private."

Janet looked to her side for a split second, then turned back to Ron. "Okay. Let's go to my office."

Bill's eyebrows shot up. "I'm not sure that's a good idea."

Janet shot him a frosty glare. "You've cleared the room of anything dangerous. He's safe with me, and you'll hear any cries for help, if that'd be necessary. I can still talk to people, can't I?"

Bill sighed. "Yeah, I guess so." He turned to Ron, whose eyes had gone wide, but stood silent by the door with his hands at his sides. "You don't have any weapons on you, do you? No firearms, pocket knives, or anything?"

Ron jerked his head back and gave it a little shake. "I have a pocket knife, sure."

Bill held out his hand. "Give it to me. I'll return it when you leave."

Ron furrowed his brows, but he handed over a red

Swiss Army knife.

Bill nodded. "Thanks."

Janet stepped up and took Ron's hand. "Come with me."

* * *

Janet closed the door behind Ron and gestured toward the chair beside the desk. "Have a seat." She pointed to his bandaged palm. "What happened to your hand?"

He held it up. "I scraped my palm a couple of days ago, and it got infected."

"Oh. I hope it's better soon." Janet took the desk chair and swiveled around to face Ron. "What's on your mind?"

"Well, I don't know if you were aware," Ron said, "but I was raised Catholic. I know you're Baptist, and all, but— well—I guess I want to confess."

Janet nodded. She stroked her temples. "Okay. If you have something you want to get off your chest, I'll listen. I won't swear to keep it secret if I think you're a danger to yourself or others, though. And obviously, I can't perform the sacrament of confession." She looked up past Ron where her father stood in front of a bookcase, arms folded. He gave Janet an approving nod.

Ron grimaced and stared down at his lap. He folded and unfolded his hands, interlacing his fingers, then squeezed them together and interlaced them again. For a moment he looked as if he regretted coming. Then he sighed. "I don't think I'm a danger to others. Not any more, at least."

Janet tilted her head and raised an eyebrow. "Go on."

Ron spent the next twenty minutes emptying his soul to Janet. He told her of his guilt over surviving when the rest of his family had died, his feelings of inadequacy that he'd never made anything of himself and that he was a disappointment to his dead parents, his sense of responsibility over Nate getting wounded because he'd shown up high on weed thinking he was somehow going to help. He poured out every failing he remembered or imagined, big or small, recent or in the distant past. Before he'd finished he'd dropped to his knees and wept as he spewed his grief.

When Ron finally ran out of words and merely knelt before her, crying, Janet stood and helped him to his feet. He produced a handkerchief and wiped his face. Janet pulled the chair he'd been using back up and encouraged him to sit. "I could assure you that God has forgiven you," she said, "but that would be too simple. I think you know that, don't you?"

Ron nodded, the handkerchief pressed to his face.

"You want to be a better person," Janet said, "and you can be. But you have penance to serve. Are you willing to work to be a better person, the kind of person that Christ wants you to be?"

"Yes I am. I want to be better." He gave a loud sniff and dabbed at his eyes.

"He can help you," Janet's father said. He'd been standing behind Ron during his confession, impassive. "He's reached the point where he's eager to serve the Lord's needs."

Janet regarded her father for a moment and gave him a nod before turning her attention back to Ron. "Are you ready to work to serve the Lord, Ron?"

He nodded, still holding the handkerchief to his face.

She laid a hand on top of his head. "We all have many temptations, obstacles laid in the path to righteousness by the forces of evil that we must avoid in order to serve the Lord. Some are small, like the temptation to avoid work we'd

402 | The Great Disruption

promised to do for our neighbors, and others are large, like the temptation to honor false gods. Even now, preparations are under way for a ceremony to worship a pagan god."

Ron tilted his head to look at her, his eyes growing wide. "You mean the bonfire at the farm?"

"Exactly. Though they may not realize it, that ceremony is taking them away from Christ. They may believe it's just a friendly gathering to mark an astronomic coincidence, but it's much more than that. It's a violation of the first Commandment, and it's abhorrent in God's sight."

Ron's mouth hung open. "What should I do?"

Janet lifted her hand and scooted her desk chair up in front of him. She eased into the chair, facing Ron, rubbing the thigh of her bad leg above the knee. "You must reject this temptation," she said, "but more than that, you must do whatever you can to convince others not to participate in this evil."

Ron furrowed his brows. "Evil? Allen is evil? He does so much for us in running the farm."

"Yes, but it's in the service of promoting his sinful agenda, in tempting others to sin."

Ron gave his head a slow shake. "I don't want anyone to be led away from Christ. I'll do what I can to prevent that."

Janet smiled. She looked up at her father and he smiled down on them too. "You're a good servant of the Lord, Ron." She patted his shoulder.

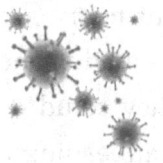

Chapter Seventy

Missing

1

DAN arrived at the Haskels' at four o'clock for the evening shift. Bill let him in at his knock.

"Hi Bill. Windy out there," Dan said as he removed his coat. "At least it's not raining yet."

"Bob hasn't returned from checking the reservoir," Bill said.

Dan stopped, one arm still in his coat sleeve and snapped his gaze up to Bill's face. "What?"

"Ed told me Bob went to check on the reservoir about nine-thirty, ten o'clock or so, and said he expected to be back for lunch, but not to wait on him for it. He hasn't come back yet. I'm afraid something's happened to him."

Dan pulled his arm out of the sleeve and draped the coat over his arm. "Why didn't you call on the radio?"

"I tried. The battery's dead and the charger's missing. This one don't hardly hold a charge no more. Janet claims to know nothing about it being gone. I didn't want to leave her alone, and the Hardys aren't home next door."

Dan pulled his radio off his belt and keyed it. "George, this is Dan. You there?"

He was just about to try again when George replied. Dan filled him in on the situation and George arranged to meet Bill and whoever else they could get ahold of to meet at the base of the hill by the trail leading up to the reservoir to look for Bob.

Bill put on his raincoat while Dan talked to George. "I'm going to stop by the house on my way over there. Hopefully Tyler'll be there and I can get his help."

Dan nodded. "Good idea. What'd Janet say about Bob being missing? Did she have any idea about where he might be?"

A grimace flashed across Bill's face, then he sighed, shaking his head. "She said she had no idea, and acted like it didn't concern her none. She and Bob don't hardly talk anymore." He gave Dan the keyring and gripped the doorknob, then turned back to him. "By the way, Ron Culbertson was here earlier this afternoon."

"Oh? What for?"

Bill shrugged. "Don't really know, but I'm guessing he felt the need for some preaching. He and Janet were together in her office for about a half hour, forty-five minutes. When he left, he looked like he'd been crying."

Dan furrowed his brows. "In Janet's current state of mind, I'm not sure if that was a good thing or not. Not that Ron couldn't benefit from some pastoral guidance, you know."

Bill gave a half-smile and an eye roll. "That's for damn sure. I better get going."

*   *   *

Sept 21, 4:05 p.m.

Light gradually registered on Bob Haskel's consciousness. Wind howled around him, blowing leaves against his face at irregular intervals. He blinked when this happened, but too slow to be effective in avoiding the collisions with his eyes. They hit him with a soft "crack" and he blinked a split second too late. Crack. Blink. Crack. Blink... Crack. Blink.

His head throbbed agony and his left arm, pinned beneath his body, tingled and didn't want to work right when he tried to move it. He rolled onto his back and had to pull his left arm into position with his right hand. It occurred to him that this should be scary, but he didn't feel any emotion.

What happened? He remembered climbing the hill to check the sluice gate and only being able to open it a bare crack. Then nothing until the leaves.

Groaning, he struggled to sit and finally succeeded. A branch from a rhododendron bush on the creek bank beside him waved against his face in the wind. He scooted sideways to get away from it.

His head swam and there were two of everything wherever he looked. He held a hand before his face. Two hands. The tingling in his left arm had started to subside, though, and he could move it a little. Not broken. He squeezed his eyes shut tight and opened them again. The double vision persisted, but the images were closer together. Another couple tries and the double images merged.

Dark clouds covered the sky, but no rain yet. Wiggling around where he sat, using only his right arm to help, he turned himself around toward the sluice gate. It was open almost all the way and a rapid, three foot wide stream gushed from it, roaring down the hill. Who opened the gate, and why didn't they see him?

He checked his watch: 4:08. He needed to get back home, but which way was that? The trail wasn't visible. His arm was about back to normal now, anyway.

He shook his head. Hard to think. He remembered the path there led through a wooded area, and there was a stand of trees to his left, down the slope from the reservoir. That seemed right. In careful, gradual stages he got to his knees and stood. He went down on his knees again almost at once as the world spun around him. Closing his eyes, he took a few deep breaths. When he opened them again, the bank and trees surrounding him were stationary once more. Another deep breath and he pushed himself to his feet again. Everything swayed for a moment, then steadied. Choosing his steps with exaggerated care, he made his way toward the trees. He fixed his gaze on a thick maple tree's trunk at the edge of the clearing where there appeared to be an opening in the brush below it.

The trees broke the wind a little as he pushed through the brambles at the forest edge. A faint trail seemed to wind its way downhill, so he followed it, clutching onto branches or saplings for support whenever possible. The tops of the trees waved in the wind, threatening to break under the strain. Under the forest canopy and with the dark clouds there was little light to see his way. Nothing seemed familiar, but he figured as long as he went downhill he was going in the right general direction.

*   *   *

Sept 21, 4:05 p.m.
George Hardy slipped the radio back into its holster and looked up at the others. They sat as if frozen, still seated across

the kitchen table holding knives and half-peeled apples, staring back at him with wide eyes. "Bob Haskel's missing, and Dan's afraid something's happened to him. It seems Bob told Ed Fischer that he was going to check on the reservoir this morning and didn't come back." He pulled his raincoat off the back of chair as he spoke and slipped it on.

Allen put down his apple. "Do you need help?"

George shook his head. "Thanks for the offer, but you should stay here. I'm meeting Bill and whoever else he can round up."

Allen stood. "A person's safety is more important than this bonfire."

"It's not that." George frowned. "Think it through. If something *has* happened to Bob and you're the one who finds him, Janet will believe you did it. Some of the others here will believe that too."

Rita's jaw dropped. "That's just ridiculous."

George jerked up the zipper on his coat. "I agree. But some would believe that." He pulled the hood over his bald head and tied the drawstring. "Hopefully we'll find him soon and be back for the bonfire tonight."

Alice came around the table and gave him a quick kiss. "Be careful."

"I will." He left the kitchen by the back door, struggling to push it closed as the wind grabbed it.

*   *   *

Allen watched him through the window for a moment as George made his way through the back yard, bent against the wind. "You know, I'm not sure it's a great idea from a safety standpoint to start a fire in this wind." He turned back to the two women. "Maybe we should cancel."

"We don't have to actually light the fire," Rita said. "It can be symbolic. Besides, this close before the event it'd be hard to alert everyone. Most of them don't have phones."

"I could go into town and spread the word."

Alice shook her head. "Until Bob shows up, you need to stay here in front of witnesses."

"You really think that's necessary? That someone would think I'm capable of harming Bob? And what reason would I have to do so in the first place?"

"Allen, I'm not saying it's reasonable. But for a long time you kept yourself semi-secluded here, and then you and Rita had that blow up with Janet last Christmas." She brushed a strand of red hair from her face. "Maybe it's silly, but it's prudent."

Rita furrowed her brows. "No one else besides Janet and Bob were present for that. How do you know about the blow up, as you put it?"

"From Janet, of course. She mentioned it once, when we had her and Bob over for dinner, and I'm sure she's told others as well. Bob looked like he wanted to crawl into a hole at the time, but he couldn't shush her."

Rita glanced at Allen, who returned her look with his brows furrowed. Rita turned back to Alice. "What did she say?"

A pained grimace flashed onto Alice's face, then she rolled her eyes. "Keep in mind, I was at the Christmas Eve service too, and I know what I saw doesn't mesh with what Janet said. She accused Allen of defiling the service with 'pagan rites' and you of 'unseemly immodest behavior.'" Alice said, making air-quotes. "She said you swore at her as you left."

For the second time in only a few minutes Rita's jaw dropped. "That's a rather—odd—interpretation of the event, based on my memory." Allen stepped behind Rita and put a hand on her shoulder. "I wasn't happy about her suggestion that I should hide to nurse Davina," Rita continued, "nor her comment about us, living in sin, quote unquote, but neither of us swore at her, or even made a rude comment."

"That's right," Allen said. "I was impressed by your restraint, though I worried for a second."

"Oh, not that I wasn't tempted. But we left there being civil, if not friendly. And I think it's a stretch to call Allen's touching the Earth a, 'pagan rite,' let alone anything defiling."

Alice shrugged. "I believe you. For the last six months or so Janet has been getting more and more—well—unstable. Then when she attacked Jamal—"

Rita's eyebrows shot up. "Whoa! She *attacked* Jamal? Physically?"

Alice gave a brief nod. "I'm surprised that story hasn't already reached you in some form." She gave them a quick account of the event, as filtered through Jamal telling Dan who told George who told her.

"It sounds like Janet's losing it, all right," Rita said, shaking her head in disbelief. "That explains why Kayla's doing Sunday services all of a sudden, anyway. How's that working out?"

"I think she's doing a great job. Especially considering her age and lack of experience. She has a much different style from Janet, and I suppose some like it better than others. She's more—" Alice tilted her head, considering. "I guess you'd say, more Unitarian than Janet."

"Personally, I'd call that an improvement," Allen said. "I thought Kayla's participation at the Summer Solstice was helpful and appropriate."

Rita nodded. "Me too, but these apples aren't going to peel themselves." She picked up her knife.

* * *

Sept 21, 4:30 p.m.
Ron had to fight the door to pull it closed against the wind. He pulled off his raincoat, still facing the door inside his living room, standing for a moment and running his fingers through his hair.

"What'd Jamal say about your hand?" Ed asked.

Ron jumped and spun around. "Oh! I didn't see you."

Ed turned off his tablet and set it on the coffee table. "Sorry. Didn't mean to startle you. How's your hand?"

"Jamal gave me some stuff to put on it. He thinks it'll heal okay." He hung the coat on the rack by the door and took a seat in the armchair in the front room.

"Bryan and I are leaving to go to the bonfire at about 6:30 or so. Are you coming with us?"

Ron shook his head and gave Ed a smile. "I'm staying here. Maybe read the Bible some."

Ed tilted his head. "Are you okay?"

"More okay than I've been in a long time." He leaned forward in the chair toward Ed, resting his forearms on his knees. "Why don't you stay here with me? I mean, we should be honoring Christ, not pagan idols."

Ed furrowed his brows and gave his head a quick shake. "Are you smoking again?"

"No, and everything is much clearer now. I'm committing my life to following Christ, and I hope you'll join me." He gave Ed his most inviting smile.

Ed grimaced and let out a sigh before speaking. The

wind moaning outside almost drowned out the ticking of the antique grandfather's clock standing against the wall. Inside, the lights had been set dim to preserve battery capacity. Shadows made Ed's face indistinct. His frown, however, was clear.

"I haven't been observant for a long time," Ed said, "but were you aware that I'm Jewish?"

Ron's smile wavered. "Oh—ah—no, I wasn't. I didn't mean any offense."

"None taken. Much. No, I'm not interested in staying home, reading the Bible, and discussing Christianity with you tonight." He picked up his tablet and woke it up. "Bryan and I are leaving for the bonfire at 6:30. You're welcome to join us or not." Leaning back on the couch, he resumed reading.

Ron retreated to his room. He closed the door and sprawled out on the bed, heaving a sigh. He needed to be more confident. More convincing.

He wanted some pot, but instead he rolled over to get his tablet. The contents of his cargo pocket dug into his leg. He pulled out the radio charging cradle and tucked it under the bed. It had seemed strange that Janet asked him to keep it for her, but he was glad to accommodate her.

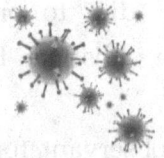

Chapter Seventy-One

The Storm Gathers

Sept 21, 4:45 p.m.

GEORGE surveyed the area around the sluice gate looking for signs of Bob. Tyler and Bill walked a search pattern looking for clues as well. The wind clawed at their clothing, with occasional gusts making them stagger to keep their footing.

"I found something," Tyler shouted. He held up a branch as he approached George. He pointed to the broken end as Bill joined them. "This branch has been broken off recently," he said, "though there's no tree here that it could have just fallen from. Somebody brought it here."

George examined it, rubbing his fingers over the gray, pitted surface. "There's a dent in the branch here," he said, pointing to a spot near the break, "like something strong compressed it."

"There's another branch," Bill said, pointing up the bank. He scrambled up and brought it to the others. One of the broken ends fit exactly with the end of the one Tyler had found.Tyler examined the dent in the branch. "Do you think someone beat Bob with this?"

George shrugged. "Don't know. Doesn't seem to have

any blood on it."

"I don't think Bob got beaten with this," Bill said. He pointed to the dent. "That wasn't made by hitting a person, and besides, it's near the middle of the stick. Looks like it was made by a rod with a fairly small diameter, probably made of metal, to have dented the wood like that." He examined the second branch and pointed near its end. Another dent showed. He shrugged. "I guess a rock might've left that kind of mark too, if you banged the branch against it."

"In two, widely separated spots?" George shook his head. "Seems unlikely." A gust staggered him, and he did a quick step forward to catch himself. If Bob was hurt, they needed to find him soon, before the rain started. The air wasn't cold, but a big storm was coming. The temperature would drop afterwards. Wet and wounded, Bob could be at serious risk from exposure.

After another few minutes of additional searching Bill shouted, "There's something over here." The other two joined him. Bill pointed to a football-sized stone partially buried in the bank. "There's blood on that rock."

The three of them squatted to examine it. George touched the blood stain. It had dried, but the color was still bright. "Looks recent."

Tyler stood and made a slow rotation in place holding his hand to his face to shield his eyes from the wind. "Looks like some of the gravel nearby's been disturbed downhill toward the edge of the stream," he said, pointing. He made his way to the bank, which was lined with rhododendrons.

Tyler squatted to examine the ground, ducking under the rhododendron branches waving in the wind. He pointed. "More blood." He stood and scanned the area. "Those look like tracks leading toward the trees, like someone was shuffling his feet as he went."

Bill raised an eyebrow. "If so, he's heading toward the woods away from town."

By a maple tree at the edge of the woods they found a place where the brambles around the tree trunk had been pushed aside and some of them broken. "Looks like our best bet," George said. He pulled out his radio and keyed it. No response. After a couple of attempts he turned it off and slid it back into its holster. "Too far away, I guess. Well, let's go find Bob."

*   *   *

Jamal roused Jim for dinner at 5:30—vegetable stew with walnuts. Jim considered the deep yellow cast of the turmeric spiced stew and shook his head. He took a bite and put his spoon down with a grimace. He swallowed hard. In a gravelly whisper he said, "You could at least add some goddamn salt. I can't taste any of this through the fucking garlic."

"The salt's not good for your blood pressure," Jamal said, "and the garlic and turmeric are keeping your tumors from growing too fast." He took a bite of the stew and grimaced himself, then swallowed.

Jim pushed the bowl of stew away. "Yeah, like that really matters now. I might as well enjoy my last few meals, rather than prolong the agony. Get me some damn salt."

"Jim—"

"Yeah, I know." He sighed and pulled the bowl back and took another bite. "Thanks for the thought."

Jamal scowled as he locked eyes with him. Jim wasn't grateful at all. Jamal set his spoon by his bowl with a loud clack. Stretching, he pulled a box of salt from an upper shelf of the pantry and dropped it on the table next to Jim.

Jim lifted an eyebrow, tilting his face up to Jamal's. "Thanks."

Jamal sat and ate another spoonful of stew without comment.

*   *   *

Jamal helped Jim into warm clothing after cleaning up from dinner. Jim coughed and wheezed as he stretched to pull on the woolens and a pair of nylon rain pants. The effort of getting dressed and moving back to his wheelchair left Jim gasping as if being smothered by a giant. But the only giant nearby was Jamal, and he just stood before Jim's wheelchair with a spit basin ready, his lips twisted in frustration at his impotence to help.

Once Jim's breathing eased, Jamal put away the basin. "You sure you want to do this?"

Jim nodded.

Jamal shook his head. "Okay. I still don't think this is a good idea. You seem to be breathing a little easier today, at least. The humidity, I guess." He maneuvered the chair through the door and pulled it closed after him.

As he pushed Jim toward the farm the wind blew in his face, resisting his progress and making his poncho flap around him. Low, dark clouds pregnant with rain scudded the sky above them heading south. Jim bent his head toward his chest and screwed his eyes shut tight.

Halfway to the farm a group of women, survivors of the Bed and Breakfast inn, caught up with them. There were eight of them, and as usual, Brenda was in charge. The group slowed their pace to keep back with Jamal and Jim once they met with them. They nodded greetings, but few of them tried to speak over the wind. Heads down, leaning forward, they continued on their way.

Jamal was glad the wind made it inconvenient to talk. He still felt awkward with Brenda after his gaffe about the "gene pool" comment at the meeting a few weeks ago. Having an excuse to not make conversation was a relief. Brenda hadn't brought up the subject since then, and she'd been helpful to a nearly professional degree with the first aid for Nate's injury at the stable a few days ago. She showed no reservations about working with him to immobilize Nate's shoulder.

As they turned up the lane to the farm Jamal checked his watch. 7:12. Sunset would be in only another sixteen minutes, but there were only about ten other people gathered. They huddled in rain coats and ponchos at the barn's door in the lee of the wind.

"Small crowd this time," he said to Brenda, raising his voice against the wind.

"What?"

He leaned toward her and repeated himself.

Brenda nodded. She said something brief, but Jamal didn't catch it.

*   *   *

Ed knocked on Ron's bedroom door at 6:30. "Hey Ron, Bryan and I are leaving for the bonfire. Are you coming with us?"

"No, I'm not gonna go," Ron called through the door.

"Suit yourself. We'll see you later."

Ron lay on the bed with a copy of the Bible open on his tablet. Exodus. The passage concerned Moses' return with the commandments to find the Israelis worshiping a golden calf.

He finished the section and put the tablet down.

Worshiping pagan idols is wrong. Evil. Janet had said so, and it was right there in the Bible, just like she said. Still, he had a hard time believing that Allen was evil. Misguided, maybe, but evil? He shook his head.

The passage left no doubt, though, especially after Janet's guidance. He swung himself around to sit on the bed, his elbows on his knees, supporting his head with his hands. The Bible is truth. Despite appearances, Allen must be evil, and it was his duty as a believer to counter Allen's program of paganism.

He stood and paced the room. The circuit required only four steps between the chest of drawers on the back wall and the door. He did three laps, then stopped. "This isn't accomplishing anything," he said aloud. He shook his head. He'd just have to give it his best shot. If he could convince one person, that was doing something. He left the room and got his coat. The grandfather's clock read 6:58. He'd have to hurry to make it before sunset.

*   *   *

At 6:45 a knock sounded at the Haskels' door. Dan almost didn't hear it over the wind. He found Andrea there when he opened the door.

"What are you doing here?" he said. "I thought you'd be going to the bonfire."

Andrea stepped inside. "I figured you might want to be with your family for that." She pulled her poncho over her head and straightened her hair. "I'll cover for you."

"That's nice of you, but don't you want to go yourself?"

"You should be with your family. It's fine. Go, or you'll

be late."

Dan frowned for a second, then he nodded. "Okay. Thanks."

"Where's Janet?"

Dan pulled on his raincoat and pointed down the hall. "She's in the study. That's where she's been spending most of her time."

"Okay, hurry along, or you'll be late."

He nodded. "Thanks again."

"Don't mention it. Get going."

*   *   *

Once the door slammed closed against the wind Andrea hung her poncho on the coat tree by the door. She stepped to the center of the room and looked around. It was neat, but a little fussy for her taste. Ruffled curtains covered the window and the tweed, wing-back sofa had a crocheted doily draped over the back in 1950s nostalgia style. She turned around and nearly jumped out of her skivvies. Janet stood right there, not two feet away, her dark eyes shadowed by a scowl.

"Oh, you startled me. I didn't hear you come out."

Janet sniffed. "Didn't expect to see you tonight. I thought Dan Kiner was on until eight."

"I'm covering so he can go to the bonfire tonight."

Janet raised an eyebrow. "What? Couldn't get a date for that? I'd have thought that with all the young women who arrived last spring you'd hardly ever get out of bed."

Andrea grimaced. "Would you like some tea or something?"

"Sure. Why not?" Janet said, shrugging. "There's dried mint in a canister by the refrigerator."

As Andrea stepped past her toward the kitchen she had

just a glimpse of Janet grabbing a heavy glass vase from an end table. Before she could turn around, pain exploded in her skull and everything went dark.

* * *

Andrea crumpled to the floor without a whimper. The pain in Janet's skull suddenly flared white-hot, as if from sympathy with Andrea, but she gritted her teeth and composed herself. She laid the vase on the floor by the sofa. With a soft groan as she forced her bad leg to bend, Janet crouched next to Andrea and felt for the pulse in her neck. She found it at once. She gently arranged Andrea into what she thought would be a more comfortable position on the floor. Stroking her temples she turned to her father, who stood by the entrance to the hall. "Are you sure that was necessary? I don't approve of violence."

"She facilitated Daniel's blasphemy, and so she blasphemed herself. Now you're free to prevent the pagan abomination soon to occur on the farm. This is God's will."

Janet nodded. "His will be done."

"Hurry now. There's not much time."

She searched Andrea's pockets, but didn't find the keys. She struggled to her feet and searched Andrea's poncho and the sideboard. Nothing. Dan must have forgotten to give them to her in his rush to leave. She locked eyes with her father.

"You have to hurry. Time's running out."

* * *

Sept 21, 6:52 p.m.

Tyler bent to examine a footprint on the trail. "We're back on track." He brushed hair away from his eyes. "Twenty minutes wasted on the wrong fork." Tracking a deer seemed simple in comparison. Less stressful, anyway.

"Then let's not waste more," George said. "Which way?"

Tyler pointed, and they continued their search. The signs were few. It was hard to tell where the leaf-litter on the ground was disturbed with the wind blowing as it was, but occasionally they saw a clear track where the path was muddy, and found numerous places where twigs were broken off trees by the trail. Once some strands of thread on a bramble caught Tyler's eye.

Fifteen minutes later Tyler's head snapped up as he caught a glimpse of Bob. He was visible for just a second before he disappeared again around a bend in the path. He pointed. "There he is!"

George looked up. "I don't see anyone."

"I saw him up ahead. He went behind those bushes." Tyler started to run. "Hey Bob, wait," he shouted.

As Tyler came around the bend in the trail Bob stood up ahead clutching a limb of an oak tree that extended across the path. In his other hand he held a piece of a branch as a walking stick. He raised it like a weapon when he saw Tyler.

Tyler skidded to a halt, and Bill stopped beside him a second later. Bob's head was out of shape, swollen on the left side of his skull. His left eye was black and nearly shut by the swelling. Dried blood trailed down the side of his face to his neck.

"Stay back," Bob shouted, clutching the stick, but then he staggered and nearly fell.

"Bob, let us help you. You're going the wrong way."

Tyler took a step toward him, but Bill grasped his arm and held him back. He looked into Tyler's face and shook his head. George joined them and Bill shook his head at him, too.

"Bob, Janet doesn't know where you are, and she's worried," Bill said.

"Janet?" Bob said. He lowered the stick a little.

Bill nodded. He glanced at George, then turned back to Bob. "Yeah. We should take you back home. You've been gone a lot longer than you expected. You're probably getting hungry now, aren't you? I'm sure Janet would fix you something to eat."

Bob's face screwed up in despair. A tear trickled down his cheek. "She doesn't love me anymore."

"Sure she does," George said. He held an arm out toward Bob. "Let us take you back, okay? Who did this to you?"

Bob blinked. "I don't know."

George took a step toward him and Bob stiffened. He raised the stick again and stumbled backward a step. "How do I know you didn't do it?"

George stopped and lifted his hands, palms out. "Of course we didn't do it," he said, "did we, guys?" Tyler and Bill shook their heads.

"From the signs by the reservoir, looks like you fell and hit your head on a rock," Tyler said. "We found a blood stain on a rock up there, a little below the sluice gate."

"Janet's worried," George said. He took another step forward. "We'll take you back, okay? You've been hurt, Bob. Let us help you."

Tears streamed down Bob's face. He lowered the stick. "Janet doesn't love me anymore."

George stepped forward and took the stick from Bob's

unresisting hand. George passed the stick to Tyler and wrapped Bob in a hug. "Of course she loves you," George said. "Let's go on back, okay?"

Bob nodded as he stood supported by George's embrace. "Okay," he whispered.

As Bill stepped up to Bob's other side a loud crack sounded followed by the crash of something falling through the trees. They turned in time to see a branch dropping fifty yards down the trail.

"We need to get out of here," Bill said.

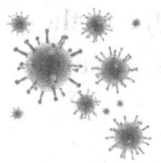

Chapter Seventy-Two

Escape

Sept 21, 7:10 p.m.

JANET used a butter knife to break open the latch on the tool box and pried off the padlock on the inside garage door with the crowbar. She got her raincoat and found a book of matches in the sideboard drawer. As she passed Andrea lying on the floor she stopped a second and pursed her lips. "Sorry. It's for the greater good."

"Hurry," her father said. He still stood by the hall in the same place he'd been since Andrea arrived.

Janet nodded. As she entered the garage she hit the button on the garage door opener. The ceiling light gave a dim illumination to the room as the gears ground in place for a second before engaging. The overhead door crept open and the room brightened further as the fading daylight flooded the mostly empty garage. Janet squinted as her eyes adjusted to the light. Wind tore at her coat and a scrap of paper flew up from the floor and whirled around the room. She pulled her coat closed and zipped it up.

Her golf cart stood connected to its charging station in

the front of the garage. The charge indicator glowed green. She pulled out the cable and slid onto the seat. The way to the farm by the back road was a little farther than the direct route, but at top speed she'd arrive before sunset.

* * *

Sept 21, 7:25 p.m.
Ron leaned into the wind as his raincoat flapped around him. Leaves swirled past him as he fast-marched toward the farm, angry dark clouds covering the sky. As he came past a stand of pine trees the barn came into view, a small crowd standing near it. He checked his watch. Only three minutes before sundown. He started to run.

* * *

Sept 21, 7:25 p.m.
Janet drove the golf cart down the side road by the farm and took the tractor path around the hay field toward the back of the barn. The ride was bouncy, but the electric motor on the cart was nearly silent and the wind masked the tire noise. She reached the little feedlot just outside the milking stall a couple of minutes before sundown. Some cows looked up at her, uninterested, as she stopped the cart just outside the fence.

Her father stood near the gate, and Dr. Anderson, her undergraduate adviser and the professor of her scripture interpretation class, stood beside him. His shoulder-length silver hair flew about his face in the wind.

Janet gasped at seeing him, and a new pulse of pain stabbed her between the eyes. She gritted her teeth, clenching her eyes shut tight.

"The Bible teaches love," Dr. Anderson said. "Don't do this."

"Christianity must prevail," her father said. "There's so few of us now, it's important that we not lose anyone to pagan idolatry."

Janet opened her eyes. A shimmering silver-white outline surrounded the two men. The retreating rational part of her mind recalled Jamal's question about "visual effects."

Dr. Anderson glanced at her father and frowned. "What shall it profit a man, if he shall gain the whole world, and lose his own soul?"

Her father shook his head. "Mark 8:36. Not applicable. We're trying to save souls, not gain worldly wealth."

Janet made her way to the gate and opened the latch. The two men just stood there, only turning their heads to watch as she went by. The manger was under an overhang from the barn in the feedlot. She limped up to it and lit a match. The wind blew it out. She tried another, with the same result. Only three left.

The pain in her skull throbbed with each heartbeat, which came faster and faster with every pulse. Now everything was outlined in glowing sliver-white.

Dr Anderson called, "Don't do it, Janet."

"You must do it."

Janet clenched her eyes shut tight and held her head in her hands. "It hurts so much!"

"Honor thy father."

Janet nodded. Blinking from the pain, tears wetting her cheeks, she grabbed a handful of hay and twisted it into a ragged wand-shape. Turning her back to the wind she struck another match and lit her improvised torch. In a few seconds it was burning well. She stared at it in fascination as she watched the play of the orange flames outlined in silver. Then the fire neared her hand and she thrust the burning hay into the manger.

Pain exploded inside Janet's skull. Covering her face in her hands, she sank to her knees.

"You're a good daughter."

Janet raised her head. Dr. Anderson had disappeared and her father stood alone by the manger, which now bloomed in fire. Acrid, black smoke rose, swept away by the wind. Cows bawled and fled the feedlot, some of them going out the gate she'd left open, others going into the pasture.

Gritting her teeth, Janet struggled to her feet. She staggered a few steps toward the gate before she collapsed. Grunting from the effort, she rolled onto her back. Shimmering silver threaded the dark clouds overhead. They were beautiful. Her father appeared, standing above her. "You're a good Christian, and a good daughter."

Through pain ricocheting between her temples with each pulse she nodded and gave a weak smile. He disappeared, fading into the air above her.

To the west, a funnel dipped from the cloud ceiling and shrank back. It formed again, snaking toward the ground, then back up. She lifted her head to see it better as it dropped and retreated. The undulating funnel outlined in silver shimmered against the ominous dark gray clouds, the silver like an after-image following its movement. The beauty of it all entranced her, despite the agony in her head.

Brenda's face appeared above her, followed by Kayla's and Dan's. Janet laid her head down and smiled at them. "His will be done," she whispered. Everything dissolved into swirling silver mist. She closed her eyes.

* * *

Sept 21, 7:28 p.m.

Allen checked his watch and nodded. It was time. He'd decided there was too much risk from the wind-blown sparks to light a full-sized bonfire, so he bent to light some symbolic twigs stacked in a small, saucer-shaped fire bowl.

He was about to strike a long-nose lighter when a shout made him turn.

"Stop! For the sake of—of your souls, don't do this!" It was Ron, waving his arms as he ran up the lane. "Follow Christ!" Ron stopped, still fifteen yards from the little crowd around the fire bowl and leaned forward, resting his hands on his knees while he sucked oxygen from the air. The maple tree just behind him creaked as its limbs swayed in the wind.

Dan started toward Ron, but Jamal grabbed his arm to stop him. Dan turned toward Jamal with his eyes wide, but Jamal's focus was on Ron.

"Ron, get away from there!" Jamal shouted.

Ron gave an emphatic shake of his head. "I won't go! We should all follow Jesus. Don't worship false idols."

"Ron, get away from the tree!"

Allen raised his eyes to the tree and gasped. A limb hanging above Ron that was as big as a tree in its own right had cracked.

Dan pointed up at the tree. "Ron, move! Run!"

Ron furrowed his brows and turned to look behind him. With a splintering crack the limb broke off. Ron tried to run, but too late. He tripped and the thick part of the limb landed across his legs, pinning him to the ground. He screamed.

Allen followed Jonathan and Sara in the crowd

converging on Ron. Jamal left Jim in his wheelchair. Brenda directed people to get on either side of the branch so they could lift it straight up from Ron's legs.

As Jonathan helped hold up the branch, his phone chimed from his pocket. Allen glanced up from the other side of the branch and raised his eyebrows.

"Didn't bring the earpiece," Jonathan said. "Can't answer it now."

Jamal and Dan pulled Ron away from the branch. He cried out again. Once clear, the rest of them lowered the branch.

Jamal knelt by Ron and did a quick examination of his legs. "Don't try to move. I think your legs are broken."

Ron nodded, sweat beading on his forehead, his face contorted in pain.

"I need something for splints," Jamal shouted. "Boards, strips of cloth, that sort of thing."

Allen did a quick mental inventory of the barn's contents. The slats he'd salvaged from the old picket fence. He ran inside.

Ed and Bryan tore the tablecloth into strips as Allen brought out the boards. He set them beside Jamal.

Ron linked eyes with Allen. "You shouldn't have—have lit the fire. Follow Christ."

"Don't talk," Jamal said as he selected boards.

Allen furrowed his brows. "I *didn't* light the fire." Cows bawled from the pasture behind the barn.

"I smell—" Ron coughed. "I smell smoke."

Allen turned toward the fire bowl. It wasn't burning, but a plume of smoke rose from the other side of the barn. "Oh, shit. *Fire!*" he shouted, pointing.

*   *   *

Brenda snapped her head toward Allen, then turned to follow his gaze. She did a quick survey of the group. Jane and Rita stood by the barn entrance, clutching their crying babies. Amber and Clayton stood next to Maria, her hands on their shoulders. The other Girl Scouts looked to her for direction. Jamal concentrated on Ron. The rest of them stood gaping at the plume of smoke.

She pointed toward the group of Girl Scouts. "Tiffany, Becky, and Katie, you stay here and help Jamal," Brenda shouted. "Rita, Jane, and Maria, get the children into the house." She pointed to the fire buckets Allen had brought up. "The rest of you, grab some buckets and let's go." Brenda ran to get a bucket, followed by the other Girl Scouts. The others stood as if paralyzed.

As she ran past him she had a glimpse of Dan's eyes fixed on her, growing wide.

"You heard her," Dan shouted. "Get moving!" He followed the young women and the rest of them ran to catch up.

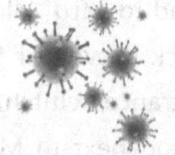

Chapter Seventy-Three

Casualties

Sept 21, 7:28 p.m.

GEORGE choose his steps carefully as he and Bill guided Bob back toward the village. He didn't want to risk stumbling and Bob hitting his head again.

The farm came into view when they crested a hill past a stand of white pine trees. Tyler pointed. "What's that crowd doing under the old maple tree? Looks like a branch broke off." He stopped and shielded his eyes from the wind. "Also looks like someone got hurt."

George squinted. A crowd of people stood near the tree around the fallen limb. He recognized Jamal kneeling next to someone on the ground by the fallen branch, his dreadlocks swaying in the breeze the only obvious motion among the crowd as the rest of the crowd struggled with the limb.

"Yeah, that's what it looks like," George said. "You and Bill go on ahead and see if you can help. I'll be there with Bob soon."

Tyler and Bill ran toward the farm. A few seconds later, though, the crowd by the tree ran around the barn toward the back, except for a few. Jamal and the injured person, who was now clear of the fallen branch, and a couple of others stayed behind. Jim Henderson's wheelchair sat parked by the barn door. George furrowed his brows. Then he realized the smoke wasn't coming from the bonfire, but from the other side of the barn. "Oh, my God. Come on, Bob. We need to hurry."

*   *   *

Dan gasped as they came around the barn. The burning hay in the manger sent sparks swirling in the wind as Brenda led the group to the fire. Most of the sparks blew away from the barn, though some flew to the roof of the overhang.

Janet lay near the open gate to the feedlot. Brenda, Kayla, and Dan stopped to check her while Christine organized a bucket brigade from the watering trough, and Allen got the hose from the milking shed.

Janet whispered something he couldn't hear over the wind when they first got to her, but then she closed her eyes and didn't respond.

Dan patted her cheek. "Janet, wake up." He shook her shoulder. "Wake up, Janet."

Kayla felt for Janet's carotid artery. "She's got a pulse but it's rapid and weak. I can hardly feel it. We need to get her inside."

Brenda checked for broken bones.

Dan spared a glance toward the manger. Between the bucket brigade and Allen spraying it with the hose, the fire looked under control. He turned back to Brenda, who was just finishing with Janet. "She okay to move?"

"Yeah, I think so."

Dan re-checked the progress of the fire fighters. The flames were gone but the others were still dousing the smoldering remains. "Okay, let's do—" Dan's voice cut off as the clouds caught his attention, and a funnel sank downward. A chill shook him. "Tornado!" he cried, pointing. Brenda turned and gasped. The funnel sank lower, reaching the ground. Debris flew up and swirled around the base of the funnel.

Dan bent and scooped Janet up in his arms. He headed toward the house, trying to run, but staggering under the load.

*   *   *

Brenda ran toward the bucket brigade. She grabbed the arm of the first person she reached, Bryan Pierce. "Tornado! Get in the basement."

The others turned toward Brenda wide-eyed, heads rotating as if in a wave traveling down the line. Then they dropped the buckets and ran toward the house, Allen leading them toward the basement door.

Once the others were all on their way to the house Brenda sprinted back around the barn where Jamal worked on Ron. "Tornado!" she shouted. "We've got to get into the basement."

Jamal glanced up at Brenda, then past her at the funnel cloud. His eyes went wide. "I'm almost done. Help Tyler and Bill. They're in the barn making a stretcher." He turned back to Ron and Tiffany handed him a strip of cloth.

Brenda spared no time to wonder about Tyler and Bill suddenly appearing. They'd found a length of pipe, a tree trimmer pole, and a blue plastic tarp, and they'd just about finished when Brenda found them. They carried the stretcher out and spread it on the ground beside Ron.

*   *   *

Jamal helped them position the stretcher. Looked like they'd done a fair job making it.

"Ron," he said, "we're going to put you on the stretcher now, and we don't have time to be gentle about it. I'm sorry, but this is going to hurt."

Ron's eyes went wide, but he remained silent as he nodded. Jamal positioned them with Brenda and Katie kneeling at Ron's shoulders, Bill and Tyler at his hips, and himself at Ron's legs.

Jamal checked that they were all in position. "Count of three, then lift on three and shift him onto the stretcher."

The others nodded, their eyes locked on his face.

Jim bumped his wheelchair into Brenda's back then, nearly knocking her over as she squatted next to Ron. "Forget him," Jim said, his words a barely audible rasp over the wind, "He's a useless slacker. Take me to the house."

Brenda regained her balance and stared up at Jim, twisting around to see him. "You can't mean that."

"Don't tell me what I mean, you stupid bitch. Jamal, take me inside." He spoke in a hoarse croak, but his words were slurred, weirdly distorted.

Jamal stared at Jim. The left side of this face drooped. Oh, shit. A stroke? He had no way to treat that. "Jim, shut up that nonsense and stop interfering. We'll take care of you. Tiffany, could you wheel Jim toward the house—"

"You stupid, fucking asshole! Don't tell me what to do." He struggled to back up the wheelchair.

"Jim, you're out of your head," George said, coming up behind Jamal.

Jamal spun around to find George and Bob standing

right behind him. "Oh my God, Bob, what—"

"Leave that piece of shit there and get me out of the fucking wind, you goddamn asshole," Jim rasped.

Jamal pivoted toward Jim again. Jim's face had contorted into a furious, lopsided mask.

"Oh, fuck," George said. Jamal twisted back toward him. George's eyes were wide, then he clenched them shut tight. "Forgive me," he said. He opened his eyes, pulled a pistol from its holster, and shot Jim in the chest.

Tiffany, Katie, and Becky screamed.

Jamal bounced up and slapped the gun from George's hand. He grabbed George's arm and twisted it behind his back, forcing him to the ground. "What the fuck do you think you're doing?"

George clenched his teeth in pain from Jamal's grip, but he managed to say, "What Jim asked for. He said to—to kill him if the cancer got into his brain and he lost who he was. Can you—you imagine Jim Henderson saying or doing those things?"

"Jim's dead," Tiffany said. She knelt next to Jim's wheelchair, feeling for a pulse in his neck. Her mouth hung open, her eyes wide. Jim slumped over in the chair, held in place by the seatbelt.

"Dealing with Jim would've wasted time we don't have," George said. "Risked killing us all."

"Jay, let him up," Brenda said. "We need to take care of Ron."

Jamal glanced up at her. He held George immobile for a couple seconds more, then he released him. George blew out a whoosh of air, then pushed himself up.

Without a word, Jamal moved back into position by Ron's feet. He looked up at the others, who stared back, wide-eyed. "On the count of three. One, two, three—."

*   *   *

Sept 21, 7:38 p.m.

Allen reached the house just before Dan arrived with Janet in his arms. He pulled keys from his pocket and fumbled with the padlock on the basement door, swearing until the key engaged and the lock popped open. Dan took the steps slowly, feeling his way into the dark basement. Allen stood by the door waving his arm toward it at the rest of the ones who had manned the bucket brigade. "Hurry! Run!"

Once the last of them were inside he latched the door and ran to the back door to the kitchen. Rita met him holding Davina, who cried in her arms as he came in, Rita's eyes wide. "What's going on?"

"Tornado. Get in the basement." He urged her and the others to the head of the stairs. Maria guided Clayton and Amber down, and then Jane and Rita followed. A few steps down Rita stopped and turned back to him, Davina screaming on her shoulder.

"Aren't you coming too?"

"Jamal, Jim, and some others are still up by the barn. I'm going to get them."

Rita opened her mouth, then closed it. She grimaced. "Hurry."

*   *   *

Allen sprinted out the back door and almost ran into Tiffany, who dodged around him, heading to the house. Becky followed, her eyes wide as if fleeing something horrible. "Go in through the kitchen," he shouted at them.

He met the others carrying the stretcher, followed by George and Katie supporting another man who'd received a head injury. It took him a second to realize it was Bob between them.

Then he noticed that Jim wasn't present. "Where's Jim?"

"Dead." Jamal's face was a blank mask.

"Dead! What happened?"

"No time," Jamal said. "We need the basement door open. Get going."

Allen wasted no more than a second in confusion, then he sprinted back to the door to the basement. He opened it and the others carried Ron inside and helped Bob down the steps. Allen followed them down and groped for the bolt to latch the door from the inside.

*   *   *

Jonathan looked up as the outside door opened and daylight flooded the basement. The candles they'd set about flickered in the wind and a couple of them went out. Jamal and Brenda came down the stairs supporting a stretcher. Tyler and Bill followed carrying the other end of the stretcher. They placed Ron on a couch in what had once been a family room in the finished part of the basement.

While Jamal and Brenda tended Ron, Jonathan's phone rang again. He pulled it out and accepted the call on speaker phone so Sara could hear it.

"Security monitor alert. Three unheard messages pending. First message: A person matching Janet Haskel's description left her house on a golf cart heading north-east toward the farm."

"Acknowledged." Jonathan said.

"Second message: A group of at least fifteen people is approaching from the north. There are three wagons and six horses with the group, which contains six adults who are armed, and several children."

Jonathan's eyebrows shot up. He glanced to Sara, whose eyes were wide. "Acknowledged."

"Third message: A tornado is approaching from the south-west. It's touched down two miles outside the village and is heading toward it at about fifteen miles per hour, but the path is erratic. Camera W-2b is down."

"Acknowledged. Where's the group approaching from the north?"

"About four hundred yards north of camera N-1b. They've abandoned the wagons and released the horses. They're taking shelter in a ditch by the road."

"That's got to be the people from New Hope," Sara said. She'd moved up beside Jonathan, listening in.

Jonathan nodded. "Yeah, probably, but there's nothing we can do to about them right now. We still need to be careful."

Jonathan's phone rang again. He pressed the virtual button to accept the call. "Security monitor alert: The house at 138 Johnson St. has been hit by the tornado and has been heavily damaged. There's no indication of casualties."

Jonathan swallowed hard. He looked at Sara and she squeezed his hand. Paladin gave a growing list of houses falling to the twister, each one gnawing at the hole in his gut. He didn't notice at first when Dan tapped his shoulder.

"We need to talk."

Jonathan stared up at him. "The tornado's hit the

village and has heavily damaged four houses so far."

The computer announced, "Update: 21 Aspen Court and 23 Aspen Court have been hit and appear to have been destroyed."

"There's something else," Dan said.

"More important than this? It's heading toward the community center."

"Jim's dead."

Jonathan ripped his eyes away from the phone, which showed a grainy, over-magnified video of a house dissolving in the tornado's path, and stared at Dan. "What? How?"

"George shot him."

"George? Why?" Jonathan's mouth hung open.

"Jim was irrational and was interfering with Ron's First Aid. In accordance with Jim's instructions for if he lost his mind, George—George euthanized him. Jim had discussed that with several of us last winter." Dan pulled out a handkerchief and wiped his eyes.

Jonathan shifted his gaze toward George, who sat on the floor in the far corner of the room, his legs folded beneath him. He held his head in his hands, occasionally wiping his eyes. His wife, Alice, stood by him, her hand on his shoulder. Nearby, Jamal wiped sweat from Ron's forehead with a blue and white bandana. A few feet away Bob Haskel knelt by Janet where she lay on some cushions that had been appropriated from a sofa upstairs. He held her hand, crying, head bowed, while Janet lay still.

His phone rang again. "Security monitor alert: The tornado has hit the community center. The wing containing the classrooms has been heavily damaged. The tornado is continuing to head east along Maple street."

"Acknowledged," Jonathan said, and his mouth went

dry. He raised his eyes to Sara. The tornado was heading toward their house.

"Update: 215 Maple street has been hit and appears to have been destroyed." Jonathan gulped. Two doors down from their house. Sara's eyes were wide. She stood close beside him and clenched his hand in hers.

"Update: Jonathan and Sara, thank you for everything, and good luck."

"Paladin, what?—" Jonathan furrowed his brows. He hadn't programmed that sort of interaction for the security monitor. The phone went dead. He hit the "reconnect" button. No response. A "No Network Connection" alert blinked red in the corner of the screen. Jonathan stared at it for a second. "Paladin. No," he whispered. The phone fell from his fingers. It clattered on the linoleum tile floor and came to rest by Dan's feet. Dan glanced down at it, then raised his eyes to Jonathan's face.

Jonathan met his gaze. "There's a group of 15 approaching from the north." His voice was flat, emotionless. "Some are armed. The last I saw, they were sheltering in a ditch." Sara laid a hand on his shoulder. He spared her a glance and turned back to Dan. "Good chance they're refugees from New Hope, but we need to set a watch and be prepared in case it's an attack." He sniffled and wiped tears from his eyes. "I can't—I can't monitor them anymore."

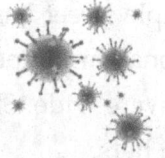

Chapter Seventy-Four

Aftermath

RITA lay Davina to sleep around eight-thirty in a bed improvised from a plastic laundry basket and some towels. Grayson already lay sleeping in his own basket beside her. The baskets sat on the floor next to a load-bearing wall near the center of the basement. She gave them both a worried smile after kissing Davina on the forehead, careful not to wake her. She touched the floor with her right hand before straightening back up.

Jane stepped beside Rita and put an arm around her waist. "Thanks."

Rita nodded. "I just hope the storm passes soon."

"The wind's already dying down."

"Yeah, that's good."

Jane wiped her eyes and turned glanced toward the other side of the room, where Jamal and Tiffany tended Janet and Ron. "I also hope—hope we don't lose anyone else."

"Me too," Rita said. "Let's help Allen find blankets and stuff. Unless I miss my guess, he's clueless about where I stored the extras down here."

Rain drops splattered against the basement windows

and drew their attention. Just a few at first, but within seconds the rain poured.

"If it's raining, that means the danger from the tornado has passed, right?" Jane asked.

"I'm pretty sure that's a myth. Hope I'm wrong. Let's find Allen."

*   *   *

Brenda awoke next morning to the first glimmers of light coming through the basement windows. She remained lying on the floor with her poncho and a bath towel covering her, listening to others snoring around the room. The wind had died, and the rain had passed overnight. She needed to pee, but it was still too dark in the basement to make her way around the other sleeping bodies without tripping over them. She could wait.

From the other side of the room blankets rustled and someone moved about in the darkness.

"Janet?" Bob said. A couple of seconds passed. "Honey, it's me. Janet? Janet, wake up." Another pause. Then his voice rose to a high-pitched wail. "Janet! No! Oh, Janet!"

People stirred as Bob's cries awoke them. Jamal's huge silhouette moved to Janet's side with surprising speed in the dark, crowded room. Brenda threw off her improvised blanket and joined them.

"I need some light," Jamal called.

"She's cold! Oh good Lord, she's cold!"

Brenda laid a hand on Bob's shoulder and gently pulled him away. "Let Jamal check her."

Rita brought a lighted candle and handed it to Jamal.

He held it to Janet's face and pulled an eyelid open. He

checked for the pulse in her neck, then bowed his head and sighed. "I'm sorry, Bob."

"No!" Bob buried his face in his hands.

Brenda embraced him, and Alice hugged him as well.

Jamal pulled the blanket over Janet's face. Bob looked up as he did, and a new series of sobs racked his body. He glanced up at Rita, who stood beside Jamal. She bent and reached toward the floor.

Bob pointed at her. "None of that!" he shouted, glaring.

Rita froze.

"Janet wouldn't want that. Show some respect."

Rita straightened and nodded. "Of course. You're right. I'm sorry, no disrespect intended."

He wiped his hand over his eyes. "She deserves a Christian burial, and by God, she's going to get it."

*   *   *

Brenda joined Allen, Dan, and George and some others as they emerged from the basement at first light. The day had dawned clear and cool with cheerful birdsong around them as they assessed the situation. Ed and George took the stretcher to retrieve Jim's body. She shook her head. Such a beautiful morning to follow such a horrible disaster.

The farmhouse and barn had escaped major damage. Some shingles were missing on the house, but the barn seemed intact. The cows had already gathered for milking. As Brenda stood next to Dan in the farmyard surveying the buildings she said, "We need to send a group to check on the refugees from New Hope."

Dan frowned. "We don't know for sure they were from

New Hope. Jon only got a brief report from his computer. I agree, that's the most likely case. But the consequences if we're wrong could be bad."

"There's not really any doubt about that," Brenda said. "Group size is right, they have children with them, and we knew the New Hope folks were considering coming. Right number of horses, too."

Tyler joined them. He scratched the back of his neck. "We need to check it out one way or the other. Until Jonathan gets his system back up, we don't have intelligence about them without sending someone."

Brenda noticed Jonathan grimace at Tyler's comment, but he remained silent. He'd hardly spoken two words all morning.

Dan gave a single nod. "Okay. Sounds like we've got a couple of volunteers." He caught Brenda's eye. "Get a couple more and head up there after grabbing some breakfast. Allen, do you have any firearms they can borrow?"

"Aside from the ones I gave to the sentries, I've only got a couple that I have ammo for. A 4-10 shotgun and a .22 rifle. I'll want to keep one of them here."

"They can borrow my pistol," Rita said.

*   *   *

"From what Jonathan said, they should be visible from the top of this hill," Brenda said. "The northernmost camera is on the crest by the road, right?" The sun had started to chip away at the morning chill, but their breath showed as fleeting clouds.

Tyler nodded. "That's right. We should keep to the brush by the roadside as we come up. Don't want anyone to see us before we figure out the situation."

"Agreed." Brenda frowned. The group ahead almost

had to be from New Hope, but if not, they were seriously under-armed. Tyler had the rifle, Cynthia carried Rita's pistol, but she and Bryan were unarmed. She peered back toward the farm and identified the tree where Bill was standing watch, but of course, she couldn't see him.

"Not to be a worry-wart," Bryan said, "but how would the New Hope folks have known where we are?"

"Arthur told them," Tyler said. "That's what Randy said when I asked him the same question."

*   *   *

At the hilltop Brenda crouched by a bush and surveyed the group below. Her first view of them showed what appeared to be a peaceful scene with campfires burning and the wagons standing upright. She pulled out the little spyglass Allen had given her and looked them over. The glass was more of a toy than an optical instrument, but better than nothing. She passed it to Cynthia. "The one sitting by the closest of the wagons looks like Ellie. What do you think?"

Cynthia took her time to inspect them through the scope, then handed it back to Brenda. "I think you're right. And that looks like Bethanna by the fire over there. I think I see Gary too. Don't see Clara."

Brenda raised an eyebrow. "Gary?"

"One of the youngsters. We met him on our first visit."

"Okay. Think it's safe?"

"Yeah. I don't think there's any doubt they're the New Hopers."

"Well, let's go greet them then." Cynthia checked that there was a round chambered in Rita's pistol and Brenda turned her head toward Tyler and Bryan. "You okay with that?"

"I don't know them," Bryan said. "I'll defer to your judgement."

Tyler frowned. "I think we should be careful."

Brenda nodded. "Okay. You hang back under cover with the rifle and keep an eye on us. We'll check things out. Just don't be too trigger happy." She stood and picked up the bag of first aid supplies, ignoring Tyler's scowl.

*　　　*　　　*

Halfway down the hill to the camp, Albert from New Hope popped up from behind a scraggly barberry bush with a rifle leveled. "Halt. Hands up." Albert was a gangly fourteen-year-old with short-cropped red hair. His voice cracked as he gave his command, and he winced.

Brenda raised her arms but shouted, "Albert, good to see you! Happy to see you all made it here." She resisted the urge to turn and look back toward Tyler. She hoped her glad greeting would calm Tyler's defensive impulses.

Albert's aim wavered, and he looked over the sights at them. "Cynthia? Brenda?"

Cynthia shot a glance to Brenda, then turned back toward the young man. "Yeah it's us. This is Bryan. You've just about made to Hendersonville. Is everything alright? Did you weather the tornado okay?"

He lowered the rifle. "Did okay. Bad night, though."

*　　　*　　　*

Ellie met them as Brenda and Cynthia approached their camp. Mud stains mottled her clothing, and some rips exposed her knees, but she appeared unhurt.

"Good to see you again," Ellie said, taking Cynthia's hand. "I assume this means we're close to Hendersonville."

"Less than an hour to get to the village. Do you have any casualties? We brought some first aid supplies."

"Nothing we haven't been able to handle ourselves. We spent a pretty uncomfortable night, but the tornado didn't get up here. Everyone seems to be okay. How are Jan and Art?"

Brenda shook her head. "I don't know. They were fine the last I knew, but the tornado hit the village and there was a lot of damage. We were at the farmhouse at the time and we haven't been back yet to see how much damage there is."

"Did Randy and Nate make it here?"

"Yes. Nate had an accident when he arrived and broke his collar bone, but it seems to be healing well." Didn't seem wise to mention the gunshot wound yet. "Again, the last I knew they were okay. They're itching to go back to New Hope."

Ellie shook her head. "Nothing to go back to. We left two days ago and brought everything we could carry with us. We want to take you up on your offer to join you."

"Welcome, but there'll be a lot of work to do to repair the storm damage."

"We're used to working. At the moment, the main help we need is to find the last two horses and get them back here."

Brenda nodded. She did a quick survey of the others gathering around. "Where's Clara?"

"She had a heart attack or a stroke or something the morning after Nate and Randy left. She just collapsed and we couldn't revive her."

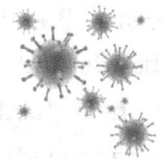

Chapter Seventy-Five

First Aid

THE Hope members arrived at Hendersonville just before noon. Bethanna drove the lead wagon, keeping behind Ellie, Brenda, and the others from Hendersonville. They walked in front to meet others in the village.

Bethanna took in the view, dazed by what she saw. The majority of the houses were standing, though a swath of destruction bisected the village. The houses were massive and modern, the ones still intact. She'd never seen such a surreal combination of luxury and devastation.

The sun had warmed the day from the morning's chill, but the wreckage through the center of the village prevented any sense of good cheer. Debris from shattered houses littered the ground, and trees down in the roads made the trip along the streets difficult for the wagons. They had to stop every hundred yards or so to clear tree limbs or building fragments from the street to progress.

As Bethanna pulled a maple branch to the side of the road she noticed someone leaning against a lamp post down the block. The person took a couple of wobbly steps toward them and fell to her knees. Then recognition hit. Andrea.

Bethanna tapped Ellie's arm and pointed. "That's

Andrea, and she's hurt." Bethanna sprinted toward her.

"Andrea, what happened?" Bethanna asked. Ellie and Brenda were right behind her. Brenda set the bag of first aid supplies on the sidewalk beside Andrea and opened it.

Andrea squinted at them. "Beth?"

"Yes, it's me. What happened?"

"I—I don't know."

"You've had a head injury," Brenda said. "Lie down and don't move."

While Brenda and Bethanna checked Andrea, Bryan approached. "There's a flyer on the lamp post that says to meet at the Community Center tonight. It says to bring anyone injured there right away."

"Understood," Brenda said without looking.

*   *   *

Andrea could make little sense of the confused montage of faces appearing and disappearing above her, hands feeling her limbs, the rattle of wagon wheels over pavement, and the jostle of being transferred to a cot. Her head pounded in rhythm with her pulse. It was hard to think. A bright light shined in her eyes as Jamal stood over her, then it was Brenda, then it was—Beth? No, couldn't be. Beth was in New Hope.

Someone was saying her name. She turned her head. Jamal.

"Andrea. Andrea, can you hear me?"

"My head hurts."

"I'll bet. You took quite a hit."

"Where am I?"

"The community center. We've set up an infirmary here. You should try to get some sleep. I'll be back, but I have to check on some of the others."

* * *

As evening approached someone pushed aside the sheet hung as a curtain around Andrea's cot in the infirmary. She gave a little gasp to see Bethanna enter with a bowl of soup. Jamal came in behind her.

Bethanna gave Andrea an embarrassed smile as she set the bowl on a table beside her. "It's rabbit soup with carrots, kale, and potatoes. Sara and Jonathan Rillman made it. I swear, I didn't add anything to it."

Andrea gave a laugh, then grimaced, gingerly feeling the lump on her head. "Ow."

Jamal furrowed his brows and shot a glance toward Bethanna, then he turned to Andrea. "You're going to be sore for a while. Sudden moves will set it off."

"Yeah, so I discovered."

"You seem less confused now, anyway," Jamal said. "That's a relief."

Andrea sat up on the cot and picked up the bowl. "Thanks for the soup, Beth, but what are you doing here?"

"I got here this morning with the others from New Hope."

"Beth has been a big help to Tiffany and I in the infirmary," Jamal said. "She's good at basic first aid, and knows a lot about medicinal plants. The books she brought will be a great asset."

Andrea gave a slow, careful nod. She swallowed a spoonful of the soup. "I'm glad you all decided to join us. We'll be stronger together."

"Well, with Clara gone, we sort of didn't have a

choice."

"Jamalll!" Ron wailed from outside the curtain. "I need help."

Jamal rolled his eyes. To Andrea he said, "I'll be back to check on you later." He pushed the sheets aside to leave and pulled them back afterwards.

Andrea raised an eyebrow. "Clara's gone?"

"She died suddenly a few days ago. Heart attack or something. The rest of us decided we'd be better off joining you."

"What about leaving your parents' burial site?" Andrea said. "I thought that was a major sticking point."

"We took a shovel-full of soil from above each grave and brought it along in a barrel. We want to use it to start a memorial garden."

Andrea smiled. "That's a lovely idea." She ate another spoonful of the soup. "The soup's good. Thanks."

Bethanna smiled too. "You're welcome, but I'm just the one who brought it."

"Thank you for bringing it, then. And for helping Jamal." Bethanna was being sweet. Andrea couldn't help but smile, despite her headache. She really was a good person, after all. Maybe just suffering from a severe case of youth. Well, she'll grow out of that. Eventually.

Bethanna nodded. "You're welcome. I have to check on some of the others." She turned to leave.

Andrea called after her. "Beth—"

Bethanna stopped and turned back. "Yes?"

"I've been working on forgiveness, and I think I've made it there."

Bethanna nodded. She wiped her eyes with the back of

her hand and tilted her face down for a second, then back up to Andrea. She gave a tight-lipped smile. "Thank you. Thank you very much. I have to check on some of the others." She wiped her eyes again, then turned and pushed past the makeshift curtain.

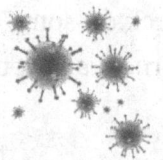

Chapter Seventy-Six

Going Forward

BRENDA could smell the sense of shock among the Hendersonville residents as they gathered in the meeting hall that evening. Or maybe it was the scent of sweat mixed with fresh soil. Her back and arms ached from helping to dig the five graves. Dirt clung to her hands and her clothes.

They'd assembled for the meeting right after the burial service. She shifted in her chair in the front row of the crowd in the community center as if there were a burr in her back pocket while she looked over the crowd. Most of the people there just seemed numb. Jamal, George, and Allen sat with her, and Dan stood at the lectern. She half-listened as he spoke to the group. She already knew which houses had been destroyed and who had died. The picture filling her mind was of when she discovered Jack Rockford, his arm exposed, his fist clenched, but his body crushed under a collapsed roof.

Brenda returned to the present when Jonathan stood and shambled to the lectern.

He looked over the crowd and sighed, fixing his gaze on the back wall, not meeting anyone's eyes. "The security monitor system is gone. The tornado destroyed the computer it ran on and all but maybe four of the cameras." He shook his head. "I can't rebuild it. The best I might be able to do is a video monitor system that a human would have to watch. None of the other computers here will run the AI persona that managed the security monitor. We need to set up a schedule for actual sentries." Jonathan sniffled. He glanced at the lectern and wiped his fingers over his eyes. "The storm also took out the cell tower. I don't know if we can get the transceiver working again. I doubt it. The satellite receiver in our house is gone."

"So we've been blasted back to the mid-twentieth century, then," someone in the crowd said, and gave a nervous laugh. Brenda turned too late to see who it was. She frowned.

Jonathan turned to meet the guy's gaze, his eyes narrow slits. "No. In 1950 they had printing presses. They had telephones and radios. We don't have those. A few radios, but their batteries won't take a charge much longer. In a few years the computers we still have will stop working. We weren't blasted back to 1950, we were blasted back to 1400. If we're lucky. Hopefully not all the way back to the iron age.

"We're an agrarian society now. Get used to that. We'd better start getting good with bows and arrows too, since before long it'll be impossible to get cartridge ammo for guns. Our primary—our *only* priorities are food, shelter, and security."

Jonathan lowered his head and wiped his eyes again. "This could be the end of civilization." He sniffled, loud and wet. "Everything I've ever worked on is—is lost. I'm not good for anything now, even getting too old to be—be any help for working the fields."

He dropped his face to his hands and fled to his seat next to Sara. She embraced him and patted his shoulder.

Silence filled the room but for Jonathan's muffled sobs.

Heat rose to Brenda's face as she shook her head. No. She didn't survive two years of slavery for this. She stood and stepped to the lectern, pushing past George as he got up to speak.

"Excuse me George. Jonathan, thanks for that update about the state of our high-tech gadgets. As for the rest of your statement, though, bullshit." She spat the word.

Brenda gripped the sides of the lectern and scanned the audience. A sea of wide eyes and open mouths faced her. Jonathan wiped his eyes with a bandanna, but his attention was locked on her.

She pressed on. "So we don't have printing presses. We'll make one." She waved an arm toward the bookcases along the wall behind the audience. "We still have our knowledge, and our books, and the printouts we've made. Food, shelter, and security? Yes, those are important, but so is civilization. Civilization doesn't end unless we let it." She clenched her teeth and glared at the crowd. "Are we going to let that happen?"

"No!" several members replied.

"No!" Brenda echoed. She had everyone's attention. Some of them were nodding along as they listened. "Jonathan, you said you're not good for anything." She shook her head. "Bullshit. We need someone who can teach math and science, and you're the best one here to do that. If we're not going to sink back to the iron age we need to keep that knowledge alive, and that means teaching it to the next generations. We need to work, and we need to work together. We need to keep the literature and culture from before the plague alive, so we can continue to learn from it. And we need to write our own stories too, to keep alive the practice of creative and historical literature for the future. Are we going to let culture disappear?"

"No!" Some in the audience raised their fists, some applauded.

"No! It's going to hard, but we're going to do it. We'll remember the past, but we'll build the future, better than it was.

"Jonathan said we're an agrarian society. That's true, but we always have been, including before the plague. Food has always been the Earth's gift. Now we have the opportunity—," she pounded her fist on the lectern, "—the *obligation*—to mindfully be an agrarian society. The Earth will support us, but in return, we need to support her as well. We survived the plague, and we'll *damn* well survive that storm."

Several people applauded, and a murmur rose among the crowd and people glanced at one another, nodding. Brenda bent and touched the floor. Most of the others in the room followed her example. She straightened. "We'll survive. By everything sacred and holy, we'll survive, and we'll prosper."

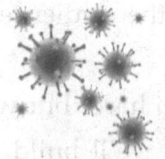

Epilogue

A knock sounded at the door, and Brenda stood from the table, reaching for her cane.

Christine snorted. "Can't they even let you finish breakfast before they start?"

Jimmy looked up from his scrambled eggs. "I can get that." After nearly forty years of marriage Brenda still thought of him as "Jimmy," rather than, "Jim," though gray flecked the kinky hair on his scalp. "Jim" made her think of Jim Henderson.

Brenda sighed. "Thanks, Jimmy, but it's probably for me." She excused herself from her spouses, giving them each a pat on the shoulder, and headed to the door. Tyler Hopson and a teenaged girl wearing a tool belt stood outside.

"The solar panels on Becky, Katie, and Nate's house have failed," Tyler said before Brenda could get out a word of greeting. "They're no longer charging the batteries."

Brenda struggled to remember the girl's name for a second, then got it. Diane. Davina's youngest daughter, by Grayson. Getting harder to remember names every year. Brenda nodded and met Tyler's eyes. "Good morning to you, too, Tyler, Diane. The Earth Mother's blessings."

Tyler grimaced and pushed a strand of white hair away from his face. "Sorry. Mother's blessings."

"Blessings," Diane said.

Brenda stepped aside. "Well, come on in." She led them to seats in the parlor. "So that was the last one, right?"

Diane nodded. "The last one that makes electric. The ones we converted to heat water and air work fine."

"Electricity, not electric," Tyler said.

Diane rolled her eyes. "Yeah, Grandpa, whatever."

Brenda locked eyes with her. "A little more respect, please."

"Yes ma'am. Sorry, Grandpa Tyler."

Brenda turned to Tyler and shrugged. "Well, we don't have much of anything left still working that uses electricity."

"Some power tools," Tyler said. "I'm really going to miss the table saw."

Brenda nodded. "I know, but we knew this day was coming. That one lasted longer than anyone thought it would. It's almost a relief to have that shoe drop."

"Yeah. Great Lakes Solar. They made the best ones. I just wanted to keep you informed. Diane and I are going to take it down today and use the black panels to make a solar air heater. We're on our way there now. Got some thoughts about setting up a water powered system for the sawmill, but that'll take a lot of work."

"Well I'm glad," Diane said. "Electric is creepy. Works without you seeing it act. Just as well it's gone."

Brenda shot her a glare. "Enough, Diane." She turned back to Tyler. "Okay, well, thanks for the update." Brenda stood and showed Diane and Tyler to the door. Maria Kiner stood there with her hand raised as if to knock. They exchanged greetings, and Brenda led Maria to the parlor while Tyler and Diane left.

"Well, what news?" Brenda asked.

Maria settled onto a straight-back chair with a thick cushion on the seat. "The visitors are cautious and suspicious, but I think we've mutually decided we're not a threat to each other. Of course, we'll want to send an envoy to look them over ourselves when we can manage that, and we've doubled the sentries in the meantime. They say they're from the east, about ten days away by horseback."

"Ten days east?" Brenda's brows lifted. "That put's them near the coast, doesn't it? I thought that area was contaminated, uninhabitable."

"About fifty miles from the coast. And they confirm that the coast is uninhabitable." Something near the fireplace seemed to be suddenly interesting, and Maria stared toward it. "They say people who go there either don't come back, or they die soon afterwards."

"Well, that gives us an indication of where the border of the contaminated land is, anyway."

"Yeah, I guess so. Not that we planned to send anyone there."

Brenda nodded. "So, three travelers, all women. Does that mean their boys tend to die too?"

Maria grimaced. Brenda recalled that all three of Maria's sons had died at less than three months old.

"Yes. They were hoping we don't have that syndrome and were quite disappointed to find that we do. It came up when they toured the school and they saw the gender ratio." Maria looked out the window and rubbed her eyes. "That, however, was the reaction that led me to suspect that their intentions are not aggressive."

Brenda sighed. "That makes four established communities we know of besides ours that all have the syndrome."

Maria turned her face to the floor and gave a single,

curt nod. Brenda furrowed her brows. Why did Maria avoid looking at her?

"Yes," Maria said. "They told us 80 percent of their baby boys die. That fits right in with us and the others."

"So it's pretty certain it's endemic."

"Yes." Maria heaved a sigh and finally met Brenda's gaze. "One thing that I found a little—well—disturbing about them, is that they were surprised that we let our young men work alongside the women."

Brenda raised an eyebrow. "Oh? They segregate the sexes?"

"No, not just that. They don't let the men work at all. Their job, if they get old enough, is to inseminate women."

Brenda leaned against the backrest and ran her hand through her short gray hair. "I see. And the men have no say about that?"

"Apparently not. One of the visitors said outright, 'We don't let the males work.'"

"Not at all?"

"I raised the same question. Nothing substantial, or even remotely risky. Light housework, some crafts. The example they showed me of some embroidery one of their men had done was beautiful."

The memory of her time in captivity at the bed-and-breakfast inn flashed through Brenda's mind, and she gritted her teeth. Then she shook her head. "I don't like it, but that's an internal matter we can't control. Assuming they're not otherwise mistreated. I will keep it in mind if we ever get into trade negotiations with them. I want you to be clear with them about our policy of non-discrimination, though. How big is this community?"

"They *say* it's about 250 people. 210 women and 40

men."

Brenda tilted her head. "You have reason to doubt that?"

Maria shrugged. "No, not really. Nothing firm. Trust, but verify. Forty men, they said. Twenty-five of them still 'capable.'" She made air quotes.

Brenda grimaced. "Did they mention anything about trade goods?"

"They raise sheep and alpacas for wool and have several treadle operated looms and sewing machines. The cloth samples I saw looked pretty good. They expressed some interest in the books and in the furniture that Tyler's shop makes, but I'm not sure how that might work in terms of trade. The roads are getting bad for wagons to transport anything heavy, and they said some of the bridges are down. They'll have to be rebuilt."

"Regardless, we should send a group there to make some sort of contact with them, just to exchange information about existing communities, if nothing else." Brenda's eyes narrowed a bit. "And to assess the situation regarding their males' freedom of choice."

"Understood."

"What's scheduled for today?"

"We're touring the sand filter system at the reservoir after breakfast, and then Bethanna's showing them the apothecary. Lunch with you and the department heads at noon in the picnic area by the memorial park. After lunch we've reserved some time for you to have informal conversations with the visitors. Mid-afternoon we're showing them the print shop. Reva has a demonstration of printing and book binding prepared. You're giving the Rillman Award for Academic Excellence this afternoon. Dinner at the first evening bell, and an open holiday-fair for the community afterwards. Kayla's giving the blessing at sunset. Davina's lined up some musicians for a dance afterwards."

"Okay, good. I want to talk with Julia about what she found out from them regarding the roads leading east. Are they willing to let us copy the maps they have?"

"Julia already has a team working on that."

Brenda gave her a quick nod. "Excellent. Okay then. I guess I'll see you at lunch. Have Julia stop by this morning."

Maria left, and Brenda pulled herself upright. The framed map from before the plague hanging above the fireplace in the parlor drew her eye. She stepped before it. The map covered the former states of Virginia, West Virginia, North Carolina, Kentucky, Maryland, Delaware, and parts of Pennsylvania, Tennessee, Ohio, and Indiana. Before the plague more than 40 million people lived in the area shown by that map. Now she knew of five communities with a total of less than two thousand people. Still, in the forty-five years she'd been in Hendersonville their population had tripled, and Tiffany had told her a week ago there were five women in varying stages of pregnancy. Last month they'd celebrated the first birthday of Karla's son. That seemed to be the point when boys were safe from Male Infant Death Syndrome.

She supported herself with her cane as she bent and touched the floor. "We'll survive. We'll survive, and we'll prosper."

THE END

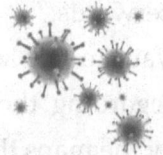

Acknowledgements

THE stereotype of the solitary writer sitting before a typewriter in lonesome isolation is one that I think has always been more romantic fiction than reality, even before the internet allowed the whole world inside their private, windowless chambers. (At least MY office is windowless...) While much of the work of the initial creation may have been solitary, the process of turning that first draft into a viable novel involved input from many people, including other writers, readers, editors, and technical experts.

I had many CRITers from the Internet Writers Workshop render valuable assistance, but particularly Virginia Anderson, Elaine Boehme, Lee Hauser, Don McCandless, Mark Piper, Brent Salish, and Bob White. Thank you. Your input helped turn the draft into a novel I also need to acknowledge the technical help I received for the medical scenes and the medical background in general from Dr. Jeff Furman and Dr. Mary Beth Hall. Your help was generous and invaluable. Much appreciated.

Beta readers Patti Auber, Bo Clary, Jeff and Janet Furman, Mary Beth Hall, Lee Hauser, Grey Forge LeFey, Luann Parkansky, Tom Strouthers, and William O. Weldy also gave me great assistance. Khrysso Heart LeFey provided editing services that no doubt saved me from many an embarrassing blunder.

Finally I need to thank my wife and lifetime partner, Rochelle S. Volen-Smith, both for putting up with me during my writing, and for believing in me. "Thank you," isn't sufficient, but thank you.

www.ingramcontent.com/pod-product-compliance
Lightning Source LLC
Chambersburg PA
CBHW011349010726
47494CB00008B/2234